THE SECOND SIGN

A SEAN WYATT ADVENTURE

ERNEST DEMPSEY

138 PUBLISHING

This story is in honor of the incomparable Clive Cussler. I never had a chance to meet him, but he had a profound impact on my life. Mr. Cussler was one of the primary influences on my writing style, and gasoline on the fire raging in my soul for adventure. And I will forever be his fan.

PREFACE

"And it came to pass, when they were gone over, that Elijah said unto Elisha, Ask what I shall do for thee, before I be taken away from thee. And Elisha said, I pray thee, let a double portion of thy spirit be upon me."

"And he said, Thou hast asked a hard thing: nevertheless, if thou see me when I am taken from thee, it shall be so unto thee; but if not, it shall not be so."

2 Kings 2:9-10

PROLOGUE

LADAKH- INDIA, 53 AD

A strong wind charged across the rocky slopes surrounding the trail and funneled through the mountain pass. The traveler cinched a dark blue scarf up over his mouth and nose to protect against the chill and the dust.

It was nearly summer in the mountains of North India, but the weather there never seemed to get the message. The pack mules didn't seem to mind, though they rarely expressed anything. The animals could have been just as miserable as the people.

The traveler narrowed his eyes against the onslaught of the wind and kept pushing forward. He was over sixty now, but he moved with the deftness and speed of a man in his twenties. His fitness level impressed his guides, who struggled to keep up as they held on to the reins and continued ushering the mules up the mountain.

The man had arrived on a boat two months before in the port town of Muziris, far to the south. With minimal funding, getting passage to the northern mountains had been tricky, but God had provided him a way, taking care of both fare and food for him to make the long journey.

That was how he'd lived his life for more than twenty years. He sighed through the scarf as he considered how fast the time had passed. *Over two decades since...*

He pushed the thought aside and leaned headlong into the wind as it gusted for the hundredth time. His thick, graying beard kept his face warm from the cheeks down, but his eyes stung from the harsh air and the frozen sand. Blown by the mountain wind gusts, it felt like being jabbed by tiny razors. He occasionally dipped his head low to keep the minuscule projectiles from his eyes. The frigid gales streaked tears across his cheeks.

This place certainly didn't offer the same climate as his homeland.

He found himself lingering on that thought, the thought of home, a place where the sun warmed the rocky hills surrounding the City of David. He pictured the olive trees swaying in a much calmer, far warmer wind than the one he was pitted against. That place might as well have been on the other side of the world.

It was a wonder people survived in places like this. He'd heard his friend speak of this area, where men from another religion came to dedicate their lives to prayer. Initially, the traveler had been concerned about coming here. He wondered if he would be welcome, if his friend had been correct in surmising that they would treat him as one of their own. His friend had never been wrong before, not once, which was one reason the traveler had been such a devout follower.

He pushed aside his doubts and kept going, trudging ahead through a thin dusting of snow that covered the ground. Nearly summer and there was still snow. He hated to think of how cold it must be here in the dead of winter.

Why anyone had built a monastery in such a remote location remained a mystery, however the traveler understood solitude as being a necessary part of truly deep meditation. His master once taught the same thing. Indeed, the traveler's own studies revealed similar practices among some of the greatest miracle workers and prophets of the past. The one thing they all had in common was that they preferred—even required—solitude, a fortress of quiet where they could calm their minds and separate from the distractions of the secular world. Up here, high in the mountains, they were far from temptations and distractions and could devote their entire focus to the obligations of meditation and prayer.

The traveler allowed himself a tight grin at the thought and caught himself looking up into the bright sky as he rounded a bend in the path.

That is when he saw it.

The monastery rose from the rocky, dusty earth ahead and to the left of the trail. The buildings were impressive only in that it must have taken an incredible amount of work to complete them. With few natural resources or materials in the area, everything had to be brought in.

A yak stood next to the white-painted structure of the monastery and eyed the visitors with casual disregard before it went back to eating hay out of a trough that looked as old as the mountain.

Few visitors dared the cold of the late spring, but in the summer, this place would be crawling with pilgrims. The traveler noted one such person, a young man bundled up in layers of fabric standing by a row of prayer wheels.

The traveler had heard of these objects before. In the past, he'd have scoffed at such a notion. His friend had explained to him the theory behind the strange metal wheels, though, and after hearing that explanation the traveler could see how it made sense to devout worshippers.

The idea was that these bell-shaped objects imprinted reality with their intricately carved prayers and reliefs. The traveler recalled wondering at the notion, asking his teacher how carvings could imprint the air.

"Not the air," the teacher had corrected with a calm smile. It was a look perpetually worn by the man, save one instance in the temple in Jerusalem. That was the lone moment he'd seen his friend overcome with fury. For some reason, that vision of the teacher's torrential anger always caused the traveler to smile. It was one of his favorite memories of his long-gone friend. He took the traveler's hand and pressed his own against it. "The air contains nothing. The ground at your feet, the trees, the rocks, they all contain nothing. It is they that are contained by something else."

"What?" the traveler had asked. "What contains these things?"

"The conduit."

He hadn't elaborated further since their discussion was cut short by a dozen children who showed up to meet the teacher. He'd always had a soft spot for the young ones. The traveler appreciated that about him. Ever patient, the teacher always made time for children. They brought a sense of joy to an otherwise dismal world.

These memories resurrected the tears he'd cried a thousand times since the teacher disappeared. While their journeys and ministry had been difficult, the traveler wouldn't trade those times for anything. The camaraderie he and his eleven companions experienced with the teacher, the wonders they'd seen, and the responsibility they'd been granted, was worth it all.

The traveler continued forward. The wind here weakened, blocked partially by the tall peaks of the hills around them and the four-story structure of the monastery to his left.

The sparse collection of people on the plateau eyed him and his guides suspiciously as they made their way toward the entrance of the great monastery of Himis. A woman clutched a child in her arms under a canvas tarp. She was selling yak butter, as well as candles made from the same material. Her offerings were slim, and the traveler wondered how she made any money during this time of year with so little foot traffic.

The child coughed and started to cry. The toddler's face was barely visible, the head wrapped tightly in dark scarlet fabric to keep away the cold. The traveler paused and cocked his head, eyeing the child curiously. Then he turned to one of his guides, a short man with light brown skin and a face worn by countless trips up this very mountain. Guide life, the traveler thought, took a similar toll to the ministry.

"What is wrong with the child?" the traveler asked, pointing at the young one.

The guide looked confused but stepped away from the mule for a moment and asked the woman the same question.

She replied, and the guide translated. "She said he has the fever. Very sick."

"How long?"

The guide once more relayed the question, and again, the woman replied.

While the traveler couldn't speak the language, he understood the woman's tone. It brimmed with a desperate sadness that only a mother's heart could feel.

"A week," the guide said. "She says they've tried everything, but no one can make him better."

The woman cut in, continuing her explanation. She sobbed and moaned, clearly afraid that the boy's time on earth was coming to an untimely end.

"She said he may not make it through the night," the guide finished.

The traveler inclined his head, acknowledging the problem. He took a deep breath and allowed his eyelids to fall shut for a moment. He envisioned the child, not as he was at that moment, but as a virile young man, full of energy, healthy. Then the traveler opened his eyes and shuffled close to the woman and her little market table.

She eyed him with suspicion but didn't withdraw as he neared. The traveler stopped a foot away from the woman and leaned over the modest table. He stretched out his hand and touched the boy's forehead with his index finger.

"Your son is healed," he said and retreated to the thoroughfare.

The mother stared at him with wide eyes. She didn't understand the words he'd spoken, but there was something about him, about the way he'd said it. She smiled at him with eyes that both thanked him and pleaded with him.

The boy's coughing spasms ceased and he appeared to relax in her arms, nuzzling closer to her breast. She looked down at the child and then back up at the traveler, as if she could find an explanation for what he'd done, but he was already twenty feet away and walking toward the entrance to the monastery, his overclothes flapping in the breeze.

"What did you do?" the translator asked as they neared the gate into the monastery's courtyard.

"Me?" the traveler asked, glancing back at the man with a curious glint in his eyes. "Nothing. I have no power of my own. I simply believed the boy was healed. I still do."

The conversation was done. The traveler chose not to elaborate, instead allowing his companion to reach his own conclusions.

A monk stood just within the gate of the monastery. He was far enough inside to avoid the brunt of the wind but close enough to the opening to be seen from the street. The monk's head was shaved, as was customary. He wore red and orange robes that folded across his body, tied off by a simple ribbon around his waist. The monk looked to be in his forties, but the traveler knew the man to be much older.

"He knows you're coming?" the second guide asked.

The traveler regarded the man with a simple nod. "Yes. He knows. Stay out here," he ordered in a kind tone, easing the abrupt command with a demure smile. "Get yourselves some food and drink; the mules may be hungry as well." He noted one donkey hungrily eyeing a trough of straw.

The guides didn't have to be told twice. They turned and ambled toward one of the small market stalls where an old man with loose skin hanging off his face sat like a statue behind a table of dried fruit.

When they were happily preoccupied, the traveler walked through the entrance and into the monastery. The monk greeted him with a weary but welcoming smile. He put his hands out wide and bowed his head.

"We have been waiting a long time for you," the monk said. "Your friend told us you would come."

The comment caused a thread of pain to snake through the traveler's chest. He missed his friend, and there was nothing that could take that pain away except the promise that one day they would be reunited.

"He was funny like that," the traveler said. "Of all the things he taught me, prophecy was the one I couldn't grasp as firmly as some of the others. He, however, could see it all with remarkable clarity."

The monk merely nodded and motioned toward a set of stairs leading into one of the buildings. "Please, let us get out of the cold. You must be hungry."

"How long have you been standing out here?" the traveler asked. He expected to hear something fantastic.

"About twenty minutes," the monk said with a mischievous glint in his eyes. "One of our ranks saw you coming around the bend from the south corner."

The traveler chuckled. The answer was anything but fantastic.

"Did you think I'd been standing in this place for twenty years?" The monk laughed and slapped the traveler on the back. "Come. Hot food. Tea. Then we talk."

The monk led the way up the stairs and through a set of huge wooden doors. Once inside, the traveler finally realized how cold it really was beyond the walls. The foyer within the monastery confines hugged him and he didn't want it to let go.

His eyes surveyed the interior with a single pass. Wooden beams ran horizontally overhead, supported by thicker posts and buttresses. Yak-butter lamps lined the walls on shelves and in sconces. The scent put out by the lamps was rumored to help focus the mind, a paramount objective in a place like this. He took in the myriad colors, or tried to. There were so many all around him in images, curtains, and wreaths hanging from the walls, as well as scarves that featured most of the hues of the rainbow. Even the wooden pillars had been painted, though a more subtle maroon instead of the wild array displayed by the rest of the little room.

Two inner doors blocked the way into the room ahead, with more doors on either side of the foyer. The traveler heard chanting echoing from beyond them.

"The prayer room is there?" he asked, pointing toward the doors with a bony finger.

"Yes," the monk replied. "Would you like to see?"

The traveler didn't know how to respond at first. His inclination was to refuse out of respect for those who were in deep meditation and prayer, but his curiosity begged to see.

"If it won't disturb the others, I would be honored."

"Of course. And you need not worry." The monk stepped over to the doors and pulled on one of the iron handles. It swung open silently, save for the slight whoosh of thick, warm air that poured through the portal. The traveler thought the foyer was warm, but the inner confines of the monastery seemed untouched by the frigid cold of the bitter winter outside.

Beyond the doors, monks sat in rows facing toward the center of the room where a path divided the space. The floor was elevated halfway to each of the side walls so that the monks on those raised platforms sat slightly higher than those in front of them. The air was filled with an assault on the senses.

Incense burned in censers in each corner. Dozens, perhaps hundreds of burnished silver lamps lined the floor along the walls. In the center of the room, at the far end, a statue of the Buddha sat on a raised platform overlooking the space. Vibrant tapestries dangled from the platform at the statue's feet. The colors seemed to spill across the room, ordaining ribbons, paintings, and even the wooden pillars in a cornucopia of shades. Buddhists, it seemed, appreciated variety in their temple adornments.

"Your friend," the monk whispered, "would not pray in this room with us because of the idol." The gentle man twisted his head another inch to catch the traveler's reaction. "He was not disrespectful. Quite the opposite. He even tried to get us to remove it." The monk chuckled softly.

"He studied here with you, prayed with you?"

"Of course," the monk said, as if the answer should have been obvious. "He traveled all over the world to learn as much as he could from other religions and belief systems. He was Jewish, though, the same as you, and believed that to be his path. I feel like he always knew. Too many people blindly choose their faith. Your friend did not." His eyes roamed up and down, searching the traveler for the answer to an unasked question. "Yes, I can see him in you, the same curiosity, the same questions."

"I am not a tenth of the man he was," the traveler confessed. He briefly considered saying more, but decided against it. Instead, he got to the point of his visit. "I apologize for being curt, but I fear time is not our ally."

The monk nodded his understanding and closed the doors to the prayer room. "He said that someday one of his followers would come with something, something important."

The traveler acknowledged with a nod and slid a satchel off his shoulder. He clutched it by the straps and held it aloft so the monk could see it better.

"Not here," the monk warned and looked around. "I trust my brothers, but I do not trust the world. If anything were to happen and our monastery sacked, my brothers could be tortured for information. While they are resolute, there may be a few weak ones in the herd."

The traveler questioned him with a twist of his brow.

The monk smiled and shrugged. "That's every herd, isn't it?" Then he turned and motioned toward another hall. "This way."

The robed figure led the way through a darkened corridor where the sunlight never touched a surface. Only the dim glow of butter lamps offered any semblance of illumination to the passage. The smell of wood and yak butter and resin filled the air, stronger now in the more confined space. The hall ran the length of the building, offering a few right turns at intersections. Quick looks down the branched passages revealed dorm cells where the monks spent their evenings. The traveler could see into the nearest one as he passed and noted the sparse decor, the minimal bed on the floor, and the little shrine for personal prayer and worship. Whether or not he agreed entirely with their beliefs, the man could appreciate their devotion.

The hall seemed to go on forever. In truth, it was probably only a minute's walk, maybe two. At the end of the vast corridor, the monk turned right and then left into an alcove where a stone statue of the Buddha sat with arms and legs crossed, a broad smile on his face.

The monk slipped in behind the sculpture, twisting his body sideways to get between the object and the wall.

"What are you doing?" the traveler asked, craning his neck to get a better view into the back of the shadowy alcove.

"You speak our language well," the monk said, avoiding the question. "I wonder how you learned it. Your friend knew it as well. Not many from your part of the world speak our words, as far as I know."

The traveler briefly considered telling the man the entire truth, but he didn't want to take the revelation to that level. "We are... quick learners," he said instead. He wouldn't lie. If the monk pressed, he would reveal everything about how he'd acquired the ability to speak multiple languages. Fortunately, the monk decided his answer had been good enough.

"I can tell," the man said. Then something like the sound of two stones grinding on each other resonated from the alcove. A heavy click came next.

The traveler took a cautious step back as the statue, previously inanimate, began to move. The base slid forward on the wooden floor, revealing the monk standing in the recess, a three-foot-wide opening at his feet.

The monk motioned to the dark cavity and then took a lamp off the wall. "Will this suffice as a hiding place?"

The traveler gave a solemn nod. "That will do nicely."

"Take one of those lamps—" he paused, realizing they didn't know each other's name. "I'm sorry, what are you called?"

The traveler's eyes narrowed slightly, the only sign of his mind's toil on an otherwise emotionless façade. "Thomas," the traveler said. "My name is Thomas of Galilee."

1

HYANNIS, MASSACHUSSETTS

The piercing sound of sirens tore Sean Wyatt kicking and screaming from his evening slumber. He would have thought that aboard the yacht he would be impervious to such interruptions. He rose and twisted, planting his feet on the floor. There he waited for a moment for the fog of sleep to wear off, aided by rubbing his eyes and forehead.

"Why are we hearing sirens?" Adriana asked. She stood at the foot of the bed, as if she'd been awake for hours. "And why do you always wear a T-shirt to bed?"

"I told you before. I get itchy at night if I don't have a shirt on."

"You know, they make nice sheets that prevent that." She stared at him with a seductive curiosity and rounded the corner of the bed, sliding closer to him.

"I'll look into that," he said and turned around to plant a kiss on her forehead. "For now, I want to see what all the hullabaloo is."

"Wow. You *have* turned into your father," she joked. "Never heard you use that word before."

"Funny. I'll be right back. Keep your mind exactly where it is."

"Okay," she relented, letting go of the fabric. She rolled over onto her other side, turning her back to him. "I'll be here."

He knew she'd be asleep before he reached the deck. One thing a few years of marriage had taught him about his wife; she loved her sleep like a lion loves its steak. He glanced back at her from halfway up the stairs. Her sleek form was outlined by the white wall next to the bed. *How was I so lucky to land such an incredible woman?*

Her backstory was a bizarre one, and read like a tragedy in some ways, a comedy in others. Her father owned the family vineyards and winery, but brokered information to the United States and its allies. He'd worked as a consultant with several agencies and departments to help bring down terrorists, stop coups, and keep the peace in various countries around the world. All the while making time to press grapes and sample the fruits of his labors.

She'd gone through the process of schooling, though hers differed from most. Her passion, though, had been art, and with the training she'd received since childhood, she became adept at an art form all its own: thievery.

Adriana didn't steal from innocent people, though, and not for personal gain. Money would never be a problem for her. Instead, she tracked down and stole art that had itself been pillaged or looted during World War II. Much like the Monuments Men in the 1940s, she made her life locating and recovering art that was lost during the war and returning it to either the governments or the families who were the rightful owners.

Sean drew a deep breath and continued up the stairs. The whining sirens drew nearer with every second. He knew they couldn't come much farther. The road came to a dead end with the only option being to turn into a parking lot or turn around.

The Kennedy compound was located just across the dunes, at least two thousand yards from where Sean's yacht laid anchor. He knew better than to try to get too close to that property. Now, though, he wondered if something was going on at the renowned homestead.

Sean pulled himself by the rail and stepped onto the deck, whirling around to face the shore in one motion. He peered into the darkness of the shoreline, the beach and much of the land behind it illuminated by the moon overhead. It was nearly full, making details on the beach much easier to discern.

He worked his way forward to the yacht's bow and climbed onto the roof to get a better view. Two headlights raced toward him. He couldn't make out the model of the vehicle, but whatever it was, it was going fast.

Sean heard the engine whining from all the way out in the bay. Seconds after he saw the racing car, the blue lights of police cruisers appeared on the horizon of the dark street leading into Hyannis' historic downtown district. His eyelids tightened as he tried to focus harder on the scene playing out before him.

The fleeing car screeched to a halt, sliding sideways for a second before stopping. The driver must have believed he could find another way out because he backed up and started to turn. There was nowhere to go. Five police cars swarmed around him with lights flashing incessantly.

Once they had the driver pinned down, the sirens cut off. Sean could make out the figures exiting their vehicles and knew they would have their weapons trained on the car, probably shouting for the driver to get out with his hands up.

Sean yawned and turned back toward the stern. He had only taken a single step before freezing in place. Out beyond the bay, perhaps a half mile out to sea, a ship gently rocked back and forth in the waves. It was a research vessel; much larger than the yacht Sean had chartered. The ship was in the same location, or close to it, when Sean and Adriana decided to drop anchor in the bay.

Upon arriving, Sean had seen the name of the ship and who it belonged to: the Marine Archaeology Foundation. He'd planned on hailing them the next day to see if he and Adriana could come aboard and ask them what they were doing. He figured it was some kind of shipwreck survey, but his curiosity beckoned him to find out for certain.

That wasn't what caused him to freeze in place. He focused, peering into the night, drowning out the lapping waves against the hull. Just beyond the research vessel, another ship crept up to its stern. The second boat was smaller, about the same size as Sean's chartered yacht. The similarities stopped there.

It looked like a modified cabin cruiser from the outline, but details were sparse because the boat was covered with dark panels, making it nearly invisible at night. Moreover, the panels almost appeared to absorb the light of the moon and the waves around the ship. Sean had seen something like it before, but it was still in research and development. So, what was it doing here?

His answer came as he reached the stern and leaned over the gunwale to get a closer view.

Shadows appeared on the top of the mystery vessel. In two breaths, the shadows launched grappling hooks over the gunwales of the research vessel. Sean watched in rapt paralysis as the men climbed the ropes up to the hull and disappeared over the edge.

A gust of wind blew through Sean's dirty-blond hair, tickling the follicles. It was cool for a summer's night, a fact for which he was glad. The chill heightened his senses, shaking him free from slumber's grasp. If the sirens and car chase on the shore hadn't done the trick, spying on what appeared to be a clandestine operation certainly would, and the cool air only sharpened him.

In an instant, Sean swung around the railing and over to the stairs.

"Addy?" he whispered loudly.

She appeared at the bottom of the stairs within seconds. Despite being a deep sleeper, she too possessed the ability to spring into action at a moment's notice.

"What is it?" she asked, her voice still dragging.

"Come take a look at this."

He turned back to the stern and peered through the moonlit night at the other ships.

His wife joined him at his side. "What are you talking about?" She then realized what he was focused on and followed his gaze. "The research ship?"

"See the other one?"

She leaned forward, bracing herself on the rails. "Barely. Looks like a cabin cruiser."

"Yeah, but modified. Notice how it looks camouflaged?"

"Black panels. Military?"

"That's the thing," Sean said. "Why would the military be conducting a covert operation on a civilian research vessel?"

Adriana turned toward him. "What do you want to do?"

"Get on the radio and hail the Coast Guard." Then he realized she was in her underwear and grinned fiendishly at her. "You may need to put on some clothes, too."

She shook her head, rolling her eyes. "Good call. What are you going to do?"

He stared at the two ships for a second. The moonlight blazed off his gray eyes like fiery ice.

"I'm going to take us in for a closer look."

HYANNIS

Sean steered the boat through the four-foot swells, guiding the vessel toward the stealth ship. He'd briefly considered going around to the starboard side, looping in front, and then dropping anchor to conceal their yacht, but immediately dismissed that idea as ridiculous. The bright white yacht stood out in the moonlight like vodka at a bourbon tasting.

There was only one way to play this: direct. He assumed the men in the stealth ship were armed even though he couldn't see weapons as the boarding party climbed their ropes. *Of course, they're armed.*

The question was, why? Their target was an ordinary marine archaeology boat. What could they possibly have of value, unless they'd uncovered a pirate treasure of some kind?

So, what could it be? Was there a high-value target on the ship, an asset stowed away in an otherwise innocent science vessel? Sean doubted that.

He needed to get a closer look at the men still on the stealth ship. He reached down into the cooler at his feet and pulled out a beer the yacht's owner had left for him. Sean wasn't a drinker, though he entertained a finger or two of bourbon now and then. The boat's owner had thrown in a twelve-pack of local ale as part of the package, and while that wasn't really Sean's bag, he decided to make use of the props since they were available.

He held the can in one hand and cracked it open with his index finger as he steered the nose of the yacht directly at the port side of the stealth boat. He revved the engine and turned on several of the cabin lights so that no one aware of his approach would become suspicious of his intent.

Adriana had called the Coast Guard and let them know what was happening, and Sean hoped it wouldn't take them too long to arrive.

When he was a hundred yards from the two ships, a spotlight appeared on the stealth vessel. From the way it wavered and moved, Sean knew someone held the light in their hand.

He pulled back on the throttle and the yacht's motors quieted to a steady rumble. The bow dipped forward for a moment, then rocked back up with the next swell, tipping high into the air prior to its next dive toward the sea.

Whoever had control of the light wasn't doing anything with it. They simply kept the beam locked on the yacht's bridge, partially blinding Sean. Fortunately, the window tinting permitted him to continue by shading his hand from the glare.

"What is this guy doing?" Sean asked himself out loud. He reached over to a panel on his left and flipped two switches. A pair of bright spotlights illuminated on the top of the wheelhouse, both pointing straight at the figure holding his own light.

The man squinted then shielded his face from the bright beams, forced to lower his own against the blinding glow. The second before the guy put his hand over his face, Sean took in a sackful of details. The man had red hair, based on his facial hair color, and semi-pale skin, indicating Western European roots, perhaps Scandinavian. If Sean went with his gut, he'd guess Ireland or Scotland, but Denmark wasn't out of the running. The man was medium height, maybe five-nine, and built like a brick.

Sean also noted the two weapons on the man: a military-grade rifle slung over one shoulder and hanging across his chest, and a pistol on his hip.

Why were these men leading an assault on the research boat? Sean's senses heightened as he made out the shadows of the attackers moving across the deck.

"What's happening?" Adriana asked, ascending the stairs. She looked out at the boat directly ahead of them and saw the armed man on the deck. "They're attacking a scientific vessel?"

"Looks that way."

"What's your plan?" she asked.

"I was thinking about ramming them, but then we'd have no boat."

"Sure we would," she suggested.

He followed her eyes to the research ship and the ropes dangling from the stern gunwale.

"You know I love you, right?"

She gave a nod. "I know."

Sean switched off the lights and allowed the man on the deck of the stealth boat a moment to recover. When he did, he raised his light again and looked back toward the yacht just in time for Sean to fire up the lights again. This time, the beams shot directly into his eyes. At that range, the light was nearly blinding and seared bright, colorful orbs into his field of vision that wouldn't go away for several minutes.

Sean slammed the throttle forward and the yacht lurched ahead. The twin engines roared, and the waves crashed hard into the bow.

The yacht rapidly closed in on the stealth ship, chewing through the waves at top speed.

"Okay," Sean said, ushering his wife over to the port side of the wheelhouse. "We jump at the same time, then take a rope and head up."

"Race you to the top," she said with a wink, patting the pistol in her right hand.

Sean snorted and stepped over to the side of the boat. "I guess we can kiss that security deposit goodbye."

He took her hand and watched the stern as it plowed through the water. Salty mist sprayed over the two of them, blown harder by the wind. Three seconds before the yacht collided with the stealth boat,

Sean and Adriana leaped over the gunwale, using their free hands to vault farther away from the two boats.

They hit the chilly waves with a splash.

Sean's face barely went under, and he immediately kicked for one of the nearby ropes that dangled from the large research ship. A loud bang, followed by a crunch, filled his ears, and he glanced back while still kicking his feet.

The yacht smashed into the port side of the stealth boat with incredible force. He thought he heard the gunman on the deck fire at least a few shots before he was knocked out of sight by the runaway yacht.

The motors whined harder, protesting the object in the yacht's way. The hull caved in against the hard edge of the target boat, but the yacht didn't sink. Not yet. The tear in the hull actually bit down on one of the cleats sticking out on the side of the stealth ship. The cleat held on like a viper, clinging to the other ship even as the motors propelled the yacht forward and sent the target ship into a spin.

Sean felt Adriana next to him, a couple of feet ahead, and he pushed himself harder until he felt the rope touch his fingers.

He shoved his gun into his belt and wrapped both hands around the rope, squeezing hard on the knots as he climbed.

Adriana made quick work of the climb, ascending at an incredible pace until she was halfway up the rear of the ship. Sean could see the name of the vessel now. *Dirty Laundry* marked the hull on the stern side in big, bold letters.

"I guess someone's an Eagles fan," Sean muttered, even as his muscles strained to elevate his body. At the halfway point, things got easier when he could put his feet against the hull and relieve some tension on his arms. He'd climbed ropes before, not just in high school gym class, but many times after. This one, though, was taller than anything he'd ever done, and Sean knew it was likely he could drop into the water before reaching the top. With some of the weight on his feet, he was able to let go of that concern and embrace a new one—precisely at the moment he made the mistake of looking down.

Sean's fear of heights was a demon he'd battled his entire life. He'd taken on some of the most dangerous people on the planet. He'd solved ancient mysteries while facing incredible odds. But heights? Heights were the one thing he couldn't seem to get past. He also didn't care much for snakes, but at the moment, that wasn't a problem.

The churning waves of the Atlantic might as well have been two hundred feet below, even though the reality was a fraction of that. It didn't matter, it *felt* like two hundred.

Sean reined in his concentration and locked it on the rope in his hands. Beyond that, he only allowed himself to see the boat's hull. He pushed the moon, the stars, the ocean, and anything else that could cause him anxiety out of his mind and beyond his field of vision. There was only the rope and the ship attached to it.

He kept pulling and walking his way up. The muscles in his back strained harder as his forearms weakened from the exertion. Then he could see over the gunwale and onto the deck.

The sounds of the skirmish they'd heard before had changed to something more like a panicked effort to find out what happened. He hauled himself over the rail and found his wife already there, crouched behind a metal box with her pistol gripped in her right hand. Sean crawled over to her, colder now that the wind scraping across the deck caught him head-on.

He scooted next to Adriana and pulled the pistol out of his belt. "I didn't see anyone on the deck, but I'm sure they would have left at least one or two out here somewhere to keep a lookout."

"Agreed. You go left. I'll go right."

Sean never liked splitting up with her. He knew she could take care of herself, but the instinct to protect the ones he loved was stronger than logic.

"Okay," he relented. "Be careful."

"You always say that," she replied. Her dark eyes drew him in. Then she turned and sprinted to a crane, staying low as she crossed the deck.

Sean sighed. Every time something like this happened, he said a silent prayer that she would be okay. There was no sense in trying to rein in that wild mustang, though, and he knew it.

He darted in the other direction, heading to the left of the entrance to the cabin. He stopped under an overhang and pressed his back against the column supporting it. Sean took a breath and leaned around the metal pillar. He pulled his head back immediately upon seeing a guard standing at the door.

Across the work deck, Adriana had taken cover next to a similar contraption. She'd seen the guard at the door, but what she didn't see was another one patrolling the deck. And he was heading right for her.

Sean had a decision to make, and he had to make it fast. The patrol guard was on the far side of the deck, talking furiously on a radio to find out what just happened as he made his way toward the ruckus. From her angle, Adriana couldn't see him coming. He was too far away for Sean to hit with his pistol—unless he got lucky. He was as accurate a shot as anyone he'd met, pulled off a few miracles now and then too, but the guard was easily forty feet away. Between the distance and the rocking boat, the likely outcome would be a miss, and then every one of the invaders would be alerted to the new threat.

The guard paused for a second and looked out over the gunwale into the moonlit sea, scanning it for more trouble. The man must have suspected another attack while the rest of his team dealt with the crash. The momentary stop afforded Sean a couple of extra seconds to make his decision.

A row of metal containers ran along the deck between the middle and the edge near the port side. Because they were four feet tall apiece, he could move quickly behind the containers and sneak up on the guard by the door. Sean estimated that when he rounded the corner of the containers, he'd only be around twenty feet from the target, which made his odds of success exponentially higher.

His mind made up, he took off and ducked behind the long metal boxes. Once there, he straightened slightly so he could move closer at full stride. His legs pumped hard while at the same time he stayed on the balls of his feet to minimize any sound.

There was no time to look over the top and see how close the patrolling guard was to Adriana, but since there was no commotion, no sounds of a struggle or gunshots, he had to figure she was okay for the moment.

When Sean neared the end of the container row, he slid like a baseball player stealing a base. His momentum and wet clothes carried him beyond the corner as he raised his weapon and aimed at the dark figure by the door. The man noticed the movement too late. Sean cracked three shots before the guard could raise his rifle. Two rounds struck the target—one in the chest, one in the neck. The other plinked off the cabin wall.

The guard's body shuddered and then dropped to the deck. Sean rushed to the opposite corner of the container and looked back toward the patrol guard he knew would be hurrying to help his fallen comrade. The next sound was an expected one as Adriana unleashed a volley of her own, striking the patrol guard in the back at least three times before he fell to the deck in midstride and slid to a deathly stop.

Sean didn't have to see what happened to know the flow of events. His shots had sacrificed his position but drawn the guard away from Adriana. It was a gamble with his life, but it had been the only way to save hers. Deep down, he had a feeling she'd react to the shots fired, look around her cover, and instantly realize what he'd done.

Although when he thought about it in those terms, Sean was smacked in the face with the reality of how long those odds truly had been.

Adriana sprinted all the way across the deck to Sean's position and took a knee next him. "Door?" she asked.

"Door."

The two scampered over to the entrance leading into the ship's interior. They took up positions on either side of the doorframe and glanced over at each other.

"They probably heard those shots," Adriana informed him, checking her magazine out of habit.

Sean agreed with a nod. "Yeah, but my money says they're all rushing to find out what caused the collision." He collected the rifle and pistol from the dead guard next to the door. He extended the rifle toward Adriana, but she cocked her head to the side, as if questioning his proffered weapon.

"I'll take the pistol," she said.

"I just thought you would—"

"You don't think I'm good enough to brandish two pistols?"

"No, obviously, that's not it." He felt himself trying to dig out of a hole he never dug in the first place. "Of course you can. I just—"

"Lara Croft uses two."

"That's a video game."

"So, a game is better than me?"

"You know that's not what I meant."

"Sean, I'm messing with you." She reached out and took the pistol from his hand. "Not about the gun, though."

His lips curled. He shouldered the rifle and kept his pistol out. Then he leaned in toward the door, turned the latch, and shoved it open. He was about to step through when he heard a faint thumping. It was far away at first, but with every passing second, the sound swelled. He turned his head and looked down the coastline. Far in the distance, he made out the flashing lights of a helicopter coming their way.

"Looks like the cavalry didn't waste any time," he said.

"Should we wait for them?" Adriana wondered.

"No," Sean said with a snap of the head. "The longer we wait, the worse things could get for the crew."

He stepped inside, and she agreed with his assessment by following close behind.

They carefully made their way down the passage, checking every open door they passed to make sure no one was waiting to ambush them.

From somewhere ahead, a woman's scream pierced the corridor. Adriana and Sean shared a concerned look, and then sped down the hall toward the sound of trouble.

3

HYANNIS

The masked leader stalked down the corridor, five members of the assault team tucked in close behind. They opened doors and checked rooms as they went, barely slowing as their leader marched fearlessly toward the sleeping quarters.

As expected, the research vessel held no security presence or system to prevent entry. The scientists would be unarmed, save for a rogue cowboy here or there, but that was unlikely. The assault team had done their due diligence, and what they had found was a soft target, one that could be infiltrated with ease.

At an intersection in the passage, the leader held up a fist and the five operators instantly froze. The leader gazed down the corridor in both directions, then motioned with two fingers to the left and two to the right.

Immediately, the men split up, two down one hall, two down the other. One remained with the leader and continued straight ahead through the crossing.

They reached a set of steps and climbed to the next level, then proceeded toward the bow where the bridge and observation deck waited. Ahead, the leader saw the control panels inside the bridge and the wide windows looking out over the dark Atlantic.

The leader stopped in the center of the bridge near the helm. Black eyes stared out through the windows, unwavering and resolute, and waited with crossed arms.

The delay was less than three minutes. One by one, the crew of the *Dirty Laundry* were wrangled up and brought to the bridge, then forced onto their knees at gunpoint.

The captives' faces were awash in confusion, fear, and for some, the lingering fog of slumber. One of the young women sobbed uncontrollably, probably still hoping she was in a nightmare from which she could awaken. Two others knelt silently next to her, one wrapping an arm around her shoulders to comfort their bewildered colleague.

Four men were held on the other side of the room, and while they also cowered in fear, none of them cried. Most appeared too sleepy to fully understand what was happening.

The leader waited to address the prisoners until everyone had been accounted for. The last one brought in was a blonde woman wearing loose-fitting red pajamas. Her wavy blonde hair dangled around her neck as she squinted up at the leader with icy indignation flaring in her blue eyes. After a momentary struggle with one of the guards, the leader motioned with a finger, and the gunman smacked the blonde on the back of the head with his pistol.

The woman grimaced at the sudden pain, but she didn't pass out. If he'd hit her any harder, she wasn't sure that would have been the case.

She raised her head defiantly and glared at the leader. "Who are you? What is this about?"

The leader said nothing, but motioned to one of the men standing two feet away.

The gunman spoke immediately, understanding the order. "Where is it?"

The woman cocked her head to the side in confusion.

"Where is the tablet?" he clarified.

"Tablet? What on earth are you talking about?" The woman's face bent in genuine bewilderment.

"You recently discovered an ancient tablet aboard a shipwreck you scavenged. Don't play dumb with us. I'm going to ask you one more time before we start killing your crew. Where is the tablet?"

"What tablet?"

Instantly, the gunman raised his pistol and squeezed the trigger. The long suppressor barrel puffed a tiny cloud of smoke as it expelled the round. The muted pop echoed in the confined space. One of the men, a burly guy with a reddish-brown beard and matching hair, fell prostrate to the floor, the back of his skull now a mangled crater.

The women screamed. The rest of the male captives shouted, some of them obscenities.

The gunman turned the pistol to the sobbing woman to the left and tensed his finger on the trigger. She howled in protest. "No! Please, no!"

The man with the gun looked down at the blonde woman in charge of the research team. "Dr. Kelley, do you wish me to kill everyone on your team? You have seen I have no problem doing so."

Kerry Kelley's face flushed red. She knew they were probably all dead anyway. She didn't have much experience with such violence or hostage situations. A hunting excursion or two with her father when she was younger was about the most gun action she'd seen up to this point, but she didn't let that show.

Dr. Kelley's nostrils flared. Her anger at the situation was twofold: first, she couldn't get her people safely off the ship, and second, she knew these killers wouldn't like the truth.

She decided to tell them anyway. At the very least, her team wouldn't be tortured and would receive a quick death. Most likely, the second she gave the assailants the information they wanted, she would be the first to die, having worn out her usefulness.

"Wait," she said, seeing the trigger finger of the gunman squeezing tighter. "The tablet from the shipwreck near Gibraltar? That was nearly a month ago."

"Yes. We are aware of that. Where is it?" the gunman demanded. His voice sounded serpentine: slithery and cold. She couldn't place the accent. The man was clearly American, but which state eluded her. If she had to guess, she'd have thought Midwestern. Not that it mattered. He was an executioner here to claim his next victims.

"Please, lower your weapon," she pleaded. She held out her hands, palms facing the killer.

"Where is the tablet?" The man's voice boomed throughout the bridge, his frustration reaching a boiling point.

"You're scaring her," Dr. Kelley insisted. "Point it at me. Please. I don't want that thing to go off. There's no need for more senseless bloodshed."

The leader watched the interaction with emotionless intensity, like a sculpture staring out at the millions of visitors it could never see. The figure's head twitched slightly to the right at a strange sound. It was distant, like muted popcorn in a microwave. After a moment, though, the sound was gone and didn't resume. The leader gave a nod, and the gunman lowered his weapon.

"The tablet—or I kill everyone in this room. Believe me when I say that the rest will not have the luxury of a quick death like that one." He motioned to the dead man on the floor.

Dr. Kelley tilted her head back. "It's not here."

"What do you mean, it's not here?" The gunman hadn't shown any lack of conviction until that moment. He glanced at the leader, but the figure didn't move, the eyes remained locked on Dr. Kelley.

"We sent it away for analysis," she exclaimed. "We couldn't decipher it. The thing had been underwater for who knows how long. Maybe thousands of years. Most of the script had faded or eroded away. Even the best labs in the world may never be able to interpret it. The best I could guess was that it was some ancient form of Aramaic or Old Hebrew. I'm pretty good with those things, and even I couldn't tell."

"Where did you send it?" the gunman pressed.

"Did you not hear me? Most of the script was unreadable. There were mere fragments of it even detectable by the human eye."

"And yet you deemed it worthy enough to keep and then send off to a lab for analysis?" He made it clear he didn't buy her story.

"It's the truth," Dr. Kelley urged.

The man raised his weapon again, returning the sights to the sobbing woman huddled with the others.

"No, please. You have to believe me. Don't hurt anyone else. Please. We sent it to the International Archaeological Agency in Atlanta. They have an underground lab there with some of the best technology in the world. If they can't decipher the tablet, no one can."

The gunman's eyes flinched, the only sign of conflict within him. He wasn't sure what to do and turned to the leader for guidance.

The silent figure turned toward the gunman. A head bob was all he needed. It was the unspoken order to execute everyone on board.

"Thank you for your cooperation," he said sardonically. Then he tightened his aim on the squalling woman and tensed his trigger finger a final time.

"No, please!" Dr. Kelley begged. "I gave you what you wanted."

The leader's head snapped to the right, this time certain of something over the usual sounds of the sea lapping against the ship's hull. It was a steady thumping that grew closer by the second.

"Coast Guard, sir," another gunman said, touching the radio in his ear. The others heard it, too. One of the men they'd left on the stealth boat was urging them to abort the mission and get out of there.

The leader gave a subtle nod and then twirled a gloved finger in the air. Immediately, the gunmen retreated out of the bridge and into the next corridor. They slammed the door shut and barred it with a metal rod found leaning against the wall.

A door slammed below deck, signaling that intruders were already aboard the ship.

"They must have already had a ship nearby," the second-in-command offered.

The leader pointed ahead toward the rear of the cabin. At the end of the hall was another exit with a ladder leading down to the main deck.

The group moved quickly and quietly down the passage until they reached the closed metal door. One of the men holstered his pistol and opened it, swinging it wide so everyone could go through quickly. When the rest of the team were outside, he turned back and saw a man's head appear over the edge of the floor where the stairs entered the second level.

Just as the man noticed the movement, the enemy raised a weapon and fired, a mere second before the henchman slammed the door hard into the frame.

Bullets bounced off the thick metal bulkheads, unable to penetrate. One of the other men already held a metal broom handle in one hand and immediately shoved it through the latch to bar entry.

At the rear of the second-level deck, the leader waited as two of the men descended a ladder. Black eyes stared out at the sea and the approaching helicopter. A boat raced toward them as well, though easily a half mile or more behind the chopper.

The leader slid down the ladder with expert ease and followed the others to the ropes leading down to the stealth boat.

In the choppy sea below, the two men who had been left to watch the boat had barely managed to untangle the yacht, but it still hadn't completely detached and was clinging to one of the cleats with extraordinary stubbornness. One of the men was trying to cut the hull free with a tool that looked like the Jaws of Life used by firemen.

The assault team descended the ropes to the bow deck of the stealth ship. The leader looked down at the mess, assessed the damage, and then motioned for the two men to return to the cabin. They obeyed, along with everyone else, and speedily disappeared into the ship's interior.

The leader bent down, inspecting where the cleat so desperately clung to the other boat. There was a piece of the boat's frame caught on the cleat. The thing would be too heavy to lift, and the waves hadn't already set it free. No amount of strength would loosen it.

Then the figure reached into a pouch, withdrew a small device, and positioned it precisely against the frame where it met the cleat. The leader pressed a button ten times on the detonator, and then rose and stalked to the cabin.

"Get us out of here," the leader ordered the man at the helm. "Full reverse."

"How?" the man at the wheel wondered. "We're stuck."

"Only for three more seconds. Do it."

The pilot obeyed and shoved the throttle backward.

The engines groaned for a second, then an explosion erupted outside. The boat shuddered, but it remained afloat and suddenly shot backward, sending most of the men stumbling toward the bow.

The gunwale broke free of the yacht's hold as the frame disintegrated and the captain slammed the throttle forward, sending the stealth ship surging through the waves on the port side of the research vessel to shield it from view of the approaching Coast Guard boat and chopper.

Then the man at the controls eased off on the throttle and pressed a blue button on the control panel. The roaring engines abruptly went silent. The boat continued forward. When they reached the bow, he pulled back on a small lever next to the blue button and the boat eased to a near halt.

Everyone on board listened, their eyes gazing up to the ceiling as if that would give them a view of what was going on aboard the research ship.

The sound of the chopper's rotors cutting through the air grew louder.

"They will land on the helipad," the leader said in a voice so calm it passed as nonchalant. "When they do, engage the silent drive again and head north."

"Aye, aye," the helmsman said with a nod.

As predicted, the helicopter swooped in from the east and came over the starboard side of the research vessel, which effectively kept the stealth ship out of sight. The Coast Guard's boat was still far behind. Some of the men from the assault team peered out into the darkness, tracking the blinking lights as they approached the tail end of the larger ship. They would drop anchor and go up the back while the team in the chopper went in from the other side.

Something struck the leader as they waited on a knife's edge. The figure turned and looked around, taking inventory of the team. Two were missing.

"What happened to Marley and Henson?"

"No response. We think they may have been compromised."

The leader knew what that meant. The men were dead. But how? Then the realization hit—the yacht that struck their boat. Whoever was aboard made their way onto the research vessel. The man who had shot at them as they narrowly escaped must have killed both assets.

The chopper's rotors eased and the beating sound in the air faded slightly. There was nothing that could be done about the men on board the *Dirty Laundry*. They were expendable and knew what they'd signed up for.

The team may not have gotten what they came for, but they were leaving far from empty-handed. They knew exactly where the tablet was. Now they just needed to get to Atlanta and take it off the hands of the IAA.

4

HYANNIS

S ean peppered the door with bullets until he realized the
rounds were ricocheting dangerously off the metal.

He darted to the exit and tried to open it, but the
heavy door wouldn't budge. He turned back toward the bridge,
keeping his weapon ready. He joined Adriana at the door to the
bridge, and that's when they heard the screams for help from
inside.

Someone had barred the door shut to prevent escape. Adriana
pulled the rod free and dropped it on the floor with a clank. When
they opened the door, they couldn't believe what they saw.

They swept the room with their pistols first, checking every
corner until they were sure the threat was gone. Adriana lowered her
two pistols when she saw the body of the man on the floor.

"What happened here?" Sean asked, doing his best not to sound
callous. Sympathy was a difficult expression to pull off in times of
urgency.

Nobody said anything at first, uncertain if the two newcomers
were friend or foe. A cluster of women huddled together on one side
of the room; the men were separated next to the body. One woman
stood defiantly in the middle.

No longer on her knees, Dr. Kelley gazed at Sean as if she'd seen an archangel. "Sean?" she breathed.

"Kerry?" Sean echoed her question.

"What... what are you doing here?"

"I'm on vacation with my wife. What happened?"

Adriana closed the door to the bridge and locked it.

The sounds of the helicopter's rotors chopping through the air reverberated through the control room. Blinking lights flashed through the windows and were followed by bright spotlights shining down onto the helipad.

"This is the United States Coast Guard," a man's voice crackled through a radio. "*Dirty Laundry*, what's your situation?"

Sean took four long steps over to the radio and responded to the call. "US Coast Guard, this is Sean Wyatt. We have secured the survey crew in the bridge. There may be more of the ship's crew down below. The threat has been neutralized here, but I would do a full sweep of the ship just to be sure. We have one casualty."

"Status?"

Sean hesitated to respond. He'd seen plenty of innocent lives lost. It never got easier, but it was routine in a macabre sort of way that bothered him deep down. Dr. Kelley and her crew were the ones he was worried about. He didn't want to have to say the words in front of them, but the Coast Guard pilot would need to know.

"Bridge, you still there?"

"Yes, sir. One dead."

The words hung in the air like a thick, red fog, swirling and seeping into the pores of every person in the room.

"Copy that. Help is on the way."

The helicopter descended into full view. The bright flashing lights seared through the darkness, a welcome but blinding sight for everyone on the bridge. The rotors churned loudly with an intimidating, thumping cadence.

Dr. Kelley rushed over to her old friend and wrapped her arms around him. Sean flinched at the unexpected show of emotion. He patted her on the back. Then she stepped away and rubbed her eyes.

Behind her, the helicopter touched down and a team jumped out of the aircraft. The members of the Coast Guard unit hurried across the platform, making their way toward the bridge.

"Dr. Kelley, it's okay," Sean said. He put his hands on her shoulders, but he couldn't help noticing the one member of their team who hadn't made it. Over her shoulder, the body still lay prostrate on the floor.

She noticed his eyes teasing toward the victim and nodded. "Tim Meyer," she said. "He... he was a deckhand, not part of our team directly. We hired him. I... I don't even know if he has a family or who his next of kin is."

"It's okay," Sean reinforced. "We'll take care of all that. I need you to slow down for a second. The Coast Guard is here. They'll sweep the ship and get us to safety. We can talk then about what happened here."

She nodded at the encouragement and bit back the tears. Up to that point, she'd been strong, the leader of the expedition, but every dam has a weakness, and hers had given way.

Sean turned and set his weapons on the floor near the helm. Adriana did the same. The last thing they needed was for the Coast Guard to come in and incorrectly assume the couple were a threat.

"Everyone, put your hands up," Sean ordered. "It's going to be fine."

After the Coast Guard unit arrived on the bridge, they got the story from Sean and Dr. Kelley, then continued their search while some of the rescue team evacuated the crew. Sean's instincts told him to assist the Coast Guard with the sweep of the vessel, but he knew that wasn't allowed and it would be a strange request.

They were taken to the local base where they were given water and snacks. Sean knew food to be one of the best ways to help people who had just experienced a terrible crisis. He'd learned that long ago, both in college and in the field.

Sean and Adriana waited in a room by themselves, sipping on bottles of water and nibbling on potato chips. They were fine; this sort of thing was old hat to them, but the food was there so they ate it.

The nondescript office looked like it hadn't been used in a year or so. The chairs in which Sean and Adriana sat were the only furnishings besides the minimalist metal desk that was probably a relic from the 1950s.

They heard footsteps coming down the hall. There was a steady click, the unmistakable sound of military boots, along with a gentle shuffle. Dr. Kelley appeared in the doorway with one of the Coast Guardsmen who had been part of the rescue team.

"Do you need anything else, Dr. Kelley?" the young man asked, sounding sincere.

"No, sir. Thank you."

"Yes, ma'am." He gave a curt nod, spun on his heels, and disappeared down the corridor.

Dr. Kelley made her way over to the empty chair near the door and eased into it. She looked over at Sean first, sitting behind the desk with his fingers steepled and a bag of half-eaten potato chips next to a water bottle near his elbows.

"I told them what happened," Dr. Kelley began without prompt. "They... these people, they were wearing masks that wrapped around their faces and covered their noses, mouths, and their heads. I could only see the eyes."

"Difficult to get an ID on anyone like that," Adriana said.

"Yes." Dr. Kelley nodded and continued. "They are doing all they can to track the boat that attacked us, but so far they've turned up nothing. I—" She cut off and sniffled. Then she looked Sean in the eyes, tears welling in hers. "Do you think they will come after us again? How will we be safe?"

Sean lowered his hands to the desk. He understood. She was a civilian. Always had been. This wasn't supposed to happen to her. Attacks like this should never happen to the innocent. His blood boiled upon seeing his old friend in such emotional shambles. He knew how strong she was, too, which made it all the worse.

Dr. Kelley was as tough as nails. She'd grown up on a ranch in the mountains of Wyoming, and worked the land with her parents. Farm life hadn't been for her, though, and she'd gone off to the University of Wyoming in Laramie to study ancient history, anthropology, and archaeology.

Her passion had always been those fields of study, but something else called to her, something she'd never seen in person growing up —the sea.

During her sophomore year in college, Kerry took a trip to the Gulf Coast with friends. She was hooked on the ocean from the moment she laid eyes on it. After that, her studies steered further toward maritime archaeology. She joined the Marine Archaeology Foundation soon after graduating and had been with the agency ever since.

They'd worked on projects with the IAA on several occasions, which was how Dr. Kerry Kelley and Sean Wyatt met.

"You're safe, Dr. Kelley," Sean reassured.

"I told you a long time ago not to call me that. It's Kerry."

"And I told you a long time ago I don't take prestigious titles lightly, Dr. Kelley."

She huffed. "You are insufferable, Sean Wyatt."

Adriana cackled. "So, you know him well then, huh?"

The wisecrack broke the wall of emotions Dr. Kelley was holding back. She laughed hard for nearly a minute.

"Oh, yes. I know your Sean. It's been a while, though, my boy. It's been a while."

"I'm in my forties now, so... I'm hardly a boy."

"You'll always be a boy to me. I remember when you first got into archaeology, with Tommy." Her smile faded instantly as the epiphany smacked her like a falling piano. "Tommy." The name came out as a whisper, lathered in fear.

"What about him?" Sean asked, his tone taking on sudden concern.

Adriana leaned forward, too.

Dr. Kelley's blue eyes danced from Sean to Adriana and back again. "The group who attacked the *Dirty Laundry*, they wanted something. A tablet."

"Tablet?" Adriana asked.

Dr. Kelley nodded. "We were in the Mediterranean several weeks ago. On our way back, we stopped near Gibraltar on a tip from a friend about some anomaly they'd found about a mile off the coast. They weren't sure if it was a shipwreck or just a natural rock formation, but they were leaning toward the shipwreck hypothesis." She took a breath and went on. "Turns out he was right. It *was* a shipwreck. The thing was covered in a few thousand years of silt and who knows what, but it was definitely a ship. Based on the structural design—what's left of it—we think it was a Roman vessel from around the time of Caligula or possibly Claudius."

"What was a ship doing so far away from Rome?" Sean asked.

Dr. Kelley snickered, though the look in her eyes remained thoughtful. "Rome was everywhere back then," she explained. "The Romans would have had outposts, harbors, even shipyards in southern Spain and Gibraltar. They'd expanded all the way to Britannia and south to Morocco and much of Northern Africa." She snapped her head. "Anyway, doesn't matter. The tablet. We found a tablet on board the shipwreck. It was nearly unreadable, but there were a few markings I could make out. They were written in ancient Aramaic."

"The language of Jesus," Adriana breathed.

"Yes, the same. Again, I can't be certain. That was my assessment based on a very small sample. The rest was too faded to read. I don't know what the tablet says or what it could mean. We found nothing else like it on board that ship, either, which we believe was a merchant vessel."

"Why would a bunch of terrorists want an ancient stone tablet?" Adriana wondered out loud.

"Perhaps they thought it could be sold on the antiquities black market," Dr. Kelley offered. "Hundreds of millions of dollars pass from one hand to another there every year."

"That's possible," Sean partially agreed. "But how did they know you had it? You said you found it off the coast of Gibraltar several weeks ago."

"Yes, that is correct. I don't know how they found out about it. I've been so distraught over the events of the evening that I can't think straight."

"Understandable." He lowered his head and rubbed his temples. They should have been asleep hours ago, sleeping soundly on a yacht —a yacht that was now at the bottom of the ocean. He decided to try a different question, one with an easier answer. "Where is the tablet now?"

Dr. Kelley's eyes remained locked on the floor. Her mood lifted with her eyes as they rose to meet his. Sean recognized the mischievous look.

"That's what's so... no, funny isn't the right word. That's what's so strange about all of this."

Sean's forehead wrinkled. "What do you mean?" he asked with a twist of the head.

"When we discovered the tablet and realized we didn't have the equipment necessary to determine its age, the language, what it meant, I made the call to have it sent off."

"The MAF has plenty of resources. You're one of the top marine archaeology agencies in the world."

"That's true," she assented with a nod. "But there's another agency with a better lab than anything we have to offer."

She waited for a breath until she saw the light go on in his brain.

His eyes widened. "You called Tommy?"

She shrugged, tilting her head to the side. "See why this is so strange?"

"Yes, ma'am. I definitely do." He looked to Adriana.

She already knew what he was going to say. She saw it in his eyes. "Vacation's over," she said without a hint of regret.

"Yeah. Vacation's over."

5

WATASCO, WYOMING

Darkness. It's nearly all the man inside the cell knew. *Appropriate*, he thought. He'd always believed himself to be a light in a dark place, a torchbearer leading the way down a path of righteousness. Now, the only light he could see was a sliver that somehow managed to sneak through the top of his cell door.

Footsteps from outside told him it was time for his daily exercise, a scant fifteen minutes of walking around inside another room that had been converted from an old dining hall into what passed for the facility's exercise area. It was, perhaps, fifteen hundred square feet.

The footfalls struck the concrete floor louder with every passing second. When they reached the door, a shadow passed in front of the narrow beam of light shining into the room, momentarily casting the inmate into total darkness.

Theodore Milner stiffened his back as he sat on the floor with his legs crossed. He'd been meditating for over an hour, and while the practice helped hone his focus, relaxing his mind and body, he also felt tired from being in the same position for so long. He wouldn't let the orderly or the guards see that, though. Milner was a proud man, one who refused to allow himself to be degraded or humbled.

He humbled himself before no man. He was the sword of the Almighty, and a shield of righteousness.

The narrow panel near the top of the door slid open. Dark eyes glowered on either side of a thick, stubby nose. Milner recognized the eyes of the orderly, a man named Stan with a superiority complex. The irony oozed through Milner. A mentally unstable orderly charged with caring for the criminally insane—only the government could be so ridiculous.

Milner didn't need to know Stan's backstory to understand the way he acted, the way he treated the inmates. Of course, that's not what they were called—not always. Milner didn't care how they sugarcoated it. He and the other tenants of Morrowfield Asylum were prisoners.

"Wake up, Teddy!" Stan barked. His baritone voice had a Southern twang to it. Which was strange, because Milner had learned Stan was from Nebraska.

And he hated it when the orderly called him Teddy.

Locks clicked and metal slid against metal. Every day, it was the same routine. He'd get one fifteen-minute period of exercise. Once a week, he was permitted outside for five minutes, but only under intense observation on a tiny patch of grass on the eastern side of the building. The minuscule yard was barely forty feet square, surrounded by two chain-link fences and a concrete block wall beyond those. Each one of the barriers featured razor wire along the ground and on the top.

Today wasn't his day to go outside, which was fine. Spring still hadn't arrived in that part of Wyoming despite what the calendar said, and Milner detested the cold. Being from Florida, the hard western winters didn't suit him.

The door to Milner's cell slid open and light poured in, dousing him in its warm glow. Silhouettes of two more figures stood just behind that of Stan. The guards were big, much like the orderly. While they liked to flaunt their physical strength, the men were hardly fit. All three were slightly overweight, with most of their muscle hidden behind a thick layer of flesh. Still, they knew how to subdue the prisoners. Milner had seen the results of disobedience firsthand when another inmate had been crippled during a fit of rage.

The man, whose name Milner didn't know, had been screaming for hours in his cell at the end of the hall. Milner had done everything he could to drown out the noise. He had a high degree of tolerance for such things, higher—it seemed—than the guards.

Without knowing the circumstances, Milner guessed the man was experiencing a schizophrenic episode. He'd been yelling at people who were neither in his cell nor in the hall right outside. Of course, random screaming wasn't exactly a rarity in this facility. Most of the people in Morrowfield truly were insane. Milner was the exception.

"Good morning, gentlemen," Milner said in his nondescript accent.

He held his hands out wide and the shackles attached to his wrists jingled, the sound echoing off the walls.

Long, shiny chains ran to the wall on either side of the prisoner. Similar restrainers kept his legs secure. His meager bed rested on the floor to his right—little more than a four-inch-thick mattress with sheets and a pillow.

"Shut up, Teddy," Stan groused. "On your feet."

"Of course, sir," Milner replied. The words escaped his lips like a serpent's hiss.

Milner did as ordered and stood. He waited while the two guards stepped into the cell. One drew his taser and kept it trained on the inmate while the other loosed the shackles and attached them to shorter chains behind Milner's back.

"You know the routine, Preacher," Stan said. "Fifteen minutes."

"Yes, thank you for that reminder, Stan. I do appreciate you telling me that every day for the past several years. It's not at all annoying." Milner made no effort to hide his sarcasm.

Stan's eyes flamed. "Maybe you'd like to stay here in this box the rest of the day instead of getting your exercise time in."

"No," Milner said, lowering his head in faux humility. "I would very much like to get in a good stroll."

"I bet you would," Stan spat. "Get a move on. Clock's tickin', and I got—"

"Four more sickos to walk like dogs?" Milner finished.

"Yeah," Stan grumbled. "Something like that." Then he punched the prisoner in the kidneys.

Milner knew he deserved that one. Sometimes he couldn't keep his mouth shut. But what was he supposed to do? He was surrounded by inferior intellects. None of his victims had been so dim. Since the day he arrived at Morrowfield, Milner had set his mind to correcting that mistake.

He grimaced and his knees buckled from the blow, but he didn't fall. He never had. Not once. And this was far from the first time he'd taken a fist to the kidneys. One time, three years before, he'd spent most of the night pissing blood from multiple blows to his lower back. That night, the guards and the orderlies had had their fun with him, beating him up for no other reason than they were able to do it.

The orderly ambled down the sterile corridor toward the place that passed for a recreation room; at least for Milner. As far as he knew, most of the other prisoners here were permitted to go outside once a day if they desired, and they weren't limited to the "yard" Milner knew. There was—he'd heard—a larger courtyard some-where on the grounds. Incredible to think that he'd been here so long and never seen the entire place. He was fine with not seeing the rest of it. How grand could it be? It was a prison for the insane. Except that he was not insane. Theodore Milner was definitely right in the head.

The group turned right and then stopped midway down another corridor. Milner stared at the white-painted cinder block walls. They were the same everywhere he'd been in the prison, and it was a safe assumption the rest of the joint was painted similarly.

He averted his eyes to the orderly as the fleshy man unlocked the door to the room and stepped through. He held it open to allow the prisoner and the two guards to come through, and then closed it behind them once they were inside.

Stan looked at his watch. "Looks like you only got thirteen

minutes today, Teddy," he said with a twisted sense of pride. Then he turned to the guards and chuckled. "I told him he had to move faster."

"Yeah, he always was a touch slow, wasn't he?" one of the guards chirped.

"Well?" Stan asked, looking at the prisoner. "You gonna get to walking or just stand there for the rest of your exercise time?"

"Thirteen is my lucky number," he said and held out his hands to be unshackled.

"I'll take the hall," one of the guards volunteered, the same one who had said Milner was slow. The other gave him the thumbs-up and went to work unlocking the cuffs on the prisoner.

The first guard waited until Milner was free of the cuffs. The orderly kept a close eye on the man and a grip on the taser at his side. It wasn't police issue, but would do the same thing—incapacitate an unruly patient.

Milner slid his feet along the smooth concrete floor and proceeded to walk to the end of the room, turn at the corner, follow along until the next wall, then make his way back. He'd followed that exact pattern hundreds of times since arriving at Morrowfield.

He didn't say it, but he appreciated even the smallest amount of exercise. It got his blood flowing. While he wasn't old, Milner could feel the effects of age creeping in on him when he turned sixty. Joints were stiffer than before. Muscles were more prone to soreness after a day of intense activity—not that he got much of that in here except for occasional beatings.

The first guard watched for a moment and then stepped outside the room. Milner knew why they did that. If someone were to try to escape, they wouldn't get out of the room even if they overwhelmed the two men inside. Even that was unlikely because of the armed guard and the orderly with the taser.

Milner doubted Stan was a skilled warrior with his shock toy, but all it took was one lucky stab and the prisoner would be down for the count.

No fanciful dreams of escape danced through Milner's head. He would have loved to kill both of the men, and the one outside, but the risk was too great. They were armed and he wasn't. It was unlikely they'd kill him if he tried something, but there were fates worse than death, bitter delicacies he'd been forced to endure during his stay at Morrowfield.

"What was the deal with this one again?" the guard asked Stan. He made no attempt to conceal his conversation, happy to speak in full voice so the prisoner could hear. "Killed a bunch of people or something?"

Stan snorted. "You really are green, rookie. This here is one of our more famous patients. Don't let him fool you; he's a shady character. But he has his uses." Stan bit his lower lip, a gesture Milner had seen far too often, its meaning unfortunately known.

"You don't have to be a jerk about it. Just tell me what he did," the guard pressed.

"I'm only messing with you, rookie. This here is Theodore Milner. He's the one who killed all those people down in Florida several years ago."

"Oh, like with a gun? One of those berserk killers?"

Stan guffawed. "No, nothing like that. This here was one of the most sought-after serial killers in the United States. Took the police months to find him. When they did, he was hiding out in the mountains. Some of the people involved with the search party are certain they walked right by him on several occasions."

"Even with dogs?" the guard asked, wide-eyed.

"I guess."

"Dogs," Milner interjected, "can be easily confused. Such is the way of things with creatures led by one dominant sense."

"I don't recall asking you a thing, boy!" Stan roared. "You just lost yourself another minute of walking time. If you want to make it two, keep running that mouth."

Milner feigned fear and shrank back for a moment before continuing his laps.

"Anyway, killed a bunch of people," Stan continued. "Men and women. He didn't discriminate. Claimed they were sinners and he had to purge their sins through pain and death."

The guard's mouth hung open. His scathing glare remained on the prisoner as he kept walking his path.

"Sounds like he should have been put in the chair," the guard offered.

"Oh, they tried to get the death penalty for him, but he found a loophole. Didn't you!" He added a few choice words from the depths of his vocabulary to emphasize his distaste for the patient. "Got a good therapist and lawyer, I guess. They convinced the judge that he was mentally ill. One of those insanity deals."

The disdain on the guard's face swelled. "Those make me so sick."

"Tell me about it. Although this one has a few things to offer." He added a wicked laugh after his comment.

Milner cringed internally. He knew what Stan meant. He and the other guards preyed on the inmates of Morrowfield, made them do things, horrible things. The beatings were often a welcome break to the other forms of torture the patients were forced to suffer.

"Oh, yeah?" The young guard's interest piqued.

"Definitely." Stan lowered his voice, though Milner could still hear it. "Especially after lights out. The ones in a box like him can't do a thing about it."

Milner reached the other end of the room for the umpteenth time and turned. He strolled to the opposite corner and then began his return trip to the end nearest the entrance.

Halfway to the corner, a rapping at the door interrupted his march.

"What?" Stan shouted. His voice bounced around the cinder block room like a tennis ball. "He still has seven more minutes."

No answer came. Instead, another knocking.

Stan rolled his eyes and motioned to the door. "Go see what he wants. He probably forgot his keys. Idiot."

The rookie snorted, then turned and walked to the door. Stan kept his eyes locked on the patient as Milner slowly picked up his pace again. He watched the door with keen interest as the guard stopped and pulled on the latch.

"What's the problem, Johnson? Forget your key?"

The door swung open and the guard got his answer in the form of a 9mm slug through the forehead and out the back of his skull. Drops of blood splattered on Stan's face and white uniform, speckling it like a piece of abstract art.

Stunned, he looked down at his clothes for a second, then ran a bewildered collection of fingers across his face, smearing the red droplets along his cheek. His eyes darted to the guard on the floor. The rookie lay on his back, blank eyes staring up at the ceiling, his head resting on a growing pillow of liquid crimson.

"What the—" Stan started to use an expletive, but he immediately felt his belt lighten. He spun around in time to see Milner with the taser. The blue arch zapped between the metal prongs the moment before Milner pressed it into the bulbous man's gut.

Stan's body shook violently as the voltage coursed through it and exited into the floor. Milner kept the device on the man longer than he needed, but he wanted to make sure the orderly would go down.

When it seemed Stan's strength and will were gone, Milner yanked the taser away and watched the big man collapse to the floor. His body still gyrated and convulsed on the tile as the aftereffects of the electrocution continued to stunt his bodily controls, one of which Milner noticed was the man's bladder.

Two men with pistols stepped into the room, their faces covered with black masks that revealed only their eyes. Milner still knew who they were.

The one in front moved quickly to the patient and checked the man for wounds.

"Are you hurt, sir?" the masked leader asked.

"No, Jeff. I'm fine. Give me your gun."

Jeff passed the weapon to Milner without a second thought. Milner then turned the weapon on Stan and fired a bullet into his groin. The man's stunned reaction to the electricity immediately changed to one of absolute agony. He clutched at the bloody patch on his white pants and howled like a wounded wolf.

"I'm sorry I can't stay to enjoy your misery," Milner said. "But I really must be going. Don't worry. The pain won't last long."

He passed the weapon back to Jeff with a callous disregard. "Lead the way," Milner ordered.

"Yes, sir."

They stepped out into the hall and were greeted by half a dozen others dressed the same as Jeff and the other intruder. The six were dragging asylum guards along the floor toward Milner's recreation room.

"Efficient," Milner said, noting the dead as they were pulled by. He mentally noted the lack of blood on the floor, or visible wounds of any kind. He assumed his men had used covert methods of taking out the security guards. Of course they had. They were assassins, death dealers who knew a hundred ways to kill a person without a weapon.

Milner was glad they were on his side. Then again, he wasn't surprised. The Almighty had always watched over him in that regard. Even here in this dark place, he'd considered the trials of Joseph when his brothers betrayed him and handed him over to slave traders. Joseph had been wrongly accused by his new master and sent away to an Egyptian prison. The place was little more than a dungeon and far worse than anything Milner had endured here in Morrowfield. That thought kept him going, pushed him forward. He could suffer anything, just as some of the most blessed men in the Bible had. Joseph went on to become the governor of Egypt, second only to Pharaoh himself.

Now, Milner's time in the dungeon was over.

He strode behind Jeff Rudolph, the second-in-command, who was in charge of field operations and security. Jeff led the way through the corridors to the raucous sounds of cheering inmates. Some begged to be set free; others screamed unintelligible sounds common to an asylum such as this one.

"Thank you, my friends," Milner said. "Soon, I will set you all free."

Jeff glanced back at Milner and they exchanged a knowing look while other members of the team began to set charges.

Once they were outside, Jeff led the way down a set of stairs toward four white vans parked in the circular drive that looped in front of the building. Milner looked up at the worn sign carved into a concrete arch over the entrance. It read; Morrowfield Asylum.

The building was a relic. Completed in 1905, it featured a Gothic-style façade. The stone-and-brick structure was designed like a cross, with the large central intersection housing the cafeteria—a place Milner had only seen once in his years of incarceration.

He looked up at the sun as he reached the first van. Jeff slid the door open, but Milner held up his hand and closed his eyes as the rays of sunlight warmed his face.

"It's good to be free again," Milner said.

"Yes, sir. It's good to have you back." He knew better than to rush the man in charge. If he ordered it, they would all stand right there on the curb and wait to be arrested. There would be no protest from Jeff. His loyalty remained unquestioned to the man he believed to be his personal savior, a modern-day prophet.

Milner opened his eyes once more and lowered his head. He nodded and climbed into the back of the van. Jeff hurried around to the front while the other mercenary closed the van door and waited.

Within a minute, the rest of the team poured out of the building and down the steps. Each van had a driver already behind the wheel, and transmissions were shifted into drive as everyone poured into the vans.

Jeff's partner climbed into the front seat and slammed the door shut. Jeff punched the accelerator and the van's tires squeaked on the asphalt, sending the vehicle out onto the road heading east, away from the mountains.

Three minutes out, a muted rumble shook the road. Milner grinned devilishly and looked back over his shoulder toward Morrowfield. A black plume of smoke billowed into the sky. Clouds of dust shot out in several directions, trailing behind debris as it sailed through the air.

Jeff barely gave a tick of the eyes in the rearview mirror, noting his team's handiwork.

"The official story will be a gas main explosion, sir," Jeff informed.

"Shame some of these older buildings aren't up to code with stuff like that."

Milner smirked and leaned his head back. He took three long breaths and then opened his eyes to watch the scenery fly by in the window. There wasn't much to see, just rolling plains and a few barren hills. Occasionally he'd see a knoll with a collection of evergreen trees atop it. But to Milner, the views were spectacular. He was finally free, and now he could pursue the thing that could set it all right and shape the world the way he knew it should be.

6

IAA HEADQUARTERS, ATLANTA

Tommy Schultz plopped down behind his desk and leaned forward, resting his head on the desktop. He closed his eyes and exhaled. It had been a hard week and he was ready to get home and take it easy. It was only Thursday, though, and Tommy almost never took a day off.

Usually, he didn't have to. He loved what he did. Running the International Archaeological Agency was hardly what he'd call work, at least most of the time. Now and then, however, it could be stressful, especially when new stuff landed on his desk.

He'd received a dozen new items from various countries in the last three days: three from China, five from Israel, two from Brazil, and two from France. And each of the senders was eager to have their artifacts analyzed and returned with full reports.

Tommy's longtime assistants, Tara and Alex, were already burning the proverbial candle at both ends, although that was how they always did things. They also loved their jobs, especially their new field roles with the Paranormal Archaeology Division that enabled them to get out and investigate bizarre occurrences across the world with a focus on ancient sites or artifacts.

He inhaled deeply again and sighed. He was going to have to hire more people.

There were four other agents working various cases around the world, but they were out in the field most of the time, often working on dig sites in faraway lands. While they had offices, those were typically empty.

He needed someone else on site to help coordinate the day-to-day stuff. It would have been nice to have his wife, June, on staff. He secretly hoped she'd be interested, but she was so busy working for Emily that coming to work with Tommy was likely never going to happen.

"Well, I guess I could start reaching out to some of the regional universities and see if there's any promising young talent graduating this year." He often talked to himself when thinking or pondering a solution to a problem. Sometimes, he did it just to entertain himself.

He sat up and then leaned toward his computer, shifting the mouse to wake the machine from its slumber. The screen blinked to life, and he began to type.

Minutes turned into an hour as he scrolled through the lists of archaeology and anthropology professors at colleges in the area. By the time he was done, he'd compiled a list of more than twenty, which was plenty for a first round of emails.

The clock ticked on the wall across from him, the second hand sounding more like a hammer pounding a nail with every passing moment.

He reached over to his phone, unlocked it, tapped on the Spotify app, and then on his favorite playlist.

Pearl Jam's "Corduroy" started to play and he felt his pulse quicken, his head bobbing along to the music.

Tommy opened the email client on his computer and entered all the email addresses on his list with a quick copy and paste. Then he began typing the body of the email under the subject heading, *New Talent from Your Programs.*

He stared at the blank page for a moment. All he'd written was "Dear Esteemed Colleagues."

Tommy blinked as the cursor did the same, though it continued on in the same metronomic pattern. *What to say?*

He let out a sigh through his nose and then began typing again. Ten minutes and two quick checks for typos later, he nodded in approval at the message and sat back in his chair. The seat squeaked a little under his weight. Tommy was a beast, with broad shoulders and thickly muscled legs. He'd started a regular workout regimen years before and he'd rapidly packed on a solid frame. While his friend Sean was leaner and stronger, Tommy had turned himself into a linebacker. Sean had even joked about him trying out for the NFL's Falcons at one point because they needed all the help they could get on defense. The two had shared a good laugh over that.

Tommy stared blankly at the screen for another minute before he leaned forward and hovered his right hand over the mouse. He shifted the arrow up to the send button and was about to click it when he heard a gentle rustling in the hall outside his office.

A second later, a woman in her late thirties appeared in the doorway holding a box. She wore a red blouse with a black skirt, and her blonde hair hung loose and hooked behind her ears.

"Good morning, Mr. Schultz," she said.

"Good morning, Sarah," he replied. He'd long since given up on insisting she call him Tommy. The receptionist was as stubborn as Sean. "Got something for me?"

She extended the wooden crate and set it on his desk. "Yes. It just arrived a few minutes ago," she grunted, out a breath. "It's pretty heavy. What's in that thing?"

He shrugged and analyzed the box. "No clue. I order stuff online all the time, usually research equipment, but I don't think I've ordered anything recently."

Tommy stood and walked around his desk to get a better view of the box. The postage said it was from Dr. Kerry Kelley.

"Oh, Dr. Kelley sent this," he announced. "That's odd."

"You weren't expecting anything from her?"

"No. Not that I'm aware of." He looked at the postmark. "It came from Gibraltar. Wonder what she was doing over there."

"A dig, perhaps?" Sarah offered.

Tommy responded with a feeble laugh, the kind of laugh someone gave to a naïve person when they didn't want to call them that.

"I doubt that," Tommy said. "Dr. Kelley is a marine archaeologist for the MAF. They don't do a lot of digs on land."

"Oh. So, is it something from an underwater excavation?"

"Could be. I see you had to sign for it."

"Yes, sir. I hope that's not a problem."

"It hasn't been in the past, Sarah. Don't see why it would be now." He offered a disarming smile, and the slight worry in her eyes faded. Her concern melted in an instant. "So, let's open this up and have a look-see."

He shifted back around the corner of his desk and plucked a pair of scissors from the top drawer to slice the packing tape. Then he pried open the flaps and looked inside. A mound of white packing popcorn filled the box and blocked any view of the rest of the contents. Tommy stuck his hand into the Styrofoam pile and shimmied his fingers around until he felt something solid halfway down the box. He brushed away the materials, spilling some onto his desk.

When the debris was cleared away, he stared into the container at a slab of stone wrapped in plastic.

"What is that?" Sarah asked, barely above a whisper.

"A rock," Tommy said, taking a stab at humor.

"Yes, I know that, but what's it for?"

The joke lost, Tommy turned back to his usual serious self. "Not sure," he said. He lifted the stone out of the box with both hands and carefully set it on his desk atop the leather writing pad. He released the edges of the stone and leaned over, inspecting the shallow carvings on the surface. "It looks like a message was written on this a long time ago. I'm not sure, but it appears to be Aramaic. It's too faded to tell."

"Sir?" Sarah interrupted his train of thought.

"Yeah?" He didn't take his eyes off the stone as they pored over the surface.

"There's a note in the box."

"Oh, great. Maybe that will offer some explanation as to why Dr. Kelley sent us this."

He reached into the box and pulled out a folded piece of paper.

"It's from Kerry," Tommy announced unnecessarily.

"Yes, sir. I... that would make sense, wouldn't it?"

Tommy felt stupid. "Yes. Yes it would." He cleared his throat and started reading out loud.

"Tommy, I'm wondering if you might be able to take a look at this piece. We discovered it in a shipwreck off the coast of Gibraltar. We are heading back to the States in the next day or so, but I wanted to get this to you as quickly as possible, and I'm afraid our ship doesn't allow for that.

"No doubt, the package has reached you before I've returned. I will reach out to you when I get back. I'm hoping you and your crack team of experts can figure out what the message on this tablet says. We believe it's ancient Aramaic but can't decipher much of it due to how it's aged over the centuries.

"Thank you so much for all you do to preserve the history of our world. I look forward to speaking with you soon.

"Kerry Kelley."

Tommy's eyes remained fixed on the paper in his hands. He reread it silently and then set the letter down. "Well, I guess that explains it."

"What are you going to do?" Sarah asked.

"I'm going to do what she asked me to do. I'll take it down to my crack team"—his fingers flexed in air quotes—"as she put it, and see what they come up with."

"They're usually good at that sort of thing. I'm sure they'll figure out whatever this... thing says."

"Yes, I believe they will. Thank you, Sarah. I appreciate you bringing this up here. You could have just called. This tablet is, like, fifteen pounds."

She cast him a scathing glare. "I'm not weak, Mr. Schultz."

"I know. I was just being polite. You know, gentlemanly?"

"Oh." Her face flushed again. "Sorry."

"Don't be. It probably sounded bad. Anyway, thanks for bringing it up."

"No problem. I'll head back to my desk now—if that's okay."

"Of course," Tommy said.

Sarah turned and walked out of the office. She was good, but probably not the right fit for someone to come in and start taking over portions of the operation. Sarah wasn't a leader, but she was a loyal follower, and there would always be a place for good folks like that in his organization.

He needed someone who could help with some of the pressing issues that seemed to be mounting. The IAA's reputation had spread over the last decade, and they were getting more requests every week.

Tommy ran his fingers through his hair and stopped when his hand reached the back of his neck. He stared down at the tablet and nodded. "Great. Now I have to take this all the way to the basement."

7

ATLANTA

P atton Driscoll gazed lazily at the computer screen on his desk. The spreadsheet displayed dozens of different numbers, each with their own monetary representation and assignment for expenditures and revenue.

His church, rebranded recently as the Vineyard Church, had a bumper year thus far, and the coffers overflowed with the generosity of its members. It was one of the largest churches in the region, and certainly in the city. Not only that, but several prominent local businesspeople were members and their tithes did wonders to fill the needs of the church, as well as Driscoll's pockets.

He drove a BMW 7 series, M edition, had a six-thousand-square-foot home in Buckhead near the governor's mansion, and the finest suits direct from the best designers in Italy, Paris, and London.

Those things Driscoll didn't try to hide from his members. He constantly explained to them that God had blessed him and his family, and that they were also blessed—the more they gave, the more they would receive.

Of course, some never received anything. A few actually went broke after giving all they could to the church. That wasn't his problem. Driscoll looked at his fellow pastors and wondered why they didn't dip into the same well that he did. The only conclusion he could reach was that they were sincere in their beliefs and teachings, in the way they engaged with their churches and communities. Driscoll didn't care.

He'd fallen into being a pastor more than eight years ago, and had quickly risen to prominence in the Atlanta community. His fervor for the gospel and the charisma with which he delivered the message earned him eager followers, and lots of them. The little Northside Church quickly grew the numbers of people flocking to the call of this upstart pastor.

Driscoll laughed all the way to the bank.

A toilet flushed from his personal bathroom and he instinctively looked over to the door as it opened.

His assistant, a thirty-two-year-old brunette, stepped out of the bathroom and shut off the light. She fixed her hair to make it look less disheveled and straightened her white blouse.

The affair had begun almost immediately after she applied for the position. Technically, it wasn't an affair. Not on his end. He wasn't married and had no plans to step onto that sinking ship. His assistant, however, was married—to a man she claimed she didn't love anymore. Her pictures on social media told a different story, or at least a different story to the one her husband was getting.

Driscoll didn't care. Divorced. Single. Married. It didn't matter to him. She was only one of a half dozen in his stable, and he rotated them with the deftness of an experienced casanova. Of course, rumors floated through the community and through the church itself, but Driscoll was able to deflect those at every turn. Always the manipulator, he managed to twist the truth and make it look unpalatable to anyone willing to consider consuming it.

"I'm heading home—unless there's anything else you need," the woman said.

What else could I need, he thought. *I just got what I wanted from you.* "No, I'm good, Mary. Thank you. Have a good night. See you tomorrow."

He didn't want to see her tomorrow. He was scheduled to have dinner with one of the other women, and being around Mary all day could slake his thirst. Not from guilt, obviously, but he didn't want her to cramp his style.

Still, there was no getting around it. She had her usefulness. And she was very good. If dinner happened to be canceled, another round with Mary would be good enough.

"Okay," she said, lingering uncharacteristically for a moment. "I guess I'll see you tomorrow."

She turned and showed herself out the door, leaving him to his financials.

The door closed behind her, and he went back to studying the numbers on the screen as if she'd never been there. Driscoll had become incredibly skilled at moving money around, slipping a few hundred into a fund here, a charity there, a donation drive occasionally. All the while, he siphoned money out of the church and into his various accounts, some of which were not based in the United States. Of course, he had a few cash businesses on the side as well, places that his flock could never know about—though some frequented.

He snorted at the idea. How quickly they would judge and crucify him for his misdeeds. All of them had sins of their own, secrets they never shared. There were no innocents. Driscoll figured if everyone were guilty, he may as well make a profit.

He snorted again and rubbed his nose, then reached down to the bottom drawer of his desk and pulled out a decanter of Pappy Van Winkle 15 Year, along with a tumbler. He set the glass on the desk and splashed a shot into it, then replaced the whiskey in its home and closed the drawer.

Lifting the glass to his nose, he took a whiff and let the intoxicating fumes of caramel, vanilla, oak, and leather flow through his nostrils. Then he took a long sip and let the slow burn soak his tongue and trickle down his throat. He let out a satisfied "ah" and set the glass next to the keyboard.

"One more check on things before we head home," he said to himself.

He clicked on the web browser and went to the aggregator site he used to keep a real-time view of all his accounts. He performed the double check twice a week just to make sure everything was performing as it should.

Driscoll typed in his username and password, then clicked the login button on the screen. The site blinked, and then his accounts appeared, listed down the left-hand side with their balances on the right. His heart rate instantly climbed as panic filled his gut and flowed upward to his throat. His muscles tensed, and he flicked his eyes back and forth at the account numbers and the balances corresponding to them.

"What?" he said. "That's... impossible." He clicked the refresh button, and a couple of seconds later, the same screen reappeared.

"What is wrong with this thing?" He clicked the browser again and entered the website for his primary bank. His fingers clicked on the keys as he entered his information.

When he clicked the login button, bile rolled up his esophagus on seeing what he feared. The account was empty. Immediately, he clicked on the browser again and entered a different bank. The results were the same. Over and over, he checked each individual account until he'd looked at every one.

His money was gone. *There had to be some kind of mistake. A banking error or internet error. This couldn't be right. There was no way millions of dollars had just vanished.*

He swore out loud, blaspheming.

"Where is my money?" he shouted at the computer screen. Then he slammed it off the desk. The thing hit the floor with a crunch, the cracked monitor now blinking in the dimly lit room.

He gasped for air. His heart pounded and a sharp pain pulsed with it. He felt his face flush and knew he was having a panic attack. Desperate for a salve, he grabbed the high-end bourbon and emptied the contents of the tumbler into his mouth. He sucked down the whiskey without even noticing the mild burn. Then he bent down and took out the bottle again to pour himself another drink.

As he removed the cap, the door eased open. He looked across the room in the pale lamplight. "Mary? I thought you left." *Maybe she didn't get enough the first time,* he thought, though at the moment he was far from interested in the carnal temptations she could offer.

The door inched farther, finally allowing the light to strike the face of the intruder. It wasn't Mary.

A man stood in the doorway, his beard a patchwork of gray and black. Thick eyebrows matched his facial hair, as did the dense forest of hair on his scalp that ran to a sharp point above his forehead. He wore a white button-up shirt with the sleeves rolled up to expose strong, bronzed forearms. Black slacks covered his legs. It would have been a business-casual look if it hadn't been for the black cowboy boots on his feet.

"I'm sorry," Driscoll said, even more unnerved as a result of the stranger's appearance. "The church is closed for the night. I thought Mary would have locked up, but I guess she forgot. Would you like to come by tomorrow? What do you need, stranger? Prayer? A scriptural promise?"

The stranger's vapid stare sent Driscoll's nerves straight over the cliff. "Unless, of course, you're in desperate need, my son. Please, come in. You want something to drink?"

The older man took a slow step forward and shut the door behind him. Then he returned to standing with his hands folded in front of him, fingers wrapped around the handle of a whip. "Are you offering me some of that Pappy Van Winkle 15 you have in the desk?"

Driscoll's eyes shot down to the drawer, then back to the man—as if he'd seen a ghost. "How did you... Did you break in here? I'm calling the police."

Driscoll reached for the phone on his desk. A crack shot through the air, immediately followed by a sharp pain in his wrist. The whip wrapped around faster than the preacher could blink. Metal shards glinted in the lamplight a fraction of a second before they bit into his skin and tore the flesh. He dropped to his knees, grasping at his arm to release it from the jagged bonds. He yelled out from the pain, but his words were intelligible.

"You have been weighed in the balance and found wanting, Pastor," the stranger said.

"Wh... what?" Driscoll cowered on his knees.

"Surely you know that verse from the Bible," the man said. "You teach the gospel here, do you not?"

Driscoll looked up at the man, eyes brimming with tears. "Yes. Of course I do. Now please, take this thing off of me."

The stranger ignored the request. "Then you will know that it's from Daniel 5:27 when the heathen king of Babylon refused to change his ways."

"Oh. Yes. Obviously. I know that one."

"I'm sure you do," the stranger sneered. "And yet you haven't changed your ways. Have you, Patton?"

"I... I don't know what you're talking about."

The intruder's eyes flashed to the computer screen on the floor. "It looks like you had an accident."

Driscoll's eyes followed the man's and then back. "Yes. I... I was looking for something, and it fell over. I guess I knocked it off. Please, let me go."

"Looking for something? I don't suppose it was all that money, was it?"

Dread filled Driscoll's eyes. His face washed a pale white. His fear quickly gave way to desperate indignation. "Why did you... how? No, you know what? Fine. You took it. Look, just let me go, and we can work this out. Okay? You keep a percentage. I keep a percentage. And the money will keep coming, too. Look around, man. This gig is a honey pot."

The stranger sighed. "I dust my sandals of this place," he said, referencing a verse from the book of Matthew.

"What? What are you talking about?"

"You have been weighed and found wanting," the stranger repeated. "By suffering shalt thou be cleansed. By his stripes you are healed. By death shall you be reborn."

The intruder jerked on the whip and a new surge of pain cut through Driscoll's arm as he felt himself pulled forward onto his face.

His jaw hit the floor and sent his brain into a haze. Blood trickled down his forearm and onto the floor. He looked up through the fog to the man stepping toward him. The black cowboy boots tapped rhythmically, slowly, toward Driscoll. They stopped with a dramatic click in front of Driscoll's face. The preacher twisted his head, desperate to plead with his attacker to let him go.

He saw the face looming over him, darkness filling the man's eyes. Then the stranger swung his boot into the side of Driscoll's head. The daze dropped like a curtain over his eyes. His eyelids drooped lazily.

The intruder held his head up and smacked his cheek several times. "Oh, no, Preacher," the man said. "You don't get to pass out. No, sir. You got to be purified first. But don't you worry. If you do pass out, you'll wake up soon enough. I guarantee you that. But you're an example. You see, I need to get a certain person's attention. So, this here is what we call two birds with one stone. I save your soul. And you help me get what I want."

"What do you want?" The words barely dripped out of Driscoll's mouth.

"Oh, that's a secret, Preacher. But when I have it, I will cleanse the entire world of sin, and then the New Jerusalem will be born on Earth."

Driscoll stared into the man's zombie-cold eyes and tried to process what was going on.

The answers would come soon enough.

8

ATLANTA

Tommy stared at the screen, eyes squinting. The computer monitor displayed several lines of text written in Aramaic, a language he recognized but was unable to interpret fluently.

"What do you think?" Tara asked, enlarging the image on the screen so he could better focus on the script.

"It's definitely an ancient language," Tommy mused.

Alex looked over at him from behind his black-frame glasses. When he shook his head in disbelief, his dark brown hair jiggled a little. "Um, yeah. You think?"

Tommy offered up a quick laugh. "Of course I'm kidding, you two. It's obviously Aramaic."

Tara peered at him with her green eyes. A single strand of her auburn hair dangled over the right arm of her tortoiseshell glasses. "And?" she urged.

"And we probably need to get an expert in that language in here to interpret it for us."

Tara and Alex exchanged an eye roll.

"I saw that," Tommy said. He pushed himself away from the desk he'd been leaning on and stood up straight. "Just because you two are married doesn't mean I don't know it when you're making fun of me."

"Half the time, you don't," Tara countered with a mischievous wink.

"Anyway," Tommy continued, "I have someone who can help. And the good news is they're just up the road at SAU near Chattanooga."

"That's useful. Would be even more useful if we could set up the quantum computers to translate those images." Tara pinched a thumb between her teeth as she pondered how that might be done. "Oh, wait. We can do that."

Tommy's eyes lit up like a kid at the bottom of the stairs on Christmas morning. "Wait, really?"

"Could have sworn we'd done that for you before, but yeah. These machines run pretty much all the time. They're always learning." She motioned to the row of computers on top of another table. Blue LED lights glowed on the front of the black towers and through transparent side walls.

Alex took over. "We set them up to compile databases of all the old languages the world has ever known. Or at least the ones we know about. Sanskrit, Latin, Cuneiform, Old Greek, and yes, Aramaic."

"Fascinating," Tommy gasped. He knew their computers were good, and they were updated every six months with the latest hardware. Software updates were far more frequent, but also taken care of —in large part—by the machines themselves.

He straightened and looked around with his hands on his hips. He'd come a long way from the lab in the old building. Back then, they had resources, but as time moved on, his investments grew, and revenue for the agency grew, too. And since it was a nonprofit, he poured a hefty segment of their proceeds into the lab—after rebuilding the entire facility.

"We will do a few more scans to make sure we get an accurate image of all the script, but it shouldn't take long. We can have it translated in less than an hour. Maybe even thirty minutes."

"Awesome," Tommy clapped his hand on Alex's shoulder, who

looked up at him from an office chair. Tara sat similarly and also wore a look of pride on her face.

The phone in Tommy's pocket vibrated and he held up a finger to excuse himself. "Keep going... with the... thing you just said." He fumbled for the words. He glanced down at the device and saw it was the receptionist.

"Hey, Sarah. What's up?"

"You have an old friend here to see you, Mr. Schultz."

"An old friend, huh? I don't have many friends."

"He says he knows you. And sir, he's with the police."

"Oh, I see." Tommy flushed. What were the cops doing here? It wasn't uncommon for a cop to come wandering in now and then, strolling along their beat near Centennial Olympic Park. "I'll be right up."

He ended the call and slid the phone into his pocket. "I'll be back down in a bit. Have a visitor up top."

"Okay, boss," Tara said playfully. She knew he didn't like it when they called him that, which is why they called him that. Antagonizing Tommy was one of the perks of the position.

He rolled his eyes and started toward the door. "Just get working on that translation. You'll save my friend in Chattanooga a drive through Atlanta traffic."

"Sure thing. We'll call you when it's ready."

Tommy thanked them again and left the lab, making his way along the wall of windows looking back into where the young couple sat talking with each other excitedly, probably about the translation. They loved that kind of stuff.

While Tommy was still young, barely in his forties, he knew that someday—probably a few decades from then—he'd have to turn over the reins to someone else. And he could think of no one better than those two.

For now, though, he apparently had a visitor from law enforcement.

He rode the elevator up to the lobby and stepped out onto the shiny marble floor. The IAA lobby bore the look of an official government building, but with touches of a more modern aesthetic in the lights, the reception desk, the plants, and some of the display cases and picture frames that showed off some of the less valuable artifacts and works of art in the agency's possession.

Tommy chuckled to himself at the thought. *Less valuable.* Everything in the building was valuable to him. Just because it wasn't priceless to some buyer didn't mean it lacked worth.

His shoes clicked on the hard floor as he stepped away from the elevator and sauntered across the large space toward the reception desk. A smile crept across his face when he saw who was standing there, absently eyeing a painting hanging from a column across from Sarah.

"I feel like I should have at least tucked my shirt in," Tommy said as he approached. He wore a white button-up shirt with navy blue pants and brown Cole Hahn shoes.

The visitor was a black man with a striking jaw and dark, serious eyes that commanded authority. He stood an inch or so under six feet tall with broad shoulders and a slender torso.

The guest turned and grinned back at Tommy, eyeing him up and down in a second. "No need to worry about that," the man said. "I'm retired, remember? Not that it mattered when I was still on the force." He motioned to himself and the untucked polo he had donned over a pair of khakis.

Tommy chuckled and extended his hand to his old acquaintance. "Good to see you again, Trent. Been a while."

"Our fishing trip to Carter Lake last year," Trent reminded.

"That's right. You wouldn't take the boat over to shore so I could take a leak. Made me go right there in the water."

"As it was meant to be."

"Not for a guy who's shy about that sort of thing."

Trent's eyebrows lifted, and then he bellowed a hardy laugh. His laughter boomed through the lobby, echoing off the hard surfaces.

"Who's your friend?" Tommy asked, suddenly aware of the third party in the room.

The woman had been standing in the corner near the entrance, checking something on her phone, when Tommy appeared from the elevator. Her long dark hair hung in a ponytail that dangled over the back of her neck. Her tanned skin signified long hours in the sun. Whether that was from work or leisure remained to be seen. She was tall, nearly as tall as Trent and Tommy. She wore a sleeveless black dress that looked like it might have been more appropriate for dinner at a nice restaurant as opposed to... whatever work she did.

That last thought brought Tommy back to the reason for Trent's visit. The woman strode across the floor, her tall boots tapping methodically on the surface.

"This is Kimberly Henderson," Trent said, extending an arm to the approaching woman.

She responded by offering her hand, which Tommy took. Her grip was stronger than he'd anticipated, and as she shook it, her triceps and forearms flexed slightly.

"Good handshake," Tommy said, recovering and gripping a little tighter.

"CrossFit," she said. Her nondescript accent made her origins difficult to place.

"Ah. Be careful with that. I have a friend who's in orthopedics. She said CrossFit pays most of her bills."

Kimberly offered an unconvincing smirk. "I'll try to remember that."

Tommy decided it was probably time to move on to the point of their visit. "So, to what do I owe the pleasure?

"As you may recall," Trent began, "I may be retired, but I'm still doing some consulting work for the Atlanta PD. Mostly when they have a... special case."

"And that brought you here?" Tommy put his hands on his hips and displayed a look that expressed both confusion and concern. "I don't think we broke any laws."

Trent pursed his lips together and twitched his head. "No, I don't think you did, either. Although maybe I should have the guys come have a look around." He realized his mistake and corrected. "Or you know, gals, too."

"I know what you meant," Kimberly said. "You don't have to walk on eggshells with me. I'm one of the guys, too." She took a step closer and held out her phone for Tommy to see.

"What's this?" he asked and tilted his head to get a better view. He instantly withdrew. "Whoa! What the...? Why would you show me that? Is that real?" He looked like he might puke.

"Sorry," Trent said putting out a hand to ease his friend's reaction. He also gave Kimberly a scathing glare. "You gotta give civilians a heads-up with that kind of thing, lady."

"My apologies, Mr. Schultz. I didn't really think about that."

Tommy held his hand over his mouth for several breaths and then held up his palm. "It's okay. I'm... I'm fine. Just need a few breaths here." He bent over at the waist and sucked in four huge gulps of air before standing up straight again. "Okay, I'm good." He held up a thumb. "But yeah, maybe a heads-up before you just pop up your phone with an image like that. We regular folks aren't used to that sort of thing."

"She's a forensics investigator," Trent said. "Fed."

"Oh, well that explains that."

"Atlanta PD special investigations called me in," she said. "The man in the picture was a local pastor of one of the largest churches in the entire Southeast."

"Okay," Tommy said, still collecting himself.

"This photo was taken yesterday. The custodian found the body. Do you know the man in the picture?"

Tommy considered a response that bordered on comical, but decided it wasn't the time. "Let me see it again. I'm okay now."

"You sure?" Trent asked.

Tommy blew off the question with a dismissive wave of the hand. He cocked his head again and looked at the image on the phone. Kimberly extended it once more so he could get a better view.

The disturbing image featured a middle-aged white man with thick, curly black hair. He hung from a large wooden cross behind the pulpit. All of his clothing had been stripped from his body. Deep gashes covered his skin, as well as an awful lot of blood, as if a blade had cut him multiple times. As Tommy stared harder at the image, he realized that the wounds weren't from a knife or sword but from a whip. The man had been flogged repeatedly.

Splattered blood covered patches of the man's swollen face. His eyes were pinched shut by the swollen skin on his forehead and cheeks.

"You said he's... was a pastor?" Tommy asked.

"Yes," Kimberly answered.

Tommy put his hand over his mouth.

"That's his church," Trent said. "We're... trying to keep a lid on this as far as what the public sees and hears. With so many members in a church that size, these things can get out of hand quickly if even one person finds out."

"What about the custodian?"

"He doesn't speak English. Guatemalan immigrant."

"He okay?" Tommy asked, genuinely concerned.

"Seem to be. The guy has seen some messed-up stuff back in his home country. Nothing like this, but some pretty gruesome things. He told our translator the cartel did some messed-up stuff in his town."

"Well, I guess that's... well, it's not good, but at least he's not going through PTSD or anything." Then a thought occurred to Tommy, pricking his mind like a thorn. "Wait a second. If I don't know that pastor, why are you two here?"

The two visitors cast a sidelong glance at each other, and then Kimberly pulled her phone closer and swiped to the right. Another image of the pastor appeared. This one was zoomed in. She held out the device to Tommy. The curious look on his face turned sour even as the color left his skin. "What in the world?"

On the man's chest, surrounded by bloody gashes, the letters *SWIAA* were carved into his flesh.

"You think—" Tommy started.

"I don't think Sean had anything to do with it," Trent clarified, firing a glare at the forensics detective.

"Had anything to do with what?" The familiar voice cut through the room, the Southern accent warm yet curious.

Everyone turned to see a man with bronzed skin in a Led Zeppelin T-shirt, khakis, and weathered brown boots standing in the doorway.

"Speak of the devil," Trent said.

"What are you three talking about? I assume Sarah isn't involved. Morning, Sarah." Sean diverted his icy-gray eyes toward the receptionist. She yawned and waved back at him.

"I just answer the phones and tell people where to go, Sean," she replied.

"So, Sarah's innocent. What about you three?" Sean ambled across the lobby to where the group stood in front of the big desk.

"I was just about to ask you the same thing," Kimberly said dryly. She held out her phone so he could see the image of the pastor.

Sean tilted his head and peered at the grisly photo. "You know, you really should warn civilians about pictures like this before you show it to them. You could get vomit all over that black dress." He kept his eyes on the phone, not allowing her to think he was checking her out. He'd already assessed her before he was halfway across the floor. Probably a federal officer. Clearly took good care of herself. And since she was here with Trent, who had been working as a police consultant, that meant something special was going on, though he hadn't anticipated a gruesome murder.

"Do you know this man?" Kimberly asked bluntly.

Sean studied the photo for another two seconds then shook his head. "Afraid I don't," he said. "Looks like this was done in a church."

"It was," Trent confirmed. "One of the largest in the city. They have tens of thousands of active members on their roster."

"That's going to make it tough to keep quiet," Sean said with a whistle.

"We're working on it."

Kimberly brought the conversation back to the victim as she pulled up the zoomed photo again. "Can you explain why this man would have your initials and the initials of your agency cut into his chest?"

Sean narrowed his eyelids and peered at the image. "No. I can't say I can explain that, but good for you coming to that conclusion. Clever."

"Your explanation as to why a dead pastor has your initials on his chest is that it was clever?" She sounded disgusted and insulted all in one tone.

"What?" Sean choked. "No, clever that you came up with that solution. Makes sense. Pastor from Atlanta. Initials look like mine and the IAA with it just confirms everything. I get it. But no, I didn't kill that man. Didn't know him. I only got back into the country a few hours ago. You can check the passenger manifest for the flight, and please, feel free to evaluate any and all video footage from Hartsfield-Jackson. I'm sure they got a few hundred good shots of me as we left the terminal and came through customs." He turned to Tommy. "On our commercial flight." He spat the words in staccato.

"Hey, we needed the company jet."

"For what? You know what? Never mind. It's your plane anyway."

"Sorry first class wasn't good enough for you," Tommy snarled, "princess."

"Actually, we flew Delta Comfort," Sean corrected. Then he abruptly stuck out his hand toward the detective. "I'm sorry, I didn't catch your name. Sean Wyatt. Nice to meet you, Ms...."

"Henderson. Kimberly Henderson. I'm a forensic investigator with the FBI."

"FBI, huh?" Sean said, sounding impressed. "Awfully quick for them to pull the trigger on a federal investigation, isn't it? When did you say this murder happened?"

"The body was found yesterday. Estimated time of death was ten p.m. the night before."

Sean peered at the body. He felt bad for the victim. He didn't recognize the pastor, though that wasn't a huge surprise. There were more churches in Atlanta and the surrounding area than he could count.

"He was one of the pastors from television on Sunday mornings," Trent said.

"Well, that's why I don't recognize him."

"Because you go to church on Saturday?" Trent laughed.

"That, too. But mostly because I watch football on Sundays. Even the pregame stuff." He didn't let his voice shift to an around-the-water-cooler tone for fear of being corrected by the newcomer detective. "Looks like he was whipped," Sean detoured, pointing at the wounds around the letters.

"He was," Kimberly said. "Severely beaten, too."

Sean didn't say it, but the thought crossed his mind that the victim looked like he'd been on the losing end of a heavyweight fight.

"The letters aren't the only reason we're here, Sean," Trent spoke up. He held out a sheet of paper. Sean looked at it and then took it. Tommy hadn't seen that yet either and shifted his position so he could see what it was.

"That's a copy of what was found on the pastor," Trent said. "The original is in evidence lockup."

Sean scanned the page. The sentences were typed and printed out, probably from a word processor. For decades, murderers and kidnappers feared being tracked down using such methods to convey their demands, instead opting to cut out letters from magazines to paste to sheets of paper. That, however, was time consuming. This killer clearly didn't concern himself with such tracking techniques.

Across the top of the sheet, were three words: Lust. Greed. Pride. Below that, the note got more personal.

"Hello, Sean," the letter began. "This sinner has been cleansed of his sins, the sins listed above. Only through suffering and death can a sinner truly be cleansed if they won't confess to the Almighty.

"I will cleanse another in three days, and every three days thereafter unless you solve this ancient mystery.

"Do I have your attention, Sean? I hope so.

"There are three legs to this mystery. Three pieces you must solve. When you have done so, I will cease this part of my ministry and begin the next with a double portion of the spirit to guide me."

Sean paused for a second. "Ministry?"

"We had the same question," Trent said. "Pretty sick gospel if you ask me."

"Indeed," Tommy added.

Sean kept reading.

"Three pieces of one and one of three, great messengers of God in the prophet's tree. The first denied his rightful place and cursed his lot, though pages forgotten tell the truth of his fate. Now he rests above the palace grounds, his piece of the key underneath, within the nave of the winged horse."

The note came to an abrupt end. Sean read it again to make sure he got all the details, then handed it back to Trent.

"Well?" Kimberly insisted. "What do you think?"

Sean looked over at his friend and stuffed his hands into his pockets. "I think you have a serial killer on your hands."

9

ATLANTA

"**S**erial killer?" Kimberly's words hung in the lobby along with the lights that dangled from the ceiling via steel cylinders. She made it sound like the most ludicrous suggestion she'd ever heard.

"Is there another name for someone who's targeting a specific type of people to murder them in a predetermined sequence?" Sean shrugged as he asked the question.

"No," Kimberly huffed. "I suppose not."

"This guy killed a local pastor. I don't know anything about the guy, but this murderer included a note to me, along with a threat that there would be more bloodshed to come if we don't jump through the hoops he says."

"Do you have any idea what the clues could mean?" Trent asked.

Sean took a deep breath through his nostrils. He pulled his hands out of his pockets and ran his fingers through his hair, letting his lips flap dramatically as he exhaled. "Tommy? Thoughts?"

Tommy had read the note twice, too. He sighed before he answered. "There's a lot to unpack there. I guess the first thing we would address is who this letter is about?"

"The next victim?" Kimberly asked.

"No, although that might be something the police want to start looking into. It didn't appear that the killer offered any sort of clue as to who the next target might be. That makes things a little dicey."

She nodded her agreement.

"I was actually talking about the person in the riddle, the one of three and three of one."

"Any clue what that means?" Trent pushed.

"Off the top of my head, not really. It's obviously talking about the prophets, but which ones? That's not a short list, Trent. There were dozens of prophets, and those are just the ones the biblical scriptures tell us about. Several more didn't have their books included in the canon or were simply never found to include."

Silence descended into the enormous room, and for nearly a minute, no one spoke. The words from the letter kept rattling around in Sean's head, his persistent memory unwilling to let them go.

"The first denied his rightful place and cursed his lot," Sean murmured.

"What?" Kimberly snapped.

"Sorry," Sean looked up, realizing he was staring down at the shiny white tiles. "Just thinking to myself. Sometimes I think out loud. Helps me process information faster."

"Oh," Kimberly looked embarrassed that she'd sounded rude.

"I know; it's a weird thing. My wife makes fun of me for it now and then."

"What does your wife do?" Kimberly asked, trying to make amends.

"That's a complicated question, one that doesn't have a simple answer." He moved back into the discussion regarding the riddle. "If we're talking about prophets from the Bible, which ones were denied their place and cursed their lot?"

"I can't think of any off the top of my head. I mean, there were so many. And that's not including the various priests that also served. Not to mention that the Kingdom of Israel was divided after the reign of Solomon."

"That's right," Sean affirmed, holding up a finger. "The kingdom was split in two, Judah and Israel. Each received their own prophets, too, though it seemed like Israel had them earlier on in their history."

"Could be because they strayed from the teachings of God," Tommy offered.

"True, but which one cursed his lot?"

"Elijah put a curse on the land, didn't he?" Trent offered. "Wasn't there a famine or something he predicted to the king?"

Tommy and Sean looked at their friend, impressed by his knowledge. "Looks like someone's been studying," Tommy said.

"The only issue I have with that is Elijah didn't deliberately curse the nation or his lot, so to speak. He warned the king that if he didn't change his ways, he would be punished with famine. Ahab's wife, the illustrious Jezebel, convinced him that Elijah was the problem and that he should be hunted down. I'm paraphrasing, obviously."

"We get the gist," Kimberly said. "So, if it wasn't Elijah, who was it?"

"Well, like we said, he's just one from a whole list of prophets. Many of them were involved with curses of the kingdom. The leaders continued to do the opposite of what they were instructed by their religious leaders, and so the curses kept coming. But all of those were results, not initial curses placed on the people in general." Tommy's explanation seemed to help her question, but only in part.

"What if by lot the riddle doesn't mean the prophet's people? What if it's talking about his lot in life?" Sean asked.

Tommy's face lit up. "Why didn't I think of that?"

"Because you're not as smart as me," Sean chirped with a wink. "But yes, that should narrow it down a bit. So, think for a moment. Which of the prophets were big complainers, people who were reluctant members of the ministry who would have rather done something else?

"Jonah whined a lot," Trent groused.

"Yes!" Tommy said, clapping his hands together far louder than he intended. "Jonah. That's right. He complained about having to go to Nineveh to preach the word of salvation and repentance. He didn't want to give the message of *teshuva* to the Ninevites because he was afraid they would kill him. Or worse."

"Worse?" Kimberly asked.

"They were a heathen bunch," Tommy explained. "Known for some serious degradation throughout the region."

"What's Teshuva?" Trent asked. "Is that what you called it?"

"Yes. Teshuva is the teaching that if a person repents of their sins, they can be forgiven. Teshuva means return, as in a return to God and the path of righteousness."

Kimberly took a moment to process the information and then offered her solution. "So, does that mean we're looking for the burial place of the prophet Jonah?"

Sean's brow tightened at the question, specifically the way she asked it. "Well, it could mean that. We'll need to do a little more research before we can say for sure, but he's certainly the lead suspect at the moment."

"The only problem with that is that the tomb of Jonah was destroyed several years ago." Tommy winced as he said the words. He detested being the bearer of bad news, which would have—ironically—made him a terrible prophet since it seemed so many were almost eager to complete such a task.

"What do you mean, it was destroyed?" Trent asked. "I'm surprised anyone knew where it was. All those tombs have been around for thousands of years. I'd think they would be buried under centuries' worth of dirt."

Tommy nodded. "That's true. Many of the tombs are that way. The Valley of the Kings in Egypt is a prime example. However, many ancient tombs have been venerated for millennia all over the Middle East. We've visited a few of them in the past. Most have had shrines or mosques built over them and are used in religious rituals. They've become places for pilgrims of multiple religions to visit. The tomb of Jonah, or Yunus as he's known in the Koran, was a holy place for Christians, Muslims, and Jews. The terrorists that destroyed it claimed they did so because it had become a place of apostasy instead of prayer. Most believe they thought that because multiple religions were permitted to visit."

"That's such a shame," Trent said, his forlorn tone matching his facial expression.

"Tell me about it. So much history and tradition gone in seconds because of a terrorist's bomb. And that doesn't even factor in the loss of life."

Sean recalled reading headlines about other sites the extremists had destroyed during their war against apostasy. Many sites in Mosul, and indeed all over Iraq, had been blown up for the same reasons. The tragic loss of life often seemed to take a back seat in a part of the world where violence seemed to reign supreme. Whenever Sean read one of those articles, he couldn't help but think of all the families destroyed by the attacks.

"The mosque was located on a hill called Nabi Yunus," Tommy said. "It was one of the more visited tombs in Mosul. There was an interesting piece of information that pertains to the attacks, though." He thumbed his bottom lip as he recalled the story. "The explosion actually opened up a hole in the mosque's floor, where the attackers discovered a series of ancient tunnels—corridors built by the property's previous tenants."

"Which was who?" Kimberly urged.

"An Assyrian king. I can't recall his name off the top of my head but definitely Assyrian, a descendant of Sennacherib, who's mentioned prominently in the Bible—in at least three books of the Old Testament if I remember correctly. I'll have to look it up or it will drive me crazy tonight when I try to go to sleep."

Sean didn't recall hearing about the tunnels, but it piqued his interest. "What was in the tunnels?"

Tommy rolled his shoulders. "We really could have this discussion in my office where we could sit down, but to answer your question, the tunnels were part of the ancient palace. Anything of value down there was looted by the terrorists. They took everything, at least we assume. It's really up in the air as to what might have been down there all that time."

"Terrorists stealing artifacts," Sean mumbled. "Now I've heard it all. I guess they have to pay for bullets and explosives somehow— although that funding usually comes from private resources, occasionally government backing. Okay, often government backing."

"So, what are we supposed to do?" Kimberly asked. "The killer said that if we don't find the first part of the key or whatever that he's going to kill another person."

Tommy and Sean exchanged a questioning look, but Tommy fielded the question.

"I wish we could figure it out, I really do, but I don't know what to tell you. The tomb was destroyed, and anything of value was picked clean, assuming there was anything of value there, as I said."

Trent looked at his two friends and then to the federal investigator. "I can make a few calls, see if this murder matches up with anything else out there. Maybe we'll get lucky, but my guess is that this is a new killer. Certainly is for the city of Atlanta. We haven't seen anything like this before. Whoever this person is, they have it in for you, Sean. So, you'd better watch your back."

"I always do," Sean quipped.

Tommy's phone buzzed in his pocket. He fished it out and pressed the green button. "What's up, guys?"

"We just finished the analysis of the tablet," Tara said.

Kimberly heard the comment and her attention perked up.

"What does it say?" Tommy asked.

"It's interesting, I'll say that. It has some pretty obscure references. They're like directions, but it feels as if whoever these instructions were meant for would already have some important bits of information."

"Such as?"

"Well, it gives some details such as how many steps to walk before making a right turn or a left. It also describes strange images, like a winged horse or something. There's no reference, though. We don't know the exact location to begin."

"Wait a second," Tommy interrupted. "What did you just say? A winged horse? Sounds like Pegasus, but that wasn't an Assyrian legend."

"We thought the same thing. Kind of weird, huh?"

"Very." Tommy considered the translation. What did it all mean? Sean and the others were staring at him, so he quickly recovered. "Thank you, Tara. I'll be down in a bit to examine the results more thoroughly."

"No problem, chief. You know where to find us."

Tommy ended the call and looked at the others.

"Well?" Sean pressed before Kimberly could. Her intense interest seeped from her eyes; eyes so dark they were nearly black.

"That tablet sounds like a description of a specific place." Then his head snapped up. "We need to go down to the lab."

10

ATLANTA

T ommy's heart pounded every bit as hard as his shoes did against the floor as he led the group through the basement corridor toward the lab. He looked in through the glass wall and saw that, unsurprisingly, Tara and Alex were still there, hovering over the computer station where they'd been twenty minutes before.

"Are you going to tell us what's going on?" Trent asked, doing his best to keep up.

Even Sean, who was slightly taller than his friend, had difficulty matching Tommy's pace. His mind was set on something. Sean knew that look. It was a look he'd seen before when his friend was onto something big.

"Something Tara said about a horse with wings," Tommy answered vaguely.

"A horse with wings? Like a unicorn?"

Tommy let out an audible huff. "No. But close. Winged horses have featured prominently in many ancient belief systems and mythologies. The most famous is probably Pegasus, but other cultures had similar creatures. In China, Tianma is a winged horse that flies through the heavens. The Valkyries rode winged horses into battle in their defense of Asgard in the Norse mythologies." Tommy reached the door to the lab, entered a code, and pulled open the door when the keypad beeped.

"And," he continued, "in ancient Islamic cultures, Al-Buraq was a mythical flying horse that carried the prophet Muhammad from Mecca to Jerusalem, and even into the heavens."

"Sorry I asked," Trent coughed.

Tommy held the door open for the others to enter first, and then he followed as they gathered around Tara and Alex at their workspace.

"What's going on?" Alex asked, noting the two newcomers.

"My trip was fine; thanks for asking," Sean chimed.

"Oh, hey, Sean. Sorry. Yes, how was your trip? I mean, other than the whole running-off-an-assault-team-on-a-ship part. I heard you wrecked a rental yacht."

"Charter. It's called a charter, Alex. This isn't some chainsaw we picked up at the local hardware store for a little weekend tree cutting. It was an expensive yacht. Luckily, it was insured."

Kimberly's head turned at the story. She said nothing but was obviously curious about what happened.

"All righty, then," Alex said as he blew air through tightly pursed lips.

"The rest of the trip was nice, though. Had a chance to relax for a couple of days with Adriana. We enjoyed it." He cast a disarming grin at Alex, and the younger man's tension eased.

"That's good to hear."

"Where is Addy?" Tara asked.

"At the house taking care of some things. Unpacking. Told her I was coming down here to check on the progress with the tablet."

"Ah. Well, we have the translation. Did Tommy tell you?"

"Sort of," Sean hedged. He arched an eyebrow at Tommy, his signal that there was still more to the story yet to be revealed.

"Yes, now if you guys are done catching up on Sean's vacation memories, can we continue?" Tommy blurted.

The others giggled at the comment.

Tommy ignored it and went on. "As I was saying, there are many flying horses in the religions and mythologies from the ancient world." He slid into an empty chair at an unused computer station and rolled into place. He moved the mouse around with his right hand, and within seconds, the screen bloomed to life.

Tommy set to work, typing in a search for the tomb of the prophet Jonah. As expected, the page of results mostly suggested links that pertained to the Nabi Yunus mosque destroyed in 2014. He clicked on one of the articles that featured a story about the archaeological discoveries in the palace beneath the demolished shrine.

The next page filled in the screen, and Tommy dragged the mouse down, scrolling through images and text until he saw something peculiar.

The rest of the group silently maneuvered around the station until they were all huddled behind Tommy, bent down and looking over his shoulders at the screen.

"What are you doing?" Sean asked.

"Going on a hunch, like a good friend taught me to do a long time ago."

Sean smirked at the reference. "Very good, young one."

Tommy simply shook off the comment and zoomed in on the image that caught his eye. Then he clicked it, and the screen blinked before it took the user to a new site. The photograph filled the monitor, and Tommy sat back in the chair while the others looked on.

"Flying horse," Trent murmured.

"Yep." Tommy sounded proud of himself, but he knew they were far from getting any answers. "You said you found a translation for the tablet?"

"Yes," Tara said. "I made a printout of it in English as well as a copy of the original, the way it would have appeared if the grooves hadn't been so worn down."

She passed the sheet of paper to Tommy, who read the lines out loud for the others. Most of the document was as Tara had said, nothing but directions to something. Numbers of steps and turns in various directions to an obscure location were hardly helpful without context. Then Tommy stopped at the last line and went silent.

"What?" Sean asked. "What is it?"

Tommy read the last sentence. "There, you will find the piece of three beneath a winged horse." Then he held up the sheet for the others to see. At the bottom of the paper, two images filled in the footer. One was a curved rectangle with the image of a strange fish on it. The other looked like a side view of the same object.

"It looks like a piece of a bracelet," Tara noted. "See the clasp receivers there?" She pointed at the two notches on either end.

"I think you're right," Tommy said. "But why? And where is the other piece?"

"Pieces," Sean corrected. "One of three."

"So...." Alex started but obviously wanted Tommy to finish his thought for him.

"So," Tommy obliged, "it's a good bet that the tablet our friend Dr. Kelley found was referring to the tomb of Jonah. I mean, it's possible there are other tombs out there with similar carvings and reliefs adorning corridors and burial chambers. But as it relates to the riddle we just received from our friends in law enforcement, I'd say it's a good bet that this is the place."

"Riddle?" Tara asked.

Tommy filled them in on the murder of the pastor, how it was designed to get Sean's attention, and how the killer threatened more bloodshed if the demands weren't met, demands to solve an ancient puzzle within a tight timeline.

"So, there's a serial killer out there who's forcing you two to solve a couple-of-thousand-years-old mystery in a few days?"

"Three, actually," Sean clarified. "Although, with the time that's expired, I'm pretty sure we're down to maybe two."

"Which is why we should be moving." Kimberly finally spoke up after five minutes of total silence. "We need to get over there and search those tunnels. Surely there is something there we can use, something that could help."

Sean shook his head. "Not a chance, lady." She took exception to his tone, but he didn't care, as exhibited by his continuing on with the train of thought. "Have you ever been to Mosul?"

Her face flushed dark red, and she caught her breath. "No. I can't say that I have."

"Well," Sean said with a casual drawl, "let's just say it's not the safest place in the world to raise your kids. It's gotten better since the allied forces pushed the terrorists out, but it's still a dangerous place. They live under the perpetual threat that more insurgents, more terror groups, could come in and make a mess of everything again."

"I think I can handle myself, Agent Wyatt," she replied. "I'm a trained United States federal agent."

"That may be true, but I'm telling you, even with all of my field experience and expertise, I don't think I'd want to volunteer for a trip to Mosul. Not like this, anyway. Now, if I was going with a convoy of hardened soldiers or a security detail? Maybe. Maybe," he repeated for emphasis. "But just this group? I don't think so." He looked at the others. "No offense."

"None taken," Tommy and the young couple answered in tandem.

"So, that's it?" Kimberly threw her hands up in the air with the question. "We're just going to sit here and do nothing? Someone is going to die in the next"—she looked at her watch—"two and a half days. And you guys are just going to sit here and let it happen?"

"Are you finished?" Sean asked. He crossed his arms over his chest, tanned arms that rippled with muscles and veins under a smattering of freckles.

When she said nothing, instead only giving him a fiery glare, he went on. "I didn't say we're going to do nothing."

"What do you have in mind?" Tommy wondered. "That artifact is long gone—if it was ever there in the first place. And we don't know that it was for sure."

"You're right," Sean said, jabbing a finger at his friend. "It's a risk, and one that may not pay off. That key piece, or whatever the riddle mentioned, could be anywhere. It'll be like finding a single grain of sand in the Sahara."

"That's my point," Tommy said. He sounded a touch exasperated on the topic. "Those terrorists looted everything. They picked it clean and left nothing but the walls and fixtures."

"Wait," Trent jumped in. "What kinds of fixtures would an ancient palace like that have?"

"It was a joke," Tommy corrected. "Figure of speech, Trent. My point is, there's nothing left. So, we take the next step in the investigation, which is coming up with a theory as to where the artifacts could have been taken."

"And we don't know where their headquarters is or was," Sean said.

"Exactly. Which means, those artifacts are most likely now among the thousands of others that were moved around in the antiquities black market."

"So?" Kimberly said, shaking her head vehemently. "We track it down. We figure out who would have the money for an artifact like that and hunt them down."

"It's not that simple," Sean said. "First, you know that. You're a fed. Second, you don't want to mess with the guys who have enough money to afford black market artifacts and relics. They usually have a big payroll of dudes who know how to inflict copious amounts of pain. Their mansions—and they always have more than one—are equipped with state-of-the-art security systems and armed guards with a ruthless penchant for taking life."

"So, that's it? We're just going to walk away and let this madman kill more innocent people?" Kimberly couldn't believe what she was hearing.

"I never said that," Sean answered with a patch of gravel and a sprinkle of salt in his voice.

"You said it would be like finding a grain of sand in the desert," Tommy reminded. "There's no way we can handle that kind of scope for a search. It's the entire planet."

"I know," Sean said.

Everyone waited, their collective breath held as they stared at Sean expectantly, waiting for his response.

"So, what do you do when you need to find single grain of sand?"

The group said nothing, their blank expressions doing all the talking for them.

Sean sighed. "You talk to the nomads, the people who live there."

The others exchanged bewildered looks and then returned their gazes to Sean.

"I guess I have to spell everything out for you guys." He took a deep breath, still hoping someone would catch on, but he was being too vague. "We know a couple of guys who deal in the antiquities black market, remember?"

The lightbulb went off in Tommy's eyes. "Oh, Dak!" he exclaimed. "That's right! He does that sort of thing all the time. If anyone can find out where that artifact went, it would be him."

"Who's Dak?" Kimberly asked.

"Yeah. Who is this guy?" Trent pressed.

"Dak Harper," Tommy said. "He runs security for a kid up in Chattanooga. The boy made a bunch of money playing video games and running livestreams of his plays. He has a few million subscribers to his channel. His name is Boston McClaren. The kid loves ancient historical stuff for some reason. Most of the artifacts he's acquired aren't super valuable and are things that no one would miss. Every now and then, though, he probably comes across something of interest. Dak is the one who gets the stuff for him. Made a name for himself while he was in Delta Force several years back."

"Yeah," Sean agreed, "before things went sour."

"Right. After he got out of the military, he realized he had a knack for navigating the antiquities black market and for finding things that can't be found. They call him the Relic Runner. At least that's what Boston and a few other people call him. Not sure if he got that title before the boy hired him or after."

Kimberly looked optimistic for the first time since arriving at the IAA building. "How did these two meet? Can we set something up with them? Can you call them?" Her questions flew frantically from her mouth. "We need to get that piece. Someone's life could be hanging in the balance," she added quickly.

"I'll give Dak a call and see what he's doing," Sean said. "But these things can take a lot of time to track down, and that's when they're able to. I'm sure Dak has way more misses than hits when he's chasing down leads. So, even for an expert like him with a vast underground network, we may strike out."

"A second ago, you acted like this guy was our savior. Now you're saying he may not be able to help? Which is it?" Kimberly cocked her head to the side, accusing him with her eyes.

"Just telling you to lower your expectations. Dak's our best bet, but I doubt he'll have anything for us soon."

11

ATLANTA

"I can't believe how quickly you found that," Sean gasped into his phone. "How is that even possible?"

It had taken Dak a little over four hours to get an answer.

Dak chuckled on the other end of the line. "I did get a little lucky, but it helps that you were asking about a fairly unique artifact." Dak's accent did more than hint at his Southern origin. Certain words were long and drawn out, while others ended sharply. "Knowin' the origin of it also helped. I've been tracking ISIL pretty hard the last few years, whenever they hit a place. Recovered several important historical pieces from their loot bins and warehouses."

Sean knew about some of those recoveries because the IAA had been called in to transport several of the items to various places around the world, including here in Atlanta.

Dak had an unrelenting vendetta against extremists, especially the ones who vandalized historic or sacred places. It wasn't a religious thing for him. He respected the beliefs of others. In his mind, what they believed in or how they worshipped was their business. But when evil men attacked the innocent and destroyed places of worship or important landmarks, he made it his business.

The Mosul attack on Nabi Yunus happened a year before he left the military, so a direct line to that particular artifact wasn't available. His connections, however, had yielded a rapid result on his inquiry.

"One of my guys in China pinged me first. Said he knew exactly which item I was talking about because he'd seen it with his own eyes about five years ago. Said a guy he knows in the market brought in some Middle Eastern stuff, specifically Assyrian. They naturally figured it was the fish god, Dagon, which was one of the primary ancient deities of that region, including parts of Iraq."

New research suggested that the old theory of Dagon being a fish god may have been misinterpreted. Instead, a new theory offered that the deity's name was an adaptation for "grain," which would mean the god was one of agriculture and possibly fertility.

Sean didn't feel the need to correct Dak, so he cut straight to the point. "You don't happen to know where I can find it, do you?"

Dak hesitated for a moment. "Yeah. I knew you were going to ask that. Problem is, that thing is on the other side of the world. Literally. The man who bought it is a Chinese oil tycoon. He's worth tens of billions. Has a little place on the Macau island of Coloane."

"Little?" Sean asked.

"Twelve-thousand-square-foot cottage on the South China Sea."

"Some cottage."

"Yeah," Dak agreed with a grunt. "Anyway, it's surrounded by walls, guards, all that. If you want to get in and get that artifact, you're going to have to be subtle."

"Subtle is my middle name," Sean said with a wink to Tommy.

His friend scowled at the notion. *Sean was anything but subtle.* The recent incident with the chartered yacht was proof enough of that.

"Well, I'd suggest not going in with guns blazing," Dak said. "Too heavily fortified."

"Sounds like this guy is either paranoid or he doesn't just deal in oil."

"That's the other thing I was gonna tell you. Apparently, he runs drugs from his home and distributes them through all of South China. Having a house on the water makes it easy to transport tons of product back and forth with the mainland in Hong Kong. Word on the street is he uses his personal leisure vessels for the job."

"Why would a guy with billions of dollars risk getting in trouble for drug money? There's no way he moves enough volume to make it worthwhile."

"He's a power player," Dak explained. "Likes to be the man, if you know what I mean. He's also an avid gambler. You can find him at the casinos pretty much every night. Likes high-stakes poker. His games of choice are Omaha and Texas Hold 'Em."

There was the sliver of opportunity Sean needed. It shone on him like rays of sunlight through roiling storm clouds. "Texas Hold 'Em, huh?"

"Yep. And he has a ravenous appetite for rare antiquities, especially ones that have to be acquired illegally."

"Sounds like someone who wants to get caught."

"Could be. The guy's name is Wang Wei. Hope this helps. I can put my guy on him if you like. He owes me a couple of favors."

"Actually, that would be very helpful," Sean said. In his head, he was already calculating how much time they had left. The exact hours were a bit blurry, but he decided to estimate on the short side. "Thanks, Dak. I appreciate the assist."

"Not a problem, Sean. Anytime."

"Tell the kid I said hi."

"Ha. Will do—as soon as he's done with his session. Has something like forty thousand people watching him live right now. He's playing some online game with a bunch of other people."

"I hear he does well with that." Sean knew that was a massive understatement. "Thanks again for your help."

"You're welcome."

Sean ended the call and looked at the others. They'd been sitting around in the lab for hours. At one point, Alex went out and got food for everyone. He picked an Israeli place nearby and brought back falafels, shawarma, and bags of fries. The food helped ease the tension in the room. They were actually going to leave and come back the next day, thinking there was no possible way that Dak could find out anything so quickly.

Yet here they were. They had a name, a location, and a key piece of information that Sean could use to their advantage. The target was a card player.

Sean had spent a good amount of time developing his poker skills when he was in college. While he had a job during the daylight hours he wasn't in class, at night he made money on the local circuit of underground poker games. He'd learned how to play for fun with friends, but after he developed a keen grasp of the strategies involved, he quickly outgrew the low-stakes games they hosted. Sean also understood how to manage his bankroll and never play above his means.

In this case, he wouldn't be able to do that.

The plan had already formed in his mind by the time he spoke again.

"We have a location for the artifact," Sean said.

Everyone beamed with relief.

"Not so fast, kids. It's not like the thing is up the street."

"Where is it?" Tommy asked, hesitantly.

"Macau."

The air sucked out of the room.

"That's... literally on the other side of the world," Kimberly realized.

"Yes," Sean said. "That's what I was saying. If we're going to have any shot at stopping this killer, we have to get that artifact."

"And then what?" Trent asked. All eyes shifted to him. He still carried a low-key demeanor, but also a gravitas that commanded attention and respect. His eyes were like a hawk's, a hungry predator searching for a meal.

"What do you mean?" Tommy offered as his answer.

"What I mean is, so you go traipsing around the world, find some old artifact, then what? Where do you take it? How do you get it to the guy? He didn't say anything about that in the note. And let's say we do give it to him, what's he going to do next? Keep making you run around until you find the three pieces that thing is talking about? What happens when he has all three? What does all this lead to? Some treasure?"

"That last part I don't know," Alex said, "but I just got a weird email that may answer the rest of your questions."

Everyone spun and stared at the computer screen next to Alex. He was turned sideways, looking up at everyone from his chair. "It's from a guy named Theodore Milner? I don't guess he cares if we know who he is."

Tommy and Sean shifted over to where Alex sat so they could read the message. It instructed them to click on a video.

"Did you check that for viruses?" Sean asked.

Alex snorted derisively. "Our systems check every incoming message for all that stuff."

"Click it."

The screen flashed black, and then the silhouette of a man appeared on the screen. The light almost touched the features of his face, but seemed to linger just far enough back to not allow any details to be seen.

"I'm sure by now you have received my little puzzle." The man's husky voice also carried a smooth, almost snobbish quality in the way he spoke. "Well, that isn't fair. It's not my puzzle. It was created long ago by the men of God. I will cleanse another sinner by noon on Sunday if I do not see proof that you have collected the first piece of the key. When you have it, take a picture of it and send it to this number." A phone number with an area code they didn't recognize was posted on the screen. "Tracking my ISP or cell phone is futile. I used a secure VPN, so don't waste your time. If you succeed in locating and acquiring the first piece to the key, you will receive another email. Then the game will begin again. Of course, should you fail to find it by Sunday at noon, there will be another sinner saved, and another every three days and twelve hours."

The man on the screen paused. When he spoke again, it was with a tone of eerie reverence. "Can you feel it, children?" His shadowy hands lifted with palms to the heavens. "The time has come for the

Lord to anoint another, one who will cleanse the earth by fire and suffering. Only then can we be made pure." Then his hands suddenly slapped down on the table that held the camera. The view jostled for a second, then steadied as the speaker inched his face forward until the light played over it, allowing the viewers to see every detail.

His salt-and-pepper hair was slicked back, a matching full beard framing the look of someone who could have been either a farmer or a European football manager. He wore a white button-up shirt with the top button undone, sleeves rolled up. The eyes, though, were what Sean studied. Dark, lifeless orbs stared back at him through the lens, as if they knew it was him standing there.

"Salvation is near," Milner said.

The screen went black, and for a minute, nothing was said. The man's haunting image was burned into their minds, and the sound of his voice lingered in the room, hanging there like a threatening poisonous gas.

"Theodore Milner," Tommy said, breaking the silence. "Why do I know that name?"

"Yeah, I know it, too," Trent agreed. "Sounds so familiar."

"He's a serial killer," Sean said flatly, his voice full of something it didn't exhibit often—dread.

"Yes, we figured that much out," Kimberly snipped.

"No, I mean he legitimately is a known serial killer. This isn't some newbie off the streets or a copycat. He's pure evil. And he will keep killing because he believes this is his mission—or worse, he believes it's his ministry."

"Ministry?"

"How do you know so much about him?" Tara asked.

"Several years ago," Sean began, "Theodore Milner ran a church in Florida just outside of Orlando. It was close enough to the city that he could recruit more members to his flock, but far enough away that they could hold their services the way they wanted to, without much interference from civilization."

"Civilization?" Tommy muttered.

"Some of these extreme churches don't like to be near population centers. They prefer to go about their meetings and worship services without people calling them crazy or cultish."

"Like some of the churches where they handle snakes?" Alex offered.

"I suppose. Sure. But Milner wasn't handling snakes in his church. He lured people into his church with the promise that they would learn things no other church would teach, that their lives would become abundant if they would simply repent and give up their sins, following his teachings. His church membership swelled to the point of bursting. Then, one of the members was found dead one morning in a local motel room. The man was married with two children—one in college and one in high school. His body was discovered with a woman who wasn't his wife. They were naked in the bed, as they had been while they slept. Their throats were slashed. On their chests, the word *Lust* had been carved by the tip of a knife."

Sean took a deep breath and continued. "It's believed that was the first time he killed. After that, there were at least five more before he was caught. Each one of the victims he murdered was given similar branding of their sins. It was his calling card."

"So, this guy wanted to get caught?" Tommy asked.

"I don't think so. Cutting the sins of the victim into their flesh wasn't a way to get attention for attention's sake. This man truly believes he is some kind of incarnation of the Messiah, or at the very least a prophet of God. It was surprising it took the police so long to track him down. One victim is one thing, but two from the same church? Then he piled on four more before they connected the dots? Seems like the cops could have reached that conclusion before more innocent lives were lost."

"They weren't innocent," Kimberly corrected.

All eyes flew to her, aghast at the comment.

She quickly added, "Not to him. They were evil in his eyes, sinners who had to be cleansed through pain and death."

"Exactly," Sean agreed. "He wasn't killing innocent people, not in his mind. He believes it's his mission, his ministry, to eliminate sin from the world." He pointed at the dark screen. "You notice how he showed his face at the end, held it there for us to see, to make certain we know what he looks like, who we are dealing with?"

"He doesn't want to get caught," Trent realized. "He doesn't believe he can be caught."

"Wait a second," Alex said. "You said the cops caught him. Wasn't he locked away in a maximum-security prison or something? Doesn't seem the type to be let out on good behavior."

"They did catch him," Sean said. "The prosecution wanted the maximum. They pushed hard for the death sentence, but the prosecution dropped the ball. Milner had money, a family fortune from orange farms he'd sold off before embarking on his new career. With all that money, he bought the best attorneys he could find. They made a case that their client was not mentally capable of understanding what he'd done, that he truly believed he was some kind of prophet incarnate, a messenger from God."

"And the jury bought it?"

"Not really, but there was enough doubt to question the death penalty. Once that doubt injected itself into their minds, the defense expanded that sliver into a canyon. Getting those insanity pleas became much tougher after the 1990s. Judges and juries weren't buying it. Pleading insanity was trendy before 2000. Criminals knew they could offer a plea of temporary insanity for their crimes and be sent to a mental facility instead of a max-security prison. Because of the crackdown on such rulings, it was surprising that Milner succeeded."

"So, they sent him to some cupcake facility where he got to hang out with the rest of the cuckoo's nest?" Tommy asked.

"No," Trent cut in. "I know this story, too, Sean." He looked at the others. "Everything he said is true. The judge wasn't going to let Milner off that easy, Tommy. He knew this man was a danger to society, and putting him somewhere soft would be a bad idea. So he sent him to a place he should have never been able to escape from." He paused for effect. "Morrowfield."

Sean nodded, but the others didn't seem to know what that was.

"Morrowfield," Trent went on, "is an old asylum in Watasco,

Wyoming. It's out in the middle of nowhere. And when I say nowhere, I mean the next town is an hour away. There isn't much there: a grocery store, couple of gas stations, and a few neighborhoods. Most of the people who live there work in the asylum. The place is known for its corruption, guards taking money to turn a blind eye to drugs slipping in, as well as other contraband. Out there, though, there's no one to stop them or put them in check. The administrator of the facility was in on it, too. They'd skim off the top of all kinds of funds.

"Again, it was easy to do," Trent continued. "Morrowfield was meant to be a forgotten place, somewhere no one talked about. Milner may have thought he was getting off easy by being sent there, but that joint was by no means a cakewalk. Some of the sickest individuals in our society were sent there. Many of them had done things that make Milner's crusade look like child's play."

"Why are you talking about this place in past tense?" Tara noted.

"Because it was destroyed a few days ago. There was a massive explosion. Gas leak, they think. Only a few survivors."

"Milner."

"Looks that way. And now that I see he's alive and well, it makes me think that explosion wasn't an accident after all."

"You think he staged it?" Tommy asked.

"Could be," Trent said with a shrug. "The guy had considerable resources. With his money and the loyal following he'd built up, it's possible he had the connections to pull off a harebrained escape plan like that."

"Doesn't look so harebrained now," Sean commented, still staring at the computer monitor. "He's out and now he's our problem. Kimberly?"

"Yeah?"

"Can you and Trent access the city's cameras and the church's, if they have any? We need to figure out where this guy went. Use anything you can to find out what he's driving, what direction he came from, where he went after the crime."

"We're already doing that," she said.

A touch of red swelled on Sean's cheeks. Of course they were doing that. They were cops. That was part of their process. "Good," he said. "Let me know when you find something."

"I'm coming with you," Kimberly announced.

"You need to stay here and run point on this," Sean rebutted.

"I'm not the point person on this. My job is investigating the killer and trying to hunt him down. That means I have to chase down every potential lead."

Sean could see he was getting nowhere with the woman. She was stubborn, and in a way she reminded him of his wife. He let out a sigh and rubbed the back of his neck, forcing the stress to dissipate. He knew Adriana would insist on coming along. Then again, he wondered if there might be a better way she could help. They were dealing with an insidious killer, and while he didn't worry about the man getting to her, he knew that they would have to approach this much differently than other cases in the past. This would be a chess match unlike any he'd played before, and he was going to need to have all the pieces positioned just right to give him the biggest advantage.

"Tommy, how soon can you have the plane ready?"

"I'll call the pilot. We can probably be wheels up in a couple of hours."

"Perfect."

"What are you going to do?" Trent asked.

Sean looked to Tommy and then back to the retired cop. "I'm gonna call my wife and tell her I'm going to Macau. Then I'm going to play some cards."

12

MACAU

The flight to Macau would never be considered a puddle jump. From Atlanta's Hartsfield-Jackson International Airport, the journey took right on twenty-four hours, which was an insane amount of time to be in a plane.

The IAA jet stopped briefly in Los Angeles before taking off on the long flight to the South China Sea.

Upon arriving, Sean checked his watch and phone as the plane taxied along the tarmac to a private hangar. "We have just over twenty-four hours left to get this piece," Sean announced to the others.

"That isn't much time," Tommy said. "You sure you can set this up?"

Sean nodded wearily. "Yeah. I know guys like this. We make him an offer he can't refuse, and he'll come crawling to the table."

"Yeah," Tommy said, "but what if you can't beat him?"

Sean looked hurt. "Thanks for the faith, pal."

Tommy only partially backtracked. "I know you're good, man. I don't question your talent, but poker isn't just a skill game, as you always say. There's a huge element of luck to it."

Sean reflected back on his experience in the World Series of

Poker all those years before. He'd taken what was known in the poker world as a bad beat. He'd put his money in with the best hand, but the opponent drew a better one on the river, the last shared card to fall on the table.

The opponent won the hand, and Sean was eliminated from the tournament.

"That's not going to happen," Sean said, both in an attempt to convince his friend and to reassure himself. "Besides, you weren't going to use this anyway." He held up a metal briefcase with a chain shackled to his wrist. It looked like the kind of luggage used to carry millions of dollars or diamonds or something just as valuable.

In this case, it was something more valuable: an artifact from the IAA vault that Tommy had found while on an expedition in the Scottish Highlands. It was believed to be a golden laurel worn by the Celtic leader, Boudica, a fiery woman who led a resistance against the Roman Empire.

It wasn't an insignificant discovery, and if the Brits knew Sean was about to wager the artifact in a high-stakes poker game, joy wouldn't be the first emotion they expressed over the matter.

"Don't worry, buddy," Sean said, sensing his friend's apprehension. "There's an upside to this."

"Oh, really? And what's that?"

"We can get another artifact. Two for the price of one?"

"You're assuming Wang Wei won't kill us if we win."

Sean nodded absently. "I guess. But I don't think that's going to happen. He's a businessman."

"And a drug dealer," Tommy added.

"And a poker player. There may be no honor among thieves, but there is among the poker community. Well, usually."

"What's that supposed to mean?" Kimberly asked, tired of listening to the rambling conversation.

Sean faced her, looking across the aisle to where she sat in the cream-colored leather chair.

"It means sometimes people don't like getting their teeth kicked in at the table. No one likes losing. Certain poker players detest it. They almost take it as a personal affront, especially if they lose on a bad beat."

"Yes, you explained what a bad beat is earlier." She went back to reading a sheet of paper in her lap. The page had come from a folder Sean assumed to be a mission briefing or a dossier of the man they were going to meet... at least they hoped they were going to meet.

That was the real gamble. Their connection in Hong Kong confirmed that Wei was still in town, but that could have changed in the twenty-four hours since the group left Atlanta.

But Sean had received a text from their contact earlier and learned that Wei was not only still in the city, but on his way to the casino for some early afternoon gambling.

The plane veered to the right and its occupants leaned involuntarily to the left as the wheels bounced along the tarmac. They'd need to get to the casino immediately.

"We'll be fine," Sean said, though deep down he knew there was the chance he could lose. If that happened, there'd be no other choice than to attempt a desperate break-in of the man's vast estate. Doing so would be suicide, and Sean hoped to avoid a confrontation of that nature. He checked the pistol in the bag at his feet again, as he'd already done twenty times since boarding the plane. *Old habits*, he thought.

The plane rumbled to a stop. Soon after, the door opened and everyone on board climbed down the steps to the runway. Their contact, a young Chinese woman, stood by a black, luxury sedan. She hurried toward the group and stopped short of Tommy, bowing slightly before offering to take their bags.

"No, that's not necessary," Tommy said. "Thank you."

She bowed her head and then introduced herself. "My name is Li Min," she said, extending a hand toward Kimberly. The investigator took her hand and shook it briefly.

"Pleasure," Kimberly said curtly.

Li turned to Sean. "I hope you had a good flight, Sean. It's good to see you again."

Li and Sean knew each other from years before, having worked together on a couple of projects for the IAA. Li understood local government, laws, and politicians. She knew the culture and customs far better than a couple of foreigners ever could, right down to the best street-food carts.

She was also well connected to the Macau underground, as well as in Hong Kong and Shanghai.

"Word is, the mark will be in the high-stakes blackjack room at the Dragon of Fortune Casino," she said to Sean, her eyes lingering on his form a little too long.

He played off her admiring glance. "Pfft," he huffed. "Blackjack. We'll have to peel him away from that table and get him into the poker room."

"Shouldn't be too difficult for you," she said. "And I already took the liberty of letting him know you would be in town this afternoon."

"You did?" Sean felt his voice crack and he quickly cleared his throat to sound less like a high school kid. "I mean, you did? Thanks."

Li was a beautiful woman. Her long black hair glimmered in the sunlight and matched her dark eyes, eyes that missed nothing, constantly analyzing her surroundings. She stood just under five feet eight inches. Her thin, muscular legs ran up to a black skirt that dropped down to right above the knees, with a slit that ran up the side of the right leg. Her top matched the skirt, though it displayed a silver strand that ran up the seam along the buttons and then wrapped around the collar.

"Good to see you again," Tommy said, trying to wedge his way into the conversation.

"You as well, Tommy," she said in her native accent. "And you're more than welcome, Sean. Will you require hotel accommodations for the evening?"

"We hope to be back in the air as soon as we have the artifact," Sean answered.

"You certainly sound confident. But Wang Wei is a formidable opponent," Li informed him. "He plays in the nosebleeds every week and is accustomed to eight-figure swings. Nothing you do will affect his poise. He's one of the better regular players in the area."

Truth be told, Sean didn't play in the ultra-high-stakes games Li was referring to as the nosebleeds. He actually didn't get to play that often anymore, only on the occasional trip to Cherokee, North Carolina, or the rare excursion to Las Vegas. Still, he remained confident. Skills he'd developed over millions of hands through the years had made him a monster at the table, whether he had the bankroll to match or not.

"I'll be okay," Sean said. "But I appreciate you scoping out the situation for me." Whether Li knew it or not, Sean understood men like Wang Wei. All their discipline went out the window the second they felt the slightest prick, the tiniest scrap of vulnerability. And other factors played into Sean's assessment of the oil tycoon. He was a gambler, a man who liked to take risks. Every person like that Sean had ever come up against at the table proved to be a beatable opponent. It all came down to finding the right spot to put all the chips in the middle, when the opponent was at their weakest.

Li let her eyes size him up from head to toe. She didn't hide her admiration, but she also knew he was married and wouldn't do anything to make Sean feel uncomfortable. Well, not too uncomfortable. She did enjoy watching him squirm.

"Well, follow me. It won't take long to get to the casino from here."

The group fell in behind her as she led the way over to the car, her hips swaying back and forth in a way she'd probably done a thousand times before to disarm men who were either in her way or had something she wanted.

Li was a brilliant woman. With degrees in business and history, she'd spent much of her time with her nose in books. The business side of her expertise kept her involved with many of the higher-end social circles that swarmed around Macau and South China. Her history background, however, was where she focused most of her energy, curating a museum collection in Hong Kong that specialized in the southern dynasties of China.

That combination of knowledge and skill put her in a unique position to acquire intel about both fields, fields that often spilled over into the Venn diagram's center where the black market thrived.

After they loaded the car with their sparse collection of luggage—a couple of rucksacks and a day bag for Kimberly—Li drove the car out of the airport and onto the road.

"So," she said as the car rolled down the highway toward the casino district. "I heard you got married."

She looked in the rearview mirror at Sean with flirty eyes.

"Yep," Tommy said. "I sure did. Although, I don't get to see her as much as I'd like. She's working most of the time. Classified stuff, so I can't really talk about it."

Kimberly rolled her eyes in the front seat but said nothing.

Li merely grinned at Tommy's assumption, but didn't correct him.

"I'm glad you're happy," she said, taking the path that wouldn't hurt his feelings. "You look good, by the way. It's been, what, two or three years since we last saw each other in person?"

"Yeah, I've been workin' out here and there," Tommy tried to make his voice sound huskier than normal. "Trying to bulk up a little. I hit the gym three or four times a week."

Sean rolled his eyes and looked out the window at the clustered city passing by. Narrow streets overflowed with a stew of people from the peaks and valleys of the socioeconomic map. Sean knew that Macau was a place of exorbitant wealth and wretched poverty. Wealthy elites traveled here from all over the world to gamble. Some engaged in less-scrupulous activities that made gambling look like charity work.

In the city's center, grandiose casinos towered above most of the other buildings and Sean recognized one of the more famous casinos on this side of the world. The Grand Lisboa climbed higher than most of the other buildings and stood out like a cactus in a Christmas tree lot. The building's structure started at a bulbous dome that looked like a balloon with a weight in the center. The tower itself rose high into the air like a rectangular flower, blooming outward in two directions and at multiple levels until it reached the top. In the evenings, the domed foundation flared with millions of lights, essentially turning the walls into a giant, curved, 360-degree electronic billboard.

The glitter and opulence of the casinos cast a striking shadow over the rest of the city, much of which labored under a crushing poverty. It was one of the wealthiest and also poorest areas of the world.

Sean noticed a young mother walking along the sidewalk with two children. All of them wore tattered clothing that was little better than rags. The mother kept her eyes locked forward on a destination that she probably didn't see. Blind perseverance, the need to survive, was the only thing that drove her forward. She had to feed her kids, keep them alive long enough that they could fend for themselves. There were no retirement plans for people like her, no 401(k)'s or investment strategies. She didn't get to go on vacations to wondrous places or dream of driving an expensive car or gamble in Macau's towering neon palaces.

As far as the Chinese authorities were concerned, people like this woman and her children were lucky they got to live at all.

Right on cue, a black Aston Martin Vanquish cruised by, the powerful engine crackling as it purred. Sean knew that car was worth more than that woman would make in five lifetimes.

Li stopped the sedan at a red light next to the Aston Martin and waited as pedestrians crossed the road. The mother with her two children struggled to cross as the woman was forced to drag one of them while carrying the other. The light turned green, and the driver of the Aston Martin honked incessantly, irritated that he was being held up for longer than necessary. A Russian man rolled down his tinted window and yelled at the mother, swearing at her in his native tongue. She clearly didn't understand the words, but the message was clear. He nudged the sports car forward toward the white line as if he might push the little family out of his way.

The woman held up a dirty, apologetic hand. Her desperate eyes looked back at the driver in sincere apology, as if she were a commoner required to apologize for inconveniencing the nobility.

Sean felt his blood boil. He wanted to reach into his bag and draw his Springfield. He wouldn't kill the idiot, but he'd love to pop those thousand-dollar tires with a few rounds.

The Aston Martin fired off the line and drove away to the sound of a screaming motor.

"Some people can be so rude on the roads," Li commented as she casually steered the car through the intersection, heading toward the casino district. "We are pretty crowded in this part of the world and people don't have much patience as a result. That's my theory."

No one said anything for the rest of the drive. Tommy busily flipped through messages on his phone, frequently rubbing his eyes as sleep beckoned him to return.

Kimberly also spent a portion of the short journey looking at something on her phone.

Sean assumed they were text messages from her boss or some other person at the bureau who may have been working on the case with her.

When they arrived at the Dragon of Fortune fifteen minutes later, Li steered the car into the parking lot outside the lobby's entrance and found an empty spot near the street.

They left their belongings in the vehicle, stowing the gear in the trunk so any wandering pedestrians looking in windows wouldn't see anything of interest and consider breaking a window.

Sean double-checked the passport in his front pocket, along with a wad of bills folded underneath it. He carried the metal briefcase in his left hand as they made their way through the rows of cars toward the entrance.

As they got closer to the casino, the parked cars became more luxurious. The valet parking area was a car enthusiast's wildest and most expensive fantasy come true. Ferrari, Bentley, Rolls-Royce, Bugatti, McLaren, and Maserati were all represented on the front line nearest the entrance—the latter being the least expensive of the group. There were cars along that row that Sean didn't even recognize. They may have been Chinese produced, but he didn't get close enough to tell. And he didn't care because his focus was on the Black Aston Martin at the far end. The driver was already in the building, probably headed to a high-stakes baccarat room.

The blood in Sean's veins raced through his pounding heart. He felt a high school urge to go slash the guy's tires or key the side of the vehicle, but he knew that was childish and would solve nothing. What would that do? It certainly wouldn't teach the jerk a lesson. Guys like that didn't learn lessons, not moral ones anyway.

In fact, Sean knew the man would be incensed that someone damaged his property. He'd seek out the vandal, using every means necessary to track down the perpetrator and punish them to the full extent of the law. Never once would he consider that he'd brought it upon himself. Men like that couldn't see beyond their own selfish designs.

Li led the group into the lobby where they were immediately overwhelmed by an avalanche of scents. Sweet perfume filled the cool, dry air, pumped in through the ventilation system. Sean chuckled to himself at the stark contrast to the sticky, warm air outside filled with the smells of exhaust, asphalt, and myriad odors from every restaurant within a quarter mile.

He took a deep breath and exhaled, satisfaction filling his lungs. He gazed upon the golden dragon in the center of the massive circular room. Smoke and fire plumed out of a gilded lotus flower propped in front of the enormous beast. The domed ceiling above displayed a litany of creatures, both mythical and real: a tiger growled, posed as if ready to strike; a goat stared off into the distance; monkeys dangled from vines; a stallion's mane flapped in the imaginary breeze; a pig squealed; and two birds fought over a prize or perhaps territory, with feathers flying. Not the least of all, a dragon occupied the relief, snarling at the rest of the creatures as if it were the king of all.

The dome suddenly started to move, the panels containing the creatures folding in on themselves. As it continued to shift, an oculus appeared in the center, shining a bright light down onto the golden dragon statue below like a modern pantheon in South Asia.

For a moment, all of the stress from the murder investigation, the unknown that lay ahead, and the mystery of the tablet, all faded away.

"Now that is how you do a casino lobby," Sean said out loud so the others could hear.

"Definitely... unique," Tommy sort of agreed.

"Little over the top for my tastes," Kimberly countered.

Sean couldn't be certain, but he was definitely steering toward not liking the woman.

"The high-stakes room is this way," Li said, pointing toward a wide corridor that flowed into the main floor. Dinging sounds of every kind echoed in their ears, the siren song of slot machines for people so inclined to that variety of gambling. It was mixed with upbeat electronic dance music in the background.

"Lead the way," Sean said to their host. "Let's see if we can take down a billionaire."

13

ATLANTA

Kerry Kelley walked through the door and into the lab. Alex held it open until she was inside and then let the portal close.

"Welcome, Dr. Kelley," Tara said, extending a hand to the woman. "Glad you had a safe flight. Can I get you anything? Bottled water? Granola bar? Coffee?"

"Coffee would be lovely, thank you," Kerry said with a nod and an appreciative smile.

"You got it," Tara said. She scurried over to the counter where the coffee maker sat with a half-full pot of steaming chocolaty liquid. "Just made this pot about thirty minutes ago, so it's fresh."

Kelley grinned at the explanation. "Oh, I'm not that picky."

"Please, have a seat," Alex said, motioning to a chair at one of the workstations. The computer monitor displayed the translation from the tablet alongside the original script as it may have looked without a few thousand years of weathering.

Kelley read over the translation with a furrowed brow. Her black-rimmed glasses clung to the tip of her nose, threatening to fall off at any second.

Tara returned with the proffered coffee and set the black mug in front of her. The white Black Rifle Coffee Company logo stood out prominently on the side.

"Oh, I do like their coffee," Kelley said.

"You've had it?"

"Of course. It's delicious. And I love how they support veterans. My dad fought in the Korean War, so it's a cause I appreciate." She collected the cup and took a long, slow sip, then let out an appreciative "ah."

"We also have Philz, which is our favorite," Alex said, "but we do love BRCC, too. But we didn't bring you here to talk about gourmet coffee. You're here to see what you found."

"Yes, well, it's quite impressive how quickly you were able to decipher the inscription. Those characters were nearly invisible in some places, certainly impossible to read with the human eye."

"Unfortunately," Tara interjected, "it looks like a kind of treasure map, but without any location context. Simply put, if we knew what specific city and building this thing was talking about, we'd probably have something we could use for a deeper investigation. As it is, it's simply a remarkable discovery that links us to another ancient civilization."

"And the fact you found it on a shipwreck proves that these people were indeed trading far to the west, as we've long suspected." Alex stopped talking and waited for Dr. Kelley's response.

She gazed at the screen for several breaths and nodded. "Yes, it's quite remarkable, although you're right. We did know about the western Mediterranean trade. This wreck was close to where we think the port of Tarshish may have been located. Pretty amazing to have discovered this piece on the seabed. The odds against such a find are staggering."

"Very true," Tara said.

Kelley's eyes wandered to the counter next to the younger woman's elbow. She noted the letter sitting there and acknowledged it with a nod. "What's that?"

"Oh," Tara coughed, embarrassed. "It's a copy of... well, that's a tricky question."

"Never mind, dear. I'm sorry. I just thought it might have something to do with the tablet."

"It is," Alex volunteered. He and Tara exchanged a look, both wondering if they were overstepping their boundaries by telling Dr. Kelley about the murder investigation.

"It's public news," Tara said with a roll of the shoulders.

"What is?" Kelley wondered.

"There was a murder here recently. A pastor was whipped and beaten, then crucified in his church." Alex relayed the story with as little emotion as he could allow, even though the incident caused his stomach to protest.

"That's awful," Kelley said. She covered her mouth with both hands, eyes wide.

"Yes," Tara agreed. "One of the investigators came here and brought this note. Apparently, the killer was trying to get Sean's attention."

"Sean? Why? They're not coming for him next, are they?"

Another set of unspoken words flew between the married couple before Tara answered. "We don't think so. The killer is a man named Theodore Milner. He's a serial killer who used to be a pastor. Ran a church in Florida where he started killing members of his own church to purify them."

"He thinks he's some kind of savior," Alex explained. "And his victims are sinners who must be cleansed by pain and death. It's pretty sick."

Kelley could see by the look on his face that Alex wasn't spouting hyperbole.

"The victim had the letters *SWIAA* carved into his chest. There were also other things cut into his flesh, signs of sins that Milner must have believed the preacher to be guilty of. This letter was left at the scene. Well, the original was. This is a copy, so there's no... you know, nothing gross or anything."

"What on earth could a serial killer like that want with Sean? Unless he was the one who put the man in jail or something? And why isn't he in jail?"

"He was in a mental institution called Morrowfield. It's up in Wyoming."

"Yes, I saw something about that on the news," Kelley said. "They just had a massive gas leak explosion up there. Killed pretty much everyone, didn't it?"

"That's what we heard," Alex confirmed. "Except now we don't think it was a gas leak. If Milner escaped, the timing of the explosion is way too close to be a coincidence."

"You think he somehow did it himself?" Kelley looked incredulous and horrified all at once.

"Doubtful he did it from the inside, but a connection from the outside? Definitely. The problem is nobody knows much about the guy except from the trial and the story about what he did. His parents have been dead for more than twenty years, and no one is sure if he ever had any children, and there's no record of him ever being married."

"Soooo, Theodore Milner is an alias? A false name?"

"Good question, but no. That's his real name. He had a big inheritance from when his parents died. The church he was running in Florida also did okay, even though it was relatively small. Mercenaries cost money, so if that's the kind of people who busted him out of Morrowfield, then he'd have to have some dough sitting around somewhere, probably in a place no one in the government knew about."

"Like with a shell company?" Kelley asked. She was out of her field of expertise but found herself intrigued with the investigation.

"Possibly," Tara conceded. "It could be with a person, too, someone he trusted, although I imagine that would have to be a pretty small list. I don't know too many people who have serial killers saved in their contact list."

A frightening thought occurred to Alex. He looked around the room, breathing methodically to calm his torrential thoughts.

"Guys," he started, "if this guy has enough money to engineer and execute a prison... asylum escape like that, it would stand to reason he could afford a security force, too."

"You mean like bodyguards?" Kelley asked.

"Yeah, something like that."

"You weren't thinking of attacking them directly, were you? Do you know where to find him?"

"No," he said, irritated. "I wish I did. While Sean and Tommy are on the other side of the world trying to get what this guy wants, I wish there was a way we could track him down and stop him before he can do any more damage."

Tara looked down at the letter on the counter. A thought struck her. "Dr. Kelley, this is a copy the letter that was meant for Sean, the one left with the victim."

"Yes?"

"Right," Tara blushed. "Well, anyway, have a look at it. Maybe you can make some sense of it. The boys went to Macau to find a man who supposedly possesses one of the artifacts mentioned in this riddle."

Kelley took it off the table and pushed her glasses up to the middle of her nose. Her eyes ran along the lines until she was finished. Instead of looking aghast at the horrific insinuation of the letter, she looked almost eager. Her eyes didn't look sad or forlorn, they beamed with the possibility of hope.

"This image at the bottom," she said. "Do you know what this is?"

Tara and Alex looked at each other, wondering if either knew the answer.

"No, ma'am," Alex answered.

"Other than what the letter suggests," Tara added. "We went with the assumption that it's a piece that is intended to fit with two others to form some kind of key."

"Yes, that's what the letter says. And in essence, that's what it is, a key that unlocks a door to an ancient power."

Tara and Alex again turned their heads to each other, but this time they did it much slower.

"Ancient power?" Tara asked, her tone almost joking. "We've seen a bit of that in our time here. So much so that Tommy put us in charge of a new branch. We call it the Paranormal Archaeology Division."

Kelley smiled. "Yes, I've heard. I'm certain there will be no end of wondrous things you two discover."

Tara didn't mention their inaugural excursion that led them on a harrowing journey around the world. That was for another day.

"At any rate," Kelley went on, "this key that the killer mentions is partly that, but it's also one piece of three that fit together to form a special bracelet."

"Bracelet? Seems like a weird thing to call a key."

"True. But it *is* a key. Tell me," she said, crossing one leg over the other and assuming a very professor-like pose, "have you ever heard of the Ring of Solomon?"

Tara and Alex both nodded that they had.

"Most historians don't believe it's real or that it ever existed. Many of those who believe in witchcraft or magic consider the ring to be a sacred item. Some of them aren't sure whether it's real or not, but what it stands for is the ability to manipulate reality in a way that doesn't involve actual physical force."

"You mean moving things with your thoughts and words?" Alex asked.

"Perhaps, though that isn't the point I'm trying to make. Most scholars agree that the story revolving around the Ring of Solomon was fiction. There isn't much in the Bible that can be found to back up the idea of a mystical ring of power wielded by the great king of Israel. There is, however, an interesting story about how he became one of the most powerful and respected leaders in the region... before he strayed, of course."

Tara licked her lips and nodded. "You're referring to the blessing from God he received? The one where he was told he could receive anything he asked for?"

"Yes," Kelley said. "And he asked for what?"

"Wisdom."

"Right. He didn't ask for a ring of power, or anything that would lend itself to his own selfish designs. Sadly, that ended up being his downfall anyway, but my point is he didn't ask for riches or power. He could have had anything he wanted, and he asked for one of the humblest things a person could request in a situation like that. He asked for wisdom. Is there a Ring of Solomon? Perhaps. Perhaps not. But that legend gives you a touch of insight into what could have been, what may have transpired between one of the most powerful kings in all of Israeli history. It also gives us precedent."

"Precedent?" Alex asked, confused. "What do you mean?"

Kelley switched legs, crossing the left over the right. "The precedent that there is a piece of jewelry that leads to some kind of power."

"Yeah," Tara said after a moment of thought. "I guess. But I don't see how that relates to this... bracelet as you called it. And why are you so sure that it's a bracelet?"

Dr. Kelley passed her a grin as she might have to a child who still believed in the tooth fairy. "I can see you need to brush up on your scriptures. Tell me, have you ever heard of the Armor of God?"

"Yep. I can't recall the verse that mentions them, but yes. I've heard about that much of my life, in church mostly."

"Well, there is a glaring omission when it comes to the list of items contained in the Armor of God."

"Omission?" Alex wondered.

"In ancient times, and certainly during the Roman Empire during which Jesus and the apostles lived, soldiers frequently wore gauntlets or at least some kind of plating on their wrists. The wrist was most often exposed during hand-to-hand combat with short swords, or a *gladius*, as they were known. The wrist was an easy and exposed target, so soldiers equipped themselves to keep that piece of their arm intact. Of course, that piece of armor existed long before the Romans. Until medieval times, they were typically made from leather. Only wealthy elites such as officers or nobles owned ones made from bronze."

She turned the letter so both could see the image at the bottom. "This is one of those," she said.

"Bronze?" Alex wondered.

"Probably, though if it is, I would have to wonder how well it has been preserved."

"So, that's what Sean is looking for." It was a statement not a question.

"Yes. Not only that one, but two others to complete the piece of armor."

Something about Kelley's knowledge bothered Tara, and she'd been holding back saying anything for several minutes. "Dr. Kelley, how is it you know so much about this subject, particularly the exact key that this madman wants?"

Her face drew long and regret washed over her, causing her shoulders to slump an inch. "The truth is, I don't know much about that particular piece. I ran across it several years ago when I was doing some research on the biblical prophet Jonah."

"Yes!" Alex exclaimed. "That's what we figured, too, that the fish represents him in some way."

"Ah," Kelley said. "Well, I never got anywhere with it. We first learned of that particular part of the artifact when we were doing some research with the Dead Sea Scrolls in a joint effort with a group from Cambridge."

"Why do I get the impression you know more about this than just the one piece?" Tara pressed.

Kelley sighed. "You'd be correct to assume that. The scroll we were working on was one that hadn't been translated and released to the public yet. It referenced the key and the three pieces that go along with it, though the only one it described in detail was the one with the fish, the one exactly like the image at the bottom of that letter."

"But how would Milner know what that thing looks like, or even what it is if it was never released to the public?"

Despair sank into Dr. Kelley's eyes. "It was stolen and never recovered. Unfortunately, we believe that one of the people on the research team betrayed us and took it. We never saw them again."

"And they sold it to Milner," Alex concluded.

Kelley nodded absently. "It seems that way, though I'm not sure why anyone would buy it other than for its historical value. As you can tell, on its own it's not complete."

"Indeed. It doesn't complete the puzzle, but it certainly peels away another layer of the mystery."

The lab descended back into silence, interrupted only by the constant low hum of the machines around them and the flow of air though the exposed vents overhead.

"Dr. Kelley?" Tara said abruptly. "Do you know what this might lead to, what it is that Milner guy is looking for?"

The professor had to think hard about this. She'd already assumed the question would come, but the answer sounded crazy—not implausible but certainly out there. "Well, let's take a look at the evidence we have so far. We have a piece of a gauntlet or wrist guard with a fish on it that represents the creature that swallowed Jonah in the story of the prophet's journey to Nineveh—or rather, his attempted escape from God's mission. We also have a strange message from the Dead Sea Scrolls that was stolen and bears references to the Jonah story."

"That's what we figured," Alex chimed.

Kelley pointed toward the end of the letter. "Yes. Because it says, 'Now he rests above the palace grounds.' The tomb of Jonah was destroyed in 2014 by ISIS and revealed a palace underneath, a place of ancient Assyrian origin."

Alex and Tara let her go on despite already knowing that piece of information.

"But," Kelley went on, "the next part is intriguing and problematic where it says, 'His piece of the key underneath, within the nave of the winged horse.' While I don't understand the Pegasus reference, the line before it makes it clear. That tablet is a set of directions to navigate the tomb and palace where the prophet Jonah was buried."

"Right," Tara said. "We did a little digging on the Pegasus thing and discovered that there was an image of a winged horse carved into one of the walls underneath Jonah's tomb."

"Ah, well, there you go. Confirmation." Kelley said the words as if someone told her chocolate was delicious. "The other part of the riddle also references Jonah where it speaks of how he cursed his lot. It's not obvious, not at first anyway, but at the end of the book of Jonah, he is sitting outside the gates of Nineveh, wasting away in the heat, complaining about pretty much everything. But there's another clue that it is Jonah this thing is talking about."

"What's that?"

"The last part speaks of forgotten pages, pieces of the story that tell the truth of his fate." She could see her audience was lost. "The book of Jonah ends abruptly, almost as if ending on a cliffhanger. Have you ever wondered what really happened to him after that last chapter?"

"I didn't think much about it," Alex said.

"Me, either," Tara added.

"Right. No one does. It's assumed that Jonah eventually died there or close to Nineveh, and was buried there. But the way the story ends leaves us to wonder. Did he go anywhere else? Did he minister to another nation or city somewhere? Or was that it? Some suggest that the story wasn't factual, that it was an allegory intended to teach us a lesson."

"Like a parable," Tara offered.

"Precisely. While most skeptics would say a human couldn't survive in the belly of an animal for three days, or that an animal like that doesn't exist in the region, I suppose we have to either take some things on faith or explain them away as a kind of object lesson. Still, that doesn't change the fact that the story of Jonah is incomplete. Imagine if every movie you ever saw ended at the worst point, the point where your emotions have been completely drained."

"Like *Leaving Las Vegas*?" Alex asked.

"Exactly like that, though I'm not sure why you'd have seen that movie. The point is people would stop going to movies if they never made them feel good or at least never gave them a sense of closure. Even sad movies have closure. Books are the same. You need closure."

"So, you're saying that whether the book of Jonah is true or not, we are missing something from the story," Tara realized.

"Right. And we think that there may have been something incredible, or at least a reference to it, in those last chapters. You see here where it says, 'Pieces of one and one of three, great messengers of God in the prophet's tree?'"

The other two nodded.

"Well," Kelley went on, "we can extrapolate that the tree they're talking about is actually the line of prophets. One of three could suggest that three of them were more important than the others. After all, there were certainly a large number of prophets listed in the Bible."

"Or maybe it's three prophets from a segment of the line," Tara offered. "What if it were Jonah and the two before or after him? Or one before and after?"

"Those are all valid possibilities," Kelley agreed. She turned in her chair to face the tablet and its translation on the screen, mulling it over for a couple of breaths before she spoke. When she did, her voice sounded distant, pensive.

"Now, all we have to do is figure out what it was pointing to."

14

MACAU

"Please," Li insisted, doing her best not to sound desperate. "I'm certain if you asked Mr. Wei, he would be more than interested in the piece my client is willing to wager."

"I'm sorry," the manager said, "but we don't do that sort of thing here. Your client is free to buy in to any of the tables we have to offer, both in the main casino or here in the high-stakes room if—" he stopped himself, eyeing Sean up and down as if he were a street urchin who had just walked into a Rodeo Drive boutique, "that is, if he can afford to."

Sean felt his skin burn at the insult. It wasn't the fact that the room's manager thought he didn't belong here—if he had been honest, Sean would have agreed, at least in part. He didn't belong in a place like this. Never had. Except to make withdrawals.

He'd popped into a few high-stakes rooms in the past after a certain benefactor had noticed his talent.

Sean had been finishing his degree while working his way through college as a landscaper for a wealthy local family. They'd always taken care of him, even secretly paid off bills he couldn't while earning his degree. He'd noticed of course, especially on one occasion when he picked up his car at the repair shop and was presented with an invoice that had already been paid in full.

He thanked his employers, but they never completely admitted to the deed. They didn't have to.

Their names were Mickey and Susie O'Brien. Sean still thought about them from time to time. They were probably in their mid-eighties by now, he figured. Maybe a year or two younger. They'd helped set him up for a life of success, though he never imagined the adventures, or dangers, he might encounter.

When Mr. O'Brien first learned of Sean's uncanny abilities at the poker table, he was amused. As time went on, however, O'Brien discovered that Sean was a rare breed, one who could almost tell the future when it came to cards. Some said he could play the game of Texas Hold 'Em without even looking at his own two cards.

Before Sean attempted to play in the World Series of Poker, it was O'Brien who had offered him the chance to play up the food chain. While Sean didn't really get into the super high nosebleeds where tens of millions were exchanged routinely, he did play with some uncomfortable amounts of money.

The results had been profitable for both him and his "investor," and had set Sean up financially so he wouldn't have to worry about debt ever again.

In those rare occasions he'd dared to set foot in a place similar to this, he'd felt out of place: a poor boy at the table with the rich kids. Now, it was all coming back to him. On top of that, he knew Wei was there, just beyond a maroon door with a shiny golden doorknob.

The cacophony of casino sounds filled his ears, annoying him to fury. He didn't show it outwardly, save the slight reddening of his cheeks. For the briefest of moments, he allowed a fanciful thought of slugging the gatekeeper in the jaw and charging past him. That, however, would result in Sean's arrest and subsequent imprisonment, and this part of the world wasn't a place he wanted to be in jail.

Li huffed and turned around to face the others. "I'm sorry. He already called the general manager, and they said their client has this room reserved for their personal game. Invite only. I don't know what else to do."

The forlorn look on her face said it all. Sean glanced down at his watch. Time was running out. On the surface, things didn't look so bad. They had nearly sixteen hours to acquire the artifact from Wei and send the message to Milner with a picture of the item. Even if they could go straight in and dive into the game with Wei, such a match could take hours to determine a winner.

"It's okay," Sean lied. All he could think about was how someone back in the States was going to end up dead if they couldn't get their hands on that artifact. Sean wondered if blackmail might be an option, but knew he'd lose his head or be dropped in the South China Sea before that worked.

"Come with me," Sean said and spun on his heels toward the exit.

They followed behind, though Kimberly felt the need to vocalize her protest. "What are we doing?" she asked as she accidentally shouldered a man in a silver Armani suit. At first, the man looked agitated, but seeing how tall and beautiful she was, he bowed his head and started to offer her a drink. She waved a dismissive hand and kept going, blowing him off as if he were an insect. "Shouldn't we be trying to figure out a way to get into that room?" She motioned back toward the foyer that served as the gateway into the private poker room.

"We are," Sean said as he sauntered up to the bar and eased into one of the seats.

A beautiful young woman in a sparkling black dress stood behind the counter. She worked quickly, shaking tumblers and pouring drinks, popping bottle caps and sliding them to cocktail runners, all to make sure the whales didn't leave their little pond.

Sean knew how casinos worked to make sure the big gamblers— or whales, as they were known—spent every waking second possible at the tables. In the poker rooms, casinos didn't make as much money directly as they did on the other table games, but there were still ways to pry money from those who preferred not to play against the house odds. Booze was one of them, though that hardly yielded a hefty percentage of income. Usually, poker players would spend hours at the table, sending money around and around until they were either too tired to continue or had won enough that they felt satisfied. It was this last group that would go to the craps tables or the blackjack tables and blow enormous amounts of their winnings.

"What can I get for you?" the young bartender asked in perfect English.

Sean smiled back at her. "I'll have a hot tea with a touch of honey and lemon."

Tommy pulled up a seat next to him and scowled at the order. "Really? That's it? Nothing else?"

"My friend will have a scotch on the rocks. He doesn't care which kind."

Tommy looked insulted, which only encouraged the laughter already leaking from the young bartender's lips.

Tommy turned to her. "I'll have a Macallan 18, please."

"Very good, sir. And the ladies?"

"Whatever they want," Tommy said with a hint of bravado. "Put it on my tab."

"Water for me," Li said. Sean knew she had a drink now and then but tried to remain focused when working, and right now they were in a tight spot.

"I'll have a vodka cranberry," Kimberly said.

Sean lifted his eyebrows at the woman as she slid into an empty seat next to him.

"What? My nerves are shot."

"No judgment here," Sean said. "That's usually Tommy's drink," he said. "Actually, appletinis are really his thing."

The ice on Kimberly's face shattered, and she let out a laugh.

Tommy's head whipped around to see what was going on. "What?" he demanded. "What's so funny?"

Sean's lips never cracked as he accepted the hot cup of tea the bartender slid in front of him, her own face displaying similar amusement.

"Nothing, pal," Sean slapped his friend on the back. "I just think it's great our new friend here is finally letting loose a little."

Tommy didn't look as though he believed the ruse, but he went with it and raised a glass. "To new friends," he said and lifted his glass when it arrived.

Li simply bowed her head and lifted her bottle of water.

"So," Tommy said, swallowing his warm sip with satisfaction. "We didn't just fly all the way around the world to have cocktails... or in your case, a cup of tea. What's the plan? We have less than eighteen hours before that maniac kills someone else."

Kimberly leaned in to hear Sean's response.

Sean raised the little teacup to his lips and drew in a long sip of the soothing liquid. It coursed down his throat, the warmth seeping through his body and easing the tension built up on the journey and the subsequent barrier standing between them and stopping a serial killer.

He gave an appreciative nod at the flavor and then set the cup down. "I have a plan, buddy," he said. "But you're not going to like it."

Tommy stared at his friend, and the good feeling the expensive scotch gave him evaporated in an instant.

"What? What is it?"

Sean took a deep breath and laced his fingers together. The sounds of dance music overwhelmed the myriad noises from outside the lounge; the random sounds of dings, dongs, and plinks that are a feature of any casino.

"I need five million dollars."

15

MACAU

"What?" Tommy said, looking at his friend as if he'd lost his mind. Then he laughed, snorting through his nose before it turned into a full-belly guffaw. "Seriously. What's your plan?"

Sean didn't say anything. Instead, he merely reached over and took his teacup in one hand, raised it to his lips, and drew another sip.

"No," Tommy spat. "No way. I can't do that." He shook his head vehemently.

"You can," Sean said. "And honestly, this is our only shot, Tommy. You know it as well as I do."

"What are you going to do with five million dollars, Sean?" He grabbed the glass and dumped more than just a sip into his mouth. He winced as he swallowed the unexpectedly large amount of liquor.

"You're going to have to trust me on this, so hear me out. Okay?"

Tommy raised the drink and finished it, then turned to the bartender. "I'm going to need another one of these if I'm going to listen to this?"

"Coming right up, sir."

"No, wait," Sean said, holding up a steady hand. "We need to stay focused here. Okay? One is fine. Loosens you up a little. But that's it. Listen, a guy like Wei may be a dirtbag, fair enough, but he built up a legitimate billion-dollar company, too."

"Yeah, and I'm sure he ran over plenty of good folks along the way," Tommy added.

"Right, but he's the kind of person with an eye for talent. And he's a gambler. Gamblers pay attention to other gamblers, especially if they get the right kind of attention."

Li and Kimberly listened intently, leaning close to hear Sean's plan.

Tommy, however, returned his attention to the bartender. "I will have that second scotch, please."

This time, Sean didn't stop her as she poured the amber liquid into the clear glass. The laser-cut dragon on the side glimmered as the light played off the whiskey.

"I need to buy in to the high-stakes game," Sean pressed. "It's the only way Wei will notice me. When he sees I'm a player, he'll want me in that room."

Tommy followed Sean's eyes toward the high-stakes poker room off to the left. It was guarded by a man at the door wearing the same kind of illustrious costume worn by the cocktail runners and dealers.

Tommy frowned as his second drink nudged his wrist, the bartender pushing it gently toward him. "That table is a million-dollar buy-in. Why do you need five?"

Sean slurped another sip of tea. "Because," he said, "you never sit at the table with one buy-in. You need to have a few in reserve, in case you take a few bad beats."

Tommy slammed the second drink down his throat and roughly placed the tumbler back onto the counter. "Yeah, no kidding. Look, maybe you think that five million isn't a big deal to me, but it is."

"I know it is, Tommy. You have never stopped appreciating the value of a nickel. You don't spend extravagantly. I'm not asking you to do this because I want to test out my skills at another level. And I'm not asking because I know you can afford it. A friend wouldn't do that. I'm asking because outside of the four of us trying to invade

Wei's mansion, I don't see any other way of getting a shot at that relic."

Tommy twirled his finger around in the air, signaling the bartender for another round. He usually wasn't such an avid drinker. To be fair, it was Macallan 18, and Sean had always preferred the stuff from Kentucky and Tennessee, but this was no time to be losing his mind.

"Thank you," Sean said, dismissing the bartender. "Just hold on to that for one second."

She nodded and flashed the same smile she probably gave to every patron who sat in that stool.

"Hey," Tommy complained.

"Stop it." Sean grabbed his friend by the shoulder and forced him to look him in the eyes.

"Okay, fine," Tommy relented. "What's your plan, Sean? Go into the high-stakes room and make a bunch of money? Then what? Pay off the security guard so we can get into the private room with Wang Wei?" His voice grew precariously loud with each word until he nearly shouted the last sentence. Li and Kimberly turned their heads; their faces burned with embarrassment as they tried to focus on their drinks.

"Would you just take it easy?" Sean ordered, looking around the room. Only one person had seemed to notice, and they immediately went back to their cocktail.

"A man as powerful as Wei would know I'm here. He knows we asked for an audience with him and for a chance to play against him. Guaranteed."

"So?"

"So, like I said, he has an eye for talent. And a guy like Wei loves a challenge. But he also wants to know that he's the best. It's one of the reasons he got into drug running even though he didn't need the money. It's just another conquest for him. Maybe it makes him feel powerful. All I know is that the ego inside that room"—Sean jabbed a finger in the general direction of the private room—"is bigger than this island. If he sees what I can do at the table, I'll be one more conquest he needs to be triumphant. But I have to get to the table first, Tommy. I have to sit with the big dogs if I want to get noticed."

Tommy listened to what Sean had to say. Deep down, he knew his friend was right. It was a good plan, the only plan that had a real chance of success. The alternative would be an assault on Wei's mansion, and while Sean was probably one of the few on the planet capable of pulling it off, it simply wasn't a good idea.

After nearly a minute of deep consideration, Tommy sighed. "Five million."

Li smiled.

Sean's stone-serious face shattered into a relieved grin. He slapped his friend on the shoulder. "Now we're talking."

"Are you two serious?" Kimberly asked, reverting to her old self. "The man who has what we need is on the other side of that door, and your plan is to goad him into letting you in by playing at another high-stakes table?"

Sean turned around and faced her. "Well, yeah."

"This is insanity."

"You gotta be a little *loco en la cabeza* to do what we do, lady," Sean quipped. "You're either all in or you're not. But I'll tell you what: If you don't want to ride the rail and watch me play, why not work on the backup plan?"

"Backup plan? What backup plan?"

"Hit the blackjack tables and see if you can make enough money to buy our way into Wei's game."

She rolled her eyes and huffed before raising her drink to her lips. She took a drink and shook her head. "Just don't screw this up. We're running out of time."

"I know."

Tommy and Sean found the high-stakes cage and went through the process of transferring the five million from his personal account. The realization hit Sean; he was taking five million bucks from his best friend to play a poker game. Not only that, someone's life depended on whether or not he did as well as he believed he could.

After collecting his chips from the cage, a middle-aged man

escorted him to a private room with a velvet rope hanging in the doorway. A beautiful young woman with her hair pulled back in high pigtails stood guard. She stepped to the side and pulled the latch on the rope to grant them access. The usher motioned for Sean to step inside and follow him to an open seat at the end of the table to the dealer's right.

Six people sat at the poker table. Four of them had about the same amount of chips, while one looked to be nearly tapped out. Two were women, one in a shimmering gold dress, and the other in a skintight leopard-print number that accentuated her curves. Sean had seen women dress like that frequently at these games. He could never be sure, but he always got the impression they did it to distract their male opponents. Or maybe they just liked the look. He didn't judge, but he wasn't going to let their appearance distract him from his mission.

The last player sat behind a mountain of chips. He was a plump man with a fleshy face and neck. His torso reminded Sean of an apple with legs and arms, and the guy wore a flashy scarlet blazer that emphasized that impression.

He laughed loudly, his voice booming annoyingly around the room. The other players clearly didn't like the man's demeanor, but there was nothing they could do about it except hope they got a lucky run of cards and ended his night with a series of beatdowns.

The man raked in a pile of chips from a victorious hand and laughed harder, taunting the others with a thick French accent.

Their annoyance swelled as he casually tossed a single chip to the dealer as a tip.

"Thank you, sir," the dealer said, unimpressed with the meager offering. It was a twenty-dollar chip from another part of the casino. Apparently, the annoying player had a stash of them from some of the lower-stakes games he used to tip the dealers. Sean was surprised the man tipped at all, and that was just his initial read on the man's persona.

"Plenty more where that came from," the bulging gambler roared.

He reached for a glass of cognac as Sean eased into his seat.

"Ah!" the big man exclaimed. "Fresh blood."

He took a healthy swig of the cognac and then burst into laughter again. He was the only one.

"Welcome, sir," the dealer said to Sean as he placed his chips in front of his seat in a neat, orderly fashion. "You're the big blind."

"Ah, sat right into it, huh?" Sean said, embellishing his slight Southern accent.

He shoved two chips out into the middle and waited patiently as the dealer flipped cards across the felt to each player until everyone had two. Sean watched each of their reactions closely. His eyes darted from one player to the next and back.

The Frenchman was the first to act and announced a raise.

Sean wasn't surprised. He'd already assessed every player at the table within ten seconds of sitting down.

The huge man tossed eight chips onto the table, quadrupling Sean's required two. Each chip was worth ten thousand dollars.

Kimberly, Li, and Tommy watched from a bar on the other side of the room, each with varying levels of concern and curiosity on their faces.

"What just happened?" Kimberly asked. "I've never played this game before."

Four of the other players folded. The one with the dealer button in front of them called the raise.

"So," Tommy began explaining, "there are two blind bets that circle around the table, clockwise. So, to play the hand you, at minimum, have to put ten thousand into the middle. Or you can raise it in ten-thousand-dollar increments, which is what that guy just did." He pointed at the Frenchman. "He raised it to forty thousand."

"Can Sean get his ten thousand back?"

"No," Tommy snickered. "It's mandatory. But it cycles around so everyone has to do it."

"And they don't get to look at their cards first to decide if they should play the hand or not?"

"No," Li answered. "That's why it's called a blind bet. Big and small blind. The small is half the big blind, so five thousand at this table."

Kimberly choked at the numbers. The amount of money on the table at this very moment could buy a luxury sedan.

The small blind folded, and the dealer pointed to Sean. "Big blind, the bet is forty."

Sean had waited until that moment to look at his cards. He never looked as soon as he got them. That was what most players did. They were eager to see if they had a good hand or not, and their faces always told the truth.

Sean only lifted his cards by the corner so he could see only the numbers and the suits. He lowered the cards and looked at the chips in the middle of the table.

"What does he have?" Kimberly asked, suddenly extremely interested in the game.

"Don't know," Tommy said. "That's the game. No one knows what each other has."

"So, you just risked five million dollars and potentially someone's life on luck?"

"Not hardly," Tommy quipped. "Just watch."

"Raise," Sean said.

"We have a raise," the dealer echoed.

"Eighty thousand." Sean said with a nonchalance that suggested the amount was a pittance to him. He tossed the chips into the middle as though they were nothing more than sticks of chewing gum.

The Frenchman frowned, his face flushing red. "Big American cowboy doesn't like to be pushed around, huh?" he blathered, spittle spraying from his chubby lips. "Well, welcome to the party, cowboy. Raise." He shoveled a stack of chips into the front, taking down one piece of his towering wall. "One hundred and sixty thousand."

Everyone at the table sat up a little straighter. After hours of being bullied by the Frenchman, this new player had injected a new, brash resistance.

Sean could tell they were all wondering if he had the hand or not, if he'd sat down into a monster pair of cards. All this action and the first three community cards hadn't even been dealt.

.at is he doing?" Kimberly asked. "That's almost two hundred
." She sounded aghast. Tommy doubted she made that much
ιey in a year, though he hadn't checked the salaries of federal
aₒents in recent years.

"Couldn't tell you. He's doing this thing. But if I had to guess,
Sean's feeling this guy out."

"Feeling him out?" The words came out in a hiss. "That's a lot of
money, your money, to be feeling someone out."

"All in," Sean said. He shoved his entire stack of chips into the
middle.

"All in for one million," the dealer announced. With the procla-
mation, the air sucked out of the room. Even the usher at the door
turned inward for a moment. The bartender leaned forward on her
elbows. Things had just got interesting.

The heavy Frenchman's eyes raged and his chest swelled and fell
with rapid breaths. Beads of sweat rolled down the side of his pudgy
face and dangled on his double chin, clinging on for dear life.

He thought about the bet for nearly two minutes before he reluctantly pushed his cards into the middle of the table.

"Fold," the dealer announced.

The mood in the room instantly lifted, except for the Frenchman, of
course. He stewed in his seat, no doubt vowing to himself that he would
make the new American player pay for taking his hard-won chips.

Sean raked in the pile and tossed a five-thousand-dollar chip to
the dealer. "Thank you," Sean said.

"Thank you, sir," the dealer replied, clearly overjoyed at the
generous tip. He'd probably just paid the mortgage for the next three
or four months with that money.

"Did he win?" Kimberly asked.

"Yeah," Tommy said. "And he just chopped one of the bully's legs
out from under him."

For the next hour, Tommy, Kimberly, and Li watched along with
the bartender and a growing crowd of curious onlookers as Sean
continued hacking his way through his competitors. He carried on

friendly conversation with the other players but ignored the big Frenchman, instead letting every lost hand or every big bet missed send the man spiraling into a tilted vortex.

The other players didn't seem to mind losing money to Sean. That's not to say they wanted to lose, but he acted the part of the graceful winner and loser—the few hands he lost—to win the hearts of the rest of the table. It was a war waged with roses and candy on the surface, while he fired nuclear missiles under the cover of darkness, all the while building up his Great Wall of chips to a size that may well have been seen from the space station.

In two hours, Sean had amassed over three million dollars in winnings, leaving the Frenchman with almost nothing.

Eventually, after a desperate attempt at a bluff, Sean took the rest of the man's chips with a full house of nines over threes. Infuriated, the petulant gambler shoved away from the table and stood. He grabbed what must have been his sixth glass of cognac and raised it to his face. Some of the amber liquid sloshed over the rim of the glass, spilling onto the floor. He issued a series of curses at Sean and the others, who merely sat quietly with faux somber expressions concealing their joy at the man's departure.

He emptied the contents of the glass into his mouth and stumbled away. At the door, the usher attempted to extend a hand to guide the man out, but the gambler raised a dismissive hand and staggered by into the main high-stakes lobby.

Sean collected the remnants of the Frenchman's chips, adding to his already daunting construction.

"Thank you," the woman to Sean's right said. "He was extremely rude." Her accent was thick, local, possibly from the mainland. She was roughly Sean's age, though probably a couple of years his senior. She had an elegant grace about her, which most likely caused her to lose often at a table like this where the sharks swam. No ring on her finger indicated she was either single, divorced, or playing a part. It didn't matter to Sean. She was being friendly, and so would he, as well.

"I had a good run of cards," he said humbly, still placing chips on top of others.

She tilted her head at an angle, still offering the same warm beam. "I don't think so. I've been on good runs. Bad ones, too. No one runs as well as you have. You're clearly a phenomenal player."

Sean offered a meager *aw shucks* grin and cocked his head. "I like to play cards," was all he could muster. "It's an interesting strategic game. But with that guy"—he indicated the direction the man went with a nod—"it's just like a bully in a playground. Someone has to stand up to the bully, no matter how big he looks." He didn't tell the woman he had another four million behind the one he'd used to buy into the game. Sean knew that insanely aggressive players were prone to huge swings of wins and losses, but that also meant so was anyone who dared to fight back against them.

"Sir?" a man's voice asked from behind Sean's chair. A gentle tap on the shoulder accompanied the word.

The woman Sean had been talking to averted her eyes to the newcomer, and Sean could see in an instant that she was genuinely surprised. A sense of respect, or was it fear, burned through her eyes, and her mouth gaped.

Sean didn't look back, still counting his chips while showing a flash of bravado he'd yet to display to anyone at the table. "Is Mr. Wei ready to play with me now?" he asked, cockily.

"Yes, sir," the man said. "Mr. Wei would very much like to hear about this rare artifact you spoke of."

Sean didn't have to look back to know it was the gatekeeper to Wei's private poker room.

"What took him so long?" Sean asked with chagrin.

"He is very selective about the... opponents he chooses."

"Tell him I'll be there in ten minutes. I need a break." He pointed over at Tommy and the women accompanying him at the bar. "My associates over there will follow you in. I'll be in shortly."

"Thank you, Mr. Wyatt," the usher said. He turned and fluttered away, disappearing into the lobby to return what he must have felt was an urgent message.

Sean looked over at Tommy and gave a nod. *Step one complete. And it only took four hours off the clock.* Sean knew, however, this next leg in the race was going to be far tougher. And he wasn't gambling for money.

Someone's life was at stake.

16

ATLANTA

Father Bill Worthington slid into his vestments with the same graceful ease he always had. The fit and fabric of the cassock felt like a lightweight blanket around him, filling him with a sense of peace and warmth. Once he was dressed, he switched off the main light in his office, leaving only the lamp on his desk glowing with a reverent yellow corona.

He floated down the corridors of St. Peter's Cathedral, his feet making no sound as they padded on the stone tiles. The strands of dark brown hair that rimmed his bald head fluttered in the breeze as he walked.

This part of the day was his favorite. The vacant church filled him with a sense of anticipation, but also of gratitude for the quiet that permeated the building. At fifty years old, silence was one of the things he loved most. Soon, it would be full of people gathering for the morning mass.

His ritual was the same nearly every day. He arrived at the church before anyone else, getting there in time to enjoy a cup of coffee and a bit of prayer prior to taking morning confession. He didn't exercise, except for the occasional stroll through Piedmont Park or the Atlanta Botanical Gardens, where he was an annual member. There was no reason for him to stay in athletic shape or work out, not that he saw. He was of medium height and twenty pounds overweight, but he didn't worry. He didn't indulge in many vices with regard to food or drink. In his mind, that balanced everything out.

He turned right into the men's restroom, pushing the wooden door open wide as he passed through, his fingers pressing into the smooth grooves of a four-sided cross carved into the dark oaken surface.

The bathroom stank of pine and bleach, burning his nostrils as he crossed the floor to one of the stalls. The pungent aroma assaulted his senses, stinging his eyes and tingling his forehead.

"Ugh, Maria. I must have a talk with that woman about how much disinfectant she uses."

Maria was the custodian who came through every evening to clean. She took care of the bathrooms and offices, while a larger crew took care of the sanctuary on Mondays. She didn't speak much English but was a good worker. An immigrant from Chiapas, she did her job with pride and diligence. In this particular bathroom, perhaps too much diligence.

He shoved open one of the stall doors and slipped inside, pulled up his robes, and plopped down on the toilet. He pulled out his phone and started to scroll through the pictures he'd taken the evening before, deleting each one.

It wouldn't do to have anyone find the evidence, no matter how unlikely. Still, the wolves were circling in nearly every town and city in the nation. The righteously angry mobs made it clear they would no longer tolerate the kinds of tastes in which he indulged, but Father Worthington couldn't help himself. With such delicious delicacies at his fingertips, how could he not have a taste every now and then?

He sighed with regret every time his thumb pressed the delete button on his phone. There would be more, of course. There always were. And his participants would keep their mouths shut. He had something on every one of their families and used that to get what he wanted—no, what he needed. He knew what he was doing was wrong and struggled with himself over it, often spending hours in prayer to overcome his vice. It was all in vain, though, and he always returned like a smackhead to a drug dealer.

He finished deleting the images—piped in through cameras cleverly concealed in his office—and shoved the phone into an empty pocket before taking care of his business in the bathroom. He was about to stand and flush when he heard the door open.

That's odd, he thought. *No one should be in the building yet. Perhaps Maria left something last night and thought it might be in here.*

"Sorry, Maria," he guessed. "I'm in here. Be right out."

Oddly, he didn't hear the door close.

"*Occupado,*" he said, hoping the use of her native Spanish would make it clear she didn't need to come in.

The door eased shut and hit the frame with a gentle thud. He shook his head and rolled his eyes. Maria was a sweet woman, but not the brightest.

Then he heard a footstep. It was loud, almost deliberate. Then another. The third footfall hit the floor with the same cadence.

"Maria?" Father Worthington said. "Please, I need some privacy. I'll be out in a moment. Did you leave something here last night?"

He tried to recall some of the Spanish he'd picked up through the years, but it was a meager collection of random words—at best.

The intruder's shadow stopped in front of the stall. Father Worthington looked down at the black cowboy boots circled by the cuffs of black denim jeans.

"I'm sorry, my son," Worthington offered. "The church will be open in a few minutes. I'll be happy to take your confession then." His voice cracked, a sign of discomfort and confusion.

"I'm not here to confess anything to you, Padre," a man's voice said. It was an unsettling sound, full of gravel and malice. The man hadn't made a threat, not directly, but it was there nonetheless.

"Okay. Just... let me finish up in here and I'll be happy to assist you. I'd prefer not to talk through a metal bathroom stall if that's okay. I'll be done in a second, and then—"

"Way I see it, Padre, you finished your business already."

Now the priest was totally baffled. He flushed the toilet and stood up. Just then, one of the boots left the floor and smashed into the stall door, bashing it open. The force struck the priest's knuckles on both hands and sent him reeling back onto the toilet seat.

He landed clumsily and nearly fell to the floor next to it, but managed to steady himself against the cubicle walls.

In the doorway, a man with thick salt-and-pepper hair and matching beard stood wearing a white shirt with the top button undone to expose a tanned, hairy chest. The pectoral muscles tightened threateningly.

"What... what is this?" Worthington demanded, suddenly overcome with righteous indignation. "I am a man of God. You don't just storm in here like this. This is assault." His voice climbed louder with every word.

"Oh? Assault, you say?" The man sounded like he was from a rural part of the country, but not entirely Southern. His accent was difficult to place, but the man's roots weren't Father Worthington's primary concern at this moment.

"Yes. It could be," the priest retreated a little. "But... I am a man of forgiveness. Let's go to the confession booth and I will be happy to talk you through any troubles you may be facing."

"You don't listen, do you, Padre? I ain't here for confession." He sounded like the grim reaper, come to collect.

"Yes, that's right. You did say that." Then the priest's eyes fell to the man's waist and the bullwhip in his right hand. Shards of metal dangled from a cat-o'-nine-tails. "What are you going to do with that?" He raised a chubby finger toward the leathery weapon.

"This?" The stranger held up the whip. "Oh, this is for your confession, Padre."

"My confession? I don't confess to anyone but the Almighty." He almost shouted the words, enraged by the unwelcome visitor.

"Oh, that's precisely what I mean. You speak of assault as if you would press charges against one of your flock, yet assault is exactly what you did to some of those innocent lambs you were supposed to shepherd."

The priest's eyes flashed wide with fear. "I have no idea what you mean."

The stranger then reached into his pocket and withdrew a phone. He held it out so Worthington could see the screen. The image sent a chill through his body that struck every bone at its core. It was one of the pictures he'd just deleted from his phone, an image of the ecstasy he'd enjoyed the night before in his office.

"How did you get that?" He did his best to sound accusatory.

"You were tasked by the good Lord to be a shepherd, Padre. But you have sinned. And now it's time for you to be purified through pain."

Then the realization hit Father Worthington. "It's you," he said. "You're the one who killed that pastor a few days ago."

"That's right," the stranger said. "Although there's a chance you get to live."

A strange sense of hope dripped into Worthington's veins. "Yes. Please. Tell me. I'll do anything. Just don't kill me. I swear; I won't do it again."

"Oh, I know you won't, Padre," the man said, his eyes falling to the priest's crotch. "I'm gonna make sure of that. But your livin' or dyin' isn't dependent on anything you can do."

Worthington felt his heart sink. For a second, he forgot the man's insinuation regarding his nether regions.

"What do you mean?"

The stranger squatted like a baseball catcher, clutching the whip in both hands. "See, I got myself an errand boy, too, Padre. If he gets me what I want before noon today, then you get to live. But if he doesn't...." He let the cowering priest figure out the rest.

"No," Worthington said. Then he began to yell at the top of his lungs. "Someone! Help me! Please!"

"No one is going to hear you, Padre. Church is closed off. Signs out front say it's going through a renovation due to fire damage."

Then Father Worthington started to sob. Tears streaked down his pudgy red face and fell to the tiles at his feet. "Please, you can't do this. Please. I'll give you whatever you want."

"What I want is for you to be forgiven through pain." He stood and inched forward even as the priest tried to retreat farther into the wall. The stranger ran the back of his hand against Worthington's cheek, brushing away a stream of tears. "Don't you see? I'm here to save you, Padre." He looked down at the toilet. "The good news for me is you won't piss yourself when we get started. Much obliged."

Then, in the blink of an eye, he snatched the priest by the back of the hair and yanked him up.

17

MACAU

Sean prowled into Wei's private poker room with the confidence of a lion.

He noted the setting was similar to the other room, though the bar was off to the left. Another striking difference was the entourage of guards who circled the table; eight of them stood against the wall, staggered ten feet apart. Sean didn't see the weapons, but he knew they were there despite any prohibition the casino or Macau might have against such possession.

A man as powerful and important as Wei never let his guard down.

Sean saw the mark immediately, though he had his back to the room. He stood perfectly still in front of a window that ran from the floor all the way to the ceiling. That entire part of the wall was made from thick glass to give a panoramic view of the city and the sea beyond.

"Very impressive," Wei said as Sean stopped next to the table where a dealer sat with his fingers steepled. "I can appreciate talent when I see it."

"I'd say I got lucky," Sean replied casually. "But we both know that's not true."

Wei snickered. "Indeed."

His focus remained on some distant point in the city. The night sky glowed with the radiant light shining upon it from the sprawl below, making it impossible to see all but the brightest stars.

"Do you need to take a break?" Wei asked. His voice was mellow, smooth, with just a touch of snobbery that might have betrayed a wealthy and entitled upbringing. "I know it's been a long day for you, coming from America."

He turned with all the slow drama of a movie villain, keeping his hands behind his back at all times. The man wasn't tall, but he wasn't short, either, probably a few inches under six feet. His torso was slight, as were his legs, all covered by a garish violet suit that shimmered in the light.

"I'm fine," Sean said. In truth, he was exhausted from the long journey and lack of quality sleep. There was no time for a break, though, but he couldn't tell Wei that. Even with plenty of time left until noon back in Atlanta, there was no telling how this game was going to play out, and it could take longer than they had.

Wei crossed the floor with an elegant grace. His expensive clothes, welcoming demeanor, and the way he moved, all played into his guise as a hydra in sheep's clothing.

"Very well," Wei said with a nod at the dealer.

The man at the table took a stack of cards and spread out all fifty-two across the felt in an arc. He waited for Sean to inspect the deck, which he did within two seconds, making sure there was one of every suit from two through ace.

"They're good," Sean acknowledged.

"Excellent," Wei said. "Wash them."

The dealer ran his hands across the cards and ruined the neat rainbow he'd created, turning it into a mangled mess of cards. When he was satisfied they were adequately mixed, he scooped them up, stacked them neatly, and inserted them into the shuffling machine. With a push of a button, the elevated device sank into the table. After a few seconds of a quiet whir accompanied by rhythmic flapping, the machine raised up again to offer the stack to the dealer.

"Do you have something to show me?" Wei asked.

"Yes," Sean said, momentarily forgetting he had an entourage of his own. He turned and motioned to Tommy who was carrying the case with Boudica's laurel.

He set the metal case on the poker table, entered the combination, and flipped it open.

Inside, a golden laurel sat cradled in foam specifically cut to house the artifact.

Wei's eyes visibly widened with pleasure. He stepped close to the table and reached out his hands to touch the item, then realized it was not yet his.

"What a prize this is," Wei said reverently. "The crown of the great Celtic queen."

"You know your history," Sean said. He'd made it clear that the others were not to speak to Wei, as a sign of respect to the man. His business was with Sean, not the others, and any intrusion into the conversation would be treated as a hostile act.

Wei's head snapped to the right, his eyes prying Sean with questions. "You thought I did not?"

Sean passed an easy smirk to the man, along with a gentle snort through his nose. "Oh, I know you do. It was merely a concession on my part, a show of admiration."

Wei accepted the compliment with an easy smile and returned his gaze to the golden artifact. "Yes. This will do."

Wei closed the case and handed it to Tommy. "Thank you, Thomas. This is a fine piece."

"Yes, sir," was all Tommy offered in reply. He didn't bother wondering how the man knew his name. Wei probably knew all their names. How was irrelevant. They were here, and that was all that mattered.

Tommy withdrew to the side of the room where Li and Kimberly stood, then watched as Wei ordered one of his men to retrieve something from a closet near the bar.

The guard, a man in his mid-thirties, turned and opened the door, then retrieved a black case. He walked over to the table and set it down with the greatest of care, stepped away from the table, and hovered a few feet away.

Wei flipped open the briefcase and twisted it so Sean could see the contents. Sean's eyes rested on the object. The gold glimmered in the bright overhead lights. A shimmering chandelier fitted with thousands of pieces of Waterford crystal caused the light to dance and play on the bracelet's surface. It looked as it might have two thousand years ago, virtually untouched by man or time.

Sean moved closer to the relic and loomed over it. His eyes passed over the golden surface of the piece, inspecting every inch. A bizarre-looking fish was carved into the smooth surface, the animal rising slightly. To the right, an image of a tree drooping to one side stood out against the wrist-guard, while on the left, an ancient ship rode atop choppy waves. The latter two images hadn't been part of the riddle, but Sean knew this was the correct artifact. Three pieces of Jonah's story were prominently displayed on the gauntlet segment, three important moments in the great minister's life.

The ship represented his attempt to flee from God's instructions. Sean recalled the story easily. Jonah fled to Joppa where he boarded a boat heading for Tarshish. He realized, silently, that there must have been a connection between the ship's destination and the one Dr. Kelley excavated recently. The locations were too close to be a coincidence. The ancient port of Tarshish would have been close to what is now Gibraltar.

The fish symbol was easy enough to correlate to the prophet's journey, but the tree was more subtle, a hint at Jonah's final days in his ministry to Nineveh. He'd complained about the heat, about being thirsty, and about God's unwillingness to destroy the heathen city-state when it—as a whole—repented of its sins and turned its ways to the path of righteousness.

Jonah pouted and complained, so God caused a tree to grow out of the ground to give him shade from the heat. Still he whined. So a worm came and bit the tree and caused it to wither and die. Right in line with his entitled mindset, Jonah griped about that, too, and that was where the story ended.

"An exceptional piece," Sean said. "I have to ask, though, Mr. Wei"—Sean raised his head and locked eyes with the man—"you knew we were coming. Yet you made me walk that little dance in the high-stakes room." He didn't sound rude, merely curious.

"Your friend Li over there contacted me as to the possibility of a wager between you and me," Wei confessed.

"Yes. Still, I flew a long way to get here. If I'd lost in the other game... would have been a shame."

"I was never concerned about your ability to beat that game. I've heard from others that you're more than capable. Word gets around the poker circuit, whether you know it or not, Mr. Wyatt." Wei turned and strolled over to the bar. He stopped and gave a single nod to the bartender, who immediately produced a drink from behind the counter. He cupped the martini glass with one hand, balancing the stem delicately between his fingers. "Martini, Mr. Wyatt?" He raised the glass in offering.

"No, thanks, Mr. Wei. That's Jim's drink."

"Ah. I didn't realize you knew James, or that you were on such... friendly terms. He's particularly reclusive, even for an MI6 agent." If Wei was surprised, it barely showed.

"Our paths have crossed a few times in a casino here and there. He usually frequents places that are... too pretentious for my style." Of course, he knew much more about Jim than he let on, and he had no designs on spilling the beans to the billionaire.

Wei nearly spit out his drink in laughter at the last part. He looked over at one of his guards to get a reaction, but the man merely stared straight ahead into the center of the room.

"Too pretentious," he said loudly. "I like this guy. Yes, you're right, of course. James does have... high tastes. Much like myself. I don't like to think of myself as pretentious, though." He sauntered back to the table, his martini coming precipitously close to spilling with every exaggerated step.

Sean noted the touch of powder under the bottom of the guy's nose and realized why he was acting so dramatically. At least Sean hoped it was an act.

"Back to your comment," Wei said, his voice returning to a steady drone. "Of course I have to vet my opponents; even the ones I know are bringing exceptional items to wager. I can't have fish coming to swim in this shark's tank."

He ambled over to the end of the table. The chair was designed for luxury, made from leather with a high back and short armrests, which was unusual for a poker table chair. This place clearly did all they could to make their wealthiest clients comfortable and happy for the sole purpose of keeping them in the building long enough to grift them for every possible nickel.

"Sit wherever you like," Wei said, emphasizing his invitation with an extended hand toward the other chairs.

Sean's eyes narrowed to match his smirk, and he shifted to the seat to his right at the opposite end of the table. "If we're going to duel, it might as well be a few paces apart, no?"

"I like your style."

Wei eased into his chair while his guard removed the case containing the gauntlet piece and strode over to the wall where he'd been before.

"Dealer?" Wei announced. "Let's play some cards. Shuffle up and deal." Wei rubbed his hands together. "Winner takes all."

18

MACAU

S ean stared down at his meager supply of chips. What had begun as an equal share had dwindled down to almost nothing.

They'd been playing for hours. Sean had honestly lost count at several points during the game. Night had fallen over Macau, and the city lit up through the window, a bright and silent beacon on the South China Sea.

The game started well enough. Sean took an early lead, knocking down his opponent's supply of chips four or five thousand at a time. That momentum, however, shifted quickly.

A dead run of bad cards didn't help. As good as Sean was, dead runs were difficult to overcome even for the best players.

Tommy's look of concern was nothing compared to Kimberly's expression of absolute horror. From the look in her eyes, Sean could tell she thought the battle was already lost. And the war, too.

Sean knew better, though. One of poker's greatest players, Doyle Brunson, once said, "All you need is a chip and a chair to have a chance."

Sean had more than one chip, but they were bleeding rapidly to the other side of the table. And in this game, there were no rebuys where he could go to the cashier cage and exchange cash for more chips. This was it. A fight to the death. Which caused Sean to wonder about their immediate safety were they to lose—or win, for that matter. Then again, he'd taken precautions for that issue should it arise.

Even with most of his chips gone and a towering wall in front of Wei, Sean kept his usual jovial demeanor. It was part of the ruse; the persona he put out to other players. He'd learned that by acting happy and talkative, he gave other players the impression he was loose, played too many hands, and didn't have a clue what he was doing. Of course, nothing could be further from the truth, but they didn't have to know that.

The dealer flipped the cards to the players, and Sean waited until his opponent had his second. Playing heads-up against a person was different than playing multiple people. It had to be approached differently, with more aggression. He also couldn't wait for the other player to look at his cards before he made a decision—since both he and Wei clearly understood that little tactical gem.

Sean peeked at his cards, barely bending them up from the corner. Another terrible hand—nine of spades, five of hearts.

He took a deep breath and decided he had to make a play, not necessarily with his cards, but with the man. Normally, he would tighten up in a situation like this, wait for something decent and then shove all his chips in the middle—and hope for the best.

"So, Mr. Wei," Sean began, absently fingering three chips in his minuscule pile. "I know about all of your legitimate businesses, but I have to ask—and please, don't think I'm being rude—but why would you build up such a massive empire in the private sector only to risk it in the drug trade?"

Sean didn't care what the man said next. It was the precursor to a deeper question; an unspoken poker inquisition he ran with his eyes. Truth or lie, there would be something Sean could use against the man.

Wei smiled pleasantly, somehow not offended by the brash inquiry. "I see that rumors are now flying over the ocean, Mr. Wyatt."

"Rumors?" Sean asked. "Raise," he said and shoved three chips into the middle of the table.

"Triple the bet," the dealer announced.

"Yes," Wei replied. "Rumors." He absently thumbed a gargantuan sapphire ring on his right ring finger. "Some people have suggested that I am running an underground heroin ring. I've even heard ganja from a few lips, which I must admit, I use to help me sleep but have never considered selling for profit. It's a shame it's illegal in most nations. The profit margins are quite good from what I've seen and heard. But no, I do not run a drug organization. That would be a foolish enterprise for a man in my position, would it not?"

Sean watched him carefully, his eyes locked on Wei's but peripherally noting the man playing with his ring.

"Call," Wei said and tossed in three more chips.

Sean's opponent had been calling a wider range of hands as his stack climbed to the stratosphere.

"I wasn't passing judgment one way or the other," Sean said. "I just thought it was an odd decision, like you said, for a man in your position. As you also suggest, rumors seem to fly everywhere."

"Indeed they do."

The dealer flipped over the first three community cards: an eight of spades, jack of hearts, and a five of spades. Neither player flinched. Their eyes gave away nothing. Sean always made the same movements, the same gestures, when cards were turned over. He learned early on in his career that consistency to all body language was the key to eliminating tells that another player could use against him. Wei must have learned from the same school of thought. The man was an eternal statue at the table, and Sean caught himself admiring the man's discipline.

"Action to you, Mr. Wei," the dealer said.

Wei inclined his head as he did every hand, and reached for a stack of chips. He thumbed six of them, held them for a second or two, then plopped them across the betting line.

"Check," Wei said.

Sean only had a pair of fives, the lowest pair possible, and his nine wasn't going to help things. He looked down at his stack, pondering a potential bet. Throwing any more out there would take him down to pretty much nothing, so he tapped the felt and announced a check as well.

"Button checks," the dealer announced and flipped over the fourth card, known as the turn card.

The ace of diamonds appeared. Again, Wei gave no indication he was either happy or disappointed about the card. He continued absently rubbing the sapphire with his thumb as he tapped the table again. "Check."

Sean's lips twitched. The guy was basically giving up on the hand, but he could also be slow-playing a monster—two pair, three of a kind, or simply a pair better than Sean's fives.

"Check's good," Sean said with a rap on the surface.

"River card," the dealer said plainly.

He turned over the two of spades.

It wasn't the card Sean hoped to see, and he cursed himself for not even considering the possibility that if a spade came out on the board, his opponent could have picked up a flush, which would have Sean's hand crushed—not that it was strong to begin with. If Wei was trying to catch the spade draw, he just hit it and the hand was lost.

Sean inwardly let out a sigh, knowing he could have bet the turn and probably taken it down. Then he noticed something, a tick he hadn't seen before, or at least considered.

As Wei reached for a tall stack of chips that represented more than Sean had left, the man stopped rubbing his sapphire. He splashed the chips into the middle of the table and called out his bet.

"I bet the pot," Wei said with a smug grin.

Sean's lips curled upward wickedly. That was it. That was Wei's tell. When the man was talking about the rumors regarding his dealing drugs, he rubbed the sapphire. When he checked the first four cards on the board, he did the same. Now, he wasn't. And he was betting.

Sean's background in psychology had kicked in during Wei's explanations about the false rumors, and he'd believed the guy. Now, he knew Wei was bluffing.

"Looks like you got me covered, Mr. Wei," Sean said.

"Looks that way, Mr. Wyatt," Wei replied demurely.

Sean took a deep breath and clutched his cards in both hands, feigning tossing them in the middle. Doing so would only leave him one, maybe two hands to play before he had no chips left to cover the blind bets.

He looked the man in the eyes, noting in his periphery that Wei was still not rubbing the precious stone. "Well, I'm gonna have to call."

Wei snorted a derisive laugh, and Sean pushed the remainder of his chips into the middle of the pile. "All I have is a pair of fives with a nine kicker," Sean announced as he flipped over his hand for the entire room to see. "It's not much, but I'm betting it beats your king high."

The stone sculpture across from Sean cracked as Wei's eyes widened slightly. His lips parted. Then he narrowed his eyes again to slits and flipped over his cards. It was followed by a broad smile. "Excellent read, sir," he said with an appreciative nod.

Sean returned the gesture. "Thank you, sir. But you're still way ahead." That was true, but Sean had just doubled up in one bold play. In the poker world, what he'd just done was referred to as a hero call.

He sensed the question in Wei's expression, a silent inquiry he would never speak. Any self-respecting player would never ask how he knew the man was bluffing.

Then Sean let his eyes peek at his watch. They were out of time. He thought he could grind Wei down, and now that he had something to work with, there was no doubt in his mind how the game would play out were he to have even another hour. But he didn't. He had minutes until the deadline. Back in Atlanta, it was nearly noon, and someone was going to die. Maybe it was fatigue catching up to him. He knew he probably had dark circles under the lower eyelids. His brain churned from a combination of adrenaline and sheer exhaustion. Out of time and out of plays, Sean did something he would never do in a regular poker game. He gave away his opponent's tell.

"Your ring," Sean said.

Wei frowned for a moment then looked down at the blue stone. He returned his gaze to Sean. There was no anger, only admiration.

"You rub it with your thumb when you're telling the truth. When you told me about the drug dealing rumors, you did it. When you checked the first four cards, you rubbed it. When you bluffed the river, you didn't."

Wei glanced down at the ring again and then met Sean's gaze. He bowed his head low. "I never realized," he said.

By the bar, Kimberly couldn't believe what she was seeing and hearing. She turned to Tommy. "Why did he just do that?" she hissed. "If he found a tell on the guy, he could have used that to take every last chip in the man's stack."

Tommy kept his gaze on the table for two breaths before he twisted his head toward the woman. "Well, one, because we're out of time and if he doesn't throw a Hail Mary soon, someone is going to die in Atlanta."

"And two?"

He held her stare in his as he answered. "Because Sean Wyatt has something too many people in this world have forgotten."

Her frown deepened, creating lines across her forehead. "What's that?"

"Honor."

Mr. Wei stood abruptly and planted his hands on the table. He peered at Sean, searching him for the truth. "Why would you do that?" He begged the question Kimberly had also asked. "When you find an edge over an opponent, you don't tell them." He kept his voice even but spoke with urgency. His eyes wandered down to the ring on his finger and fixed his gaze on the gem. Seconds ticked by, and Sean wondered what the man was thinking, though he had a pretty good idea.

It was a tactical mistake as far as the game was concerned. Of that there was no doubt. But Sean was out of time.

"You're right, of course," Sean admitted. "Normally, I would let you just keep rubbing that gem of yours all night until I had every last chip from your stack. But you're too good a player to allow that to happen. It wouldn't be fair. I can tell you have honed your game, your strategy, all of it over years of play. You're an exceptional opponent, and I'm certain if we played ten heads-up matches, we would split them down the middle, fifty-fifty."

A look of appreciation softened Wei's face.

Sean continued. "It would feel like cheating if I didn't tell you. And I don't cheat. I win straight up, or I lose straight up."

Wei straightened, holding his head high. He looked over at the guard protecting the black briefcase. The man had long since given up holding it and had rested it on a nearby high-top table. Wei motioned to the man with his right hand, beckoning him to come.

The guard did as ordered and brought the black briefcase over to the table. Tommy's eyes widened as he realized what was about to happen. Li stood close to him, holding her breath. Kimberly's scowl remained frozen on her face.

Wei collected the case from his guard and turned it so the clasps faced him. He flipped open the lid and stared at the piece with no small amount of admiration.

"They say this was from ancient Assyria," Wei began. "Though there is something about it that makes me think it could be from another culture, another civilization." He looked up at Sean, meeting his gaze. "I don't know what it could have been used for, but it appears there might have been other pieces that fit with it."

Sean nodded. "Two," he informed Wei, risking more truth than he felt comfortable sharing, but there was no turning back now.

"So, you know what this is?"

"I do," Sean confessed. "It's a piece of an ancient gauntlet, something that was lost long ago. We're trying to locate all three pieces to reunite them."

Wei nodded appreciatively. "This rod that protrudes from the end..." He looked down at the object again. "I've never seen anything like that on old gauntlets or wrist guards before."

Sean studied the odd piece. It was attached to a hinge that flipped out, bending with a slight curve before straightening again. At the end of it, the golden rod flattened into the shape of a fish's head, similar to the fish on the plating. "I don't know what that's for," he concurred. "But I aim to find out."

Wei spun the case back around. His eyes fixed on the artifact within, a sort of regret filling them.

"I wanted this the first second I laid eyes on it," he said, his voice distant. "I didn't know why. I have many pieces that have a higher monetary value." His head shook. "This one, though. It called to me."

Sean wanted the man to hurry up so they could get back to the game. He had a feeling that wasn't going to happen. "There are no coincidences, Mr. Wei," he said.

The man searched Sean's icy-gray eyes. Then he surrendered a nod. "No, I don't believe there are. I don't know why you want this item so badly, bad enough to fly halfway across the planet to play me for it—especially when you thought I was a drug dealer."

Sean blushed noticeably.

Wei held up a hand. "Don't feel bad about it. I'm not offended. Many men in my position have gone down such a path. I suspect, in the end, it will be their undoing. I'm too busy enjoying what I've built to risk it all on some ridiculous ego play."

He closed the case and shoved it across the table. Sean stopped it with a deft hand.

"It's yours," Wei said. "You won it fairly."

"But, Mr. Wei, you're still way ahead of me."

The man shook his head and looked down at his still-impressive stack of chips. "Let's just say, anytime you want a rematch, I'll be happy to entertain you as my guest. Perhaps we'll pick up where we left off. But it seems to me that you're in a hurry. Am I correct?"

"Yes, sir," Sean said as he stole a glance at a clock on the wall. He didn't elaborate further, though if he felt the necessity, Sean was willing to throw it all on the table.

"Then take it," Wei said. "We can finish our game another time."

Kimberly watched in rapt amazement, her chin nearly hitting the floor. Tommy looked down at his watch. They were nearly out of time, only two minutes from the deadline.

Tommy pulled up the phone number they'd received from the killer and tapped on the part to send a text message, hoping that he could buy a few seconds before the man went through with the murder. His heart beat like a jackhammer, and he could feel his blood pulsing to the same cadence.

He worked his fingers as fast as he could. "We got it," he typed before tapping the send button.

"Come on," Tommy said, stealing a glance back over at the table where his friend pried open the lid to the case, admiring their acquisition. The text message took longer than it should have to go through. Tommy let out a relieved sigh as the progress bar at the top disappeared, signaling the message had been sent.

"Tommy," Sean said, his voice suddenly urgent. "Come take a picture of this, quick. We don't have much time."

Wei and his entourage watched as Sean turned the case toward his friend. Tommy rushed over to the table and opened the camera app on his phone. He focused on the object inside the case and then tapped the button. The device vibrated and a preview of the incoming message appeared at the top. It was from the killer.

"Sixty seconds" was all it said.

Tommy tapped the message, and his phone switched back to the text-messaging app. He typed the word *Here* and hit the send arrow. Then he tapped on the image icon to add the picture of the artifact from his camera roll. He selected the image and then hit the send arrow again.

The previous message had just gone through. Now he watched with horror as the phone tried to process the image through the device and then the cell network.

Li and Kimberly stepped close, huddling with Sean and Tommy to watch as time ticked by.

"Come on," Sean said, echoing Tommy's previous frustration with the technology. "Why is it taking so long?"

Then another message appeared at the top of the device.

Too late, Sean.

19

ATLANTA

The group had been poring over the document for hours, analyzing the letter, the tablet, and back again. They'd scoured the internet using their powerful quantum computers to search for something that might give them a clue as to the answer to the riddle. The machines pulled down immense amounts of data from every available source, all the while filtering through it to find possible correlations.

Still, with all that effort and power behind their work, their search came up empty.

Alex leaned back in his chair and stretched his arms out behind him. He made that Wookie-like sound everyone makes when they stretch.

Dr. Kelley rubbed her eyes and took a few deep breaths.

Tara reached over and picked up a coffee mug, pressed it to her lips, and took a sip. It was her fourth cup in two hours.

"What is it we're missing?" Alex asked, still reaching his arms out until he heard a low crack in the middle of his back. "It has to be here. Right?"

"Not necessarily," Kelley said. "The assumption about the tablet's directions are that the reader will know where to be. It's possible, likely even, that we won't find anything about where this is telling us to go."

"Unless we can figure out the riddle," Tara chimed in.

"Yeah, but our searches haven't come up with a solution for that, either," Alex said, sitting upright again with his hands on his lap. Then he frowned as a new realization hit him. "This guy knows that the relic was taken from Jonah's tomb. He has to."

"You think he knows who has it?" Kelley asked.

"Probably not; otherwise he'd have just gone for it himself."

"Yes, I suppose you're right. Unless he is enjoying making Sean his errand boy."

Tara chewed on her lower lip for a minute, the pensive gaze in her eyes locked on the far wall. "He has to. But why? Let's assume that Milner is killing people he deems sinners. Sean's not perfect, but he's not really guilty of any of the deadly sins Milner's message insinuated."

"Maybe it's not because he thinks he's a sinner," Alex offered. "Could be that Milner merely knows that Sean is the best at what he does—recovering artifacts."

"So, in a sick sort of way, he's like a client?"

"I guess. Didn't really think of it that way, but sure. In Milner's psychotic mind, maybe."

The room descended into silence again. Alex twisted around in his chair, flapping his lips with the air blowing through them. He leaned forward and hovered over the riddle again, studying the sheet of paper—hoping for some other piece of the equation to reveal itself.

He was about to give up and go get another cup of coffee when something at the bottom of the page caught his eye. "What the—" He cut himself off. At the bottom of the page, fragments of dots occupied a small space in the corner. He'd seen them before, thinking they were just a result of poor copier quality, stray ink. Now, though, as he peered at the anomaly, he realized it wasn't accidental at all.

"Guys?" he said, his eyes never leaving the page. "You need to come look at this."

"What is it?" Tara asked. She sidled up next to him and looked over his shoulder. Dr. Kelley rolled to his side.

"This." He pressed the bottom of the letter with his index finger. "See anything strange about those dots?"

"Not really?" Tara admitted. "You see that all the time with old copiers and printers. The quality isn't always the best."

"That's what I thought too. Look closer."

The women did, tilting forward to get a better view.

"See how some of those dots appear longer than others?"

"Wait," Kelley said. "Do you think that's some kind of Morse code?"

"Not some kind. It is," Alex said definitively.

Energy brimmed in him now, catalyzed by the caffeine pulsing through his veins. His mind raced, clarified by a single purpose. He slid his chair to the keyboard a foot away and began typing. A list of links appeared that offered either Morse code translation software or information on how to do it. He clicked the first link and was immediately taken to a website with a free tool for translating the code.

The two women watched with rapt attention as Alex began entering the code by clicking on the images of either long dots or short ones. The process took less than a minute.

"Are you sure about this?" Kelley asked, looking down at the paper. "Some of those are barely visible."

"I know," Alex said. "But maybe this is a clue to what we're looking for."

He finished clicking the corresponding dots and then clicked the translate button on the screen.

The software worked in seconds and produced a line of words that started with four numbers and then a street address, followed by the city of Dunwoody, Georgia, and the zip code.

"That's strange," Alex muttered. "It's an address."

"Maybe it's stationery he took from there and used for the letter. It's not the address of the first victim's church?"

"No. It isn't." The perplexed tone in Alex's voice mirrored the others' sentiments. "And I don't know of any place, church or otherwise, who puts their address on stationery in Morse code."

"Fair point," Tara surrendered.

"So," Dr. Kelley said, then paused as she considered the implications, "are you saying this is from the killer? Why would he put this here unless he wanted us to find the—"

"Oh, no," Alex gasped. "That's the address for his next victim."

His fingers flew across the keyboard, tapping the keys as fast as his mind and body could connect. Back at the search engine, he entered the address and clicked the search button.

The screen blinked and then displayed a huge stone cathedral. The name *St. Peter's Catholic Church* hung over the image in bold black letters.

Alex turned to Tara, his face awash with fear. The color in her face had also drained, turning her cheeks and forehead pale.

"That's where his next victim will be," Tara said.

"But... that doesn't make sense," Alex disputed. "Today is Sunday. They'll be having mass there in—" he glanced at his watch. "Now."

"He wouldn't kill someone in the middle of mass," Kelley argued. "That would be stupid."

"And mass killings aren't his thing," Alex added. "Not yet, anyway."

Tara lost herself in a tornado of thoughts swirling through her mind. "That has to be the place," she said with certainty. "Call the church and see if everything is okay."

Alex looked at the number on the screen and then took out his phone, entered the numbers, and pressed it to his ear. Five seconds passed, then ten, each with the same monotonous ringing. Then a voicemail message kicked in.

Alex looked up at his wife, the phone slowly lowering from his ear. "No answer," he said.

"There has to be someone manning the reception desk," Kelley insisted. "It's the busiest day of the week for them."

Alex ended the call and tried again with the same result. Still no answer.

"Something is very wrong here," he concluded.

Tara agreed with a nod. "Yeah. We need to get over there."

"What?" Kelley blurted. "Go over there? To where the killer might be?"

"Good point. We need to call Trent."

20

ATLANTA

A lex swung the Audi S5 into the parking lot adjacent to St. Peter's Cathedral. He whipped it around under an awning that stretched out over a side entrance and flung open the driver's side door.

A confused mob occupied the sidewalk, a safe distance from the main entrance near the street. Some of them were talking, probably trying to understand what was going on and why they couldn't take mass. There were only twenty or so of them, most having read the sign and decided that mass wasn't going to happen that day.

With lights blazing, two police cars sped into the lot, followed closely by another vehicle, a Jaguar F-Type, with Trent behind the wheel.

The former cop barely slipped his car into park before pushing open the door and getting out.

He pointed at the doors as the cops hurriedly exited their rides. "Inside. Quick," Trent ordered as if he still wore the badge he'd donned all those years ago.

Two uniformed cops sprinted to the door, drawing pistols as they neared. One pulled open the door and the other stepped inside and checked the foyer. Then the other followed behind.

Another squad car arrived along with a blacked-out Dodge Charger.

A tall man with pale skin and red hair stepped out of the passenger side of the Charger. Trent motioned to him and he strode over, his long legs quickly chewing up the asphalt to cover the distance between the two.

"Captain Donaghy," Trent said. He didn't bother extending a hand. They were against the clock. "Two of your men just went inside."

"What do we have here, Trent? You said it was big." The captain peered through the bright midday sun at the building. The third cop rushed to the doorway and peeked in through a window before stepping into the building.

The captain stood six feet eight inches tall. He was a gangly man, a former college basketball player for Kennesaw State University. He was only thirty-nine years of age, but he commanded the department with the leadership and savvy of someone twenty years older. The freckles probably didn't do him any favors in the bullpen, but Trent imagined very few, if any, in the department gave him a hard time.

"I got a lead that the serial killer was going to strike here," Trent answered.

"Lead?" Donaghy's skepticism oozed out of his narrowed eyes. "What lead?"

"You asked me to help out."

"With the federal investigation. Where's your contact?"

"She's... chasing down another lead." He hesitated to tell the captain where she'd gone, and the fact that she was with a clutch of civilians.

"Sir?" One of the cops who had gone into the building interrupted before Trent was forced to answer in more detail.

The captain spun around and looked toward the door. The cop, a husky fellow a few inches shorter than six feet and with tattoos adorning his arms, inclined his head. "You need to take a look at this."

The cop led the captain and Trent into the cathedral. Trent inhaled the familiar smell of church—a mix of wood, stone, old upholstery, and incense. His church didn't usually have the latter, but it was faint enough that he recognized everything else.

"What is it?" the captain asked, noting the tough-looking man's troubled tone.

"Probably better for you to see it for yourself, sir," the man replied, his accent a country drawl from South Georgia.

The captain's distress only heightened as they followed the cop to the doors leading into the sanctuary. They were closed, but through the narrow windows, Trent and Donaghy could see one of the other cops on his radio. Donaghy's radio crackled with the man's voice as he called in the crime, giving the corresponding code to the dispatcher so they could send all the necessary investigators for a murder scene.

The cop guiding Donaghy and Trent gently tugged on the big wooden door on the right side and swung it open. Trent gasped, feeling his stomach drop. Bile crept up his esophagus, but he fought it off.

Donaghy took a wary step into the sanctuary, his eyes fixed on the scene ahead.

Trent walked next to him, staring at the grisly scene with pity and horror.

In the center aisle, just in front of the presbytery, a wooden cross was propped up, fixed to the floor with a round wooden base and several two-by-fours that steadied it.

A man hung from the cross, blood dripping from his wrists and feet. He wore nothing but a pair of black boxers. Ropes around the man's biceps bound him to the cross so the spikes driven through the wrists didn't tear the body down. The victim's face was drained of color and wore a look of permanent agony, with mouth agape and eyes fixed on the first row of pews or the floor next to it.

As Trent drew near, he saw even more of the terrible details. Seven names were carved into the man's flesh, starting at the nape of his neck and stopping at his lowest ribs. On one side, a gash oozed the last remnants of the man's blood onto the floor, where the rest of his body had spilled it into a pool.

One of the first men to come into the building was standing off to the side, his hands pressed against his knees. He was doubled over, breathing methodically to fight off the nausea. He looked young, probably early twenties, and it was unlikely he'd seen anything like this before.

Trent had seen some messed up stuff in his day, but there was never really any getting used to such a macabre scene as this.

He stopped short of the second row and stared up at the dead priest, a rosary hanging from his left thumb. The saints adorning the stained-glass windows along both walls seemed to stare down at the dead man with pity, their faces drawn in sadness.

"What are the names?" Trent asked. It was an old habit he'd picked up decades before, one that forced him to focus on solving the crime so he didn't lose his lunch, which at this point would be a couple of gyros from his favorite Greek place.

Donaghy absently shook his head.

"Altar boys," one of the cops answered. He was the one who had come through first. His thickly muscled forearms flexed in anger. A tattoo of a rattlesnake on his right forearm seemed to breathe with the action.

Trent and Donaghy turned to the cop.

"What?" Trent asked first. "How do you know that?"

The cop pointed at the names. "My nephew attends this church," the man said, disgust dripping from his tongue. His head turned back and forth, denying a truth he didn't want to hear or see.

Trent followed the man's gaze to the torso in the middle of the cross. "Your nephew," Trent realized, "he knows this man?"

The cop nodded slowly.

Trent noted the name on the man's tag. "Officer Murray," Trent said, using the man's name to snap his attention away from the body. It worked, and Murray locked eyes with Trent. "What does your nephew have to do with this? Is he hurt? Where is he right now?"

It was as if the question had never been asked.

"We always wondered if something weird was going on with that priest," Murray started, his eyes focused on Trent but his mind far away in the past. "There were rumors. People always talk, though, and priests are always the target of accusations. It happens all the time. My brother and his wife... they always said they were lucky their church had one of the good ones, one that would never do anything like that."

Trent's mind instantly connected the dots. His head involuntarily twisted and faced the dead man. The names cut into his chest appeared to glow against the pale canvas of skin.

The sickening epiphany smacked Trent across the head. He didn't dare say it out loud, but he knew why this man had been murdered. And the only thing that bothered Trent more than the haunting scene before him was that a small part of him was glad this priest was dead.

21

MACAU

"No," Sean said angrily.

He looked over to a woman in a cocktail dress who had been standing in the shadows for the duration of the evening. He gave one turn of the head, and her face drooped visibly.

"What?" Kimberly asked, urgency filling her voice.

Sean raised his phone and showed the screen to her. She jumped back, so jolting was the image.

"Who is... oh, no," she said as she realized the next victim had been taken.

"Who this time?" Tommy asked, concerned.

"A priest," Sean answered as he closed out the image. "Trent said it was St. Peter's."

Tommy sighed. "I've been to that church before, but I don't know anyone there. They asked me to check a relic for authenticity. Didn't take long to tell them it was a fake." His eyes met Sean's. "Name of the victim?"

"Father Worthington."

Tommy thought for a moment and then shook his head. "Don't know the name. It's possible I met him, but it doesn't ring a bell."

Li stepped over to Tommy and touched his shoulder. "What do we do next?"

It was a good question, and she'd asked it in a hushed tone, reminding Tommy and Sean that they were still in Wei's private poker room surrounded by the billionaire's guards.

Just then, Sean's phone rang.

He looked down at the number on the screen and instantly recognized it as the one he'd seen on the email from the killer.

Sean pressed the answer button and lifted the phone to his right ear. "I guess you have a thing about punctuality," he spat.

"Now, now, Sean. Don't be that way." The gruff voice scraped against the inside of Sean's ears. "I just did the world a favor. And I saved that man's soul."

"Listen, you sick piece of—"

"No, you listen, Sean. The clock is already ticking. The priest was a dirtbag. I'm sure if you ask the parents of some of his lambs, they'll be glad he's gone when they learn about what he did."

Sean's forehead tightened, but he didn't respond. He couldn't. His mind wandered to places he didn't dare guide it on his own, and he had to steer it back to a better place.

"Now, here's the rub, Sean. You did manage to get the artifact. Well done. I knew you were the man for the job. But you still have to get it to me."

"Yeah," Sean grunted.

"Not to worry. I know you're probably thinking up ways you can set me up, hogtie me, the whole nine yards. I've made it simple for you. I'm sending you an address. Take the artifact to that address and leave it with a man named Ling. He will make sure I get it."

"And if I kill this Ling person?"

Everyone in the room shifted their eyes to Sean when they heard him say those words. For the first time, Mr. Wei even looked a little concerned, and the guards around him tensed.

The woman in the cocktail-runner's dress shifted weight onto her right foot, ready to spring into action and take out the nearest guard, who was just ten feet away. Adriana had maintained her disguise as a casino worker up to this point, but if things went south... well, that's why she was here. It had been Sean's idea to keep her identity from Mr. Wei in case he tried anything crooked, but the man had turned out to be a generous and honest person. The guards, however, looked jumpy, and Adriana didn't trust jumpy people with guns.

"You know the answer, Sean. I will find each and every one of those boys that priest defiled and give them similar fates. And let me tell you, it was excruciating. Drop off the artifact within one hour, or I start with the first boy on the list. I don't think I have to tell you where the list is. I'm sure you've already seen it."

Sean clenched his jaw, grinding his teeth against each other. There was nothing he could do—it was a bluff he couldn't afford to call from so far away.

For a second, he considered calling Trent and warning him to get all those boys to safety, but this killer would have already planned on that contingency. They were playing the ultimate game of chess, and Milner seemed to be constantly one step ahead of Sean.

"What about the next piece?" Sean asked. "Are you going to give me another hoop to jump though once I deliver this artifact to your courier?"

"Now you're catching up," Milner exclaimed. "Very good! The second Ling receives the package, you will receive the next clue."

"Why don't you figure out the riddles yourself, Teddy?" Sean sneered. "Go find whatever it is you're looking for and leave us out of it."

"Ah, I would, my son, but unfortunately, you must be the one to do it. A lesser prophet precedes the greater, always."

"Prophet?"

"Yes. But I am more than that. Just as John, a sinner from a lowly state, preceded Yeshua, I must have a forerunner to prepare the way. You have killed many. You have sinned. But you have a purpose, Sean. Do not dismay. The Almighty can use you in ways you have never imagined. And so it will be."

Sean couldn't listen to another second. He wanted to jump through the phone and beat the man until his arms gave out and his knuckles bled. He extinguished the rage scalding him from the inside and took three deep breaths.

"So, you're comparing yourself to Jesus now? Seems lofty, considering you've just killed two people."

"I've done more than that," Milner confessed. There was almost a tone of regret in his voice, but Sean took it as mocking. "He came with a message of peace and hope. I come with the whips to overturn the tables of the money changers, to rebuke the wicked, and to cleanse the world of sin."

"At least your ego is in check," Sean quipped, managing to find something light to say in this darkest of conversations.

"This has nothing to do with ego," Milner snorted. "This has to do with the salvation of the world. Soon, I will have a double portion of the spirit. When that happens, my true ministry will begin. And the end of days shall come."

"Sounds like you need to go back to Morrowfield and get some meds," Sean said. When no reply came, he realized Milner had hung up the phone. "The nerve of that guy," Sean muttered. "I'm supposed to get the last word."

"What did he say?" Tommy asked.

"We have to take the artifact to some contact named Ling. He sent me the address."

"And after that, what then?"

"He said he would send me another clue. It appears this Milner guy wants us to jump through hoops for him."

"We can't just take this to some random person," Kimberly insisted. "If he wants it, he can come take it from us with his own hands." She wrinkled her nose in derision.

"I wish we could do it that way," Sean agreed, even though it hurt him to do so. Even though they were on the same side, he didn't have to like it. Kimberly was cold, annoying, and temperamental. The last part should have been burned out during her training with the bureau.

"Why can't we? There are lots of ways to play this, Sean. We can install a tracking device. Or follow the contact person once we drop it off."

Sean shook his head. "No. We can't. If we try anything stupid, he's going to start killing innocent people, kids, Kimberly. Young people. We have to play this his way for now. All we can hope for is a break along the way."

She looked despondent, then her irritation boiled over. "Fine. But I think we're making a big mistake."

"Maybe," Sean said. "But we make big mistakes all the time." He glanced at Tommy. Out of the corner of his eye, he noticed Adriana slip out of view again and into the shadows. "Usually seems to work out okay."

"From the sound of it," Mr. Wei said, "it seems you need that piece more than I. So, I guess I made the right decision."

"I'll pay you back for it," Sean offered.

"Me, too," Tommy added.

Wei waved a dismissive hand. "Not necessary. Just keep your schedule open for a rematch," he said with a wink.

"Will do, sir," Sean agreed.

The group made their way out of the private high-stakes poker room and into the main lobby. Sean walked with purpose, clutching the briefcase tight in his grip.

Adriana appeared through a door to the left, just behind the bar, and joined him at his side. "Well, that went better than expected," she said.

He eyed her up and down, admiring her form in the glittering casino uniform. "Nice disguise."

She curled her lips. "Eyes up here, big guy," she warned, motioning to her eyes.

"Hey, you're my wife. I can admire the view if I want to."

They led the way out of the high-stakes area and back onto the main floor, where the simmering pot of sounds boiled to a roar once again. Somewhere on the second floor, someone yelled out in excitement—probably hitting some jackpot on a slot machine.

"Where is this contact you're supposed to meet?" Li asked.

Sean took out his phone and showed her the address. "Know where that is?"

"Yes," Li said with a nod. "Not a nice area. Lot of crime there. You have weapons?"

"Always," Sean said, then added, "I mean, not at the moment. We couldn't bring them into the casino."

"I did," Adriana said dryly, her lips curving up even farther. Sean sighed, knowing where she'd hidden the small subcompact 9mm. That was one of the benefits of wearing a skirt. She could strap the weapon on the inside of her thigh, and no one would be the wiser.

"Of course you did," Sean acquiesced. He turned back to Li. "The rest of our gear is in the car."

"Good. Hopefully we can make the drop without any trouble, but you never know in this town. Especially in that part of the district."

22

ATLANTA

A lex's phone rang, shaking him from the sleepy silence of the lab. He reached out and picked it up, noted the call was from Trent, and answered. "Did you get him?" He sounded hopeful, but deep down Alex expected the worst.

"No," Trent said. "And we didn't get here in time to keep him from killing again."

Alex let out an audible sigh. He was by himself in the lab at the moment. Tara and Dr. Kelley had gone out to grab some sandwiches from a nearby sub place. "Who was it this time?"

"A priest with a messed up history of doing bad things to kids; though we didn't know that until now."

Alex fought the curiosity creeping toward his lips. He didn't want to ask how the priest was murdered, but something deep inside him did.

"He was whipped, cut, stabbed, and crucified in his own church," Trent explained, simultaneously eliminating Alex's need to ask. "Beaten, too. It appears Milner kept him alive right up until noon, then stabbed him in the side and let him bleed out. Not sure if the man was still conscious or not."

"That's awful," Alex blurted.

"Be glad you weren't here."

Alex heard the sounds of traffic through the phone and guessed Trent was standing by a road, probably in the cathedral parking lot.

"The captain is here," Trent said. "He's real curious how we knew this would be the place the killer planned on hitting. And I think he wants to know if we can figure out the next location or victim."

Alex had already started to think about that, but as yet, he had no leads. "Unfortunately, we haven't received anything. No clue. No riddle. Nothing."

"So, you think it's over?" Trent hedged.

"No. We'll hear from Milner again. It's just a matter of time."

"Anything out of Sean or Tommy?"

"Not yet, but now that the deadline has expired and the victim is dead, I expect we'll be hearing from them shortly, probably with more questions. If I had to guess, Milner is setting up his next victim. He gave us three days last time."

"Which means we can expect another murder on Wednesday at noon."

"Correct, but it also means we'll be given another opportunity. Milner doesn't want to find the pieces of this gauntlet on his own. Maybe he could, but he didn't or isn't. He's making us walk the line for him. Anyone's guess as to why."

Trent pondered the thought. "He's a psychopath. He likes to be in control, make people do his bidding. Gives him some kind of a power trip or something."

"Maybe," Alex conceded. "Or there might be some other game at play here. For the time being, I'm assuming that whatever his final objective is, it's beyond his grasp or is in a place he can't get to. Maybe he doesn't know where it is and that's the piece he needs Sean and Tommy to figure out."

"Do you have any idea what it is this guy wants? What he's looking for?"

Alex had to think about that, even though that very thing had been on his mind for the last few days. "I wish I did. I've analyzed several bits from the riddle and the tablet, but nothing definitive has emerged yet. I'll let you know if I find anything."

His phone vibrated. "I have to go. Sean's calling."

"Let me know what's going on with their end of things, will you?"

"Yes, sir. Thanks, Trent."

Alex ended the call and answered the one from Sean.

"Tell me you have good news," he said into the device.

"Not really," Sean answered over the sounds of traffic. "We're on our way to drop off the artifact. Did you hear?"

"About the priest? Yes." He sounded dejected. "And we haven't received a new clue yet."

"That's probably because we're on our way to drop off the artifact to one of Milner's goons."

"Oh." Alex thought for a few seconds. "You guys didn't happen to come up with an idea of what Milner is looking for, did you?"

"Negative," Sean said. "Still trying to figure that one out ourselves. He did call me, though, and was talking about the end of the world, how his ministry is different from Jesus', while at the same time comparing himself to the Messiah."

"What an ego."

"Yeah, but he doesn't see it that way."

"Jesus didn't kill anyone," Alex said. "How could he compare himself to someone who never did anything wrong to anyone?"

"Said he's the same but different, or something along those lines. Claimed that he is here to finish the work that Christ began, not in so many words, but that's the gist I caught. Said something about the temple and the money changers there."

Alex knew the story. It was one of the few examples in Jesus' ministry that involved him using violence to make a point. Usually, he simply used parables. "In the case of the temple, Jesus went in and drove out the corruption. You think there's a clue in that somewhere?"

Sean focused on the question, and didn't respond for nearly a minute.

"Sean? You still there?" Alex pressed.

"Yeah, sorry. Just thinking. Both victims were flogged with whips.

And both were in churches. It seems he has his own method of cleansing temples. I don't know how that connection helps us, though." He paused and then continued. "There was one other strange thing he said to me on the phone."

"What?"

Sean didn't answer immediately, as if uncertain the information was at all pertinent. "He said something about a double portion of the spirit. That's the second time he's said those exact words. What do you think it means?"

Alex frowned and rolled over to his computer. He typed the phrase into the search bar and clicked the button on the screen. "One second, Sean. I'm looking for something."

The screen blipped, and a new set of results appeared with corresponding links to various websites. Most of them featured Bible verses. Alex leaned closer to the screen and read the first result that displayed a preview of what would be found on the website.

"It's from the story of Elijah and Elisha," Alex said. He clicked the link to expand it to the full story and continued reading when the site popped up. "Now I remember. Elijah asked his apprentice what he wanted from him, sort of a parting gift before the elder prophet left this world. Elisha asked for a double portion of the spirit bestowed on Elijah, to which the master claimed he'd asked a difficult thing."

"That's right," Sean realized. "I knew I'd heard that phrase somewhere before. I haven't read that story in a long time, but it's clear now."

Alex took a breath and then exhaled. "I wonder why Milner is using that phrase?"

Sean believed he had at least a partial answer. "He thinks he's the Messiah or at least an incarnation of Christ and the great prophets. It would make sense—in his mind—to use a phrase like that, especially since Elijah was considered one of the more powerful prophets. He could walk through walls, disappear entirely, heal the sick, raise the dead. The miracles he performed were incredible."

"Great," Alex said, exasperated. "So, we have a guy who thinks he's some kind of messenger from God sent to murder people he deems sinners."

"Looks that way. Any idea what it might be he's trying to make us find?"

"Not yet, boss, but I'll keep working on it."

Sean laughed. "I'm not your boss, but he's here with me if you need to speak to him."

"I'm good," Alex said. "Let us know if you guys need help with the next... whatever it is Milner sends you. First, it was an email. Then a text and phone call? What's next, sending a messenger pigeon?"

"You never know," Sean chirped. "We'll be in touch."

He ended the call, and Alex set his phone back on the desk next to the keyboard. Sliding his chair directly in front of the monitor, Alex studied the contents of the screen, resting his chin on his thumb as he pondered the question. "What is it you're looking for, Milner?"

23

MACAU

L i wasn't lying when she said the place they were going to was sketchy, although she hadn't used that exact word. Sean stepped out of the car and looked around, scanning the dilapidated apartment buildings and cracked sidewalks for any sign of immediate trouble.

There was no threat that he could detect, but that might change in a heartbeat. Long strands of colorful cloth hung from the eaves overhead, dangling so low that people walking along the sidewalk constantly brushed their heads against them.

Up ahead, a small collective of produce salesmen hawked their goods from stalls that were made of old pallets. A hookah bar to Sean's right spilled the sweet aroma of flavored tobaccos out into the open air to mingle with the smells of scallions, mushrooms, and chicken being prepared by cooks manning street carts. Across the road, the doors to a nightclub were wide open; the bouncer in black displaying his multiple tattoos on arms crossed over a massive chest. From that distance, Sean couldn't tell how tall the man was, but he looked to be under five-ten.

"It's over here," Li said, pointing to the hookah bar.

Sean was surprised the place was still open at this hour. Then again, he shouldn't have been. It seemed this city truly never slept, and he had thought New York owned that title outright.

Adriana stepped out onto the sidewalk, having slipped on some leggings and a black Ramones T-shirt during the tightly packed ride from the casino.

"A hookah bar?" Kimberly asked, uncertain they'd found the right place.

"That's the joint," Tommy confirmed, double-checking the address Sean had forwarded to him before leaving the casino. The numbers on the main front window said they were at the right place.

"I see what you did there," Sean commented, casting his friend a suspicious glare.

"I wondered if you'd pick up on that one."

Sean merely rolled his eyes and walked around to the trunk. He opened it and pulled out the briefcase, holding it firmly in his right hand.

"So, who is this Ling person we're supposed to meet?" Tommy asked.

"I don't know."

"You're just going to walk in there and ask for someone named Ling?" Kimberly wondered.

"Pretty much." He took a step toward the bar entrance, and the others fell in line behind. Realizing they were following, Sean halted and whirled around on his heels. "You guys should probably stay here," he suggested. "I don't know if Milner wants all of us going in."

"No can do, *compadre*," Tommy said. "We're in this with you."

Adriana gave a subtle nod in agreement.

"I knew you guys would say that, but I need you out here. Someone has to cover the entrance. And if there's a back door—"

"I'm on it," Kimberly volunteered. "I'll make sure it's covered."

"Thanks," Sean said, genuinely surprised at her willingness to play along.

She nodded curtly and took off down an alley between two buildings, the gun on her hip flashing into view for a moment before she tucked her jacket back over it.

"You guys going to be okay here?" Sean asked, directing his question to Tommy and Adriana.

"I guess," Tommy relented. "I don't like it, though."

"You'll live." Sean turned to Li. "I need you to come with me."

She looked surprised, and he quickly added, "In case I need a translator."

"Oh, of course," she said.

"We'll be back in a minute," Sean announced. He glanced at his watch and noted they still had more than twenty minutes to deliver the item. He allowed himself a moment of gratitude for that. While it was unfortunate the priest had been murdered, the killer insinuated the man was worse than bad. Sean found himself caring less and less about the killing with every passing second, but his concern over the boys' well-being only escalated. He wouldn't waste another moment.

He strode across the sidewalk with Li in tow and passed through a black metal gate that was attached to a fence. The four-foot-high barrier wrapped around a small sidewalk patio, enclosing six round tables. Only one of the tables was occupied, where two patrons sucked on red hoses connected to the base of a shiny red-and-black hookah. As Sean passed, he caught a whiff of the strawberry-flavored tobacco and inhaled, appreciating the aroma.

Inside the bar, the scents strengthened and filled his nostrils with a cornucopia of berries, roses, coffee, incense, and tobacco. Long seats lined the walls on both sides, hosting tables and chairs opposite them. Like outside, only three men occupied the space, puffing lazily on their hoses. Directly ahead, a counter ran horizontally across two-thirds of the room. A hall continued beyond it, where Sean figured the restrooms and business office were located. Dim candle-shaped bulbs hung from sconces designed to look like the heads of dragons.

Dragons, Sean thought. He wondered at the connection between the casino and this place, or if it was just a cultural thing. He had seen several dragons on the way here and on the way from the airport to the casino.

Maybe he hadn't been entirely correct in suggesting to Wei that there were no such things as coincidences.

Behind the counter, a man—probably late twenties—in a red tunic stood with his palms against the surface. He stared intently toward the door, through Sean and Li, and focused on some distant, imaginary object. Sean figured the guy must have been smoking something other than the flavored tobaccos the menu had to offer. When he reached the counter, Sean realized the man actually *was* staring at him.

His dark red tunic was the color of blood, the edges laced with golden fabric. Two strands of long black hair dangled down past his ears and cascaded over his shoulders, while the rest was done up in a tight bun. Behind him, darkly stained bamboo shelves were filled with a litany of fresh-seal packets containing different flavors of tobacco. To his left, larger shelves held hookahs that patrons could rent for the evening.

"Sean Wyatt?" he said demurely, his accent slight.

"I guess that makes you Ling," Sean said.

"You guessed right. That the artifact?" He motioned casually to the briefcase.

Li looked around the room, sensing something was off. Sean felt it, too, but he wasn't getting the feeling from the man behind the counter. It was... something else.

"Yeah," Sean said. "And I'd appreciate it if you told your boss we delivered it so he doesn't hurt anyone else."

"Let me see it," Ling demanded.

Sean rolled his eyes and lifted the case to the counter. He set it down gently and waited patiently while Ling pored over it, scanning every inch of the object with an expertise uncommon to a hookah bartender. Satisfied, he closed the case and took a phone out of his pocket. He typed in a quick message and sent it, presumably to Milner.

"Thank you," Ling said. "I let him know. You'll be hearing from him soon."

Ling turned and started down the hall.

"Hey!" one of the men shouted from near the door.

Sean turned and saw the three men from before standing in the middle of the room, blocking the exit.

Ling also turned around to see who had halted him.

"What's in the case?" said the leader, a short man with a bald head and tattoos running from his neck down to his exposed chest underneath a silver button-up shirt. With the black pants and matching shoes, he could have just come from a club or a drug deal. His two friends were similarly dressed.

Sean didn't know as much about Macau as other places, but it was easy to tell these guys were part of a local gang, maybe out of Hong Kong. Each of them had a matching tattoo, again... a dragon. And every one was placed deliberately under their right ear.

Either they were part of some kind of dragon-lover's club, or they were in a gang. Sean was going with the latter assumption.

"That's none of your concern," Ling answered.

Sean knew Ling's comment would only incite the three men, like throwing rocks at a hornet's nest. He gently, subtly, nudged Li to the left to keep her out of harm's way. Not that she needed it. Li was highly skilled in martial arts, even some that were only taught in the most elite and secretive of orders. Even Sean hadn't been trained in that particular school of fighting, and he'd seen almost everything. He'd actually gone online to find information about the style, but had never been able to turn up anything.

The three men blocking Sean and Li's way out immediately produced knives from their back pockets. The weapons weren't intimidating, per se, but they would make exiting the building more complicated.

"Maybe we just take it from you, hookah boy," the leader said, brandishing his blade in the dim light.

Ling regarded him curiously, cocking his head to one side as he assessed the threat with a cool gaze from black eyes.

"I can't allow you to do that," Ling said calmly. His voice was just as devoid of emotion as when Sean met him a few minutes before.

"Oh, you don't have to allow me. See, that's the thing about taking." He stepped forward and paused, then pointed the tip of his knife to the briefcase. "Show me what's in there, and maybe I let you go home with all your fingers."

"Guys," Sean said, putting his left hand up while allowing his right to drift toward his hip and the subcompact 9mm Springfield concealed underneath his belt. "I'm sure we can all come to an arrangement, but our friend here has to take that case to someone else. It doesn't belong to him, or us, or you."

The leader turned toward Sean, firing daggers from his eyes that were bigger than the blade in his hand. "Shut up, American. This doesn't concern—"

Three quick, muted pops echoed through the bar. The instigator looked absently to Ling, who held a pistol in his hand.

A river of smoke drifted up from the suppressor's barrel.

Then the leader dropped to the floor, the hole in his temple exposed. His accomplices fell in their places as well, one to his knees, the other on his back, and each with a bullet hole through their forehead.

Sean was tempted to whirl around and face the threat, but he knew any sudden movement could provoke Deadeye Ling. So instead, he barely turned his head to look at the man.

"Impressive shots," Sean said, his heart throbbing in his chest.

Li stood next to him like a statue. If she was afraid, she didn't show it.

"I will deliver this now. Someone will clean up the mess. I suggest you go."

A scream from outside agreed with Ling's assessment. Sean looked out the exit and saw the patrons who had been happily smoking a moment before stand up and run down the sidewalk, yelling hysterically.

"Understood," Sean said. But when he turned to look back at Ling, the man had already disappeared down the hall like an apparition.

Tommy stumbled through the door with Adriana right behind him. He nearly tripped on the body closest to the exit. He looked down at the corpse, aghast. Then his eyes followed the floor up to Sean. "What did you do?"

"It wasn't me this time." Sean saw the disbelief on his friend's face and added, "Honest."

"We need to go," Li interjected. "The police will be here any minute, and I don't think I have to tell you the trouble there will be if they find us here with weapons and three dead bodies—gang members or not."

Sean nodded and followed the others out the door. He slowed when he reached the relatively fresh air outside and stole one more quick glance back at the dead men inside. If Ling was the kind of person Milner had working for him, how many others like him were there? And if there were others, what grander purpose did this murderer have in mind?

They got in the car, and Li revved the engine. She was about to take off when Sean realized they were minus one.

"Where's Kimberly?" he asked.

"Crap," Tommy blurted. "She went around to cover the back."

"That's where Ling went. If he thinks she's a threat—" He let his words trail off when he saw the FBI agent sprinting down the narrow alley.

"There she is," Adriana announced.

She skidded to a stop and flung open the back door. "What was that sound I heard?" Kimberly asked as she slid into the back seat. "It sounded like gunfire, but with silencers."

"It was," Sean said. "Very astute."

Her face drained. "You didn't kill someone, did you?"

"I didn't. But our friend Ling did. I have a bad feeling Milner and his crew are far more dangerous than we thought."

Li punched the gas and the tires squeaked on the wet patch of asphalt. She guided the car around the next corner. "Where to?" she asked, looking back at Sean in the mirror.

Sean's phone vibrated in his pocket. "Airport," he said as he pulled out the phone and checked the message. "Got a new message from Milner," he announced.

"What does it say?" Tommy asked.

"The lost son of Rome sought to burn the prophet's bones and return the state to heathen ways. But sons of God stole them in secret and took them to the general's city, where now they hide from heathen eyes. Produce the artifact in two days' time, or I will cleanse another."

For several seconds, the only sound in the car was the engine purring as Li drove through the streets of Macau.

"What is that supposed to mean?" Kimberly asked first. "And why only two days this time? He's changing the rules."

Neither Sean nor Tommy had an answer. Sean copied the message and sent it to his friend's phone so he could read it for himself. He also sent it to Adriana.

"He's making the rules," Adriana answered. "He can change them if he wants. We're in his game."

"It sounds like we're going to Rome," Tommy suggested. "I do love that city, despite all the chaos."

"Not necessarily," Adriana interrupted.

"What do you mean? It says right there, lost son of Rome."

"Son, yes," she allowed, "but that doesn't mean this person is still there. We don't even know who they are."

"Fair point," Tommy surrendered. "So, where then?"

"We have to get to the root of it," Sean said, taking over the conversation again. "Son of Rome could be anyone. It could be a caesar, a noble, or—"

"A general," Tommy finished. "Like it says at the end, the general's city."

"Right," Sean agreed. "It could be that we're looking for a city named after a Roman general."

Adriana pored over the text she'd received from Sean. She studied each word like a college student preparing for a final exam.

"The prophet's bones," she muttered.

Everyone else stopped talking and looked at her in the rear middle seat. Kimberly was out of her element when it came to solving ancient puzzles, and it appeared she wanted to physically pull Adriana's thought from her brain.

Adriana raised her eyes, twin orbs glowing in the digital hue from her phone's screen, the pupils black as night. "Which prophet?"

24

MACAU

Tommy made the call to change course and head to a hotel. Li, who was just as exhausted as everyone else, happily obeyed and steered the vehicle back toward the casinos.

Time was against them, but that didn't matter if they couldn't think straight due to a severe lack of sleep.

Even Sean caught himself dozing off several times on the drive to the hotel. Back when he was younger, a twenty-hour session of poker wasn't uncommon for him. Now, though, he wasn't the spry youngster from those days. He still had plenty of energy and discipline, enough to last the entirety of the last dozen-plus hours of cards, but it hit him harder now than it did when he was younger, and he knew recovering would also take more time.

He tried to make himself feel guilty about another victim who was unknowingly in danger, that if he and his crew could figure out the riddle, they might save someone's life.

Even that couldn't keep the bittersweet call of slumber from dragging his eyes downward. Only faint traces of adrenaline pumping through his veins kept him from falling asleep fully in the car.

When the bright lights of the casinos appeared through the windshield, he found himself energized enough to sit upright as Li pulled the vehicle into a parking spot.

She called the front desk as the group made their way into the building, arranging rooms for them with Tommy's IAA credit card. She was fortunate to get two suites, which provided enough beds for all and a little additional personal space, and when she went to check in at the front desk, the concierge told her that the rooms were compliments of Mr. Wei.

The man had eyes everywhere. Not that Li or any of the others blamed him. Wei was a high-profile character, and wolves lurked in every shadow.

The suites exemplified opulence in every sense of the word. Golden filigree danced along the crown molding, accenting the walls and ceiling with leaves and vines that seemed to grow straight out of the drywall. The great rooms were furnished with lavish couches and matching chairs that looked as though they'd been painted by one of the great masters, featuring multicolored dragons swirling around ancient Chinese homes, temples, and mountains.

Sean didn't think much of any of it as he stumbled along the white marble floor to one of the bedrooms. No one else said anything, either. They were too tired to admire the beauty that surrounded them.

Kimberly and Li opted for the suite next to where Sean, Adriana, and Tommy stayed, and Sean imagined the two women were probably also too fatigued to enjoy the grandiose luxury the suites offered.

The last thing Sean remembered was thinking how soft the pillow was against his face as he collapsed onto the mattress of a king-size bed.

Five hours later, daylight streaked through long, pale orange curtains at the window. Sean snapped awake and looked around, momentarily confused by his surroundings.

Everything came back to him at once. The events of the days before crashed into his brain like an avalanche. The murder of the priest, the preacher, and the clues given by the killer. *Milner.*

Sean twisted in the bed and noticed Adriana was already up. The smell of fresh coffee wafted in through the closed doors, signaling she'd either made a pot or ordered room service.

He wearily swung his heavy legs over the edge of the bed and checked his phone. The battery was nearly dead, a result of forgetting to plug it in before his early morning nap. There was still enough charge left to get to the airplane, where he could remedy the issue, so he picked up the device and rechecked the message from Milner he'd received only a handful of hours before.

To his surprise, there was another message from the unknown number. It merely said, "Noon, Wednesday."

It didn't need to say anything else. Sean knew exactly what that meant. Milner had already chosen another victim.

Sean scrolled back up to the previous message and read the clue again. Figuring out ancient riddles and clues was one thing, but this guy was just being cliché, and atop all his exhaustion, Sean couldn't help but be annoyed at that. The stuff he'd worked on before, the adventures and danger they'd led to, were at least authentic, created by people from history with the intention of either finding their treasures again in the future, or securing them for someone they deemed worthy to discover anew.

Milner was simply toying with him, and with his friends. That fact snuck into Sean's craw and festered by the second.

He read the riddle again and then set his phone down. His skin felt grimy, oily, and he realized he needed a quick shower to wash off the filth of travel and the casino.

Since he couldn't hear anyone else in the bathroom, he padded over to the double doors and pulled the left one open. Ten minutes later, he felt like a new man as he dried his hair with what he was certain was the softest towel he'd ever felt in his life.

After slipping into the only set of clean clothes he'd brought on the trip—khakis, a Pearl Jam Ten Club T-shirt, and his Adidas Sambas—he opened the door and stepped into the living room.

He was surprised to see Tommy was already awake and dressed, sitting on the couch with his laptop on his legs. Adriana sat in one of the chairs, looking through her phone with a cup of coffee on a bronze end table next to her.

"How long have you guys been up?" Sean asked. He ran a hand through his still-damp hair and ambled over to a silver tray resting atop a counter near the window. A matching coffee pot dispelled a trickle of steam into the atmosphere.

"Half hour," Tommy answered, his eyes still fixed on his laptop.

"Forty minutes," Adriana said.

"Always have to one-up me, huh?"

She merely rolled her eyes.

Coffee in hand, Sean walked over to his wife, kissed her on the top of the head, and then found a seat opposite her on the other side of the glass coffee table.

"Anything out of the other two yet?"

"No," Adriana said. She took a sip of coffee. "But if we don't hear from them soon, I'll go wake them up."

"Good idea. Tommy, I assume you're looking for something related to the clue our sociopath friend sent?"

"Yeah," he said without looking up from the screen. "It's interesting. I'm looking through ancient Roman history, primarily its leaders from throughout their run on top. Tara and Alex are looking into it, as well. Nothing really stands out except that there were several emperors and generals—some who became emperors—who tried to eliminate Christianity entirely."

Sean nodded after swallowing a cup of the hot coffee. "That's a pretty well-known thing."

"Right. And that's the problem. It doesn't really narrow anything down. Take Caligula, for example. He was sort of a lost son of Rome. Was in hiding for most of his young life because his mother was from noble blood and they feared Tiberius, his predecessor, would execute him for fear he was a threat to the throne."

"Roman politics. Such cannibals."

Adriana afforded a chuckle at Sean's comment.

"No kidding," Tommy agreed. "Anyway, Caligula learned a ton of worldly things from his adopted grandfather—his great uncle—

during his time on Capri. Safe to say, Caligula's elder warped the young man's mind in many ways, and was likely the sole cause of Caligula's wild and often catastrophic behavior."

"So, you think he might be the one the riddle is talking about? He did have a lot of Christians executed."

"He did," Tommy confirmed, "but I can't find anything about bones or relics. And the riddle suggests that the lost son was returning the state to its heathen ways."

"So, that would mean after the conversion of Constantine?" Adriana wondered out loud.

"That's a thought," Tommy said. "In fact, that makes more sense than anything I've come up with so far."

She smiled broadly at the compliment. "You're welcome."

Tommy's pulse quickened. "Yes, that has to be it. There weren't many emperors after Constantine. Rome fell pretty fast in the next couple hundred years, ending with the reign of Flavius Romulus Augustus."

"Impressive," Sean said, his tone snarky.

"What? He was the last emperor of the Western Roman Empire."

"I know. I'm just messing with you."

Tommy sighed, annoyed, but kept going. "To Adriana's question from a few hours ago, we also need to correlate this mysterious son of Rome to a specific prophet. I guess we can eliminate Jonah."

"Good job, Captain Obvious."

"Which means we should consider other prophets around that time frame," he said, ignoring Sean's barb.

"So," Sean twirled a finger in the air, "if memory serves me correctly, and it usually does, that would mean Jonah's predecessor and his heir to the prophetic call."

"Right," Tommy said. "Which would be Micah, who followed him. The predecessor question is more complicated. Obadiah came before him, but also served in tandem with Jonah. It was Elisha who came before them both and anointed the two into the brotherhood of prophets."

"That's it," Sean said excitedly. He nearly shot up out of his seat.

"Remember last night? We were talking about Elisha and how he asked for a double portion of the blessing given to Elijah."

Tommy shook the cobwebs from his brain. "Yes," he agreed. He suddenly felt energized. "Of course. Man, I must still need some sleep because that one was right there in front of us."

"So," Adriana cut in, "the prophet's bones we're looking for are Elisha's?"

"Looks that way." Tommy's fingers flew across the keys, tapping in a fury as he entered another search query.

Sean stood and moved over behind the couch to look over his friend's shoulder. Adriana joined him and watched as Tommy clicked on the first result on the page.

That one didn't contain anything useful, so he backed out and altered the search to include different keywords.

The new results displayed one of the links from before, but also a new set with different information. He chose the second one and started scanning through it.

"There," Adriana said, pointing to the third paragraph. "That guy."

The two men followed her finger to the part of the page that talked about the Roman emperor Julian the Apostate.

"It says that Julian the Apostate, or Julian the Second as he was occasionally referred to, ordered all the relics of the prophets buried in Sebastia, in Palestine, be burned as part of some sort of purge of Christianity," Tommy said.

"A return to heathen ways," Sean breathed.

"Looks like Julian believed that Constantine was wrong to convert the empire to Christianity, and he thought that by returning to old Roman values from the ancient times they would regain prosperity and dominance over the known world."

"But someone saved the relics," Adriana said. "They took them away and hid them in the general's city. But what general?"

"Alexandria," Sean answered and pointed down to the paragraph at the bottom of the page. "We were thinking it was a Roman general, but it wasn't. It was one of the greatest generals of all time."

"Alexander," Tommy realized. "You think they mean the library?"

"I hope not, since it was destroyed. There must be another place."

Tommy scrolled down the page and stopped when he found a location. "This says that the bones of Elisha and Obadiah were moved to the ancient village of Scetes, Egypt."

"Scetes?" Adriana wondered.

"I don't know much about it, either," Sean confessed.

"I do," Tommy said. "A little, anyway. It's in the Wadi El Natrun region. The place is a desert, a basin below sea level."

"Like Death Valley."

"Sort of. Not that far below sea level, but it does get hot there." He looked through the details on the screen and then clicked a link that took him to more information about Wadi El Natrun.

"Why do you know so much about this place?" Adriana asked, genuinely curious.

Tommy's eyes stayed fixed on the screen as he answered, clicking various images and links to search for more clues. "We did an excavation there a few years back. Well, I didn't run point on it, but they requested IAA assistance with transporting some of the artifacts. Apparently, some of them were culturally sensitive. I only spent four days there, but I remember it well. Not much there, to be honest. Small town. Lots of palm trees, like an oasis. And—" He cut himself short as he clicked on an image of a church.

"And what?"

"This," Tommy said, his finger extending to the screen. In the middle of the page was an image of a church the color of sand.

"The Monastery of St. Macarius the Great?" Sean asked, curious. "I'm afraid I don't know that particular saint, although to be fair, I'm not up on my Catholic saints."

"They're not Catholic," Tommy corrected. "This is a Coptic Orthodox Church, part of a collection of Oriental Orthodox churches throughout the Middle East and Asia. They even have their own pope."

"I stand corrected."

Adriana motioned to a paragraph halfway down the page. "It says they discovered the tombs of the prophets Elisha and Obadiah during a renovation, and that there are manuscripts from the eleventh and sixteenth centuries that confirm the discovery."

Tommy looked up at Sean, then to Adriana. "The bones of Elisha are in Egypt. That has to be where we're supposed to go next."

Sean frowned. "It sounds like it, but this place is no secret, right? I mean, there are websites documenting it for everyone to see."

"True," Adriana said. "But it's unlikely the bones were disturbed during the renovations. The religious leaders of the Coptic order would have made certain of that. They would have taken every precaution to preserve the prophets as they were in their burial chambers."

"Which means our second piece of the gauntlet might still be in the sarcophagus."

"Or," Tommy said, "it was removed and put on display like so many other relics."

Sean nodded. "Either way, it sounds like we're heading to Egypt." He looked at Adriana and then Tommy. "I guess we need to wake the others."

"And pack some sunscreen," Tommy added. "Things are about to heat up."

25

ATLANTA

Alex looked down at his phone the second he felt it vibrate. Tara drove the 4Runner through the suburbs of Smyrna, Georgia, just fifteen minutes—depending on traffic, it could be an hour—north of downtown Atlanta. She noticed his phone light up in the darkness and wondered not who the message was from but what it said.

"What did he say?" she asked, knowing it was from Sean, or an outside shot it was Tommy.

Alex read the message. "Sounds like they figured out the next location they have to visit."

"They did that without us?" she joked. "The nerve of those guys."

Alex snickered. "No kidding. For a minute there, I was thinking they couldn't do anything without us. But they are the masters, after all."

"And we're still the students."

The two had just dropped Dr. Kelley at her hotel a few minutes before. Originally, she'd planned on flying out the next morning, but those plans had changed now that she felt like she was in too deep with the mystery of a serial killer on the loose.

Normally, Alex and Tara would still have been at the lab downtown. But they were tired and had been working since the early morning hours. Their beds beckoned them from the rolling hills of Smyrna, and they desperately felt the need to answer the call.

"I wish I had the energy of a student," Alex commented as he turned his head and looked out at the passing homes, shops, and cafés.

Tara acknowledged his comment with a grin.

"So, where are the guys heading next?"

"This says they're going to Scetes, Egypt in the"—he struggled with the pronunciation—"Wadi El Natrun region. He says they're flying out in a few minutes."

"So, they learned the location of the next piece," she stated. "That's good."

"Yeah, I guess." Alex sounded unconvinced.

"What's the matter? They're ahead of schedule. I don't know how long it takes to fly from Macau to... whatever place you said, but it can't be longer than the flight from here to Macau. So they'll be there in hours. That still gives them a couple of days to find what they're looking for."

"No, I mean, that's good. I'm glad for that. I'm just wondering why there was no clue about who the next victim might be. They left a clue with that letter."

"Hard to do that with a text message or email," she soothed.

"True," he agreed.

"And besides, if they get to the relic in time, no one dies. That's what Milner said."

He turned his head from the window and faced her. "You believe him?"

She took a breath and shrugged. "I guess so. I mean, we don't really have a choice. And besides, if he's lying, he won't make much of a messiah, which is what it sounds like he is trying to be."

"Messiahs don't murder innocent people, Tara," he cautioned.

"No, they certainly don't. Then again, look at the victims."

His eyebrows pinched together. "What do you mean?"

"Well, we know about the priest and what he did."

"Allegedly."

"That's fair. And we just found out that the preacher was sleeping with his assistant and embezzling money from church coffers."

"Okay, that stuff did happen."

"Right," she said. "So, this killer isn't just going after random innocent people. He's targeting religious leaders who are, at least in his eyes, hypocrites."

"It almost sounds like you sympathize with him."

"Not at all," she denied. "It's just that they're not as innocent as they seem."

He thought about what she said for a minute before responding. "I get what you're saying, but where do we draw the line? Milner's acting as judge, jury, and executioner. And he's using religion to drive his motivations. Where does it stop? None of us are innocent, Tara. We're all sinners in one way or another, whether it's through jealousy, greed, lust, laziness, deceit, murder—they're all equal even though the effect each of those has on others is very different."

"I agree with you. But Milner doesn't see it that way. At least, it doesn't seem like it. I guess the question isn't where we draw the line, it's where he does."

"Which is why we have to help stop him. But we also need to get some rest. I'm worn out."

"Me, too," she said with a nod.

The next five minutes were spent in drowsy silence as she drove the SUV into their driveway. Once the car was safely inside the garage, she hit the button to lower the door and the two went inside, both silently contemplating everything that had happened the last few days.

One thing still needled at both of them, but it was Tara who expressed the issue first.

"Why didn't he send us a clue this time?" she asked as they stepped into their craftsman-style home. The interior was decorated in a more contemporary design, with sharply angled tables, shelves, and a clean, modern touch to everything, including the 55-inch flatscreen hanging over the gas fireplace in the living room.

"Milner? I was wondering that, too. He gave us that hint on the stationery before. I don't know much about psychology like Sean, but from what I do know, these types of people work with patterns. For example," he said, taking off his jacket and hanging it over a barstool in the kitchen, "the first victim looked like it was going to be some kind of killing spree where the murderer cut sins into the victim's flesh. But he didn't do that with the priest. It was the names of those he'd violated."

"Right. I thought the same thing." She made her way over to the refrigerator and opened it, inspected the interior for, then selected a bottle of, her favorite plant-based chocolate protein shake. "Does that mean there is no pattern? Or if there is one, what is it?"

Alex stared down at the white countertop for several seconds, his eyes glazed over in an exhaustion-induced haze.

"I don't know," he finally answered. "Maybe we'll have a better view of things after we get some rest. How many hours of sleep you figure we've had in the last few days?"

"Not enough," Tara admitted. "That didn't used to be a problem. It sure feels like it now. You're right, though. We need to get some sleep. We'll process things much better in the morning."

She changed her mind about the protein shake and put it back in the refrigerator, thinking it was too late to take in more calories.

The two made their way into their bedroom, went through the process of getting ready for bed: showering, changing into night-clothes, and brushing teeth. As they snuggled into bed under cool, soft sheets and a warm blanket, they both stared up at the ceiling. Their minds didn't want to shut off, but their bodies demanded it and eventually pulled their eyes closed and into a swirling dreamland of confusion and mystery.

26

WADI EL NATRUN, EGYPT

S ean peered through his wraparound sunglasses, his arms crossed over his chest. A brisk, dry breeze rolled through the sparsely populated streets of Wadi El Natrun.

A cluster of awnings stretched out from beige buildings, offering visitors and members of the little community fresh produce, meats, and eggs. Lush trees of palm, fig, and olive danced in the gentle wind, occasionally brushing the buildings next to them with their wide leaves. Sean had been surprised at the number of trees in the area. When he found out their next destination was an Egyptian desert, he'd believed it would be something like the Empty Quarter, but this place was anything but. It was a veritable oasis springing forth from the earth.

The domes of monasteries and churches dominated the scenery, though, rising above most of the other blocky dwellings and shops. Coptic crosses were fixed to the tops of the domes, symbols of the community's adherence to the old faith that had brought so many to this barren land long ago.

The buildings themselves looked as though they'd simply grown out of the sand and formed into neat structures.

Sean detected hints of spices in the air, along with the smell of roasting meat, though he didn't immediately see the source.

He and the others had said their goodbyes to Li and left Macau earlier that day to fly to Cairo. From there, they rented an old Toyota Land Cruiser—a relic from the late 1970s—and drove the sixty-eight miles to Wadi El Natrun.

They left the truck near the center of town next to several other vehicles and ventured in on foot, as it seemed was the local custom.

It was a town forgotten by time in many ways, and Sean wondered how it managed to continue thriving despite its remote location.

"So, this place popped up in the fourth century," Tommy said, interrupting Sean's thoughts. "Christians fled Roman persecution to come here, literally in the middle of nowhere."

"Yep," Sean said. "I bet the stars out here are amazing at night. Very little light pollution must make for quite the view."

Tommy twisted his head and eyed his friend suspiciously through his aviator sunglasses. "What are you, a poet now? Philosopher? Astronomer?"

Sean remained a statue. "Maybe. I try to find something to appreciate about everywhere I go, no matter how far off the beaten path."

"Ugh," Kimberly said. "I couldn't live in a place like this."

"And there she is," Tommy chirped.

"It could be worse," Adriana murmured. "We're lucky to be here at this time of year when the weather is mild."

Sean cocked his head to the side, questioning his wife. "I thought you'd never been here."

She winked at him. "I haven't, but I looked up the weather so I could be prepared." She turned her head and peered into the promenade where the main intersection hosted more kiosks, stiles, and vendors.

"And Tommy said it would be hot," Sean quipped with a fiendish look to his friend.

Tommy shifted uncomfortably. "Okay, so maybe I was here when it's really hot. How was I to know?"

Adriana held out her phone and jiggled it in the air. "It's called a weather app. There are only like a million of them. And you were also out in the real desert," she explained. "This basin actually seems to keep the temperatures fairly stable, at least enough for the agriculture surrounding the town." She'd noted the many farms dotting the landscape as they approached, where the land went from a stark tan to a lively green in many places.

Wadi was an ancient region, dating back to the times of the pharaohs, though there was little in the way of ruins or archaeological interest to discover, save for sparse villages on the outskirts. That wasn't to say the area didn't have historical significance. The Natrun part of its name came from the abundance of natrun in the area, a naturally occurring combination of sodium carbonate and sodium bicarbonate. The material was used in mummification, sodium oxide, and for glass manufacturing. Natrun was also important in ancient Egyptian medicine and rituals. The substance occurs in a solution in the lakes of the region and forms a crust around the edges, depositing the material on the lake bottoms.

Surprisingly, Wadi wasn't just a place for religious pilgrimages. Bird-watching enthusiasts came from all over the globe to see dozens of birds in a unique location.

Sean was done wasting time, and the current conversation was going nowhere. "So, is that the place we're looking for?" He motioned to a collection of domes straight ahead on the other side of the intersection.

"No." Tommy pivoted and looked down the street. Then he pointed at a tall, skinny tower that stood high above everything else. Its crest featured a small dome atop the flat, cubical walls, and the same Coptic cross on its peak, and it was surrounded by a high wall. "That's the one we're looking for."

"Can we just walk in there?" Sean asked.

"Not sure, but we're going to find out."

"Here's the other thing I have an issue with," Adriana announced. "Let's say we go in there and find the alleged tomb of Elisha. Then what? I have a bad feeling about stealing a holy relic from a dead man's grave. Especially that dead man."

"Ironic," Tommy spat, and immediately regretted it.

"Look," she defended, "I know I steal things all the time, but they are things that don't belong to those people, and I take them to the rightful owners. This is very different, Tommy."

He backed off at the sound of her tone. "Sorry. Bad joke."

"Wait," Kimberly said. "What do you steal?"

"Nothing," Sean stopped the conversation. "We need to stay focused. Adriana is right, though. It's going to be difficult to get the relic out of there if we do, in fact, find it. If it comes down to it, I'll handle taking the thing. We're doing it to save someone's life. I can't imagine the good prophet wanting anything less than that."

Something else nagged at Kimberly's brain, and she didn't hesitate to ask. "What did you mean, *that prophet*?"

Tommy took the opportunity to answer. "Elisha was powerful, granted a double portion of the spirit of God that his mentor, Elijah, possessed. There's a bizarre story in the book of Kings where it says two men were burying a friend when they saw a group of bandits coming toward them. The men dumped the body into the tomb of Elisha and took off. When the body touched Elisha's bones, the power of God that still resided within them brought the dead man back to life. He got up, fully capacitated. Unfortunately, the story ends there, and we don't hear anything about it in the rest of the Old Testament."

"That *is* bizarre," Kimberly agreed.

"Getting in won't be an issue," Tommy said. "It's not like we're trying to sneak into Fort Knox. This is a place that welcomes tourists and pilgrims, people who come to learn or to worship. What will be difficult is getting into the tomb alone with enough time to extract the artifact."

Adriana shifted nervously. "I don't like it," she said. "But we don't have a choice."

"I don't like it either," Sean whispered to her. "But if we don't get that piece of the gauntlet, many more innocent people could die."

She nodded her assent. "I know. I don't suppose there's any

chance the monks in there will pull a Mr. Wei and simply let you have the relic?"

Sean stifled a laugh. "I doubt it. But we should have a look around to assess the place and come up with a plan." He glanced at his wife's attire with skepticism. "First, though, we need to get you something a little more appropriate to wear."

She looked down at her casual activewear and then noticed a few women across the road. They were conservatively dressed, with heads covered and long, lightweight dark robes that hung down to their ankles. A few of the women's faces were completely concealed save for the eyes, but some simply kept their hair out of sight.

While the area was mostly Coptic Orthodox Christian, locals still kept some of the same ancient Arabic traditions when it came to dress.

"Yes," Adriana said. "I believe you're right." She cast a glance at Kimberly. "You should probably pick up some clothes for both of us."

The women stayed with the car, while Tommy and Sean went across the street and up the sidewalk to a shop with women's clothing hanging in the window. They quickly picked out two sets of regional attire and returned to the car to find the women sitting in abject silence. Sean chuckled to himself, knowing Adriana was probably less than thrilled at being left with Kimberly.

Adriana was peering out the windshield of the car, scanning the area as she often did when they were involved in something like this, though he suspected it had become routine for her in much of her everyday life.

When he and Tommy neared the vehicle, the women stepped out again and slipped into their coverings. Kimberly grumbled something about how much fabric there was, but Sean didn't pay much attention. The clothes were extremely lightweight and breathable, perfectly suited to desert conditions during the warmer months.

Adriana stepped back once she'd pulled up the hood over her head and put her arms out wide. "How do I look?" she asked.

"Like you're ready to attend the liturgy," Sean said with a smile. "Come on. Let's see what we can find out about this place."

The group started the march toward the walled monastery, noting the sights, sounds, and smells of this unique place. The scent of simmering black beans and onions wafted out of a small café on the right. Inside the restaurant, a few people in black clothing huddled over bowls of the stuff mixed with white rice. It was a simple meal, but it sent a grumble through Sean's stomach as he realized they needed to eat when they were done scouting the church.

The monastery grew more imposing as they approached. The high walls were dotted with windows that may have served as lookout posts in ancient times. As a religious safe haven, the compound would have been a pure sanctuary, with no military presence and zero consideration to defensive measures. In other similar structures, the windows would have provided excellent positions for archers to fend off invaders.

Sean considered this as they reached the fifteen-foot-high metal gates at the entrance to the monastery. One half of the gate was swung wide open, allowing people to pass through freely, though there were few tourists beyond the barrier.

Entering into the serene commune felt like taking a step back in time—a huge step.

Many of the buildings, walls, and even the square stone tiles lining the streets and walkways were thousands of years old. More palm and olive trees swayed next to buildings, growing intermittently throughout a vast courtyard. The plants thrived in the dry conditions of Wadi, and played host to a vast population of birds that sang and chirped from the higher branches.

The birds' songs echoed through the corridors and alleys, filling the miniature city with the constant sounds of nature.

It was then Sean realized that while the courtyard and streets felt vast, there was also an overwhelming sense of comfort, as if the walls themselves were wrapping their arms around anyone inside. It felt safe, welcoming, and the faces of the few people walking by reflected that.

Tommy noticed a sign pointing to the church of St. Macarius the Great and pointed to it. "Looks like we go that way," he said.

"You sure?" Sean asked with a laugh.

Tommy rolled his eyes at the joke and followed the directed path toward an archway with a line of brick that accented the bottom edge. The corridor narrowed, and the group found themselves surrounded by colorful Egyptian rugs of dark red, gold, blue, and green.

They descended the steps, passing beneath the archway that had served as the original entryway to the monastery for over a thousand years. History seeped from every pore of the place. Sean felt the footsteps of those who had come before and once again felt his mind filled with a sense of reverence and peace.

As they continued to follow the prescribed path, they passed a blocky building on the left. It had originally served as a keep, a defensive fortress for the monks millennia ago when invaders would tear through the town seeking treasures to loot. The keep was positioned next to a tall structure that housed a staircase leading up to a drawbridge.

"Look at that," Adriana said, pointing to the wooden structure connecting the smaller building with the fortress.

The others followed her gaze, staring up at the bridge.

"A drawbridge," she commented. "The monks here didn't fight or try to defend themselves, so they would climb that tower and cross the drawbridge into the keep. See the recess in the fortress wall? The bridge could be pulled up and fit right into that slot so the monks couldn't be harmed. They probably had enough supplies to last a month or more in there."

Kimberly scowled from behind her black veil. "How do you know all that?" she asked.

"I enjoy studying ancient castles and fortresses," Adriana said with a shrug, though part of her past studies of such structures also had to do with her extracurricular activities hunting down lost art from World War II. More than once, she'd had to navigate an old castle's maze of corridors to find what she was looking for. "But I also looked up a little information about this place to learn more. I found it fascinating."

"Ah," Kimberly said, unimpressed.

The group continued toward the church, following the signs until they reached the tall, skinny tower they'd seen from the town. While that served as a beacon to anyone seeking the place of worship, the entrance was simply marked by a small sign on the exterior wall, just above a short set of stairs leading down to an open doorway on the right.

The smell of incense wafted out of the door and through the air, touching the nostrils of visitors and beckoning them to come and partake of the services as they'd been performed for thousands of years.

Tommy noted the shoes sitting outside the door at the top of the steps, and motioned to the others. "Looks like we go barefoot from here," he said.

Kimberly grunted her annoyance but removed her shoes with the others and left them sitting near the two strangers' pairs.

The hard stone felt surprisingly warm against the soles of their feet as they padded down the steps and into the darkened atrium of the church. The smell of incense lingered heavily inside, like a dense fog on a San Francisco morning.

Tommy stayed in front, leading the others through the somewhat crowded entryway and into a room that opened up into a sanctuary. Along the far wall, a wooden divider with painted gold filigree kept separate another room where the priests could prepare for mass and perform their daily rituals.

Along the opposite wall, a long shelf ran the length of the room with scriptural books set atop it, spaced evenly apart every five or six inches. Somewhere in the building, a man's voice could be heard chanting prayers from a ritual.

A man in black robes with a salt-and-pepper beard stood directly ahead, blocking their way. He wore a matching black hood called a *qalansuwa* in Arabic and a *koulla* in the Coptic language, a vernacular that was the target for annihilation throughout the centuries by a plethora of enemies ranging from the Romans to the Muslim invaders.

"Hello," the monk said with a welcoming smile. "Is there anything

I can do to help you?" His English was perfect, adorned with his local accent. The man sounded well educated, which came as no surprise. Many of the monks in this monastery spent much of their time studying—not just the scriptures—but languages, history, math, and science.

"Yes," Tommy said politely, his voice kept low to be respectful. "We understand that this is the place where the bones of the prophet Elisha are kept. Would it be possible to see the reliquary?"

For a second, Sean thought his friend had been too bold just coming out and stating the reason they were there, but the monk appeared unfazed. "Certainly. I would be happy to show you there if you like."

Tommy and Sean exchanged a half-surprised look and then nodded.

"That would be wonderful," Tommy said. "Thank you."

"Of course. That's why I'm here. Please," he motioned with his left hand toward a narrow corridor. "Follow me."

Sean panned the room, taking in the scenery as they followed the monk, single file, into the stone passageway. His mind locked on to one thought like a vise and wouldn't let it go. *It can't be this easy.*

27

WADI EL NATRUN

The monk led the group deeper into the monastery's church through the narrow passage. More archways of red brick loomed overhead every so often, serving as both symbolic and literal supports of the building.

"In here," said the monk, pointing to a room to the left, "is a mural of the great prophet Elisha and St. John the Baptist. St. John's bones are also kept in the reliquary here at St. Macarius."

That little nugget had slipped past them when they were doing their research.

"Pilgrims have been coming here to pray at the reliquary for centuries. The bones were brought here when the emperor of Rome, Julian the Apostate, ordered them destroyed."

No one interrupted the monk to tell him they already knew that, and Sean and Tommy both hoped Kimberly would keep her mouth shut. There was no need to sound like a know-it-all. Fortunately, she said nothing.

Maybe she has a hint of decorum, Sean hoped.

The monk continued the abbreviated tour, showing them additional alcoves and recesses that contained sacred images, carvings, and holy objects. In one, he relayed the story of forty-nine monks who had been killed in an attack centuries before. Despite the tragedy, the monastery recovered, and their sacred mission of study and service continued—their sacrifice not in vain.

Sean could see through an open doorway at the end of the hall and noticed something brown that looked like it was the shape of a box. As they drew closer, everyone realized what they were seeing.

The monk pushed the dark wooden door open the rest of the way, his hand brushing absently across a four-sided cross that adorned the front. The wall where the door fastened shut was actually not a wall at all, but a screen made from wood, half of which was carved with the same crosses, allowing visitors to peek in before entering. Tommy and Sean noted the crosses, then cast each other a wayward glance.

Tommy mouthed, "Templars."

Sean suppressed a giggle, but there was no denying the similarities between the symbols of the Order of the Knights Templar and the Coptic cross on the door. In fact, that cross adorned much in the church: doors, walls, ceilings, and even places along the floor where it had been painted.

Seeing it reminded Tommy of something else, too, a show he'd once seen on a history channel about a theory that the cross wasn't the tall, slender apparatus seen on necklaces and in churches all over the Western world. Instead, it looked more like the Templar cross, propped up with a brace on the backside, not driven into the ground like a piling.

Tommy let go of those thoughts as he entered the reliquary behind the monk, followed by Adriana, Kimberly, and Sean.

"This," the monk said, "is the reliquary of the prophet Elisha and St. John the Baptist."

He held out a hand to display the sarcophagus, allowing the room to fall into reverent silence.

A plaque on the wall indicated that the reliquary indeed contained the bones of Elisha the prophet and St. John the Baptist.

Sean stared at the box. It was made of wood, stained a deep reddish-brown color. The upper exterior edge was adorned with four-sided crosses all the way around, keeping consistent with the sacred symbol's liberal use throughout the building. Below that, on the façade, three distinct images were carved in relief. Each was contained in a rectangle where the wood was slightly faded compared to the rest of the reliquary. The image on the left was one of a chariot of fire ascending to heaven with the great prophet Elijah. The engraving in the center featured a man with a bushy beard that covered most of his face, and thick, curly hair that draped down beyond his ears, embracing his skull almost like a helmet. The third image on the right displayed two people. One appeared to be dousing a rag with water while the other bowed his head. A dove hovering above and between the two figures cleared up any questions as to who the image featured. It was the baptism of Jesus by his cousin, John.

Each of the reliefs were framed by white edges painted into the wood, and those were surrounded by hundreds of ivory-colored tiles grouped in clusters of five, all in the shape of the Coptic cross.

"The bones in this reliquary," the monk said from beside them, "were discovered under that archway long ago." He pointed to a wooden trapdoor. He bent down and raised the door, revealing a square hole in the ground. Within the cavity, a light allowed visitors to see the bedrock below and the recess where the bones were discovered so many centuries before.

Sean recalled the information about a manuscript from two different centuries documenting both the discovery and the story of how the bones had come to rest here during their evacuation from Roman jurisdiction.

Several places around the world claimed to host such holy relics. It was an easy claim to make, and with authority comes credibility. Most of the religions that made such claims had authority in spades. And who would question them? People wanted to believe, whether the relics were authentic or not.

These, however, were unlike anything Sean had seen in his time working in the field of archaeology. There were others, of course, that purported to hold various forms of evidence, but this had been documented on two occasions, each separated by centuries.

"Incredible," Sean uttered. His eyes overflowed with solemnity, and he didn't fight the feeling that they truly were in the presence of the remains of two of the most prominent men in three of the world's major religions.

Adriana brushed her fingers against his arm and then wrapped them around his biceps, squeezing gently. Appreciation and humility ebbed from her.

"It truly is," the monk said, looking down at the reliquary.

"How long have you been here?" Sean asked, turning his head from the ornate container.

"Eleven years," the monk answered. "It has been a true honor to be able to dwell in this place." He held up his hands as if showing off the entire building. "If you would like, you may take pictures. And we have a bookshop near the exit if you would like to learn more about the history of the church."

Sean smirked at the last part. Of course they did. Every tourist spot, holy or otherwise, put the gift shop at the exit.

"Thank you. I would love to pick up a couple of books."

Sean stole a glance at Kimberly, who shifted uncomfortably but bit her bottom lip. He knew she was short on patience. And there was no telling what her bosses thought of her jaunt around the world to hunt down a serial killer that seemed to be isolating targets in the greater Atlanta area.

He thought about how Emily would feel if he'd done something similar back in his Axis days. It was different, though, in that his job tended to be more international. They were a branch unto themselves in many ways, though they'd played by many of the guidelines that the department of defense adhered to.

The more he thought about it, the more he worried about Kimberly's interactions with her superiors. They would want reports, updates, anything she'd gleaned up to that point. On a few occasions, she'd used her phone to call in and let her superior know what was going on, but Sean doubted the man or woman would understand the kind of mission they were on. It was off the books, and there were no manuals about how to play it. He called it a mission because that's what he knew, that was the life he'd lived for years, time that had imprinted certain habits and vocabulary on him that would stay with him for all time.

Tommy called them cases or, if they were out helping a group or government, referred to them as assignments.

Sean supposed that was more accurate. But he'd made it his mission to stop Milner, no matter what it took. He would do all he could to stop the maniac from killing any more people, whether they were innocent or not. And deep down inside, Sean had the creeping feeling that his role in all of this was going to be much bigger than even he could anticipate.

They followed the monk through the same passages they'd come through before, and at the end he led them out a different way. As promised, a small bookshop with souvenirs and several volumes featuring information on the monastery lined the humble shelves.

"Thank you," Tommy said, dismissing the monk so he was free to help other visitors if needed. "I appreciate you taking the time to show us around."

"You are most welcome," the monk said with a bow. "Thank you for visiting."

The man turned and floated away, his priestly robes fluttering in the breeze as he moved.

Sean picked out one of the books, paid another monk for it—this one shorter and skinnier than the first—and the group left through an open doorway at the end of the room.

Once outside, they made their way over to a collection of trees at the corner of the promenade and stopped.

Tommy turned and faced the other three with his hands on his hips. "Well, that sucks."

Kimberly didn't follow. "What do you mean?" she asked, genuinely confused. "There's literally no security there. The doors into that place make it easy to break in, if they even close them."

Tommy had had enough of the woman's attitude. "You don't get it, do you?" he asked, not expecting an answer. "Didn't you hear that guy?" He pointed at the church. "That place is important to him, important to millions of people who adhere to the Coptic Orthodox faith."

"So? We need that artifact. Someone's life is in danger, and that thing can save them."

Hearing the empathy for someone else surprised the other three, but it still came off as sounding self-serving in some way. Sean wondered if she somehow thought cracking this case would result in a big promotion. He'd seen a few things like that go down in other agencies when he was with Axis. Maybe that was her angle. Still, it didn't make her wrong. No matter how important the relic was to the monk, and all the monks in the monastery, Sean and his crew needed it before it was too late. He checked his watch and noted the time. They were still good, but every passing second pushed them closer to failure and another murder.

"I'll do it," Adriana said.

The others looked at her, surprised.

"What?" Tommy asked first.

"I have the most experience with this sort of thing. It will be easier if only one of us goes after the artifact—assuming it's in the reliquary."

"What's that supposed to mean?" Kimberly blurted.

"It's possible the gauntlet piece isn't in that box we just looked at." Adriana cut herself short as a group of six men and women walked by.

Two of the men had fanny packs that matched those their wives wore.

Sean cast Tommy a sidelong look. "You think we should get matching fanny packs, buddy?"

"It never stops with you, does it?"

"I hope not." Sean turned back to Adriana. "I can't let you go in there alone. You know that, right?"

She touched his cheek with the back of her hand. "I wasn't asking permission. Besides, it will be easier if I'm alone. More people means more problems."

"Oh, so I'm a problem?" he joked. "I'm kidding," he added before she could defend her words.

"Alone, I can navigate everything faster. I'll get in and out without being detected. Then, when all this is over and we take down Milner, I'll return here and put it back where I found it. The monks will never have to know."

Tommy and Sean considered her plan while Kimberly stood there with her arms crossed.

"Radio? Camera?" Sean asked.

"No radio," Adriana stated. "No offense, but I don't want any chatter while I do this. I need total silence while I work. If you want me to wear a camera, I can do that. Then you can see everything. Do you have... a camera for something like that?"

Tommy blushed. "Well, no. And I don't think there's a Radio Shack around here."

Sean huffed. "I don't think there's a Radio Shack anywhere anymore."

Tommy kept going. "No communication isn't my favorite idea," he said. "We could be your extra ears in case there's trouble. But it's your call," he relented. "What else do you need?"

Adriana looked back at the monastery. "We just scouted the building, and I know how to get to the reliquary. Once I'm there, getting through that door won't be a problem."

"What do you mean?" Kimberly wondered. "I know that door fixes into a frame with a flimsy, decorative wall, but you can't exactly cut through it or knock it down. Then they'll know you were there."

Adriana knew all that, but she controlled herself and didn't allow irritation to bubble to the surface. "Correct. Fortunately, I know how to pick that lock."

"How do you know that?"

"Because I checked it on the way in. I know that lock. I can pick it in less than ten seconds. That won't be the hardest part."

Kimberly scowled. "What will that be?"

"Those passageways are tight. We had to move single file or two wide through most of them. There are lots of places to hide in those alcoves, shrines, and recesses, but if someone sees me, I'll be in the open and won't have many options for escape. And that takes me to the last problem."

"Only a couple of exit options," Sean realized.

"Right. There's the way we came in, which will probably be locked. Again, not an issue, but I'll be exposed from the lower courtyard. It's doubtful anyone will be out, but if they are, it will be easy to see me. So, once I'm inside the gates, just getting to the church will be tricky."

"Um," Tommy interrupted, looking over at the wall surrounding the compound. "How exactly are you going to get over the wall? You didn't happen to pack a grappling hook, did you?"

Adriana's lips stretched into a devilish grin. "No. But I don't need to go over the wall to get in. Only to get out. You don't happen to have that climbing rope you always carry with you, do you?"

It was Tommy's turn to flash the same mischievous look.

"Seriously?" Sean asked. "You're still carrying that thing around?"

"Good," Adriana cut in again. "I'll need it to get out."

"Wait," Kimberly blurted. "What do you mean, you don't have to go over the wall to get in?"

28

WADI EL NATRUN

Darkness blanketed the sky and it now twinkled with the glow of billions of stars. The moon was only a sliver, and the lack of its omnipresent radiance allowed more of the tiny lights a place in the black tapestry above.

Adriana emerged from the alcove where she'd been waiting for more than two hours since the gates closed. She wanted to make sure that every drop of residual sunlight was gone before stepping out into the courtyard and onto the promenade.

A few of the windows flickered with golden light in the buildings across the quad. Some of the monks were staying up late, either praying or studying.

Sean was right about one thing. The stars out here were absolutely spectacular. She figured he was outside the wall at that very moment, staring up at them with boyish wonder.

He'd always loved looking at the stars, though he knew very little about constellations or astronomy in general, except for the theoretical physics aspect. He enjoyed speculating on Einstein's theories, as well as on the postulates of other famous scientists who had long considered the wonders of the universe.

Adriana dispelled the thoughts of her husband and his affinity for stargazing and focused on the task at hand.

She gripped the outer edge of the alcove wall with her fingers, steadying her weight as she peeked out into the courtyard. She didn't detect any movement, no signs of life, not yet. This place didn't have some of the usual problems that came with a job like this: patrols, guards, security systems, and worst of all, dogs. The only animals she could hear were the occasional chirps or whistles of birds in the tree-tops, and most of them had already settled in for the night.

Still, the danger of being caught was ever present. While the monks wouldn't kill or torture her, like some of the more dangerous targets from the past, there was still the possibility that she could be arrested. That would be bad enough, but it would also mean another person would die back in the States. She didn't want that on her conscience. Failure, as ever, wasn't an option.

Satisfied the path to the church was clear, she stepped out from her hiding place and crept to the wall to her right, keeping low and to the edges in case someone did happen to walk by in the middle of the thoroughfare.

She stopped under a window and crouched by a planter containing a thick palm tree. She listened but only heard a few murmurs from a window overhead, prayers from a monk as he conducted his evening devotions. Again, Adriana moved forward, her feet silent as a summer breeze. She rushed around the corner toward the church, her black robes flapping behind her.

The clothes were hardly optimal for a stealth job such as this, but if she were to be caught, the apparel she had on underneath might make for a worse punishment. She imagined the monks' expressions upon seeing her skintight yoga pants and black, dry-fit top that clung snuggly to her skin.

She reached a staircase she'd noticed earlier that went into a tower and then out onto a platform above the outer wall. A raised stone garden bed in the corner provided an excellent place to stash Tommy's rope, and when she reached it, she took the looped rope and stowed it under a collection of dense bushes. The second the climbing rope was out of sight, she turned and sprinted to the corner of the next building.

Once more, she clutched the stone edging and leaned around. She immediately withdrew upon seeing two men in robes walking along the tiled street. They were engaged in a deep discussion, one walking with his hands behind his back, the other twirling a hand around as he explained something in Coptic.

Adriana didn't know what the men were saying, not that it mattered. She ducked back around the exposed steps and squatted in the shadows until the two monks passed by. She kept a careful eye on them until they were out of sight before darting back to the corner and checking one more time. There were no more monks in view, so she took off toward the tall tower and the staircase leading to the church entrance.

Adriana skirted along the edges of the buildings, the wall, and the sidewalks, moving like sleeping death as she crept closer to her destination. When the descending staircase was in sight, she stopped behind a copse of olive trees and ducked down behind the raised bed. She stole a glance at her watch, out of habit, noting the time in her mind. Moving from where she left the rope to this point had taken less than five minutes, but there were no guarantees she wouldn't encounter delays on the way out.

She took a deep breath and shed the cumbersome robes, revealing her taut frame. Most of her body was covered in black, including a mask she pulled up over her face that concealed her skin from the nape of her neck all the way up to the bridge of her nose. A matching bandanna covered her head and brown hair, making her look like a ninja on the way to yoga class.

She stuffed the robes under the trees and ran across to the opening. When she reached the staircase, she leaped down the entire set of steps and landed on the floor at the base, right next to the church entrance.

Rolling to her right, she pinned her back against the wall and looked straight ahead into the courtyard beyond. No sign of anyone.

She turned to the closed door and set to work on the lock.

Adriana produced the small kit she always kept with her and inserted the pin into the hole. Then she slid a narrow bar into it and started working the mechanism. After three tries, she started to wonder if she'd made a mistake when identifying the lock. She removed the tools from the hole and wiped her brow, even though there was no sweat to be seen. The dry air in the Wadi basin caused most perspiration to evaporate the second it reached the surface of a person's skin.

She was about to try the lock again when she heard footsteps from around the nearest corner. They were shuffled, muted, but someone was definitely coming her way.

Her heart thumped at the same cadence it always did, but her mind flashed into action. She bounded back up the stairs without making a sound and slid around the corner just as a robed monk appeared. She kept her eyes on him, watching as he approached the door to the church and pushed it open.

Of course, she thought. *That's why I couldn't pick the lock. It was unlocked the whole time.*

She wasn't naïve enough to think the door into the reliquary would be likewise unimpeded, but for now she'd be thankful for an easy entry into the building.

Adriana waited until the door closed behind the monk and then slipped out from cover again, risking a look back down the promenade to make sure no one had seen her.

Back at the door, she eased it open and stepped inside. The hinges must have been well oiled because they didn't make the slightest squeak as she entered. These monks clearly didn't expect anyone to waltz in and rob the place. The thought sent a renewed shot of guilt though her mind. Adriana had mostly purged any such doubts, but they'd returned easily, and she found herself loathing the task at hand.

No. She steeled herself against the thoughts and closed the door. Inside, the smell of incense still lingered in the air and it seemed stronger than before. The monks must have finished their evening prayers recently, although she didn't know the Coptic rituals and routines. In truth, she didn't know much about monastic life except what she'd read and heard by chance.

Adriana tiptoed ahead and stopped at the next corner, where she peeked around and saw the man who had entered before her walking across the wide room toward a door in the back.

She cut away and sprang across the floor toward the passage that led to the reliquary. Inside, she curled around the first corner and stared down the corridor. She didn't hear anyone, and there were no monks in sight. *All clear. For now.*

Adriana wasted no time and scurried through the hall on silent feet.

Arriving at the door to the reliquary, she pulled out her lock-picking tool kit again. This time, when she inserted the requisite metal pieces, she was unsurprised to find it locked. Trust, even for the monks, had its limits.

The lock took Adriana twelve seconds to open, a time that bruised her ego, but she slid the tools back into her pocket and swung the portal open. Then she stepped into the room and over to the box containing the bones of the two great spiritual leaders.

She breathed slowly, intentionally, through her nostrils to regulate her heartbeat and breathing, but also out of reverence. Adriana's family had originally been Protestant, somewhat outliers in the countryside near Madrid where Catholicism ruled, but she still had a deep respect for religious artifacts, especially if these were indeed the bones of two great men from the Bible.

She'd felt the same sense of respect earlier when she and the others were here, and she knew how in awe Sean was deep down just standing in this very place. Now she had to violate it and steal something that had been safeguarded for thousands of years by good people who honored the artifacts and bones of those they revered.

The thought made her sick, sicker than she'd ever felt acquiring art stolen by the Nazis. Getting those things back was easy by comparison, but her inner struggle here tore her apart inside.

She wrestled the guilt into submission, again telling herself that it was only temporary, that she would bring the gauntlet piece back when they'd figured out a way to stop Milner. Of course, if they failed, the piece would be lost to a madman. She snapped her head to shake off that cobweb and stepped closer to the reliquary.

Adriana wrapped her fingers around the golden handle on the near end and carefully lifted. The thing didn't budge with her effort, so she tugged harder, this time using both hands.

She felt a slight shift, and then the heavy wooden lid loosened. Its weight was overwhelming, and for a second she wished Sean *had* come with her if for no other reason than to help bear this particular burden.

A strange, acrid smell wafted into the room and seeped into her nose. It was bitter and dry, not like rotting death, more like death of ages gone by. There was also the scent of withering fabric, like a grandmother's closet that had gone untouched for millennia.

As she grunted silently, still pulling the lid to her right, she noticed the source of the smell. With the lid far enough over to prop it on the lip of the main box, she stopped her toil and looked inside.

The lights were dim in the corridor outside the reliquary shrine, but it was enough to see the bones within the container and the tattered remains of shrouds that had wrapped around them.

Two skulls were propped up, vacant ocular cavities staring out, never to see again. The rest of their remains were arranged neatly in front of the skulls atop the fragments of dingy cloth.

Other items also occupied space in the container. A withered strip of leather that may have been an old belt rested in the far corner next to what she assumed were the remains of John the Baptist. Her eyes didn't remain on that side of the reliquary for long. They were drawn back to the near side where the bones of Elisha the prophet lay. Next to them, wedged against the interior wall, was a curved yellow piece of armor, glimmering in the faint light.

29

ATLANTA

The phone call came at an hour neither Tara nor Alex knew existed. Tara was the first to respond, rolling over on her side and stretching a mile to reach the nightstand next to the bed. She tapped around in the dark three times before her fingers found the phone. She grabbed it, noticed the name on the device first, and then the time.

It was 5:30 in the morning.

She pressed the green button on the screen and put the phone to her ear as she rolled onto her back and stared through a filmy haze at the ceiling.

"Hey, Dr. Kelley, what's up?"

"Tara. Did I wake you?"

"Um...."

"Oh, sorry about that." The woman sounded like she'd been awake for hours already, and had four cups of coffee to boot. "I can let you go back to sleep if you want, and you call me when you wake up."

"No, no it's all right. I'm up now. What's going on?"

"Well," Kelley began, "I stayed up pretty late last night in the hotel. A couple of things just kept nagging at my brain about this whole murder investigation with Milner. I couldn't let it go until around midnight when I fell asleep. But I woke up about thirty minutes ago, and my brain was still in a bind over it."

"Yeah?" Tara reached over and poked Alex, who remained motionless.

"Yes. So, I've been doing some research about Milner, especially into what he did to get put in Morrowfield, but also about what he was researching both prior to that and after being put in the asylum."

"Is there any way we can talk about this at the lab? I'll get Alex up and meet you over there in an hour."

"Lab? Oh, sure. I'll be there in a few minutes. See you then."

The excited Dr. Kelley ended the call before Tara could say good-bye. She raised the phone over her body and stared at the screen for a second, shook her head, and closed her eyes. Dreams called to her from their unfinished precipices, but she couldn't fall back to sleep now. She was awake, and her brain was already starting to churn.

"Alex, wake up," she said in an unusually authoritative tone.

He grumbled some random words, or at least the semblance of words, and only stirred for a second.

She shoved him a second time. "Hey, get up. Dr. Kelley wants to meet us at the lab."

"What?" was all he could manage, and even then, it was barely English.

She whipped her legs over the edge of the bed and planted her feet on the cool wooden floor. Palms on the mattress, she lowered her head and took several deep breaths just as she always did in the morning when getting out of bed. When her head started to clear away the fog, she stood up and walked to the kitchen to begin her routine of grinding the beans, dumping them into the filter, and pouring the water in the pot before taking a quick shower.

On her way to the bathroom, she yanked the sheets off Alex and smacked his bottom. "Hey, time to go to work."

"Already?" he complained, then chased it with a yawn. Then the chill in the room slithered over his skin and he reached for the comforter that was no longer there. "Aw, man."

Fifty-three minutes and a truckload of Alex's whining later, the young couple scanned their ID cards and entered the IAA building with Dr. Kelley in tow.

When they usually showed up, the receptionist and the security guard were already there, but that was at nine in the morning. No one was there now. In fact, most of the streets in Atlanta had been similarly vacant. The drive in was actually a pleasant surprise to the two. Atlanta's traffic was world-renowned, and some of the worst in the nation. At six in the morning, though, it wasn't so bad.

"So, what had you all excited when you called this morning?" Tara asked, leading the way through the vacant lobby to the elevator.

Dr. Kelley clutched a notebook in her hand. They stepped onto the elevator and Alex pressed the button for the basement.

"Well," Kelley said, "I wanted to know more about Milner than what I'd heard on the news. So I started digging. And what I found was truly interesting."

"The backstory of a serial killer?" Alex mused, still a touch grumpy from the early hour.

"Yes!" Kelley exclaimed. "I wasn't totally surprised to learn that his parents were both religious fanatics in North Florida. They were small-town folk, from a very rural area. His father was a farmer. His mother kept the books while raising little Theodore.

"Old-school."

"Right. They were members of a local church, barely a hundred members. But when Theodore was ten, they left the church, claiming it had become idolatrous, hypocritical, and untrue to the faith."

"Wow," Tara said as the elevator doors opened on the bottom floor. She stepped out and continued toward the entrance to the lab. "Usually, those small-town rural churches are extremely conservative."

"Exactly. Which means either the pastor did something or allowed something the Milners didn't approve... or they were extremists."

Tara stopped at the door and entered her code on the keypad.

"Sounds like the latter considering the murder spree their son has been on," Alex said.

"That's the conclusion I reached, too. The Milners stopped

attending that church. They pulled Theodore out of school and homeschooled him until he was college age. There aren't many records with the state as far as I can tell, but I don't have access to such things. I have a friend who's a guidance counselor back in Wyoming who might be able to pull something like that, but it could arouse suspicion if someone noticed her looking at a file from Florida. It would be a stretch for her to find it, anyway. Milner was a student back before electronic records were implemented, and most schools don't bother to scan in anything older than 2006, not that I can tell, anyway."

They walked into the lab and Tara went straight for the coffee pot. The two cups she'd had already weren't going to be enough to fight off the effects of this ridiculous time of day. She scooped the grinds into a filter, poured in the water, and hit the button before returning to where Dr. Kelley stood over a cleared workstation.

She set the notebook down on the desk and opened it. "Do you know what this is?"

Alex and Tara leaned over the desk to inspect the notes.

"Looks like you've been taking a keen interest in our suspect," Alex quipped.

"These are notes from the doctor who was seeing Milner," she answered.

Tara narrowed her eyelids and glanced up at Kelley. "Isn't that a HIPAA violation?"

"Only if we tell anyone. I have a friend who knows the doctor responsible for Milner's treatments and evaluations. They were willing to forgo ethics in this particular patient's case due to the immediate danger Milner poses. According to my friend, Milner spent most of his time studying scriptures or peripheral manuscripts, books that deal with scriptural texts. He especially focused on the ancient prophets. Specifically: Elijah, Elisha, and Jonah."

"Good to hear we are on the right track," Alex said. "You also used the word *most* when you mentioned how he spent his time."

Kelley nodded, and the excitement in her eyes brimmed, her lips pinching into a tight grin. "Yes. Remember how I mentioned the scroll that was stolen?"

"Hard to forget something like that."

"Well, that was only part of what Milner was after. There were other books, scrolls, ancient texts that he scoured the world to find, all of which he told the psychiatrist, my friend. The doctor told me that he'd been working with obsessed people most of his career, but what Milner felt toward his mission—his ministry, as he called it— was beyond anything he'd ever seen. He called it a delusional frenzy. Milner truly believes that he's part of God's grand plan to save the world, purging it of sin through pain and suffering."

"That's a big leap," Tara remarked.

"Yes. And that's not all. There were verses from scripture written all around his cell, most of them having to do with the end of days. But he took the verses and manipulated them, saying things like, he would be the one to throw the wicked into fire, to cleanse the world of its sins, and 'through His stripes all would be healed.'"

"Stripes?"

"A verse in the Old Testament mentions that. It's a reference to the whipping the Messiah took before the crucifixion."

"Wait," Alex said, the realization smacking him in the face. "That's why he used a whip on his victims."

"Correct," Kelley applauded. "But there's one more piece to the puzzle that kept coming up." She paused and made eye contact with each of them before going on. "Along with the scriptures written on the walls, he also continued to make references to one of the prophets; the one he called the greatest of them all—Elijah."

"What about Elijah? How does he fit into all of this?" Alex wondered.

Kelley nodded at the question and raised a finger. "I wondered the same thing. Until I saw the drawings."

She took out her phone from a clutch hanging from her shoulder and showed the two a collection of images. "You see this?" She pointed at something that looked like a blanket, fluttering in the wind.

"A quilt?" Alex asked.

"Close," she said and flipped to the next picture. This one was a color illustration. It displayed something similar to the first image, but in color and with another distinct image—a chariot of fire being pulled by flaming horses with a man standing at the back, hand extended out as if reaching for the falling fabric."

"Elijah's translation to heaven," Tara realized. "We get it. The man is obsessed with prophets, especially Elijah."

"It's not just the prophet the man is after. Think about the clues. All of this is pointing to something, a source of power he craves that will make him an unstoppable force. Elijah could walk through walls; perhaps even turn invisible. When he went to rebuke Ahab, the king ordered his men to find and kill the prophet, but they couldn't locate him even though he'd just been there seconds before. He could raise the dead. Heal the sick. Give sight to the blind. Multiply the smallest amount of food into enough to sustain a family for years. And when he left, his apprentice asked for one thing."

"A double portion of his power," Alex murmured.

"Yes. And do you remember how Elisha would know that request had been granted?"

"He would see his mentor taken to heaven."

"Correct. And one additional piece."

"The mantle," Alex said, his pulse quickening. "He caught the cloak of Elijah."

Kelley plopped down in the nearest seat and exhaled a long sigh. She punctuated it by clapping her hands together once.

"That's it," Tara said, her mind spinning. "That's what he's after."

"Yes, my friends," Kelley said, her tone turning dark and foreboding. "It is said that there was still power in Elisha's bones when a dead man touched it after being hastily buried with him decades after the prophet's death. If there was that kind of power in Elisha's bones, I shudder to imagine what that mantle can do."

"And in the hands of someone like Milner," Alex said, "it could have global consequences."

No one said anything for several breaths as the gravity of recent events gripped them in a cold embrace.

"There is one thing I am curious about, Dr. Kelley," Tara said finally. "You told us that you believed Milner was the one who stole the scroll that is connected to this mystery."

"Yes," Kelley confirmed. "We believe he had a hand in it."

"But that's my problem. He would have been in Morrowfield when it was taken? How could Milner have had anything to do with it while he was locked up?"

Kelley took a long breath and exhaled. "Milner isn't working alone."

"We figured that based on the simple fact Sean had to deliver the artifact to someone."

"Oh, there's no question Milner has an extensive global network. He inherited quite the fortune when his parents met their untimely demise."

Alex arched one eyebrow. "Untimely?"

"They were murdered when Milner was in his late twenties. No one could pin him for that one. The defense worked a miracle and got him acquitted. Milner's inheritance helped him set up a world-wide following of people he called believers. He even has elite soldiers with him; mercenaries he managed to lure with money and convert with his wild promises."

"It's a cult," Alex realized. "He's built a cult that's spread all over the planet?"

"Not a cult," Kelley said. "Milner's created a new religion."

30

WADI EL NATRUN

Adriana started to reach into the reliquary, then paused. She squeezed her eyes closed tight and said a quick prayer, asking for forgiveness for what she was about to do. It was grave robbing, plain and simple, and beyond that, she was robbing the grave of two important men of God.

She opened her eyes and stared into the container at the two skulls. She recounted the story of John the Baptist's execution, and the sickening request the queen had made on behalf of one of her young relatives. The phrase *on a silver platter* probably originated from that tragic tale, but Adriana also remembered hearing that some of John's followers recovered the man's body, including the head, to give him a proper burial.

That would explain the presence of the two skulls, she thought.

"Sorry," she whispered. "I'll bring this back."

She wasn't superstitious, and not overly religious, but Adriana carried a strong spiritual side and tried to show respect. As she reached in to take the golden piece, she recalled the story of the dead man who touched the bones of Elisha and was resurrected. She wondered if there was still such power there, and what it would do to a living person.

It was probably better not to find out, so she plucked the golden plate from the corner and stuffed it in a black pouch slung over her shoulder. Once it was secure, she shoved the lid back into place, carefully lowering it until the edges were flush with the bottom.

She took a breath from the exertion and turned to leave when she stopped cold in her tracks. In the silence, she heard footsteps and voices, and with every second that passed, the sounds grew louder.

Someone was coming, and Adriana didn't have a way out. She looked around, suddenly frantic, and realized she was indeed trapped. The nearest shrine was twenty feet down the passage. Maybe she could make it. Or maybe whoever was coming would catch her in the act.

There was no time to weigh the consequences. She was about to chance running down the corridor when she caught sight of the wooden trapdoor next to the reliquary.

Within seconds, she eased the entrance shut, which bought her a few more seconds since the door blocked any view of the trapdoor. She spun around and lifted the handle. Again, she was surprised by the lack of creaking, and she immediately slid into the darkened cavity, then pulled the covering back over, immersing herself in near pitch black.

The light she'd seen in there before must be turned off at night. Even though she wasn't scared of the dark, being in this place, where the bones had been discovered so long ago, felt more than a little creepy.

The voices continued to grow louder as the monks approached. She could hear them through the trapdoor, murmuring and chanting, the sounds of night prayers.

She hoped they weren't planning on opening the trapdoor. If they did, she would have to think fast. *A lie, perhaps, about how she fell in earlier that day and... hurt her leg. Yes. Hurt her leg, and no one heard her crying for help. It would work. It had to work.*

Adriana wasn't good at lying, and now not only had she stolen a priceless relic from the grave of a powerful prophet of God; she was planning on lying to a bunch of monks.

She could feel her list of sins growing by the second.

The men unlocked the door and stepped into the reliquary. She couldn't see much save a few faint streaks of light that managed to sneak through cracks in the trapdoor's flawed surface. Even with those, she could only make out huge shadows.

The monks loitered for several minutes. Adriana didn't dare even risk a look at her watch for fear that the slightest movement would draw attention from the praying men.

The air under the archway stifled her breath. She feared that any moment, the musty oxygen entering her nose and lungs might cause her to sneeze or cough, giving away her hiding place.

The men finished their prayers and then one by one exited the little room. Relief filled Adriana as they left, but it was short lived as her nose twitched. Her body's reflexes kicked in, and she lost control as every fiber in her torso convulsed into a sneeze.

She managed to stifle it enough to keep from making much noise, but she thought for sure one of the monks heard it. Through the narrowest of cracks, she watched in horror as the last man out paused at the doorway. He nudged the door open a little farther and looked around. She couldn't see his entire face, only one eye and part of his cheek, but he was curious. Something had caught his attention, and she was certain it was her sneeze.

The man stepped back into the room and walked over to the trapdoor. Adriana knew that within seconds he would lift the covering by the handle and find her cowering inside. She looked back toward the rear of the former gravesite, but it was dark and seeing anything was impossible. Not that it mattered. She'd noticed earlier that there wasn't much room in the hole, though if she pushed as far back as possible she might be able to avoid being spotted.

Adriana wondered if there was more to the little cave, if there was a passage that connected to it she hadn't seen before. If she could just feel her way to it, she could escape. But shifting around under the trapdoor would make a sound, and if the man didn't know she was there before, it would surely give away the truth.

She decided to stay motionless and play the odds. If she had to, she would lie to the monk and explain she'd fallen and gotten hurt and eventually passed out from the pain.

To her surprise, the monk didn't open the door. He stepped over to the other side of the reliquary for a few seconds, and then left. One of the men asked what he was doing, at least Adriana assumed that's what was said. She couldn't see very well, but enough to see the man holding up a lamp with a candle burning in it.

He forgot his lamp, she realized with grateful relief.

The door closed again, and this time, no one returned.

Adriana felt the little satchel pressed against her skin and was reminded that her task was only half-completed. She still had to get out of the church, and then the monastery.

Her nerves quieted once more and she pushed the trapdoor up, careful to hold the underside so that it didn't flap loudly against the floor. She climbed out and silently lowered the lid, then looked through the openings in the wall next to the door. The monks were gone, and no sound echoed back to her.

She pulled the door open and stepped through, shutting it silently behind with one last look back at the reliquary she'd just pilfered.

Ten big steps and she was at the first alcove, where she ducked inside and waited, listening for any sign of trouble approaching. The corridor remained silent.

Adriana secured the satchel one more time, making sure it didn't move or jiggle, before emerging from the cell. She repeated the maneuver two more times, skipping by an alcove before ducking into the next until she reached the end of the corridor.

From there, she slipped around the corner and into the next hall leading to the exit. The sounds of voices touched her ears, driving her feet faster along the smooth stone floor. With every step, Adriana thought one of the monks would spot her and sound the alarm—whatever that might be in a place like this.

That alarm never came, though, and she made it to the exit without being noticed. She wrapped her fingers around the handle and was about to push the door open when another sound radiated into the confined foyer. Someone was coming down the steps outside. Their footfalls were accompanied by the jingle of metal, perhaps keys or something used in one of the rituals of worship.

She could retreat, head back down the corridor toward the reliquary and find a place to hide, but that would add more risk. At any second, another monk could appear from the sanctuary or from the dormitory. She was surprised at the number of people still awake and not in their cells.

With no time left to think, she pressed her feet against the wall with her hands in the corner and climbed up over the doorway into the eaves of the ceiling between two archways.

The door below opened and a monk stepped inside. The man never bothered to look up, and why would he? There had likely never been a thief in their midst, much less one sprawled out like Spider-Man on the ceiling.

Adriana's shoulders burned from the effort of keeping her weight stable. Her legs handled the burden more easily, but she knew she could only hold this position for so long.

Luckily, the monk didn't hang around. He closed the door and continued on his way, disappearing around the next bend into the passage.

As much as she wanted to, Adriana didn't let herself simply drop to the floor. She worked her way back down the walls until the fall was less than five feet, then let go and landed on the balls of her feet, silent as a cat.

She pulled open the door and escaped out into the cool evening air once more. It washed over her as she pulled the heavy wood closed again, realizing how balmy it had been inside the sacred confines of the church.

Perspiration dribbled down her face and soaked into the mask around her mouth and ears. Her shoulders still ached from the maneuver she'd just pulled.

Adriana flew up the stairs, taking them two at a time. Her feet barely touched the ground as she sprinted into the courtyard, aiming for the stairwell where she left the rope. The robes would be left behind. Someone would find them as they passed the planter or tended to the shrubs, but it was doubtful the person who discovered them would even consider the implications. They would be curious for a minute or two, but no one would think to check the reliquary.

Even if they did, she would be long gone. Another pang of guilt struck her heart. She shook it off and kept running full speed through the little plaza, again keeping close to the walls and shadows to avoid detection. If someone saw her from one of the windows, they didn't shout.

She looped around the last building on the left and found the rope where she had left it, hung it over her shoulder, and ascended the staircase to the top of the wall. A quick peek out from the enclosed stairwell told her there were no guards, no monks meandering about or gazing up at the stars. She left the confines of the tower and wrapped the rope around a sturdy wooden cleat jutting out from the stone. Once the knot was secure, she flung the cord out over the wall. She took a pair of gloves from her satchel and jammed them onto her hands. They were thin, but the palms were coated with a hard surface to prevent rope burns.

Adriana took one last look back over the courtyard of the monastery, then climbed over the wall, gripped the rope, and ran down face-first. When she reached the bottom, she used the gloves to brake and her speed came to an almost instant halt.

Two hundred feet away, she spotted the dark outline of the rental SUV parked near some tall bushes and a skinny palm tree. Adriana left the rope dangling against the wall, another souvenir that would no doubt raise questions to whoever found it, and took off. She galloped across the desert plains, sand kicking up in her wake. The run was difficult thanks to the loose soil beneath her.

With every sinking step, she felt certain someone walking along the wall would spot her. Why would it matter if they did? They wouldn't know what she'd done and would have no reason to be suspicious of her.

Adriana reminded herself that she wasn't on one of her typical cases, one where there were armed guards, state-of-the-art security systems, or—heaven forbid—dogs. No one was lining her up in their sniper rifle's sights to take her down. No police were on their way. She had a clear run to the goal line. Despite that knowledge, up to the point she trotted to a stop at the SUV, she expected to hear the sound of a rifle report or a klaxon blaring.

She slowed to a stop and slid into the back of the SUV through the open door, and slammed it shut. Tommy stepped on the gas, kicking dirt and sand out from behind the tires.

"Did you get it?" Kimberly asked, looking back at her from the front with accusing eyes.

Sean and Tommy each snorted a laugh at the woman's doubts.

Adriana's breath came quickly from the sprint. Tonight had been a workout all around. As her heartbeat slowed toward its normal pace, she reached into her satchel and removed the piece of golden plating inside.

She held it in her hands so the others could see, though Tommy kept his eyes on the road—mostly. He took a fraction of a second to look back in the mirror to catch a glimpse of the artifact.

The gold was in perfect condition and displayed three images just as the Jonah piece had, though these reliefs featured different stories from the life of Elisha. An ax head was the first. Another displayed a bear coming out of the woods. The third was of a flaming arrow framed by an arched window.

"Good work," Kimberly said. "I'm officially impressed."

"That's what she does," Sean said as he took out his phone and snapped a picture of the gauntlet piece. "And it looks like we got it with an hour to spare."

He sent the image to Milner and waited for the reply. Seconds passed. Then minutes. Still nothing.

"Did you send it?" Tommy asked as he steered the SUV down the road heading back to Cairo. The corona of the city's lights glowed over the horizon in the distance.

"Yeah," Sean said, a scowl of concern stretching across his face.

"What did he say?" Tommy asked.

"Nothing."

31

ATLANTA

Alex and Tara pored over Dr. Kelley's notes for the fifth time, looking for anything that might give them a clue as to who Milner might target next in his string of gruesome murders.

The man's life was an interesting case study of the bizarre. His mother and father had lived simple lives on a farm in North Florida. They saved money like chipmunks hoarding acorns before winter, socking away every nickel. Theodore's father had also invested wisely and grown the family fortune. He never spent it, though, always forcing Theodore to earn his way, working through high school and college.

Alex and Tara figured the younger Milner didn't know about his family's money until sometime in his twenties when he discovered they were actually multimillionaires.

Some of the notes from his cell at Morrowfield talk about his parents' sins and how they were now forgiven, though he never wrote down any kind of confession to the slayings. Not that it mattered. With the double jeopardy rule, he couldn't be tried for it again, and there was no chance of a civil lawsuit since he had no next of kin and his parents had no friends or colleagues.

It was all perfectly convenient.

Alex slid his chair away from the notes and rubbed his temples. He'd looked over Kelley's findings more times than he needed. If there was a clue buried in that stuff, he wasn't going to find it by staring at the pages for another hour.

He scooted up to his computer and pulled up the previous victim. The grisly visage of the priest on the cross with his bare chest engraved with the names of his victims scorched Alex's chestnut eyes. He would have preferred not to look at it, but there was something off about the image, and he couldn't tear his thoughts away.

Kelley busily scrolled through her phone, performing various web searches in conjunction with Milner's backstory to see if there was a correlation somewhere.

Tara continued looking over the notes, though Alex was certain there was nothing left to find within those pages.

The revelation concerning the cloak of Elijah had been profound. Now they knew what the madman was looking for, and they could only imagine the ways he would use such a powerful artifact, if it indeed still possessed some kind of supernatural power, or if it still existed.

Alex stared at the screen, forcing himself not to look away from the tortured priest's body. *Something is off, but what?*

He stared at the list of names on the priest's chest, and the answer glared right back.

"Guys?" he said without removing his gaze from the screen. "Take a look at this."

The two women perked up and instantly huddled around Alex's station. He pointed at the dead man's chest. "See anything strange about these letters?"

"Ugh," Dr. Kelley groaned. "Such a terrible sight. I don't want to look anymore, Alex. I'm sorry."

She turned away, but Tara didn't. "Yes!" she exclaimed. "I see it. Those letters are bolder than the others. Why didn't I notice that before?"

"I missed it, too," Alex said with a shrug.

He snatched a nearby pen and jotted down the boldface letters from the murder scene, *NWATLFP*

"What do you think it means?" he asked when he finished writing.

"It looks like a scramble," Tara said. "We've certainly seen a few of those in our time here."

Dr. Kelley had turned her head away from the computer monitor, but curiosity pulled her eyes back with its gravity.

"You think this is a clue to the next murder location?" Kelley asked.

"He gave us a hint in the last message. Maybe this time he wasn't including the clue in the message. It was at the previous crime scene."

"Wait a second," Alex interrupted. "That's not a word scramble at all."

He clicked a tab at the top of the screen and entered a new search term, northwest Atlanta churches.

The results took less than three seconds to populate on the new page. The first one displayed a mini map of the searched area along with several listings for churches. The second result in the map's box drew Alex's attention right away.

"Northwest Atlanta First Presbyterian," he read the words out loud.

"It's the next location," Tara stated. "I'll call Trent."

"He may be on the wrong side of town," Alex offered. "We need to go."

She nodded. "Yeah, I think you're right."

"Wait," Kelley said. "Why don't you call the police?"

"We're calling Trent," Tara explained. "It will be better for him to call the cops than us. If we're wrong, we look suspicious or, at best, like we don't know what we're doing. We're civilians, too. That doesn't carry as much credibility. If Trent's wrong, he's playing leads, working with the system to figure out Milner's next move."

Kelley bobbed her head. "Okay. Well, I don't want to see another corpse, but I'll come with you."

"No," Tara said. "Stay here at the lab. Keep looking for clues as to where this prophet's cloak could be. If we can get a step ahead of

Milner—and ironically, Sean and Tommy—we may be able to head him off."

Kelley nodded her acceptance of the assignment and immediately slid over to another workstation, where she set to work searching for more clues.

Twenty-seven minutes later, Alex and Tara pulled into the mostly vacant church parking lot and rolled to a stop near the entrance. A gray Honda Accord sedan sat in the spot closest to the building. The late-model vehicle screamed dependability rather than opulence and stood as a tribute to the pastor's fiscally conservative nature.

Assuming the car was his.

Tara killed the engine and they stepped out of the SUV. Alex gazed at the entrance, both enthralled with curiosity and racked with fear.

The red brick building looked like many of the churches built in the last decade. Its cubed twin towers on either side of the entrance looked more like castle parapets than anything related to worship. In the center, a steeply angled roof met at the center of an A-frame that loomed over the doors.

The design of the entire facility mimicked a cross with the length of the sanctuary making up the main body of the shape. Huge arched windows lined both sides of the main structure, pouring daylight in for those who came to worship. The clear windows represented a stark contrast to the stained-glass windows many older churches used to make worship services seem more private.

Tara and Alex walked up to the front door and pushed on the bar. For a second, they both wondered if they should have brought their weapons, but Trent had advised against that, telling them that if the cops showed up and they were there with guns, the cops might mistake them for the suspect.

After that brief explanation, Tara and Alex acquiesced, although reluctantly.

The door opened easily under Alex's force on the bar, and the two cautiously stepped inside.

The wide atrium stretched from east to west, with a reception desk directly across from the doors, men's and women's restrooms on either side, along with a collection of rooms where people could have Bible studies, prayer meetings, and one with a stroller in it for newborns and infants to attend the sermons without interfering with the peace and quiet the rest of the congregation expected.

A sinister silence permeated the building. The two visitors could feel it in the air, mixed with the smell of hymnals, upholstery, and new carpet.

"You think he's still here?" Tara asked, more than a little nervous.

"I don't know," Alex answered honestly. "But I wish we had our guns."

"You and me both."

A thud echoed from somewhere in the building.

"What was that?" Alex wondered out loud.

"Sounded like a door closing. And it came from in there." She extended a finger toward the sanctuary doors to their right.

Alex nodded his agreement. He took a step toward the door and froze.

The phone in his pocket vibrated two staccatos and then fell silent again. He drew the device out of his pocket and looked at the message.

"It's from Sean," he stated. "Says they located the second piece and sent the picture to Milner. Now they're waiting on further instructions on how to deliver it."

"Crap," Tara said then broke into a short sprint to the double doors. She hit them hard with both hands, bursting into the sanctuary.

"What?" Alex begged, hurrying to catch up.

"Milner," she hissed back to him. "He just left."

"How do you—" Alex caught up, and the question teetering on the edge of his lips fell away into the ether.

Straight ahead, behind the stage and the pulpit in the front of it, a middle-aged man hung from scaffolding over the baptismal pool. The almost-naked man wore nothing but his underwear. With his arms and legs bound tight with duct tape, he dangled from a central point in the boards overhead. His slender body showed signs of a beating: bruises, gashes, and sharp red lines on his shoulders and the few ribs that were visible under the lines of Alabama chrome.

The man's body twisted one way and then another, north, north-west, west, southwest, south, stopped, and then repeated the movement in the opposite direction, suspended by nothing more than a few thin strips of tape.

Tara noticed the baptismal pool beneath him brimmed nearly to the top with clear water.

"We're too late," she said.

Then they heard a sound from the man, the feeble groan muted by the tape stretched across his pale face. His neatly cut hair hung loose over his forehead as he twitched.

Alex saw something on the floor in the aisle ahead and moved toward it. When he reached the object, he realized it was a photograph. He frowned, bent down, and picked it up.

The image featured two men locked in a deep, passionate kiss—with eyes closed and arms wrapped around each other in a loving embrace. As he stared at the picture, Alex realized one of the men was hanging from the scaffolding in front of them.

Another picture littered the floor ahead, and another beyond it, each spaced four rows apart like breadcrumbs. In front of the last row, nearly a dozen pictures of the two men enjoying casual dates or passionate romps decorated the navy-blue carpet.

Tara reached the stage first and stepped up to the pedestal. "Are you okay?" she asked.

He nodded, but something in his eyes betrayed the truth. He worked at the duct tape on his face, gnawing at it and twitching until it fell loose on his right cheek.

"We'll get you down," Tara said. "Just hold on."

"No," the man said. "Don't."

"What? Why not?"

Tears streamed down his face, and she noticed a frayed section of tape halfway up the line to the top of the scaffold. Any sudden movement would cause the tape to tear and he would plummet into the water. She didn't immediately see the problem with that. He could thrash around or worm his way over to the side, where he could breathe until she and Alex arrived in the back to pull him out.

She was missing something.

Alex joined her on the stage, dropping the pictures he'd collected. "There's a power cord running into the water," he said, pointing to the side of the baptismal pool where a white extension cord fed into the liquid. The wire blended with the porcelain pool so well that Alex hadn't immediately seen it.

"If he moves too much, he'll fall, and there won't be anything we can do," Alex said.

Tara followed his gaze and realized the danger. "Just stay still," she ordered the man.

He replied with the same negative response. "No." His head shook slowly from side to side. "Don't you see? I'm ruined. I have a wife, two kids. When they find out about... that," he indicated the pictures on the stage by inclining his head slightly, "I will be ruined. They won't have someone like me as their pastor. My wife and kids—" Sobs cut him off. "They'll never understand. No one will understand."

"Just relax," Alex counseled, trying to keep the man calm. His eyes remained fixed on the torn section of tape stretching taut over the pastor's body. "Don't worry about that stuff right now. We just need to get you down safely, okay?"

Tara pulled out her phone and called the police.

"Don't bother," the pastor said. "I'll be dead by the time they get here. That's the only way now."

"Whoa, take it easy," Alex warned. "Don't talk like that. We're here. You're going to be okay."

Again, the pastor rejected any comfort from them. "He told me to give you a message."

Tara's and Alex's ears pricked at the mention of Milner.

"He said that you have two days to get the final piece. And then the way of the Lord will be opened." The preacher grunted, struggling to get the words out against the strain pulling on his body. "He said you must look where the great prophet ascended and returned, drink from the mouth of holy waters to make ready the way of the Lord."

"That's good," Tara said, motioning to Alex to slip around to the side door that led into the baptismal preparation chamber. "Did he say anything else?" She didn't know much about de-escalating a situation like this, but she figured as long as the man kept talking, he'd stay alive.

Alex took a step to the right, doing his best to be subtle.

"I love my wife," the pastor said. "Always have, but my needs were... different. And I love my kids." The almost mournful words fell amid choking sobs that dripped tears into the electrified water below. "I tried to be what everyone wanted me to be. I really did."

Alex shuffled his feet quicker, hedging toward the door as he sensed time was running out.

"Tell my wife and kids I loved them," the preacher said, briefly locking eyes with Tara. The intensity, the pure desperation in his gaze, held hers and refused to let go. "Tell them. Will you do that for me?"

"You can tell them yourself," Tara pressed, stealing a glance at Alex as he neared the door to the back room. "We're going to get you down, and we can take care of all of this. Okay? No one has to know. We'll get rid of all this," she motioned to the pictures.

"It's too late for me," he blubbered. "I have sinned. And only one can forgive me for what I've done."

"Hold on," Tara said, holding out a hand. "Just take it easy. There's plenty of grace for everyone. Okay?" She'd grown up in a Christian home and often heard those words from her grandmother and her mother. They echoed throughout her life during difficult times when she struggled with her own guilt. "Just let us get you down, and we'll work it out."

"No," he said. A definitive sound in his voice signaled what would come next. "My time is done."

The preacher shook abruptly, thrashing around like a fish caught in a net. The duct tape didn't stand a chance. The frayed remains gave way, tearing easily under the burden.

"No!" Tara shouted as she watched the last thread of adhesive snap.

Alex bolted through the door, but he was too late.

Tara could only watch as the preacher plummeted into the water. When his body hit the water, nothing happened. For the briefest of moments, Tara felt a sliver of relief. That feeling vanished the second he touched the side of the pool. Instantly, his body convulsed violently. He let out an agonized scream that reverberated through the sanctuary as a ghostly howl before his head disappeared beneath the surface, muting his voice forever.

Alex appeared at the top of the pool and yanked the cord out of the water, careful to toss it aside so he wouldn't also be electrocuted.

The foul stench of burned flesh and steaming water struck his nostrils. Along with the reek rose a ghastly mist from the pool. The preacher's bound body floated prostrate in the water. It didn't move save for the gentle remnants of waves hitting the sides of the baptismal, then returning to the dead man to toss him like a macabre ship in a tiny sea.

Alex stepped back involuntarily, grimacing at the smell. He averted his eyes from the visage and looked toward the back of the sanctuary just as the doors burst open. Trent stormed in with two cops behind him.

Tara whirled around to face the newcomers. Relief poured into her body from some invisible vase and she rushed to Trent, anguish written on her face.

"What happened?" Trent asked, noting the scene in the baptismal behind the pulpit.

Tara stopped short of the man, not sure if she should hug him or just stand there. She chose the latter. "We," she huffed, "we got here in time, but the preacher... he—" her words stifled in her throat, blocked by a lump that she couldn't suppress.

"He didn't want to live," Alex finished for her, emerging from the side door. "He was too ashamed to go on." He pointed at a loose collection of photos on the carpet. "I guess he figured he would lose everything, including his kids. And he didn't want to hurt his wife."

Trent bent down and picked up one of the photos of the preacher with his lover. The former cop sighed as the uniformed men with him rushed to the baptismal pool to assess the situation.

"Milner left him here," Alex said. "I think we got here just after he disappeared. If you put out a call, you might be able to catch him. I doubt he's gotten far. We've only been here ten minutes at most."

Trent took a radio off his belt and called it in using police terminology Tara and Alex didn't understand. "Set up a five-mile net around this entire area." He finished the call and tucked the radio onto his belt again. "If he tries to get anywhere, we'll find him. My guess is he'll lie low. Lots of places to hide here, both residential and rural. He could be in a forest, maybe even the one just outside this building." Tara looked out through one of the windows at the gangly trees stretching beyond the rooftop.

"I doubt he's that close," Trent assured, "but we'll check. If he's still here, we'll get him."

Tara and Alex retreated to the back of the church as more cops began to flood the sanctuary.

They'd done all they could to save the preacher. Now they were on the clock again, as were Tommy and Sean.

Tara took out her phone as she and her husband left through the double doors in the rear of the sanctuary. She brought up Tommy's info and pressed the green dial button.

32

CAIRO

"Tara?" Tommy answered the phone after only two rings.

Through the windows on the driver's side of the rental, the city of Cairo blazed in the late night sky, a stark reminder of the ancient and modern cultures that still constantly clashed in this region.

Beyond the buildings, car traffic, and modern conveniences, the pyramids of Giza towered over the desert plains. Millennia-old temples dotted the Nile all the way down to Aswan, all documented by tourists snapping photos with their smartphones.

Tommy and Sean were just discussing the fascinating cultural contradictions when Tara called.

"Hey," she said, her voice crestfallen.

"What's the matter?"

She drew a breath and sighed, trying to find the words. "We didn't make it in time," she said.

"What? But we sent the image. And we're on our way back to Cairo with the gauntlet piece."

"Did Milner tell you what to do with it?" she asked.

"No, not yet. Have you heard from him?" Tommy replied with his own question.

"No." She paused. "We made it to the third church, the place where Milner intended to kill his next victim."

"Wait. You said intended. Why did you say intended?"

Sean cast a sidelong glance at his friend but said nothing.

"Milner was gone when we got there, but the preacher..." She faltered. "He was still there, suspended from some scaffolds over a baptismal pool. He was... alive. Badly beaten but alive."

Tommy wanted to ask what happened, but he knew Tara would tell him, and by the sound of her voice, he needed to tread lightly.

"There were pictures," she continued, "dozens and dozens of photos of the preacher with another man. He... he had a wife and kids. The shame was too much for him. We tried to tell him everything was going to be okay, but he wouldn't listen." Tara choked up and found herself unable to speak for several seconds.

"It's okay," Tommy encouraged. "Take your time."

"No, I'm fine," she lied. "He gave us a message from Milner. I memorized every word of it before the man... before he threw himself into the baptismal pool. There were wires running into the water, Tommy. He was electrocuted. He killed himself because of what Milner did, exposing his private life like that. I can still smell the burning, still hear his screams."

There were few times in Tommy's life that he hadn't known what to say, but this was one of them. Guilt riddled him, incapacitating him to the point he could form no words.

Sean flipped on the blinker and guided the SUV off the highway and down onto the exit ramp. When they reached the bottom, he steered the vehicle toward the airport, following the sign with a plane and an arrow on it.

On the phone, Tara sniffled and took a breath. "Before he died, the preacher told me this. He said to look where the great prophet ascended and returned, drink from the mouth of holy waters to make ready the way of the Lord."

Tommy pursed his lips at hearing the clue. "Okay," he said. "I'll run it by Sean and see what he thinks, but it sounds like something I remember hearing before from the life of Jesus." That didn't add up in Tommy's mind. They'd been looking for something from the line of prophets of Elijah through Jonah, not the life of Jesus.

"Tara?" Tommy said after a temporary silence. "If you and Alex need to take a few days off, we'll be okay. We can figure this out."

"No," she snapped. "We'll be fine. Milner is still out there, and no matter what Trent says about throwing out a net to snare him, I have a bad feeling that they won't find him. As long as he's out there, we have to keep looking. And it's not like you and Sean can figure any of this out on your own. You need us."

The hint of her usual humor glinted like the rays of morning sunlight on a still pond.

Tommy forced a smile. "Okay. But I'm not forcing you or anything."

"I know. We'll be fine," she insisted. "You have what you need. We're going to head back to the lab and meet Dr. Kelley. Maybe she's found something you can use."

"Thanks, Tara. I appreciate it."

He was about to hang up when she stopped him. "Tommy?"

"Yes?"

"There's one other thing."

"What's that?" He stared through the windshield with the phone against his ear. Orange-yellow streetlights passed by in a blur next to slender palm trees, one more contrast Egypt offered.

"What you're looking for. We know what it is." She paused once more. "We believe Milner is after the cloak of Elijah, the mantle his apprentice, Elisha, caught when he was taken up to heaven. Remember Milner talking about the double portion of the spirit?"

The lights flashed to life in Tommy's brain, fueled by equal parts inconceivable possibility and unfathomable dread. "Of course," he muttered. "That makes perfect sense. The references to the double portion of the spirit, the prophets, the rebukes of kings and king-doms. Milner is going to try the same thing, but he can't do it without the cloak."

"I don't think there's any record of it beyond the last few references of Elisha having possession of it. He struck the Jordan River and walked across it. There was something about a miracle where he purified a town's water supply, but other than that, there's nothing about it in the scriptures or online."

"Perhaps there's a book somewhere or a scroll," Tommy hoped.

"Could be," she admitted. "There are hundreds of thousands of old texts that haven't been cataloged. Without a lead, though, we'll never find the one containing the information we need."

Tommy knew she was right. If there were some way they could locate the prophet's mantle before Milner, they could head him off at the proverbial pass. His brain churned, but no easy answers bubbled to the surface.

"I'll have to get back to you on that, Tara," Tommy said finally. "You three keep on it. Let me know when you find anything remotely close."

"I like the way you said when and not if."

"Gotta stay positive, right?"

"I suppose so."

"We'll figure this out. We always do. For now, it looks like all of us have work to do."

"Yeah," she agreed. "Okay, chief." Her tone sounded a shade brighter. "We'll get to it. Good luck. When we learn anything, I'll give you a call."

The call ended, but Tommy didn't lower the phone for several seconds. His mind spun, already searching for a solution to Milner's riddle. He wondered if the man was concocting the clues from his imagination or if they came from another source, perhaps a stolen manuscript. He knew they weren't from the scroll he'd received from Dr. Kelley, not directly anyway. Though it was possible he'd twisted some of the information contained in that text to say what he wanted in a more taunting way.

Milner had made his mocking of Sean and Tommy's work clear. They were pawns in his game. For the moment.

Tommy finally lowered the phone and held it over his lap, still saying nothing about his conversation with Tara. He knew she and Alex were probably riddled with guilt, not to mention with the awful image of a dying man seared forever into their memories. Tommy and Sean had seen horrific things throughout their partnership, but they were different—hardened.

Still, he remembered the first time he'd seen someone die. That haunting visage stood like a grisly piece of art in the back of his mind's gallery, always there in the corner if he ever allowed his thoughts to wander.

"What did she say?" Sean asked hesitantly. He sensed something amiss while Tommy spoke with his young assistant, and now that he'd fallen silent, Sean's concern ballooned with every passing second.

Tommy sucked in a gulp of air and tried to find the words. "They... made it to the church on time. I forgot to ask which one." He only realized it after the fact.

"You don't sound like that's a good thing."

"The preacher was there, alive, but Milner had strung him up over a baptismal pool. There were pictures of him and another man, and they were engaged in... romantic activities. That's how she made it sound. Tara and Alex tried to get him down, but the pool was rigged with an extension cord, plugged in to electrocute him. The preacher had a wife and kids. He was too ashamed to go on, or maybe he thought he was going to lose everything."

Adriana's lips parted in horror, already seeing where this story was going.

Sean knew it, too.

Kimberly remained unaffected, callous as always.

"She said he threw himself into the pool, and... they watched him die. There was nothing they could do."

The conversation in the SUV dropped off a cliff and into a silent void. For minutes, no one said anything. Sean's heart contorted for Tara and Alex.

Adriana, normally strong when it came to such things having

been through so much in her own life, also felt a bomb fall straight through the pit of her stomach.

After waiting for what she believed to be an appropriate amount of time, Kimberly finally spoke. "Did she say anything about the next clue?"

Tommy nodded absently. "Yes. She did. She said we have to look where the great prophet ascended and returned, something about drinking from the mouth of holy waters to make ready the way of the Lord."

"So, that's why we didn't get a call from Milner," Adriana realized. "Or a text or email."

"He's changing the rules again," Sean said. "He's no ordinary serial killer. They play by a set of guidelines that they create, and they rarely deviate from them."

"Perhaps he's simply adapting to the way we're playing the game," Kimberly offered, the rare insight from her a pleasant surprise.

"Could be. But that doesn't make it easy for us to play."

"The great prophet," Tommy said, ignoring her for the moment. "She was talking about Elijah." He left his emotional concerns behind and resumed problem-solving mode. He could deal with the intangible stuff later. Right now, another victim was in danger.

"You're sure?" Kimberly asked.

"Tara said that Milner is after the mantle Elijah dropped from the chariot of fire as he ascended into heaven." His words gushed quicker now as adrenaline started to drip through his veins. "She didn't say how they came to that conclusion, but I trust Tara. If that's what she, Alex, and Dr. Kelley believe, then it's gospel to me."

"Absolutely. It adds up perfectly," Sean agreed. "The double portion of the spirit. That's what Elisha asked for from his master. Elijah said he'd asked for a difficult thing, but if Elisha saw him go up into the clouds, that would be the sign. The mantle falling from the sky was the second sign. Only problem is, I've never heard of anything about this artifact before. Everyone has heard of the Ark of the Covenant, the Holy Grail, things like that. This one? I don't think it's ever come up."

"Yes," Adriana cautioned, "but remember, many of the things you two have gotten into over the years revolved around objects that no one knew existed. I don't think I need to go through the list for you."

A chortle escaped Sean's lips. "Fair point."

"The real issue," Tommy continued, "is that this thing is made of fabric, natural fibers. It was created nearly three thousand years ago. I can't imagine there is anything left of it."

"Unless it was somehow sustained with supernatural power," Kimberly offered. Her comment sounded unusually hopeful, at least for her.

"True," Sean said. "And we've certainly seen our share of that through the years. It's also possible the cloak may have been preserved. Whoever went to all the trouble of hiding it would likely try to keep it safe from the elements of time. We've seen documents like that before. The Dead Sea Scrolls were housed in nothing more than clay jars. And even though they took considerable damage through the centuries, there were still enough fragments of material left to piece together most of the writings from Qumran."

His words fell away into the constant groan of the vehicle's engine and the rumble of the tires along the asphalt.

"Assuming the cloak is still intact," Adriana spoke up, "at least in some capacity, we need to figure out the last piece of the puzzle." She looked down at the satchel now resting on her lap. "Based on every-thing up to this point, even if we knew where the mantle was, we couldn't get to it without the third piece of the gauntlet. It's the key. Which means we have to go to the next location to recover the last part of it. You said Milner's riddle spoke of the place where the great prophet ascended and returned."

"That's what Tara told me," Tommy answered. "But that's the prob-lem. If we're talking about Elijah, he never returned. He was 'trans-lated' to heaven in a chariot of fire, but he didn't come back."

"Is it possible we have the wrong prophet?" Kimberly asked. "There were dozens of them, weren't there?"

"I suppose it's possible," Tommy admitted. "But based on the evidence we've seen so far, there's no reason to think it's one of the others. Most of them are considered minor prophets, with only small roles in Israel's ancient history. I doubt any of them would be referred to as great, with a few exceptions such as Daniel and Isaiah."

That's it, Sean thought. *That's the answer. Or at least part of it.* "Isaiah," he groaned.

"What was that?" Tommy asked.

"Isaiah. He's the answer. Well, part of it."

Tommy stared at his friend. "What are you talking about? Isaiah lived in a different period of Israel's history. And none of the clues we've found so far bear any reference to him."

"No," Sean insisted. "You don't understand. We're not looking for something related to Isaiah. Isaiah prophesied the coming of the Messiah. And that's not all. In Isaiah 40:3, he said there will be a voice of one calling in the wilderness to prepare the way for the Lord."

"You remember the exact verse?" Kimberly asked in surprise.

"He remembers everything," Tommy quipped.

"Some things stick with me better than others, but yeah, that one I remember. It's the prophecy of John the Baptist's appearance in the wilderness where he preached to the rocks and trees, the animals, and eventually a contingent of his own followers. His intent was never to be admired or adored. He knew that his cousin Yeshua was the one their nation had been waiting on for so long."

"Yeah, but what does that have to do with Elijah?"

"That's the trick of this riddle," Sean said, glancing in the rearview mirror at a pair of headlights trailing behind them. "You have to peel back another layer to John the Baptist's story to catch it." He allowed a crease to form on his lips. "Very clever."

"What is it?" Kimberly demanded. "Would you just tell us!"

"You're not a very patient person, are you?" He didn't wait for her to answer. "John's followers initially thought *he* was the Messiah, but he later claimed the verse from Isaiah, telling everyone that he was the voice crying out in the wilderness. After that, many people theorized that he was a reincarnation of the prophet Elijah, which is kind of funny when you think about it."

"Why's that?"

Tommy fielded that one. "Reincarnation wasn't part of their theology back then. There were peripheral schools of thought that considered it possible, but not many people believed in it."

"Right," Sean affirmed. "But because of that prophecy, they thought it could have happened."

"And where is this place?" Kimberly asked, desperate for them to get to the point. "Where the prophet ascended and returned?"

"It's in Jordan from what I remember," Tommy answered. "I don't recall the exact location, but I'm pretty sure that's it."

Sean glanced over at his friend with shock in his eyes. "You don't know where Elijah ascended to heaven and where John the Baptist preached in the wilderness?"

"Well, I'm sorry I can't remember everything, Sean. There's a lot of stuff in this noggin." He tapped on his skull. "But I do know they're the same place."

A soft glow appeared from the back of the SUV. It illuminated Adriana's face. She rolled her eyes at the two bickering in the front and finished reading the results of her internet search.

"It's called Elijah's Hill," she said. "And it's in Jordan."

"Yes!" Tommy exclaimed. "That's it. I knew it was something like that."

"Really?" Sean questioned, sarcasm dripping from his lips. "You knew the place where Elijah went to heaven was called Elijah's Hill? How did you ever put those two together?"

"You think you're funny," Tommy fired back.

"So do you." Sean turned his attention back to his wife. "Name of the town?"

"Yep. Looks like it's a pretty touristy place. Pilgrims from all over the world visit it. It's where John baptized Jesus and is considered extremely sacred. Churches were built there during the Byzantine era and throughout the centuries since then. A monastery was also constructed in the area. Most of those structures have fallen into disrepair through the years and have been rebuilt, while others were left as they were found."

"At least it's in a country friendly to the United States," Tommy said. "And not a long flight. We can stay here in Cairo for the night and be there before noon tomorrow. Even if it takes us several hours to locate the mouth of holy waters Tara mentioned, we'll still be a day ahead."

Kimberly busily tapped away on her phone, making notes of where they were heading next or perhaps informing her boss.

"That does leave us with the bigger problem, though," Sean pointed out. "If we get there and find this thing, deliver it to Milner—who hasn't told us what to do with the second one yet—that still leaves the issue of him having all three pieces. If he knows where to find the prophet's mantle, and if the garment really does possess some kind of supernatural power, we'll have to find a way to stop him."

"Or do it before," Adriana offered.

"Right."

"We can cross that bridge when we get to it," Kimberly announced. "For now, I like the plan of getting some rest and taking off for Jordan in the morning."

"Agreed," Tommy said.

Sean checked the lights in the mirror again. He knew he wasn't crazy. The headlights that had maintained a cool distance behind them during the journey now closed in with deliberate speed.

Being attuned to that sort of thing from years of training and service with Axis, Sean noticed the car ten minutes after leaving Wadi El Natrum. Considering they had just left such an important tourist destination earlier, he dusted off his paranoia with justification. Many people visited Wadi every year to take in the sights and behold the alleged burial place of two highly important religious figures.

With the headlights charging toward their SUV, though, he knew the driver was either tired of cruising along at a casual pace, or bore nefarious intentions.

A flash from the passenger side of the approaching vehicle gave Sean the answer he didn't desire. The bullet found no purchase, sailing wildly into the night, but Sean knew more would follow. And the airport was still twenty minutes away.

"Hope you guys are ready for company," he said, eyes darting from the road ahead to the mirror and back. "Because it looks like someone else wants that artifact."

33

CAIRO

The other three turned and looked back as another bright flash popped from the vehicle tailing them.

The round struck the driver's side tail light.

"I think someone wants that piece of gold we picked up," Tommy said, urgency now brimming in his throat.

"No one knows we have it, right?" Kimberly asked, pointing her question directly at Adriana. "You're certain of this, yes?"

Adriana didn't hesitate. "I wasn't seen," she said. A sprinkle of doubt hung in her words.

If Kimberly sensed it, she didn't say anything or show she'd noticed.

Adriana retraced her steps through the infiltration of the monastery, replaying every second in her mind. The only possible moment she may have been spotted was when the monks went into the reliquary to say their evening prayers. She'd stayed perfectly silent, though, remaining hidden from view under the trapdoor until the men left and returned to their dorms.

There was the issue of the one who had returned to collect something he forgot, but again, he didn't see her. *Did he?*

No, that couldn't be it. The monk would have told the others, raised an alarm, called for assistance. Anything but what actually happened.

Another gunshot thumped into the back door.

"Are you guys going to shoot back at them or just sit there talking about who they are and how they found us?" Sean asked almost in a shout.

Adriana and Kimberly sprang into action and retrieved their weapons from bags at their feet. They rolled down the windows and took aim at the vehicle behind them as another bright flash briefly illuminated the gunman and his ride.

The truck following them turned out to be an old Isuzu Trooper, probably from the early 1990s. The top-heavy SUV swerved dramatically to the left and back to the right as Adriana took aim and squeezed off three shots.

Sean's task of watching the road ahead while dodging bullets grew tougher when a huge work van approached ahead.

Kimberly replied to the gunman's volley with a series of shots of her own that forced the enemy driver to apply the brakes and regroup.

The work van roared by on the other side of the road, giving Sean two empty lanes to use for at least another mile. He doubted that would last long, though, and knew this fight needed to end quickly.

The question kept coming: *Who were these guys?* Merely from the method of their attack, Sean knew they didn't have much training. Anyone with half a brain would have simply driven up behind him, turned on a blinker as if to pass, and when the front quarter panel of the trailing car was even with the rear of the lead car, a subtle turn would send the lead car into a spin. And in the lumbering SUV rental, Sean realized that spin could quickly turn into a roll.

Sean supposed they were lucky in that regard. But it had more to do with the ineptitude of the gunmen.

He'd heard of bandits in touristy areas of Egypt, places where millions of people visited every year. His initial thought wasn't one of concern. Instead, he regarded it as spin from the media. No matter what the news reported on any given day, their mission always remained the same: use fear to control.

Unfortunately, it appeared the media outlets weren't fibbing about the trouble with bandits around the outskirts of Cairo—if Wadi El Natrun could be called the outskirts.

The location actually made for the perfect target, Sean realized too late. The remote town and monastery were situated just far enough away that while many people did indeed visit on pilgrimages, it wasn't the tourist hot spot that some of the other locations were, such as the pyramids of Giza and the many temples lining the Nile.

Kimberly ducked back into the vehicle to take cover. Her move came a split second before the gunman in the tailing SUV fired four more rounds, the shots coming one after the other from a semiautomatic submachine gun. That was another clue in Sean's mind. If these guys were terrorists, they'd have fully automatic weapons, more than likely.

"Hold on back there!" Sean shouted over the groan of the engine and the sound of the wind crashing through the back windows.

Tommy grabbed onto the famously named bar hanging over the window and squeezed it tight. He felt utterly useless at the moment, but Kimberly took up space in the lane he could use to fire back at the assailants.

"I'm going to do something a little crazy," Sean continued.

"Wait," Tommy said. "What kind of crazy?"

Sean twitched his head to the side and clicked his tongue. "I only know one speed, buddy."

"Oh, no. Sean? What are you doing?"

"Grab your gun," Sean said, ignoring the question.

"I thought you said to hold on." Tommy wore the concern of a kid with his hand stuck in the cookie jar, and the only way to get it out was to let go of the cookie.

"You'll know what to do. Just be ready. You, too, Kimberly."

Kimberly reached up and clutched the handle over her window. Uncertain of what Sean was about to do, she copied her backseat partner and then looked over at Adriana.

"What is he going to try?"

Adriana smirked wickedly. "It's probably best none of us know."

"Hold on!" Sean warned again.

He jerked the wheel to the left and into the other lane. Sean stomped his foot on the brakes. The trailing car tried to fall in line behind the Toyota, but as soon as they lurched over and slowed, Sean sped up, hammering the gas pedal. The Isuzu wobbled, still trying to keep up, but they had lost momentum and Sean steered back into the right lane.

They fell farther behind, and it appeared Sean's plan was to outrun them. Instead, he gradually let his foot off the accelerator, allowing the Isuzu to catch up.

Ahead, in the distance, airplanes coasted in toward the airport while others launched steeply into the dark night sky, visible mostly due to the blinking lights on the wingtips.

Sean briefly considered the notion of outrunning the attackers, but when they reached the airport, the men wouldn't stop, or he doubted they would. Maybe the sight of airport security would scare them off. That wouldn't help Sean's case. Security would perceive him as a threat the same as they would the men in the Isuzu.

"Here we go!" Sean shouted over the road noise. He saw the flashes in the mirrors again. He momentarily thought he heard a bullet whiz by, probably his adrenaline-fueled imagination.

Sean wasn't going to give the amateur gunman another chance. He slammed on the brakes. The tires screamed against the asphalt, and for a second, Sean felt the lumbering SUV lose its grip and start to enter a twisting slide. He knew exactly how to deal with that, though, and it played perfectly into his plan. Letting off the brakes, he tapped the gas pedal and regained control just as the approaching Isuzu zoomed toward them.

Sean turned the wheel left again and guided the Toyota into the left lane at the last second before the Isuzu crashed into their tail. The enemy caught up immediately and couldn't slow down fast enough to stay behind.

"Now!" Sean ordered.

Tommy and Kimberly both gripped the overhead handles with their right hands while raising their weapons with their left. They squeezed the triggers over and over, unloading the contents of their magazines into the Isuzu's broad side. Tommy took aim at the back tire and struck true with one shot. The Isuzu's driver ducked down to avoid being hit, but one of Kimberly's rounds pierced the door and drilled through his leg, stopping catastrophically when it hit solid femur. The tire burst almost simultaneously with the round in the driver's leg, and the man instinctively let off the gas, howling in pain. His hands involuntarily yanked the steering wheel to the right.

The gunman, with no angle to fire back across his driver, could only hold on as the Isuzu dipped onto its left side and entered a horrific roll.

Sean jammed the gas pedal to the floor and the Toyota surged forward. The front-left corner of the crashing enemy vehicle missed his back-right bumper by mere inches.

Tommy turned around and watched the destruction unfold. The Isuzu Trooper's front edge caught the asphalt and bit hard, causing the vehicle to go from a roll to an all-out cartwheel.

It flipped over and onto its roof and slid to a stop with sparks shooting out behind it.

Tommy eased back into his seat and took a deep breath. Kimberly continued looking through the back window at the wreck.

"Who were those guys?" she wondered before twisting around in her seat and facing forward once more.

"Bandits," Sean said. "I doubt they knew about the relic we have with us. They've been following us since we left Wadi El Natrun, but I didn't notice them until we were on the road."

"So how can you rule them out as knowing about the gauntlet piece?"

"Because one, my wife is the best thief in the world. She doesn't get caught."

Adriana faced the other woman and shook her head. "That's true."

"And two?" Kimberly asked defiantly after a skeptical glare at Adriana.

"They're monks," Sean said. "Car chases with guns isn't their style. And I seriously doubt they were sent by Milner. Even with his extensive connections around the world, it wouldn't make sense for him to try to kill or rob us now. Since we haven't heard back from him, that must mean he wants us to keep the artifact for now. For how long, I have no idea."

"Or maybe," Tommy interjected, "he left in a hurry from the church. Assuming Milner went to the church to murder the preacher, he would have left in a hurry—probably when Alex and Tara showed up. If that's the case, maybe we just need to wait. He'll be on the run now, trying to get clear of the net Trent's setting up. With cops breathing down his neck and the circle around him tightening, it's a good bet Milner is keeping a low profile. For now."

"True," Sean agreed.

He continued to check the rearview mirror for any signs of further trouble for the rest of the drive to the airport.

No more bandits appeared on the road behind them.

Sean pulled the damaged SUV into a parking spot at the rental place.

"I thought we were going to get a room for the night," Kimberly protested.

"Not now. I don't want to hang around here any longer than we have to."

"Okay. So, where are we going?"

"We're going to Jordan," Sean said plainly. "Tommy, call the pilot and see how soon he can get us to Amman. Jordan is friendly to us, but there may still be some additional hoops we have to jump through. If we can't get there tonight, Tel-Aviv isn't far away."

"Israel?"

"Yes, Kimberly. Israel. It's the next best place if we can't land in Jordan tonight, though I don't think that will be an issue. Always good to have a contingency plan, though, right?"

She muttered something vaguely agreeable.

He didn't care. Sean was already getting out of the busted SUV.

Tommy and the others exited the vehicle, hefting their gear bags over shoulders to make their way toward the hangar. Tommy looked at the front bumper and then walked around to check the rest of the SUV. The damage was worse than he thought.

A mangled side mirror hung from a door. Part of the front bumper was bent and a dark smear of paint marked it. Then he examined the back where three bullet holes dotted the rear door. A shattered taillight accompanied the puncture wounds in the metal.

He stood there for nearly a minute, staring in disbelief at the battered vehicle. Sean sidled up next to him and nodded. He clicked his tongue and slapped his friend on the shoulder. "Yeah," Sean said, "there's no way you're getting your deposit back."

Tommy turned and gazed flatly at Sean. "Thanks for that."

"Well, I'm going to head to the plane. Good luck with this. Oh, and don't forget to call the pilot. Thanks, pumpkin."

Sean shook his friend with a tight grip and then started walking away with Adriana and Kimberly in tow.

"So, I guess I'll just pay for the damage then?" he shouted at them.

"Your company," Sean replied without looking back.

Tommy nodded absently, his lips pressing together. "Yep. That it is."

34

ATLANTA

T ara and Alex sat in their chairs in front of cluttered workstations festooned with tools for measuring, loose wires, white gloves, sheets of plastic, and an assortment of vials, each filled to the brim with a different color liquid.

They hadn't spoken since arriving back at the lab, and Dr. Kelley chose not to pry, having been told what had happened over the phone.

When thirty minutes had passed, Alex finally stood up and walked over to the water cooler in the corner. He plucked a cone cup from the sleeve and filled it halfway, drained the contents, then refilled it.

"You thirsty?" he ventured.

"No, thank you," Tara replied.

He finished the second drink and dropped the empty cone into the blue recycling bin.

Dr. Kelley sat with her elbows on her knees, fingers steepled in front of her with the tips brushing against her lips. Her eyes bore a look of deep concern for both of the young researchers. Her eyes remained fixed on Tara as the younger woman stared at the desk in front of her, the only movement an occasional blink.

"It sounds like there's nothing you could have done," Kelley offered.

"Nope," Tara said. "The man wanted to go. Actually, he wanted to be who he was. But he couldn't. The rules he played by wouldn't allow that. So he had to pretend. And because he couldn't be himself, he chose to die."

"I'm sorry."

"Don't be. I understand his thinking, why he thought he couldn't go on. But I'm angry. Not because he made me watch him die in such a horrific way. Sure, that image will be forever burned into my memory—there isn't enough tequila in all of Mexico to wash that away. I'm angry because he left behind a family that will never understand what happened or why."

"You're mad at the preacher," Kelley realized.

"Yes, I'm mad at the preacher," Tara echoed as Alex walked softly back to his seat nearby and lowered himself into it. "It's a selfish thing to do. He could have told his family the truth. He could have chosen to live. Sure, he probably would have lost his position as a pastor, but he could do something else for a living. Or he could have started a new church. Maybe he wouldn't even have had to. People are more forgiving, less judgmental these days."

"Some are," Alex countered.

"True. And some aren't. But my point remains: He didn't have to choose to die. He could have dealt with the consequences. Moved on. At least his kids would have a father, even if he wasn't who they always thought he was. His wife would be hurt, but she could move on, too. In time, things can always work out. Now," she paused, reflecting, "they never can. Those kids have to face life without their father in it."

"You feel it the most for them, don't you?" Kelley said.

Tara nodded. A tear swelled in her right eye. It breached the seal and rolled down her cheek, leaving a trail of glistening moisture in its wake.

Kelley stood up and stepped over to her. She put her arm around Tara's shoulders and squeezed her tight. "Tara, there is nothing you could have done about that. You know it and I know it. While it's okay to be angry about the pastor's decision, it's not okay to beat yourself up over it. And there is still another innocent person out there we can save. Don't forget that. We still have a chance to stop Milner before he can kill again."

Tara listened with grim determination, her focus firmly on a stew of guilt and rage simmering in her mind. She knew Dr. Kelley was right. Milner would keep killing until he got what he wanted. And just like the case with the Presbyterian minister, getting to the target in time might not make a difference. Unless they worked faster.

She slapped her hands on her knees and wiped the tears from her cheeks. The best way to help the family of the man who had just ended his own life was to stop the man who had put everything in motion.

Since they hadn't heard anything from Trent yet, Tara took that to mean the cops hadn't located the killer, and she also knew it was probably best to assume they wouldn't. Milner had evaded authorities since escaping from Morrowfield, there was no way he would let himself get caught. This wasn't a person with delusions of grandeur. Fame was not Milner's goal.

"Okay," Tara said. "What do we have to go on?"

Kelley let out a humph. "Good question. Not much from my end. I'm afraid most of what I have to offer on the killer has been used up. This well has run dry."

"Maybe not." Tara sat up straight, stiffening her spine so that it cracked. She let out a relieved sigh. "Milner is working with someone."

"More like lots of someones," Alex chimed.

"Right. But he couldn't have coordinated all of this from behind bars in Morrowfield. It's too elaborate. The planning portion of it, sure. He could have handled that. But the execution?"

"Not a chance," Kelley finished. "But we already know he has an extensive network around the world."

"Maybe," Tara hedged. "Or it might not be as formidable as we thought. A small collection of people in the right positions could make it appear as though he had a veritable army."

"So, what are we trying to do again?" Alex asked.

Tara grinned at him and proceeded. "Two things. One, I want to know if Milner has any close contacts. I'm talking cousins, parents—okay, scratch that one—nieces, nephews, aunts, or uncles. Does he have a longtime friend who may have been willing to risk everything by busting him out of Morrowfield? Or was it simply hired help; people who had become members of his cult?"

"Probably the latter," Kelley said, "but it's worth a check."

"And two?" Alex asked.

"We have to locate the next victim before Milner can get to them."

"Oh," he said with a nod. He looked down at the floor then back up to meet Tara's gaze. "How are we going to do that?"

She didn't have a clear answer, but the direction in her head was as clear as a Swarovski crystal. "It's time for us to do some old-fashioned detective work. We need to make some calls. Dig up more information from Milner's trial. Find the lawyers who were involved. This guy is not a ghost. He has a past, a long-lost relative somewhere or at least people he met along the way."

"We already learned he's lived a sheltered life, being schooled at home for much of his youth, and only getting out later when he was a young man." Alex's point struck a valid chord.

"True," Tara half agreed, "which is all the more reason we need to keep looking. Someone who grew up in such a sheltered, skewed home environment would have trouble recruiting people to his cause."

"Which would narrow down candidates," Kelley said.

"Yes. Their profile would most likely be people who were down on their luck, social outcasts, or maybe those burned by religion."

"That's still a huge population," Alex countered. "We're talking tens of millions of people, potentially. Maybe more."

"All the more reason we need to dig in and find any connections he may have had during his time between the deaths of his parents and his killing spree in Florida. And if there's anything we can find from Morrowfield we haven't already seen, Dr. Kelley, now would be the time to look for it. Did he have any visitors? Any correspondence? Even inmates like Milner are given certain rights or privileges. We need to know anyone who ever so much as sent him a card or came by to ask the director of the facility how he was doing. Even if we have to check phone records, we need to do it."

Tara finished and swiveled around to face her computer monitor. She cracked her knuckles and then started typing. The other two didn't move for several seconds. Tara realized they were still sitting there and whirled around again. "Now would be good."

A sheepish grin swept over Alex's face.

Kelley simply looked stunned, but impressed.

"Okay, then," she said. "I don't know if I can do all of that, but I'll certainly try. Maybe I have a contact who can get me some of that information." She spun around and pulled up to one of the other computers at a workstation across from Tara's and Alex's.

Alex sat there briefly, thinking about what he should do next. Then he thought about what his wife said about the rights of the patients at Morrowfield. *Patients at Morrowfield,* he thought. *I wonder if there are any who were released who may have known Milner?*

Alex decided that rabbit hole was one worth diving into. He rolled up to his computer and began the search.

They worked for hours, poring over documents from all over the world. Calls to Wyoming yielded few results, though one of Kelley's contacts relayed a promising lead, which was more than they expected at this point.

"Trent sent us the pictures," Tara said, her voice slicing the silence like one of those infomercial knives that cut through metal. She didn't sound excited, probably because she knew what the images would show: the dead pastor with his lover, the cause of the man's rash decision to end his life via electrocution.

She clicked on the email and opened the first image of six. From what she'd seen, most of the pictures that littered the floor of the church portrayed the same scenes over and over again, copies of the original six photos.

Tara opened the rest and fought off the sense of nausea rising in her gut. She kept telling herself there was nothing she could have done, but that didn't change the fact of what the preacher in the pictures had done earlier that day.

She blinked hard and clicked the rest of the images. The candid photos portrayed them both as happy and carefree, a reflection of the way the young minister yearned to live but felt he could not.

Alex rolled over to her and put his arm around her shoulders as he gazed at the images on the screen. In most of them, the men's faces were only partially visible. Only two made it easy to identify both men in the image.

"Who is the other guy in this picture?" Alex asked. "He looks Middle Eastern."

"He does, doesn't he?" Tara agreed, only now realizing the man's ethnicity. "I wonder if Trent has found him yet."

Dr. Kelley's phone rang at her desk several feet away. She picked it up, checked the caller ID, and answered. "This is Dr. Kelley."

Tara and Alex looked over at her with desperate hope brimming in their eyes.

Kelley listened to the other person on the line, occasionally saying things like "I see" and "Oh, dear." When the conversation reached its conclusion, she thanked the person for the information and then spun around, still clutching her phone.

Her eyes told of an extreme sense of fear, the whites showing bright against the fluorescent lighting. "Um, so we have a bit of a problem."

"What do you mean? We have, like, five problems right now." Tara said.

"No, no. I don't think you understand. Sean and Tommy are in grave danger. You need to call them right now." Her voice trembled as the words gushed from her lips.

"What's the matter?" Alex pressed, standing up.

"Milner has a daughter." Kelley didn't wait to build up the drama, knowing that time was critical. "It's Kimberly Henderson. Her real name is Kimberly Milner. She played us all. She's the one who set up the escape plan for her father. She planned everything."

"Wait, are you sure?"

Kelley nodded sternly. "I just got off the phone with one of Morrowfield's assistant administrators. They weren't in the building when the escape happened, out sick for the day. He said Milner's records indicated a daughter, but the admin never thought it to be of any consequence."

"How is it that we missed that before?" Tara wondered while Alex took out his phone and started dialing Tommy's number.

"I don't know," Kelley admitted.

The call went straight to Tommy's voice mail, and Alex pressed the number one on his screen. "Hey, Tommy, it's Alex. You need to call me back. Kimberly is Milner's daughter. We just found out. You guys need to get out of there, wherever there is. It's a trap. You hear me? It's a trap."

He ended the call and rapidly typed out a quick text message relaying the same dire news to both Tommy and Sean, then called the latter's number. Just as Tommy's phone went to voice mail, Sean's did, too.

"Any luck?" Tara asked, looking up at him, despondent.

He shook his head and proceeded to leave the same message for Sean. "They may be out of range for their phones," Alex guessed. "Those guys used to have satellite phones. I wish they had them right now."

"Or maybe they're not out of range and they're already in trouble," Tara offered reluctantly.

"Let's hope that isn't the case. I'll keep trying. You call Trent and see if you can find out who the guy is in the picture with the preacher."

"You thinking something?" Tara asked.

"It's a long shot, but without any other viable clue as to who the next victim might be, it's possible we've already seen him. And he's in those pictures."

35

JORDAN

Sean stepped off the airplane and onto the tarmac at the airport in Amman, twenty-five miles south of downtown. The rolling white roof and matching support structure of the Queen Alia International Airport—named for the late Queen Alia of Jordan who died in an accident in the late 1970s—gleamed in the bright morning sun behind a scattering of jets parked at the only terminal.

A man in a black suit and tie stood next to a concrete-gray Range Rover. With his hands folded in front of his waist and with sunglasses covering his eyes, the Jordanian looked like the poster child for anyone wanting to sign up for the king's secret service.

Sean stalked toward the man with a broad grin on his face. The sight of his friend in a suit struck him both as comical and relieving. The stress of the last several days wore on Sean. Even though Tommy and Adriana shared the load, he wondered if it ground them down the same way it did him.

Tommy, he felt certain, was every bit as tired and mentally frayed.

Adriana, however, never cracked. Her façade always remained the same no matter how difficult things got. He'd seen her vulnerable side before, though it was elusive.

Sean stuck his hand out when he neared the man at the SUV. "Zaid, good to see you, my friend."

The Jordanian stood an inch taller than Sean and with slightly broader shoulders. He looked like a professional linebacker for an American football team, and the car behind him didn't soften that impression.

Zaid took the proffered hand and shook it with the same hardened grip Sean remembered.

The two had worked together on a mission when Sean was with Axis. While he didn't miss his days at the elite, ultra-covert agency, he did miss some of the people he met along the way. Zaid was one of them.

"Good to see you again as well, Sean. It's been too long."

"And it's good to hear you with your native accent," Sean joked. "There were a few times I was convinced you were Russian on that one job."

Zaid stuck out his right arm and pulled back the sleeve of his jacket. "Not with this tan," he said, showing off the dark bronze arms.

"Sorry you had to wait," Sean said, "we got held up in Egypt. Sat there for several hours waiting to be cleared to come here. I wouldn't have thought this airport was so busy."

"It's not, but you're flying a private jet. Things must be cleared first." He turned to Tommy and tilted his head forward. "This must be your friend Tommy." Zaid extended the hand again and shook it.

"Thanks for taking the time to help us out," Tommy said. "Sean told me you two worked together when you were with Axis."

Zaid's right eyebrow perked up and he cast a scathing glance at his old friend. "Did you give him classified information?"

"Hey," Sean replied, putting his hands out wide to show his innocence, "not Jordanian classified information."

Zaid's firm expression softened, and then he laughed again. "You always could find the gray area, Sean."

Tommy, who appeared a touch uncertain at the accusation, relaxed and let go of Zaid's hand.

The two women stood close, just off Sean's right shoulder, and for a second he'd forgotten to introduce them. This seemed to be both a bad habit and a cause for more than one bit of chastising from his wife.

"This is Adriana Villa, my wife," Sean said, motioning to her.

He took her hand graciously and bowed his head. "A pleasure." He cast a sidelong glance at his friend. "Glad to see you lowered your standards for my friend."

Sean put on a mock smug grin and nodded. "You and me both, brother."

Zaid winked at his friend and then turned to Kimberly. "I'm Zaid...." He waited for her to say her name, but Tommy broke in.

"This is Kimberly Henderson. She's with the FBI."

"Forgive me for saying so, Agent Henderson, but this sort of thing seems a little outside your jurisdiction."

"I'm tracking down a lead," she explained.

The big Jordanian still appeared curious as he released her hand. "Oh?"

"It's off the books," she continued. "My boss knows I'm here, but it's only because we're leaving no stone unturned." She twisted her head to face Sean. "I would have thought you'd have told him about the investigation." Her insistent tone made things awkward.

He returned his attention to Zaid and laughed uncomfortably.

"Investigation?" Zaid prodded, his deep voice teetering on the edge of scary and playful.

Sean sighed. "We're trying to stop a serial killer who's running around Atlanta, killing religious leaders. That's why we're here."

"Why would something like that in Atlanta bring you here?" He put out his hands as if showing off the entire country.

"Because," Tommy answered first, "he wants an artifact. Said if we bring him that artifact—three, actually—the killing will stop."

"Yes, but something worse will begin," Adriana mumbled.

"Worse?" Zaid sounded skeptical.

"We think the killer is after a holy relic," Sean said. "The cloak of Elijah the prophet."

A jet revved its engines across the airfield and then accelerated toward the end of the runway. Halfway through its run, the nose tilted up and the wheels delicately let go of the tarmac. Within seconds, the aircraft climbed at a steep angle, soaring into the sky.

Zaid watched the plane take off and then returned to the conversation. "The cloak of Elijah? I have to say, I've heard of some of the treasures you boys go looking for, but that's one I didn't know was around."

"You have heard of Elijah, right?" Kimberly asked.

"Of course," he answered, putting his hand over his heart. "He was a prophet of God, one of the greatest." He kept his head aimed at her, but his eyes shifted to Sean. "You think you will find this cloak in Jordan?"

"Not the cloak," Sean said. "Something that will lead to it."

"Something?"

"I'll explain more on the way. You want me to drive?"

Zaid inclined his head and laughed a booming laugh. Almost as suddenly as it began, the hilarity ended, and he fired lasers from his eyes at Sean. "No. You're not driving my SUV."

The four visitors loaded into the vehicle with Sean in the front and the others in the back.

Zaid drove through the security gate, showing his identification and something else along with it, perhaps an old government-issued card from his days in the service.

"Looks like the fashion business has been good to you, my friend," Sean said, visibly appreciating the charcoal-leather interior with the brushed steel accents.

The driver cocked his head at an angle and snickered. "Wealthy people love exotic. Everyone does, I think." He stole a look at Sean and motioned with his eyes toward Sean's wife.

"Easy," Sean nudged.

Zaid let out an abrupt laugh. "I'm kidding."

"No, you aren't." Sean laughed, too.

"That's true. Still, my point remains. People like exotic things."

"Wealthy people just pay more for them."

The driver's teeth gleamed in the sun. "Precisely, my friend."

Tommy leaned forward from the middle seat in the back, which made no sense since he was the biggest of the three, but he'd been courteous and offered Adriana and Kimberly window seats. Still, Sean thought the sight hilarious.

"So, you're in the fashion industry?" Tommy asked, shifting on the edge of his seat.

"He's a clothier," Sean answered for Zaid. "Well, he owns a clothier now."

"A clothier? Really?" Tommy thought for certain his friend was playing him for gullible.

"It's true," Zaid confirmed.

"Zaid runs one of the largest clothing companies based in Jordan. Textiles and clothing are a major export here. He's always had a penchant for designing clothes, so it just made sense."

Tommy's eyebrows dropped so low they nearly covered his face. His unbelieving gaze shifted from Sean to Zaid and back again. "This guy? Is a fashion designer?"

Zaid's jovial grin evaporated and the killer from the past returned with an iron jaw. "Yes. Is that a problem?"

Tommy couldn't shake his head fast enough. "Nope, no, sir. Not a problem. I just... well, it's interesting with your background and all."

"What background?" Sean joked.

Then the front erupted in laughter again.

Kimberly rolled her eyes and looked out the window, while Adriana's eyes remained on her phone as she read an email from a contact in Prague—a lead to a piece of art that was taken by the Nazis in World War II and never heard of since.

"That's a good one," Zaid bellowed, pointing a free finger at Sean. "Always with the wit."

Sean allowed himself to catch his breath when the laughing slowed. "Yeah, well, it gets me into trouble now and then."

Zaid's head bobbed up and down. "Yes, I can see that." He giggled at his own comment, which was funny in its own right.

"But yes, Tommy," Sean said, finally collecting himself. "Zaid is a clothier, a designer, a seller of fine clothes. Whatever you want to call it."

"Only these days, I am in meetings more than I would like. Not enough time for the work I love."

"Why not hand over some of the administrative duties?" Tommy asked, having himself loathed certain aspects of running the IAA.

"Ah, it's my company," Zaid said. "It's a hard thing to let your baby go."

"Every baby grows up," Sean mused. "Sooner or later, you have to let them go for their own good."

He looked out the window, thoughtfully watching the condensed city buildings pass.

Amman rested on the undulated hills near the Ajlun Mountains, the first settlements dating to the Chalcolithic Age between 4,000 and 3,000 BC. Eventually, they became the Ammonite kingdom and were invaded by King David of Israel in the controversial battle where he sent one of his friends and best soldiers, Uriah, to the front lines where he was killed along the wall.

Later in Amman's history, Ptolemy II Philadelphus successfully sacked the city in the third century BC and even named it after himself. The name *Philadelphia* stuck until the Byzantine Era. Down through the centuries, Amman passed from the Greeks to Romans, Ottomans to Palestinians. All throughout, the city absorbed the cultures of its conquerors. A remarkably preserved Roman amphitheater sits at the base of a hill underneath tightly packed dwellings, the site of an untold number of multicultural performances through the centuries.

Sean studied some of the city's history as a refresher, though it didn't take much for him to remember. He'd spent time here, time that didn't provide much in the way of sightseeing, but still enough for him to get a feel for the rich and diverse history of this ancient place.

Zaid drove through the outskirts of the city on the highway, and soon the densely populated city surrendered to hilly countryside.

No one said anything for five minutes. Sean's comment sucked the humor out of the vehicle and replaced it with a burst of somber philosophy.

"Perhaps you are right," Zaid said. "Sooner or later, every head of a company takes a step back, often to work with a different facet of the organization."

"Yep," Sean said, his thoughts wandering far from the conversation to another one, another dozen he'd had with his wife over the last year. "That's right."

He continued to watch the rolling plains and foothills in the countryside. Mountains towered into the sky on either side, bordering wide valleys and always seeming to remain in the distance no matter which direction the car turned.

The Range Rover topped the crest of a rise, and Zaid slowed down. He turned on the blinker and pulled off the road next to a sign pointing the way to a sparse collection of ruins along the side of the hill. Other wooden structures popped up among the hills.

"Some of those are the old churches from long ago," Zaid said, motioning to the wooden buildings. "There's also a new Greek Orthodox Church over there," he added, pointing to a golden-domed church with walls the color of sand.

Zaid found an open parking space next to a red compact car and got out of the SUV, opening the back door for Adriana.

"*Gracias*," she said in her native tongue.

"*De nada*," Zaid said with a perfect accent.

Tommy didn't receive the same cordial treatment, though Zaid kept the door open long enough for Tommy to exit. Zaid slammed the door shut and nodded toward the area where the group could begin their investigation.

They walked down to the wooden shelter, following the signs along the way. The open structure had no walls and looked more like a picnic pavilion than a church. Some of the authentic ancient ruins dotted the landscape in various places, some dating back thousands of years. All told, more than twenty churches, prayer halls, and baptismal pools occupied the property under the shadow of Elijah's Hill, a small rise on the eastern side of the area.

While all were intriguing, the visitors kept their focus on one thing: finding the spring that fed into the Wadi al-Kharrar, a tributary of the Jordan River.

Many historians concluded that Jesus' baptism would have been here, on the Jordanian side of the river, and in a creek rather than the river proper since it would have been cleaner due to the fresh spring water. The Jordan River was also prone to flooding in the days of John the Baptist, so it's likely he would have chosen a tributary for his ministry rather than the main river.

The group stopped by a huge pool. The stone blocks lining the walls opened on one end to an elaborately constructed canal. The pool was bone dry, the water source long-since dried up, but the construction was impressive.

Sean scanned the area and noted the lush vegetation growing toward the river—a telling sign of water nearby.

"Over there," he said, pointing at the greenery. "Our best bet to find the spring should be in that area."

"So," Zaid said as the group marched down a narrow, rocky trail toward the creek, "you're here to find something in the spring?"

"We think a clue may have been left here a long time ago," Sean answered. "At the mouth of the water source."

"And who left this clue?"

"That is a good question. Actually, I haven't really thought about that. Thanks. Now I'm curious."

Zaid chuckled as he worked his way past a particularly large shrub that jutted out into the trail. "You came all the way to Jordan to find an artifact, and you don't know who it belonged to or who put it there? Sounds like a well-thought-out plan."

"When you say it like that," Sean agreed.

"Most of what we do involves many unknowns," Tommy said, jumping into the conversation. "Usually, we find something first and then figure out who it belonged to after the fact. That's how it works in archaeology and anthropology. It's how we learn."

"Interesting," Zaid said. "I don't know if I would enjoy that kind of work. I like to have a plan."

They rounded a bend in the path and arrived at a spot ripe with green reeds, bushes, and small trees layered with other lush foliage.

Sean took a deep breath of the dry air, and the scent of sage filled his senses. He looked around for a moment, taking in the surroundings, and noted the stark contrast between the desert earth that dominated most of the area, and the vibrant life of the creek shore.

Adriana stepped ahead of the others and walked over to the narrow stream flowing toward the river. She bent down and dipped her hand into it, letting the cool, pure water wash over her skin.

She took a moment to appreciate the gravity of where she stood; and the liquid touching her fingers and palm. The same water source had touched the skin of Jesus over two thousand years ago when John the Baptist officially kicked off Jesus' ministry.

"Looks like it flows from that direction," Tommy noted, pointing upstream through thick stands of reeds and shrubbery. He looked around for any signs of an authority figure, like a park ranger, but saw no one. "I don't think we're supposed to get off the trails here, but it's only illegal if you get caught. Right?"

"Since when are you a rule breaker?" Sean asked. He turned to Kimberly, who had been silent since getting out of the SUV. "This guy almost always goes by the book."

She didn't respond at first, instead only offered an impatient, almost nervous expression. "Well," she began after a few seconds, "like he said, if there's no one here to catch us, what's the problem?"

"I like the way you think," Sean replied. "If the head of the stream is up that way, then that's where we need to go."

He took the lead and stepped off the path and into the underbrush, maneuvering carefully through the scraggly branches and leaves that scratched and rubbed against his bare forearms.

Sean felt himself overwhelmed by the feeling of being in a sacred place, much more than he had when they were in the reliquary in Egypt. That place had born much of the same kind of sensation, but this... this was something else.

Jesus himself had set foot on this ground, perhaps on the very dirt where Sean's shoes pressed into the earth. The rocks may have been brushed by the skin of Jesus and his cousin John, two of the most important figures in all of history.

As an historian, Sean had always felt an overwhelming sense of reverence whenever he was in a place that had seen so much in centuries past. Even in Washington, standing before the Capitol, he could feel the presence of long-ago events, hear the voices, see the people, and take in the wonder of being somewhere that played host to something special.

This moment overshadowed anything Sean had ever experienced before. It humbled him, and more than once Sean considered dropping to his knees and taking off his shoes as had been done so often in Biblical times.

He pulled aside a gangly tree branch and held it back so his wife could safely pass by without getting smacked in the face, then she did the same for Tommy, who repeated the process for Zaid and Kimberly.

Sean pressed on, moving up a slight rise toward an even denser patch of bushes and tall grass. He wasn't a religious person, one who attended church often, but he felt a spiritual connection to the Almighty, and that sense reached its zenith here, in this place where the entire Christian religion truly began.

He'd been to Jerusalem and recalled feeling the same thing on each occasion there, but the noises of the city, the distractions all around, and the mere feel of tourism took away some reverence, if only by a fraction.

Here, there was nothing but wilderness, as so many of the great masters of the past preferred. Elijah, Elisha, Moses, and many more, plus several from other religions, knew that to achieve a true spiritual connection, they had to remove themselves from the distractions of the world and place themselves firmly where their focus would not stray.

There'd been times when Sean's conscience tore at him, casting guilt and blame on his soul for the things he'd done in the past. He'd always justified it as being a sword for the innocent, a righteous warrior in a world of evil.

Here, though, he felt like nothing more than a desperate sinner, eager to dispel his shame by hiding behind falsehoods.

He shook it off and refocused his mind on the task at hand. Somewhere in the States, someone was the target of a mass murderer, and Sean had the chance to stop him. Though what he would do with the gauntlet once they found it was still a mystery, as was the purpose meant for the one they had in their possession.

Since leaving the path, no one in the group had said a word, allowing the gentle desert breeze and the few birds in the area to fill the air with sounds of nature.

Less than five minutes into their off-trail journey, Sean stopped.

Adriana nearly bumped into him but caught herself short and looked straight ahead, following Sean's gaze.

The stream flowed past them, a few feet away, crawling its way downstream. The crystal-clear water trickled along, flashing fragments of sunlight at the visitors who stood next to it.

"Looks like we're not the only ones who came to see this spot," Sean whispered. He pointed to a hooded figure next to a hole in the ground where water poured out into the shallow creek bed. The man's back was to the group, and the deep auburn shawl on his head draped down over his shoulders, concealing his face. His white tunic and beige, linen pants gave away his local origins, or perhaps from nearby Israel.

"Should we wait until he leaves?" Tommy asked, leaning over Adriana's shoulder.

Just then, the man stood up and bowed his head low in a goodbye gesture.

"Looks like he's done," Sean said and took a step toward the mouth of the spring. He noted the haphazardly arranged stones on the ground next to the stream, a couple caked in dirt and mud. One flat stone displayed a yellowish hue, not like gold but certainly different than any of the others around it.

A horrible realization swelled in Sean's mind as he neared the spring's mouth. Someone had tampered with the stones.

"You needn't come any farther," the man in the hood said. "I'd say you've come quite far enough, actually."

He spoke English. Perfect English with a hint of a Southern drawl.

"I'm sorry?" Sean offered. "Is everything okay?"

"Oh, yes," the man said. "Everything is as it should be."

He turned to face the newcomers and pulled back the shawl, revealing his identity.

Sean instantly reached for the gun concealed beneath his belt. Zaid did the same.

"I wouldn't do that if I were you," Milner said. He pointed with a bony finger toward the back of the procession, where Kimberly stood holding a Glock at arm's length, the sights squarely at the base of Zaid's neck.

Sean froze in place, looking back at the woman who had been with them throughout the journey, going all the way back to Atlanta.

"What are you doing?" Tommy asked, directing his question at Kimberly. "Arrest him." He waved a finger at Milner.

"Oh, come now, Tommy," Milner said, taking a dramatic step across the stream. "You don't actually expect my own daughter to do something like that, do you?"

36

ATLANTA

"Tara?" Trent's voice came through the phone speaker with a scratchy gravel in his throat.

"Yeah, Trent. It's me." She glanced over at the clock on her computer screen and became abruptly aware that they'd been working way too long. She needed sleep, which wasn't a typical feeling for her.

"We found the guy," he said. "Name is Eslam Demir. And get this; he's a religious leader at a mosque here in town."

"Trent," Tara took on a sense of urgency as she stood up. "You need to find him and get him to a secure place. Get him into protective custody or whatever you guys do. We think he's the next target."

"Are you sure?"

"Not a hundred percent, but sure enough to risk sending the cops to his place to jerk him out of bed."

"You do realize what time it is, right?"

"Hey, you're awake. Look, worst-case scenario: You explain to the man that you fear he's the next target of the serial killer. Make up something. Don't you cops do that all the time?"

He let out a sarcastic laugh. "You think you're funny, don't you?"

"At this time of day, maybe."

Alex could hear the gears grinding in Trent's mind as the former cop breathed into the phone, pining over the decision. "Listen," he said finally, "I'm catching some flack over the other victims. Some people were asking why you two were at the scene and then wanted to know where you went. I'll do this, but anything else beyond... I'm going to have to run it through proper channels."

"Understood."

"What are you two going to do?" Trent asked.

Tara already knew the answer. If Milner was planning to take out the next victim at their place of worship, like he had the others, then the answer was clear. "What's the name of the mosque where Demir worships?"

"The Islamic Center of Atlanta," Trent said, then wished he hadn't. "You're not thinking of going over there, are you?"

"Someone has to. If we're right about Demir being the next target, Milner will be scoping out his mosque right now. He's a meticulous planner. You'd have to be to execute the crimes he's committed without getting caught. If we can get over there and catch him off guard, maybe we have a chance of ending this tonight before anyone else gets hurt."

"You could get hurt," Trent groused. "I can't let you two go over there."

Alex had a rare moment of bravado. "You can't stop us, either. Remember? Anything else and you'll have to go through proper channels."

Trent let out a reluctant laugh. "Okay, I see how it is."

"Just playing by your rules, boss." Tara added. "Of course, if you think it's dangerous to go over there, you can always send someone."

"Yeah, maybe. Just don't get yourselves into trouble. You hear? Now I have to see if the chief will let me pull one more string to get Demir somewhere safe."

"Sounds good," Alex said. "Thanks, Trent. Be careful."

"Don't thank me yet. And you two be careful."

"No promises," Tara quipped then ended the call.

Tara looked over at him expectantly.

"I think we have a location," he announced.

The two women, worn out from the nightlong investigation, perked up.

"The guy in the picture is Eslam Demir. He's the religious leader at the Islamic Center of Atlanta. Trent is going to pull some strings and try to get him into protective custody, or at the very least make sure the guy is safe."

"And what about the location?" Tara asked. "The Islamic Center. What is he going to do about that?"

Alex's eyes shimmered with mischief. "Well, about that."

ALEX PULLED the 4Runner into the empty parking lot outside of the Islamic Center of Atlanta. The white walls of the mosque were paired with limestone columns at the entrance and side doors, each rising as circular towers to their domed tops. The largest dome towered over the others in the center of the building, with a crescent moon perched on top of a metal rod.

He shifted the vehicle into park and sat there, staring at the building.

"You ready?" Tara asked, her eyes also fixed on the mosque.

"As ready as I can be," he said.

The two stepped out of the vehicle. Alex patted his hip where the Springfield XD .40 rested. Cameras watched over the entrance as well as the gate they'd passed coming in. Anyone who may have been watching a live feed would see who they were and easily be able to identify them.

With no security guard on duty, as far as they could tell, it meant most of the video was being recorded for use after the fact. Still, civilians showing up to a mosque with guns in full view wouldn't convey the right message—whether they were there to help or not.

The two slowly crept across the parking lot. Stars still dotted the early morning sky as the moon dipped over the hills to the west, gradually disappearing behind the silhouetted peaks.

The first rays of sunlight would break through soon, and Alex and Tara didn't want to be around when they did. Worshippers would be arriving soon, or perhaps the mosque's leaders. Not Demir, though. He would be with the cops, or so Alex hoped. He believed Trent could pull it off, but there were variables at play that Alex didn't understand.

A chill in the air swept across their skin. Both wore Marmot wind-breakers but were still relatively unprepared for the cool at this time of year. The warmth of the Southern summer had yet to breach winter and spring's grip on the weather.

"So, what's the plan here?" Tara asked. The uncertainty in her voice reflected in her eyes as she looked to Alex for the answer.

"Honestly? I don't know. I guess I thought we would come here and catch Milner in the act. My guess is that he showed up to his victims' churches early, maybe by as much as a day, to size things up and get a plan together. Or it could be that he did it far in advance. Given the timeframe of his escape and the way things have gone down with the other killings, my gut says he will be here."

She passed him a meek smile, one that he loved seeing from her. The sincere gesture told him that everything would be okay, that she trusted him, and that she loved him deeply. It pulled him to her, tugged at his heartstrings whenever he saw it.

"Let's check the main door first," he said, pointing at the entrance.

"After you, sir," she said, motioning with her palm up toward the doorway.

The two ambled to the doors and took a quick reconnaissance of the parking lot once more to make sure no one was watching or sneaking up on them. Satisfied they were in the clear, Alex reached out his hand and pulled on the door handle. It didn't budge.

"Locked," he said.

"Well, that's a good sign," Tara offered optimistically.

"Unless Milner is already inside and waiting for Demir to show up."

"Always gotta be Johnny Raincloud, huh?"

He shrugged. "Just realistic. And cautious. Come on," he said, twitching his head in the direction of the side door off the parking lot, "let's check the other doors."

They snuck over to a pair of glass doors with dark tinting on them. The doors were divided in the center with a square piece of glass on the top and bottom of the frame. It was nearly impossible to see inside, which was probably the point. It would give those who came to worship some privacy.

Again, Alex tried the handle, but to no avail.

"Locked again," he complained.

"Maybe it's not the right place," Tara theorized.

"This is the main mosque in Atlanta. The others are smaller, and besides, Demir doesn't run those. This is his place. If Milner is going after him next, this would be the right mosque."

"Okay, so what do we do?"

Alex's eyes wandered to the back corner of the huge building. "Come on. There's always a back door."

"Okay, but for the record, I don't think anyone is here."

"I'm starting to agree with you."

He led the way along the exterior wall to the corner of the building, then made a sharp left. In the rear, the chain-link fence that wrapped around the front of the property continued down into a ditch and up a gently sloping hill amid a thicket of pine, oak, poplar, and birch. The fence made a hard left at the end of the property line and disappeared behind the mosque's northern corner. In the center of the back wall, an awning extended out from the building, covering a rear door.

"See?" Alex said. "Back door."

She rolled her eyes. "Yeah, but no sign of our guy."

"You sound disappointed."

"Only slightly. I'm not super excited about running into a serial killer face to face."

"Granted." He reached for his pistol and loosened it in the holster to make it easier to draw if the need arose. A camera high on the far corner blinked a red light. Whether they wanted to or not, Tara and Alex were going to be on tape.

They hurried over to the back door and stopped on the concrete steps leading down to the narrow sidewalk that looped around the building.

Every question in their minds immediately fell away into a black void as they stared at the glass doors. In the center, along the seam, a note hung from a piece of tape. The words were handwritten in sloppy print, as if by a fourth grader in a hurry.

Alex drew near the door and lifted the bottom corner of the note. Initially, he feared touching it, thinking it might be some kind of trick to draw their attention.

His head snapped around and he peered into the dark thicket behind the mosque, searching for a nonexistent threat.

"What?" Tara begged.

"Just thought maybe it was a trap."

She followed his line of sight but didn't notice anything amiss in the trees.

Alex plucked the note from the doorway and read it out loud.

"If you're reading this, I'm impressed. You found the location of the next sinner's cleansing. However, I regret to inform you that you will be disappointed. His cleansing will have to wait as I have a plane to catch. By the time you read this, I will already be on my way to claim my prize as the rightful heir to the Lord's anointing. Fear not, my children. I will return, and with the glory of the Almighty at my command."

Alex looked up from the note clutched in his fingers. His eyes met Tara's, both full of fear.

"He's gone," Alex said. He scanned the note again, wondering if there might be a clue as to where the killer went; though he had a bad feeling he knew the answer.

"You haven't heard back from Sean yet, have you?" Tara asked.

Alex's head swiveled side to side. "No."

"Then it's a good bet Milner went to find him. Or rather, meet him in Jordan. And there's nothing we can do to help."

37

AMMAN, JORDAN

Sean kept his cool, his eyes boring a hole through Milner's.

It all made sense now, most of it anyway.

Kimberly was Milner's daughter. He put her in place to make sure things would go according to plan and that no one got close enough for his little game to come crashing to a halt before he found his prize.

Still, a couple of things still bothered Sean, and it wasn't like him to hold back.

"How did you get here so quickly?" he asked. "I assume your kid was keeping tabs for you, telling you our next move and such."

"Something like that," Milner confessed. "I had a feeling you would end up here, in this sacred place." He put his hands out wide as if waiting for a dove to descend from heaven, surrounded by beams of light. "Of course, I had to be certain. So, yes, Kimberly sent me a message the second you figured this part of the riddle out."

"So, you knew this was the place?" Tommy asked, bewildered.

"Obviously," Milner exclaimed. "I can tell from the stupefied look on your face that you want to know why all the riddles, why all the jumping through hoops, and all that. Well, I'll tell you. I believe this place contained the third of the gauntlet pieces, but I had to know for certain. Still, I hedged my bets and left Atlanta yesterday, before you four even realized where you were going."

"But the next victim in Atlanta?" Tommy wondered.

"I picked someone out. It was easy, actually. The idiot who killed himself had a lover who also happened to be a leader at the Islamic Center of Atlanta. Oh, don't worry. I fully intend to make him pay for his sins once I have the mantle. For now, however, he gets to continue to live in sin. Temporarily."

Sean shook his head, his eyes dropping to the ground for a moment. "So, all this was just to make us do your dirty work when you knew where those pieces were the entire time."

"Oh, Sean. So negative. I didn't know where the first two were. But this isn't the kind of puzzle you can figure out by looking at the picture on the box. The third gauntlet piece doesn't lead to the second. It's a one-way track, and you helped me navigate it. Although I have to ask how you were able to get the one from the reliquary in Wadi El Natrum. That must have been a tricky piece of work. Much more difficult than your desperate plea for help from a Chinese businessman at the poker table."

It surprised no one that the killer had heard about the poker game. For all they knew, Milner could have set up the whole thing. That was unlikely. Sean had a weird but good vibe about Wei. And a man who so easily parted with such a rare artifact in trade for nothing more than a good deed couldn't have been a monster. *Milner's daughter must have relayed the message about the game and every step they took along the way.* As the evidence compounded, Sean felt more and more fuel dumping onto the angry fire inside his mind. He'd been used before but not by someone like this, someone who claimed to be a messenger of God or doing the work of the Almighty. And certainly not by their daughter posing as a federal agent. *How could I have been so sloppy?* He cursed himself silently for not thinking, not checking at the very least to make sure she was who she purported to be.

Her murderous father would never see how blasphemous his actions were. He was a rogue zealot out to gain power for his own distorted plans that he believed to be righteous. It would do no good for Sean to mention the part in the Ten Commandments about "Thou shalt not kill." This guy believed in his core that he embodied those commandments, that every single action he took was holy. He considered himself a sword of God.

The irony of that last thought punched Sean right in the gut.

All those years he'd justified his actions in the same way. He never killed an innocent person, not that he was aware, but through it all he convinced himself that he was some kind of warrior for God. And now, this maniac was doing the same. Did that make Sean a maniac, too? Of a different breed?

"I have to say," Milner went on, unaware of the conflict boiling in Sean's mind, "I can't believe the Chinaman went for it."

"I don't think they like to be called that," Sean corrected.

"Well, I honestly don't care, Sean. Their nation, their culture, is swamped in heathen ways. But not for long. Soon, they and all the others who revel in wickedness will reap what they have sown!"

His voice rolled through the hills and evaporated somewhere over the desert plains. The madman arched his back and tilted his head upward, facing the crystal-clear blue sky.

He leveled his gaze at Sean once more and raised a finger. "Where's the gauntlet piece, Sean? I'm going to need that."

Sean started to conjure a lie, something about leaving it on the airplane or with a friend in Egypt, but Milner cut him off before he could speak.

"And don't try to tell me you don't have it with you," Milner warned. "I already know you do."

"She has it, Father," Kimberly stated, for the first time showing off her true North Florida accent. "In that little bag." She indicated the satchel on Adriana's hip with a tip of the gun.

"That right, missy? You have my prize?" He stepped closer.

"They're armed, Father," she said. "I wouldn't get too close until they put their guns on the ground. Dangerous folks here."

"Thank you, darlin'," Milner said with an appreciative nod. "I had a feeling they were. Imagine, coming here on this holy ground, armed to the teeth. Tsk, tsk, Sean. I thought you would know better."

"But it's cool if your daughter has a gun?" Sean fired back.

Milner merely snickered. "She's with me, son. She has the Lord's blessing."

"Y'all do not," Kimberly added. "Now, drop those weapons where I can see them. You do anything stupid; I blow this one's forehead all over you." She motioned to Zaid, who had remained completely silent up to that point.

"Speaking of heathens," Milner said. "I think we might have caught ourselves one here."

"You leave him out of this," Sean said.

"Testy, are we?"

"I get that way when someone is pointing a gun at me or my friends." He twisted his head slightly, not enough to bring Zaid into his periphery but enough to sense the man's figure. "Just like that time in Bangladesh."

Zaid faked a short laugh. "That was a tough night."

"Not for us. For the other guys, though."

"Shut up," Kimberly snapped. "I said put your weapons down."

"I really don't think it's a good idea, Sean."

"Seriously?"

"What happened in Bangladesh?" Tommy asked.

"I never told you? It was pretty crazy."

"Pretty crazy?" Zaid argued. "It was insane. We were surrounded by, like, ten guys."

"Eleven," Sean corrected.

"All of them armed."

"What were you doing in Bangladesh with Zaid?" Tommy's curiosity spiked, and for a second he forgot they were being held captive.

"I said, shut up," Kimberly ordered, the gun in her hand shifting slightly toward Tommy, then back to Zaid.

Sean sensed the window and started to go for his gun.

"Not so fast there, slick," Milner warned. He produced a pistol of his own from the folds of the shawl. The weapon had been hidden the entire time.

Once more, Sean cursed himself for not anticipating it.

"What happened in Bangladesh?" Tommy pressed, still interested in the story. "Why were you guys surrounded?"

He set his weapon on the ground and stepped back with hands up.

"I'll tell you about it later," Sean huffed.

He and the others removed their weapons and placed them on the dusty earth.

"That's more like it," Milner commented. "Now, you," he brandished his weapon toward Adriana. "The gold, please."

Adriana hesitated, but they were out of options. The only play here was to hand over the relic and then hope she could get it back. That could only happen if Milner figured he still needed them for something, anything.

She looped the satchel over her head and laid it on the ground with extra care.

"Good," Kimberly said. "Now step away from it. Back up. There you go."

She spoke to Adriana as though she was a child, but the treasure hunter didn't reply. She already had fantastical plans running though her brain about how she would end Kimberly Milner.

Adriana did as told and moved away from the satchel.

The group parted as Theodore Milner stepped toward it, waving his gun in the general direction of each person to keep them at a safe distance. When he neared the little bag, he bent down and scooped it up in one motion, then returned to his spot near the head of the stream. He flipped open the flap and checked inside. A bright yellow metal object glared back at him in the hot sun, illuminating his teeth with a golden hue as he grinned broadly at his triumph.

Then the man reached under his belt, pulled up the tunic, and retrieved the third and final piece to the puzzle—the last section of the gauntlet.

He fit the two pieces together and fixed the clasps down tight, then took the first golden section of armor—the one Sean took from Wei—and attached it to the others, then wrapped it around his wrist and clasped it securely into place.

Milner's eyes widened at the sight of the ancient piece of armor. He held it aloft in the sun and let the rays shine on the yellow metal, casting tiny specks of golden light onto the ground around him. He admired the artifact for nearly a minute before unfolding the curved prongs that lay against the protective wrist guard. The three rods protruded out beyond Milner's fist, each with a uniquely shaped end much like on an old skeleton key with deep grooves set into them.

"This," Milne said, "is the key to unlocking the most powerful secret in the history of the world."

"Um, yeah," Sean interrupted. "About that. We already found the Ark of the Covenant. And bad news, no one can get to it."

"And don't forget the Spear of Destiny," Tommy added. "Probably a more powerful weapon than the mantle."

"Shut your mouths!" Milner roared, even as the two friends snickered at their own humor. "Soon you will believe, when you see entire cities leveled in my wake, when you see the blood of the wicked flooding the streets of the sinful, when you see them cry out for mercy and forgiveness, repenting of their sins... Then you will know that I wield the power of the Almighty!"

His words boomed throughout the valley long after he stopped speaking.

Sean didn't let his concern show, but it was there. In all his years of studying psychology, he'd only come across a few cases where people suffered from a God complex. None of those held a candle to this, however, and worse yet: Sean knew that if the mantle still existed —somewhere—and if this guy found it, the world would be in grave danger.

"So, what's the plan now, Teddy?" Sean asked. "You going to kill all of us and leave us here to rot in the desert?"

The maniac snorted derisively. "Kill you? Oh, no, my friend. You're not going to get off that easy. I still have use for you and your friends.

Not that one, though," he said, pointing at Zaid. "You can kill him, dear."

Before Sean or anyone else could protest, the thunderous crack of the pistol's report blasted through the air, startling everyone and sending their eardrums spiraling into an abysmal ringing.

Zaid wavered for a moment and then fell to his knees. He looked down and saw the exit wound where Kimberly's bullet had torn through his abdomen just an inch away from his stomach.

He looked up at Sean with fear in his eyes and then teetered over onto his face.

"No!" Sean yelled and started toward Milner.

In an instant, Adriana shifted her feet. Sensing a split-second opening, she swept her right leg at Kimberly, driving it up toward the pistol in hopes of knocking it out of her hand.

Kimberly noticed the movement and reacted just as quickly, twitching her torso 360 degrees to avoid the strike. She used her momentum to whip the pistol around and struck Adriana on the side of the head with the base of the grip.

Adriana stumbled to her knees, catching herself with her palms against the hard ground. She didn't fall completely, but she didn't get up either, instead remaining on all fours as the desert around her spun in a haze.

Sean's concern shifted from Zaid to his wife. A quick assessment suggested she was fine. She'd have a headache for the rest of the day, but nothing serious. She confirmed his assertion when she struggled to her feet, albeit with considerable effort and a slight wobble.

"Don't move," Milner warned Sean, brandishing his pistol and pointing it directly at Sean's head. "Would be a shame for your friend's death to be in vain, now wouldn't it?"

Sean didn't understand immediately, but he quickly caught up to the man's insinuation.

"Now," Milner said, his tone much calmer than before, taking on an almost matter-of-fact quality. "Your friend there could still make it, at least for a little while, if you can give me the last answer to this ancient and sacred puzzle."

"Figure it out yourself," Tommy spat. "You'll get no help from us."

Milner pursed his lips and nodded. "I thought you might say that. Kimberly? Finish him off."

"Happy to, Father," the woman said. She took a step forward and lowered her weapon, once again setting her sights on the back of Zaid's skull. The man moaned into the dusty ground, but nothing intelligible came out of his lips.

"No, wait," Sean insisted, sticking out a hand to stop her. He stepped between the armed woman and her target. His eyes held hers and didn't let go.

"Father? You want me to kill him now or what?"

"Now, hold on just a second," Milner instructed. "Sean, I thought you didn't want to help us. You change your mind?"

Sean twisted his head and glowered at the killer. "What do you want us to do?"

"Oh, that's so much better, Sean. Thank you for understanding." He addressed his daughter. "Honey, you can step back. But if he tries anything, you know what to do."

"Yes, Father."

She shuffled back a couple of paces, keeping her weapon aimed at the bleeding Jordanian clutching his abdomen.

"Okay, Sean," Milner said, raising up the gun in his hand and then letting it drop to his hip. "Did you happen to see the lettering on the outer edge of these golden sections?"

Sean's face turned sour. "No. I don't suppose I did."

"Well, that's fine. It's very small. Fine print, if you will." He raised the golden wrist guard and pointed to the edge nearest the cuff. Sean started to take a step toward the man, but Milner held him back with a wave of the gun and a clicking sound from his tongue. "Uh-uh-uh," Milner warned. "Not too close. I'll just read it for you. It's in Aramaic, and the person who wrote it deliberately made it difficult to see. Tommy, did you notice it?"

Tommy shook his head, angry but also curious.

"I thought not. You see, along this cuff here is the inscription." He pointed his trigger finger at the minuscule lines of ancient script.

Neither Sean nor Tommy had seen the Aramaic writing because they hadn't had time to inspect either artifact. They retrieved the first piece with only minutes to spare and rushed it to a random drop-off in a hookah bar before getting a chance to look closely at it. The second, stolen by Adriana, had been in their possession longer, but they never looked at it closely.

Besides, their main task had been to keep it secure, which meant keeping it out of sight and packed away until they could deliver it, or until they were given further instructions from Milner about what to do with it.

Now Sean regretted that. Perhaps if he'd taken some time on one of the flights to analyze the relic, they could have prevented all of this.

That assumption was quickly disposed of by Milner as he read the ancient message out loud.

"The sacred mantle of the prophets awaits the end of days with those of wisdom and stature, for a new prophet to make ready the path of the Lord—Thomas of Galilee."

Milner lowered the wrist guard and stared intently at Sean, letting his gaze drift between him and Tommy.

"Thoughts, boys?"

The two friends cast sidelong glances at each other, both uncertain of the answer. One thing was clear to both of them; if they didn't come up with it soon, Zaid would die, and them along with him.

38

JORDAN

Tommy and Sean risked a look at each other before returning their focus to the serial killer before them. A dry breeze swept over them again and tousled Sean's scruffy hair. Tommy's thick, dark locks barely twitched.

"Thomas the Apostle?" Sean asked. "As in the one they called Doubting Thomas?"

"So it would seem," Milner responded cryptically.

"And you don't have the answer," Tommy stated. "So, you're hoping we can solve that little problem for you. Then what? You kill us?"

"Oh, come now, Tommy. By the way, your name is Thomas, too, isn't it? I'm surprised you don't know this one."

"Why would I? Until last week, I didn't even know that thing on your arm existed. Our friend here is going to die if we don't get him medical attention soon. But there's no way we can solve that without context. You ask the impossible."

Milner's eyes grew weary. Lines stretched out from the corners, and he took on a look of a man who had just run a marathon only to learn there was still another mile to go.

"They said miracles were impossible, you know. The Messiah and a great many of the prophets proved those doubters wrong. I suppose it's ironic that the mantle of Elijah was hidden by the one who held on to the most doubt of anyone close to Him. Perhaps that was Jesus' plan in all of this. To bestow such a great honor on the one who sought so much proof during His ministry."

Sean had been silent for over a minute, his mind in overdrive as he combined the message from the gauntlet with information he'd gathered during his life as a student of history and of the scriptures. His eyelids blinked rapidly, a mechanism that usually kicked in when he forced deeply embedded memories to rise to the surface.

It hit him with surprising clarity. Could it be that simple? Surely there was another explanation, but try as he might, another answer didn't present itself. It had to be that place. It was a long shot, to be sure—a Hail Mary if ever there was one. But if it was correct, there was still a chance to save his friends and stop Milner.

"What will you do with us?" Sean blurted abruptly.

"I'm sorry? What?" Milner asked, irritated.

"Me and my friends. What will you do with us if I can take you to the place where the mantle is hidden?"

Milner's eyebrows perked up, and he cocked his head to the side. "Look, Sean, I appreciate the sentiment for your friends' safety, but let's be honest, you're all going to die. It's just a question of when and how. I would prefer to do it after I have the mantle, obviously, but if I have to kill you all now, I will. Perhaps when you're dead, I'll pay a visit to your young friends back in the lab in Atlanta. Maybe they can help me if you can't."

Sean fought the urge to lunge at the man and drive his fist through his nose and out the back of his skull. His fingers involuntarily tightened into a ball at his right side. He took a deep breath and exhaled, letting his heightened rage settle into a simmering lava pool.

"I know where it is," Sean announced. "I can take you to the mantle. But I want you to let my friends live. You can do whatever you want with me."

Tommy's head whipped around and looked at his friend in astonishment.

Adriana groggily cast her eyes on him, curious but still recovering from the blow to her head.

"How do I know you're not lying to me?" Milner asked, raising the gun and pointing it straight at Sean's forehead.

"Like you said," Sean began, "you're going to kill us one way or the other. If I take you to the wrong place, I'm dead. If I take you nowhere, I'm dead. But if I'm right, and you kill me, there is no way anyone else will find the mantle. Sure, you could pay the kids a visit, but they're no easy target. I've trained them for years now, and they're nearly as lethal as me. Present circumstances notwithstanding." He waved his right hand slightly.

"They don't know where the cloak is, Teddy. I do. And I'm willing to bet I'm the only person on the planet who does at this very moment. I'm your quickest and easiest path to it."

"I suppose you'll want assurances? You know I can't do that. You and your sinner friends must be cleansed, purified by pain of death just like the others."

"I know," Sean said, playing along. He called on his training in psychology and his brief experiences dealing with hostage negotiations. In the latter, he typically relied on taking out the threat with a bullet, but there were at least two times when he'd had to talk his way out of trouble.

"We have all sinned and fallen short," Sean added. "Just like the scriptures say. If we have to be purified by fire, then so be it. How much better is the beautiful eternity that awaits us if we can still be saved? Right?"

Milner's eyes betrayed his pleasure at the sound of Sean's words. "Yes! Yes! You see it! Finally! A sinner, one who has killed many in the name of evil and greed, has come to the foot of the cross and is willing to be cleansed and forgiven. Tell me, Sean. Where is the cloak, that I may purify you of your sins?"

"I will take you there," Sean said. "Just let my friends come with us. Don't harm them. And let us call someone to help Zaid. He's bleeding and needs a hospital."

"Oh." Milner's tone turned insidious. "You're all coming with me,

Sean. That's the first rule in taking hostages, isn't it? Same as in poker, right? Don't let anyone take your chips. So, tell me. Where are we going?"

Tommy and Adriana bent their ears to hear the answer to the mystery.

Kimberly even lowered her weapon a few inches, eager to hear the solution to the riddle on her father's wrist.

"The reference on the band is to Christ's training as a young man, his studies from the age of twelve to thirty."

Milner's eyes narrowed. "What?"

"The missing years of the Messiah," Sean continued. "The scriptures only tell us that he grew in wisdom and stature. You don't think he spent eighteen years of his life working in his father's carpentry shop, do you?"

Milner's cheek below the right eye twitched. "Careful, Sean. I will not listen to blasphemy."

"It's not sacrilege or blasphemy, Theodore," he said, using the man's proper name for the first time. "The scripture is clear that Jesus had learned all he could from the rabbis, that their Jewish schools had nothing left to teach him. Why do you think those eighteen years, the most formative years of a person's life, were omitted from history and scripture?"

Milner sucked in a long breath and looked down at the bleeding man. "You should hurry, Sean. Your friend doesn't have long."

Sean's gaze remained on the killer. "There is research out there that suggests Christ traveled the world during that time, probably as a preliminary mission trip. Some historians have suggested that he even spent time with Buddhist monks at a monastery in the mountains of North India."

Tommy's eyes flashed wide at the epiphany. He'd heard the same story, about a young man from the Middle East who visited many religious centers around the known world, particularly one in India, where it was said he came seeking knowledge.

"You're suggesting the Son of God studied with heathens?" Milner sneered.

"I'm saying it's possible he spent time with them, most likely to teach them what he'd learned," Sean waged. "If you recall, he ended up teaching his rabbis things they didn't know or hadn't considered. It would only make sense that when he'd learned and taught all he could with his teachers, he expanded.

"Perhaps he learned a few things from the others, too. After all, the three wise men who came to see Jesus right after his birth were not Jewish. They were likely heathens, as you call them, men who studied astrology as well as astronomy, and probably worshipped in a very different way with different gods. So, don't be so quick to judge. I'm not saying Jesus prayed to other gods or took part in their ceremonies. What I am saying is that there is evidence he visited that area and that he may well have spent time with the people there, even the religious masters."

Sean didn't mention that some of that story had been disputed or even disproved, but the fact remained that if Christ was to grow in wisdom and stature, he couldn't have done it in the synagogue or in the Jewish schools in Nazareth or Jerusalem. That was the basis for the story. He left his nation to study abroad, to learn their ways, and to teach them a better one. One story Sean heard suggested he even tried to get the monks in North India to quit praying to idols.

Sean embellished this. "Imagine, the young Messiah, beginning his ministry with men who thought they had it all figured out, masters of another religion. He witnessed to them, Theodore, tried to convert them, long before he was even baptized, before his ministry truly began."

Sean watched the man carefully, assessing his reception of this hypothesis.

"Yes," Milner said. "That would make sense. The best way to defeat an enemy is to learn from them. Moses studied in the schools of the pharaoh. There are many examples of that throughout history, people learning from their enemies so that they could destroy them from within."

Milner clearly missed the point of Sean's commentary, but it seemed to be working, just not in the way he imagined. It didn't matter. If Milner bought it, they still had a chance to get out of this, or at the very least, to live to fight another day.

"Where is this monastery?" Milner asked after a moment of careful consideration.

"Like I said, it's in North India—Ladakh, to be specific, in a place called Hemis."

Milner inclined his head as if still assessing whether or not Sean was telling the truth or leading them on a pointless endeavor.

"Very well, Sean. We will go to this place, Hemis. There, you will show me where the mantle is. Come, we must hurry."

He took a step forward and urged his prisoners to retreat down the path they'd taken earlier.

"What about Zaid?" Sean pleaded. "He needs help."

"Someone will find him," Milner said callously.

"No, you have to help him."

"Sean," Zaid grumbled, still clutching his abdomen to stem the bleeding. "Go. I'll be okay. You... have to stop him." His words came out as labored as his breath, and he lowered his head to the ground again to rest.

"I'm not leaving you here," Sean said, bending down to put a hand on his friend's shoulder.

"Yes," Zaid said, twisting the hand at his gut to reveal a cell phone. "You are. You have to. I'll be okay."

Sean bit his lower lip and nodded. He didn't want to abandon Zaid here in the desert, but the Jordanian had a plan. He may have already called for an ambulance and for help, though based on what Sean had seen from the cell service here, it was spotty at best. He'd checked his phone a few times upon arriving and noted only one bar that blinked in and out.

"All right, Teddy," Sean said, standing straight again. "Let's go."

"We're leaving?" Tommy protested. "We can't do that to him. He'll die."

"We don't have a choice," Sean said. "Come on."

"You can't seriously leave him here like that."

Sean turned on his friend, fire lapping the rims of his eyelids. "We can, Tommy. And we will. There's nothing else we can do. Let's go."

Sean spun and headed toward Kimberly, who stood there with a smug look on her face, gloating. "That's better, Sean," she said. "Although I have to ask..."

He stopped a few feet away from her, near striking distance for a punch to the throat. "What?" he seethed.

"How is it you're so sure that it's the right monastery?" She stood with one arm under the one holding the gun, allowing the weapon to dangle loosely in her hand.

Sean wanted to rip it from her, put it to the back of her skull, and force her father onto his knees to watch as he executed her. He pushed away the darkness, the vengeful part of him that always lurked in the shadows of his soul. He didn't like that guy, that monster he'd tried to run from for so long.

"How do I know?" Sean repeated the question. "Because Thomas of Galilee ministered in North India, too."

The story was common knowledge in many church circles. Sean thought it strange that she seemed to have no point of reference. As the daughter of a preacher, that sort of thing could easily have been common knowledge, though it was possible that particular piece of church history eluded some, depending on denominational traditions.

As the traditional history went, Thomas, also known as Didymus, traveled to India to minister to the people there. He and the other disciples were given the sacred task of preaching the gospel to Jews and gentiles alike, which basically meant everyone.

The history suggested that Thomas was murdered by angry Hindu priests of Kali, but there were other possibilities, including a man named Eusebius, who claimed he was the one who executed Thomas along with several other disciples. A tomb in Mylapore, India, is venerated as containing the remains of the great apostle.

There were other stories, other fragments of history surrounding the subject of Thomas' ministry and death, and it seemed Kimberly didn't know about any of them.

Odd, Sean thought.

"You're unaware Thomas visited India as a missionary?" he asked with a touch of snark.

She tossed her loose hair back over her shoulders with a twist of the head. The action reminded him of every girl who had blown him off in high school. It usually came just before they laughed and walked away. It was an old memory, one that he'd quashed long ago. He didn't dwell on it, and his confidence hadn't taken much damage as a result. In fact, it had thrived. He'd developed a sharp wit as a result, and that had served him well through the years. Usually. It also got him into trouble.

"Why would I know that?" she asked.

"Be... cause you're the daughter of a pastor."

The others passed by, continuing up the trail as Milner led them at gunpoint. "Come along, dear," he said. Time is wasting."

"Yes, Father," she said and motioned with her gun for Sean to follow the others. "Not all churches believe the same things, I suppose," she offered.

Sean wasn't convinced. Maybe it didn't matter, but there was something strange about her response. The psychologist in him couldn't let it go. Not only that, the interrogator in him couldn't either. Sean had been an expert in extracting information when he worked for Axis. He usually knew when someone was lying or telling the truth. In this case, red flags were flying all around him.

"I suppose," he half agreed.

"Come on. Get moving," she said.

Sean obeyed and fell in line behind the others. The killers marched them up the hill and over to an old gray utility van. The vehicle had no side or back windows, no doubt a deliberate selection by Milner.

The killer stopped at the side of the van and looked around, careful to keep his weapon covered by the shawl to hide it from any tourists or pilgrims. There weren't many people there at the moment, probably because of the oppressive, dry heat. Just like when he visited the American Southwest, the feeling of moisture being sucked out of his body was undeniable. It was like being in an oven set to a low temperature that gradually dehydrated him like beef jerky.

Sean had joked several times in the past that he preferred the heat in the Southeast because it was a wet heat. On one occasion on Hilton Head Island, he said as much to one of his older retired military friends while playing golf. The man looked at Sean as if he was out of his mind. Aghast, he said, "Wet heat? Did you just say a wet heat?"

Sean had chuckled and said, "Humidity keeps you hydrated."

He shook off the memory as Milner unlocked the van and slid the door open. There were no seats in the back, only a mostly empty cargo area. A plastic bag containing a cluster of handcuffs sat on the rubber lining close to the opening.

"Didn't go for the leather option?" Sean quipped, trying to lighten the mood.

Tommy fired him a scathing glare. "Your buddy is probably dead, Sean. And it's our fault."

Sean leaned close. "He had his phone," Sean breathed only loud enough for Tommy to hear.

"Oh," Tommy mouthed, finally understanding.

"You first, Sean," Kimberly ordered as she grabbed a set of cuffs.

Milner kept a close watch on Sean, the hidden gun still pointed at him. He could have made a move, a quick twist of the wrists to jerk Kimberly in front of him as a human shield, then the hostage situation would be level. But he couldn't risk it. Milner had the upper hand, and one mistake would catch him a bullet in the chest.

"So, what's with the black bag?" Tommy asked, motioning to a folded canvas satchel on the floor behind the passenger seat.

"They're going to knock us out," Adriana said coolly. She spoke as if it was of no consequence.

"What?"

"I'm guessing they have some kind of tranquilizers in there," she continued. "That way, we'll be less trouble. Although that *would* make it more difficult to get us on the plane once we're at the airport."

"We have people to help with that," Kimberly said, tightening down the cuffs on Sean's wrists so that the plastic bands nearly cut off circulation to his hands.

"Not taking any chances, huh?" Sean asked. "You know, you really should tie these behind my back. Less chance of an incident."

She answered by shoving him into the van.

"So, I guess you're not doing our feet?"

"You will need to be able to walk when we get to the plane," she said. "The tranquilizers are for when we're on board. And yes," she turned to Adriana, "we need to make sure none of you try anything while we're in the air. It will make for a smoother flight for all of us."

Adriana said nothing. Her dark-brown eyes, however, screamed a thousand threats.

Kimberly repeated the process with Tommy, then Adriana, until the three prisoners were safely tucked into the van.

Then she drew her pistol again and waited for Milner to get in the passenger seat. Once inside, he resumed holding the hostages at gunpoint while she climbed into the driver's side.

"Now," Milner said. "Don't be any trouble, you three. We'll be at the airport soon, then on our way to India."

39

ATLANTA

Tara winced as she flipped down the visor on her side of the SUV. The bright rays of the morning sun would be behind them as soon as they were back on Peachtree Street and heading toward HQ. For the moment, though, they were nearly blinded as the vehicle sped along the hilly suburb thoroughfare of West Paces Ferry Road.

They left the Islamic Center of Atlanta the way they'd found it, except for the note attached to the back door. That they brought with them. Both of them pored over the piece of paper in the hope that it might yield a clue of some kind. Those fantastical hopes were for naught.

Milner was gone, and as neither Sean nor Tommy were answering their phones, it seemed the worst-case scenario was now a reality.

"What do you think we should do?" Alex asked for the second time since leaving the mosque. "We can't just sit here and do nothing."

"We go back to the lab," Tara answered as she sent another text message to Sean and Tommy. "Maybe there's another clue we can use to locate where they're heading next."

"You mean the final location?"

"Exactly."

Alex held his tongue and slowed to a stop at a red light. A school bus rumbled through the intersection, probably en route to its first pick up of the day. Alex absently watched the cars following it roll by until the light turned green again.

"I guess that may be a good idea, but we've gone through everything. Dr. Kelley is still there right now trying to figure it out. I think if there was something to find, we would have found it by now."

"Yeah," Tara said with a yawn. "You're probably right."

"You need to get some rest," he offered.

"So do you. We all do. Poor Dr. Kelley is probably worn out."

"Yeah, we should check on her."

Tara pulled up Kelley's number and was about to dial when the phone vibrated in her hand. She saw Trent's number and pressed the answer button.

"Hey, Trent," she said, throwing a glance toward her husband. "What's up?"

"I am. And I'm not happy about it," he grumbled.

"Yeah, sorry about that. We could all do with a nap right about now."

"Nap? I need a whole weekend of sleep." He paused as she laughed and then continued. "We picked up Demir and got him to a safe house with a rotation of cops guarding the place. They'll change out every few hours. I can't say for how long we can keep him like that, though. We probably have a couple of days at most before the chief pulls the plug."

"That should be enough. Although I don't think Demir is in any danger now."

"What?" The question came with a hint of irritation.

"We went to the mosque. No one was there but we found a note from Milner on the back door. It seems he's done in Atlanta and moved on."

"Moved on? What's that supposed to mean?"

Tara sighed. "Our best guess is he's gone to find Sean in Jordan.

We're not able to reach him or Tommy, so he's either found them, which is bad, or they're simply not in cell range."

"Wait. Are you saying that Milner left the country to find Sean and Tommy?"

"Worse than that, sir. We think Milner knew exactly where they were going. It's probably a trap. Unfortunately, we're stuck hoping the guys can figure it out before it's too late."

"I see." Trent fell silent as he considered what his next move should be. "I'm sorry I don't have any advice for you on that front, but I can tell you I'll do everything in my power to make sure Demir is safe for the next day or two. If Milner really is gone, I suppose he's not in any real danger now anyway. Still, better to err on the side of caution."

"Thanks, Trent. I appreciate it. We're heading back to the lab now to see if Dr. Kelley has anything new for us, but if she doesn't, it looks like hurry up and wait."

"Understood. Keep in touch and let me know if you hear back from Sean or Tommy. There's no telling what kind of trouble those two knuckleheads got into."

Tara allowed a feeble laugh at the comment. "Will do."

She ended the call and set the phone down in her lap when it started to vibrate again. For a second, she thought Trent must have forgotten something. That assumption vanished when she saw the number.

"Whoa," she said. "This number is from Jordan."

Alex took his eyes off the road and glanced over at her. "Well, you gonna answer it or just let it ring? I doubt it's a telemarketer."

"Wise guy," she remarked and raised the phone. "Hello?"

Nothing.

"Hello? Who is this?"

The phone on the other end produced a gentle rustling sound, as if the device's user was outside in a breeze. "Sean," a voice mustered. "H-H-Hemis."

"Hello? Who is this?" she repeated. "Did you say something about Sean?"

"Milner," the man's desperate voice said. "Took... Sean... to...." The voice cut off.

"Hey," Tara snapped, drawing a look from Alex again, this time with eyes full of concern. "Where is Sean? You said Sean. Where did he and Tommy go? Is Adriana with them?"

"Be... trayed," the man groaned. "Hemis. India."

Something clicked, but the call didn't end. Instead, the gentle sound of static came through the speaker, indicating wind running through the microphone.

"Hello? Hello?" Tara felt her exhaustion melt away as adrenaline kicked in. "Tell me who you are. Are you in some kind of trouble?"

No response. "Hey! Are you there?"

Again, nothing.

"What's going on?" Alex pressed.

"I don't know. They're not responding."

"And you don't know who it is?"

"No," she shook her head. "They didn't say."

The call abruptly ended and she looked down at the screen. "It's dead," she announced.

"Should you call them back?"

"I don't know if it will do any good. They sounded like they were in pain... like they were dying."

"Dying?" he said, worry flowing through his mind. "Then you should call them back."

She did, but the call went to voice mail. "Hello, this is Zaid. If you have a question about how Royal Amman can help with your clothing and retail needs, please leave me a message and I'll get back with you as soon as possible."

The .beep signaled the end of the message and Tara pressed the red button to end the call.

"I got voice mail," she said. "His name is Zaid. Do you know anyone by that name?"

"No," Alex confessed. "And if we don't know him, Tommy probably doesn't either, which means he's likely a friend of Sean's or Adriana's."

"Whoever he is, he's in trouble. The voice mail said he works for a company called Royal Amman. Ever heard of it?"

"Not that I know of. What is it?"

Tara stared through the windshield, recalling the message. "He said it was for clothing or retail. Must be some kind of textile manufacturing company based in Jordan."

Alex processed the information quickly. They reached the end of West Paces Ferry and turned right onto Peachtree Street. "Why would a textile manufacturer be involved with Sean?"

"I don't know," Tara said. "But he also said something else." She paused to recall the name. "I think he said Hemis. Hemis and India. Do those names mean anything to you?"

"Not off the top of my head, but I know someone who might be able to help."

"Dr. Kelley," she said, reading his mind.

Tara dialed the professor's number, and after four rings, a weary voice answered on the other end.

"Tara?"

"Sorry, Dr. Kelley. Were you sleeping?"

"I just dozed off. It's fine. Where are you two? Everything okay at the mosque?"

"Yeah, we're okay. Milner wasn't there. We have reason to believe he went to Jordan."

"Jordan? That's where—"

"Yes. And we can't get in touch with the guys. I just got a strange call from Jordan, though, from a guy named Zaid. He sounded like he was hurt. I tried calling him back after our call was lost, but it went to voice mail."

Alex twirled his finger in the air, urging her to get to the point.

"Zaid?" Kerry said, "If he's calling you from that region, it must have something to do with the boys. I'll check on it immediately and see what I can find out."

"Thank you," Tara said. "There's another reason we called. Is there a chance you have heard of a place called Hemis, India?"

She yawned into the phone and then made that universal

stretching sound that everyone makes. "Hemis? Yes, I believe that's a small village in North India."

"Wait, you've heard of it?"

"I can check, but I'm fairly certain there's a monastery there. Seems like... yes, there it is." A click came through the phone. "Yep. Hemis Monastery. It's in the Ladakh region in the northern part of the country. Himalayas."

"Why would the man on the phone say something about that location?" Tara thought out loud.

"What?"

"The man that called me from Jordan a few minutes ago, he said Sean's name, then said the words Hemis and India. Do you think that's where Milner may have taken Sean, assuming he and the others were captured?"

"Possibly, although I'm a little out of my element with that question. One moment."

The SUV passed the High Museum of Art on the right and merged into the downtown section of Peachtree Street. Pubs, taco and tequila bars, coffee shops, and trendy restaurants lined the streets of midtown.

"Oh, my," Dr. Kelley said. "Now I know why I've heard of this place. There was a movie done there years ago, a documentary about a theory some Russian historian had about Jesus visiting that place before his ministry began. Most of the theory was largely disproved, but there were still a few elements of doubt—enough to not completely discredit it. I thought we were looking for something that has to do with the prophet Elijah and his successors."

The woman brought up an interesting point, and Tara didn't have an immediate answer for it. What she did know was that they needed to get to India, but with the IAA jet gone, a flight at such late notice would be near impossible to obtain.

Still, they had to try.

"Dr. Kelley, we're going to the airport. You can stay there at the lab as long as you want. I know you've been in a hotel, but if you want to stick around Atlanta and help us from the lab, we have a key in a lockbox next to the front door of our place for when we're out of town and need house sitters. You are welcome to stay there if you like when you need some rest. I know it's a lot to ask, but we may need your help again."

"Of course I'll stay and help. I have this week off and don't have to report back for another few days. And thank you for the offer. I will probably take you up on it since I need a shower and a solid nap."

"Thank you," Tara said sincerely. "I appreciate all your help with this weird case."

"It's not a problem. Actually, it's quite exciting compared to my normal routine. I just wish our friends weren't in danger. And it sounds like they might be."

"I hope not. I'll let you know if we're able to find a flight to India. I have a bad feeling there won't be much available."

"Best of luck, you two. Let me know if you need anything else."

"Thanks, Dr. Kelley. I will."

She ended the call and looked over at Alex, who was already turning right to head toward the interstate.

"So," he said, "I'm guessing we need to head back to the house to get our passports and a few things."

She acknowledged with a nod and set a determined gaze through the windshield. "Looks that way."

40

AMMAN

Heat waves rippled off the tarmac as the van pulled up to Milner's plane next to an old hangar near the edge of the airfield.

The Cessna Citation CJ1 featured a white fuselage with a gold stripe down the side. While smaller than the IAA Gulfstream, the plane was light and fast, and certainly less expensive.

"Nice jet," Sean commented as Kimberly parked the van and shoved the transmission into park. She didn't reply, instead getting out of the vehicle. She trotted around to the back door and flung it open, while Milner stepped out, keeping his weapon trained on the prisoners.

"Out," he ordered.

"Whew," Tommy said. "Good. Because I have to say, that floor is not nearly as comfortable as it looks. My back and legs are so stiff."

"My butt hurts," Sean added.

"Shut up and get on the plane," Milner barked.

Adriana was the first to set foot on the tarmac. She looked at the aircraft, assessing it from tip to tail. Of the three, she was the only one who could fly it if they somehow wrested control from Milner and his daughter, but the tranquilizer case in the van meant that window of opportunity would soon be closing.

"Move," Milner ordered.

Adriana noted the pilot was already in the cockpit, visible through the windshield that wrapped around the front portion of the plane.

Hands folded, she marched toward the stairs leading up to the open door.

Sean and Tommy followed, both allowing the blood to return to their legs, though it was still notably absent from their fingers and hands.

The door of the vehicle slammed behind them, and a darkly tanned man stepped out of the jet's cabin and onto the steps. He wore a red polo shirt and black slacks that matched his hair and mustache.

He made his way down and stopped at the bottom, shifting out of the way so the prisoners could be taken aboard.

"Everything is ready?" Kimberly asked the man.

"Yes. The plane is fueled, the flight plan is filed, and you should be able to take off in the next thirty minutes. There isn't much air traffic today, so the sky is yours." His Jordanian accent rolled certain consonants as he spoke.

"Excellent," Kimberly said. "Thank you." She handed the man a thick envelope.

Sean noted the exchange. On top of that and several other little details, it was starting to look like Kimberly, not Milner, was running this entire operation—almost as if he was just a puppet.

He blew off the thought as a pistol jabbed him in the kidneys.

"Up we go," Milner said.

Sean lifted his foot and stepped onto the stairs. He ascended slowly and carefully so he didn't trip or lose his balance. Without hands to catch himself, he could easily get hurt, and he doubted Milner's and Kimberly's medical abilities.

He ducked his head and stepped through the door and into the confined cabin. "This is cozy," he muttered to himself. The cockpit door was closed and locked, a smart move by the pilot. Even with his hands tied, Sean could have taken down the likely inept pilot, although it wasn't clear if there was a copilot. The more he thought about it, the more he realized there probably was a second person in there—just because Milner seemed to have every possible base covered.

Tommy and Adriana joined him in the cabin, and then Kimberly stepped on board.

"In the back," she ordered and motioned with her Glock.

"Yeah, yeah," Tommy complained.

The three prisoners worked their way back to the rear of the plane. Sean and Adriana sat next to each other, while Tommy took a seat across the aisle.

Kimberly eased into a rear-facing seat a few rows up, leaving space between herself and the hostages.

Again, a smart move, Sean thought. If he and the others attempted a mad rush toward the front of the plane, she'd have ample time to gun them all down before they got close. Of course, discharging a firearm aboard a plane would carry its own risk. A stray bullet puncturing the cabin walls would be problematic at high altitude, to say the least.

That wouldn't be an issue, though, thanks to the syringes Kimberly began to pull out of the medical satchel.

Milner stepped onto the plane and rapped twice on the cockpit door to let the pilots know they could begin the process of taking off.

The steps folded up, and the door to the aircraft closed. Milner pulled on the locking lever to seal the opening and then turned toward the captives in the back.

"Tommy?" he said, motioning with a flick of his fingers. "Come have a seat here."

He motioned to one of the seats two rows ahead of where he was already seated.

"What now?" Tommy whined as he stood. Then he saw the syringe in Kimberly's hand and realized what was about to happen. "You know, come to think of it, I'm up to date on all my vaccinations. And I get the flu shot every year in September. Company policy."

"Sit," Kimberly ordered. "Or I will make this hurt more than it should."

Milner gripped his weapon, carefully choosing a target that would hurt Tommy the most—Sean.

"Try anything and your friends die," Milner said.

"Yeah, I get it. Thanks for the reminder, Buffalo Bill. Wouldn't want you to make a skin suit or something out of me."

The man didn't respond. Either he didn't get the reference or simply wouldn't allow Tommy to get under his skin.

Tommy slid into the seat with his hands in his lap, still shackled together at the wrists.

"So, what is this, a—"

The needle was in his arm before he could finish. He winced at the sudden pinch and then felt a slight burn easing through his shoulder and arm.

"Ouch?" Tommy said. "You could have given me a... a... warning."

His eyes glazed over and he grinned stupidly at Milner. Within thirty seconds, his eyelids drooped shut and his head slumped to the left against the headrest and his shoulder.

"Next?" Milner said. He motioned toward Adriana.

"What's in that concoction?" Sean asked, masking his concern with a sprinkling of machismo. The truth was he didn't want them injecting Adriana with any of that... whatever it was.

"Just something to help you sleep, Sean. Don't worry. Adriana is next."

"No. You don't have to do that."

"Sean?" Milner said softly. "Please, shut up. Now is not the time for chivalry."

Adriana looked over at him. She nuzzled the side of her head against his cheek. "It's okay," she said. "I'll see you in India."

"I love you," he mumbled.

"*Yo también.*"

She rose from her seat courageously, unaffected by the syringe in Kimberly's hand.

"Over here, please," Milner directed, motioning to a seat across from Tommy.

She did as told and sat down with an elegant grace that would have been impossible for anyone else with their wrists bound.

Just as with Tommy, Kimberly didn't give warning as she stuck the needle into Adriana's slightly tanned skin. Adriana gave no sign of pain or irritation. She'd learned long ago to control such outward displays of weakness. That power gave way to the drug as it coursed through her body. Her vision distorted first, followed by a feeling of floating in the clouds. Her eyes fluttered, and then she was out, head resting limp against the seat.

"Where do you want me to sit?" Sean asked. "And could you hurry? I'm in need of a good nap. Haven't been sleeping well lately. You know, since this idiot serial killer showed up." Sean had a few other choice words pop into his mind, but he kept them to himself.

"You stay right there," Milner said, taking a step toward Sean, then another. "I have a few questions for you before your little nap."

"This isn't going to be like one of those stupid twenty questions things, is it? Because I don't like those."

Milner didn't answer as he crept toward Sean with a wicked gleam in his eyes.

"Worse," Sean went on, "it's not one of those first date cliché sets of questions like where do I hope to be in ten years, or what are some of my life goals? Please tell me it's not that."

Milner eased into a seat facing Sean as Kimberly checked the other two to make sure they were truly unconscious. She poked Tommy in the hand with a needle. No response. Not even a moan. She repeated the process with Adriana to the same effect.

"Tell me what you know about Jesus' supposed mission to India," Milner said.

"That's not really a question," Sean chirped.

Milner didn't laugh. He didn't even move. His eyes blinked lazily once, but that was all.

Sean breathed a sigh through his nose. "I don't know much about it. Okay? I saw something about that theory a while back, maybe a decade ago. Seems about right."

The pilot's voice interrupted over the speaker system. "Just a heads-up. We'll be ready to taxi in a moment. Make sure everyone is buckled in. We have clearance from the tower, and it looks like we're third in line."

Milner kept his eyes on Sean, unflinching.

"I did some reading about it."

"Sounds like it changed your perspective on things," Milner said. "Perhaps your beliefs."

"It did, a little. Everything used to be black and white to me before," Sean admitted. "Now I question everything. Like I may have said before, a faith unchallenged or untested is a blind faith."

"Don't test the Lord your God," Milner quoted.

"I don't. I test the words of man, the interpretations of man. The fact is, we don't know where Jesus went for those eighteen all-important years of his life. Seems like a glaring omission to the scriptures."

"You think the Bible incomplete?"

"I think that certain people left out some details that we might have found important or that could have clarified things for us as believers. But what we have is still enough, isn't it?"

"I like to think so."

"It doesn't change what Christ is or what he did for us if he traveled the world and studied with others, learned from them, even. What he brought back to Israel and through his ministry, to us, is because of whatever happened to him during those formative years. Someone knows what happened. Someone knows where he went and what he did. It's clear he knew about India. Otherwise, how would Thomas have known to go there, who to talk to, what to say? I choose to believe Christ sent him there specifically."

"That's an interesting theory, Sean. And you're right. I don't think you're being sacrilegious. You have a clear understanding of the scriptures. I can see that. You were right about the rabbis and the Jewish schools being unable to teach Jesus anything else. So, we will give your theory a try."

"And if I'm wrong?"

Milner shrugged. "I kill one of your friends here while you watch." He motioned to the others.

"Can I go to sleep now?" Sean asked. "You're boring me."

Milner offered a smug grin and nodded. "Of course. Night night, Sean."

He stood and moved out of the way.

Kimberly approached the second Milner had passed. She held a syringe menacingly in her fingers, a dry, indifferent look on her face. Her eyes, though, betrayed a different emotion, something far more sinister. He couldn't decipher what it was.

"So, how long does this stuff last?" he asked. "Because it's a long flight to Ladakh."

"Don't worry about that," she answered. "This is the least of your problems."

The needle sank into his skin and the muscles under his eyes involuntarily twitched.

"Your wife takes this better than you," she whispered. Within seconds, the warmth in his shoulder spread. "Then again, I'm not surprised. Women have always been the stronger sex." She risked a look over her shoulder. "Regardless of what tradition says."

He blinked groggily at her, looking into her rapidly blurring facial features.

"Stronger," he babbled, then surrendered to gravity's pull on his eyelids.

41

SOMEWHERE OVER THE ATLANTIC

F irst class never sucked. Not on a train. Not in an airport
lounge. And definitely not on a plane.
 Tara and Alex had never flown in first class. In fact, they
didn't fly all that often. When they did, it was either in coach or in the
IAA Gulfstream. Both were the extremes of the flying spectrum, but
now that they were getting to experience first class, they had already
decided there was no going back.

"These seats are so much more comfortable than the ones in
coach," Tara said, leaning back into the wide blue leather cushions.
"We should travel more often."

"Agreed," Alex said as he flipped through the options on the video
screen in front of him.

After getting off the phone with Dr. Kelley, the two went straight
home, collected a few necessities, and then drove to Hartsfield
International Airport. During the drive, Tara searched through her
favorite travel app for any flights from Atlanta to Delhi. The only
ones available on such short notice were in first class, and she was
relieved to find three seats still available. After a short conversation
with another passenger, the man agreed to swap seats so Alex and
Tara could sit together.

Alex stopped looking through the collection of movies and television series and removed the laptop from the bag under the seat in front of him. They'd been in the air long enough for the plane to reach cruising altitude, and people all around them were busy on their phones, tablets, and computers. Some sent text messages. Others made calls to business associates or family members. The old man across from them, with whom they'd swapped seats, simply looked out the window at the last remnants of land passing far below.

Alex left the laptop closed in his lap and stared at the man, probably longer than he should have, but he couldn't help thinking he recognized the guy from somewhere. His bushy white hair was combed neatly to one side. The tanned, somewhat wrinkled features of his face revealed a life—or perhaps retirement—spent in the sun.

The satchel at the man's feet was the color of sand. The letters *CC* were embroidered on the side in black.

Alex put off the investigation he'd planned to conduct on his computer. He didn't know what he was going to search for anyway. Not yet.

"Have you ever been to India?" Alex ventured, leaning over the armrest and into the aisle.

Slightly startled, the old man turned away from the window and faced Alex. "Me? Oh, sure. Several times. You?"

"No, sir," Alex admitted. "We don't get to travel much. Usually we're working all hours of the day."

The old man chuckled. "Don't spend too much of your life working. Unless, of course, you love the work you do. I don't plan on ever retiring because I love what I do. There's nothing better in the world."

"Same with us. We really enjoy what we do, so it doesn't feel like work."

The man's eyes narrowed to mirror the kind smile on his face. "Then you shouldn't quit doing it."

"Agreed. So, you're heading to India again? Business?"

"Pleasure is business for me," the man said, still beaming proudly. "My catamaran is on the Andaman and Nicobar Islands. Had to leave it there for maintenance while I jetted back to the States for a few weeks to handle some administrative duties."

"Sounds like you travel a lot," Alex noted. He couldn't help but wonder what kind of work the man did where he had to leave his boat on an exotic Indian island for repairs while he flew across the world to the United States and then back again. Alex decided not to press the issue, but the comment about the catamaran gave him a clue about the source of the man's tan. "On the water a lot?"

The old man's lips stretched farther. "You could say that."

"Well, I wish you smooth sailing when you get there."

"Thank you," the man said. "That's what I'm hoping for."

Next to Alex, Tara took out her phone and flipped through it until she found the number for Emily Starks in her contacts. She removed the airplane phone from its cradle and entered the numbers. Then she hesitated.

Something had been bothering Tara since they learned that Kimberly was Milner's daughter, and she knew no one with better intel than Emily.

She hated to bother the Axis director, knowing that at any time the woman was probably spinning a dozen plates on a global scale. Still, Tara had to know.

Hesitantly, she pressed the call button and raised the phone to her ear.

It rang four times, and she was about to abandon the idea when Emily's cool, familiar voice came through the speaker.

"Hello?"

"Hey, Emily. I'm so sorry to bother you, but I have a question I was hoping maybe you could answer."

"Tara?" She immediately recognized the young IAA agent's voice. "That sounds cryptic. I take it this is something you couldn't Google?"

Tara gave up a laugh at the joke. "No. Definitely not. We are working on something with Sean."

"Oh, dear. Is he in trouble again?"

Tara deflected the question. "Probably. We're helping to chase down a serial killer."

"The one in Atlanta that's killing the religious leaders?"

"That's the one. But I have some questions about his background, more specifically, his daughter."

A pause came over the phone. "Daughter?"

"Yes. We've been trying to piece together his history, the man's backstory. His name is Theodore Milner. He was a... patient at Morrowfield in Wyoming. I was hoping you could shed some light on his daughter. If you have the time. No pressure. And again, I'm so sorry to call you about this."

"It sounds like you're on a plane," Emily said.

"We are. Heading to India."

"That explains the hum in the background." Emily wasn't one to beat around the bush with pleasantries, and as per the norm, she cut straight to the chase. "What's the daughter's name?"

"Kimberly Henderson. But she was a Milner before."

"Kimberly Henderson?" Emily asked. "I don't think she was a Milner before."

Tara crinkled her nose and looked over at Alex, who had ended his conversation and now had his laptop open, browsing information on Ladakh.

"What do you mean?" Tara asked.

"I know who Kimberly is."

That's new information. How had that slipped by before? Tara hadn't thought to seek out Emily for information because it hadn't seemed necessary, but suspicion needled at Tara's mind. Something didn't add up. What it was she didn't know.

"You know her?"

"I know who she is," Emily corrected. "I don't know her personally, though I believe I met her at a function in Washington at some point. She struck me as overly ambitious. Don't get me wrong, as a female in a career-field traditionally dominated by men, there were certainly times when I felt like I had something to prove. But not to her level. She's too aggressive, even for my tastes. I went through her file when I was considering adding an agent to the Axis roster, but decided against it and kept things as they are."

"You considered bringing her on board with you?"

"Yes. In hindsight, I still feel like it was the right call." She stopped for a second. "Tell me, why did you think she is related to Milner?"

Tara pondered how to answer that question. "Kimberly visited Milner when he was at Morrowfield. We think she was the one who orchestrated the explosion and escape at the asylum. Whoever was behind it would have had to gain access to blueprints, schematics, tons of detailed information about the place."

"Much of that could be obtained from local government sources," Emily debated. "But go on."

"You said she's not a Milner. How do you know?"

"Like I said, I looked at her file. I can't recall all the details, but Kimberly isn't from Florida. She's from Baltimore. There was something strange about her parents. Her mother died when she was young. I can't recall how old, but Kimberly wasn't yet in college. I think maybe high school age, possibly middle school. I just remember it was tragic. Possibly a murder. Yes, that seems right. I can look up the file if you like."

"No, that's not necessary." The truth was Tara wanted Emily to look up the file and send her a copy of it, though she figured that would be illegal. "If Kimberly isn't Milner's daughter, then why would she go through all that trouble to get him out of Morrowfield? Why would she be helping him to get the prophet's mantle if she—"

Tara cut herself off, the epiphany hitting her like a major league fastball.

"Tara? You there? If she what? And what is a prophet's mantle?"

"It was Kimberly all along," Tara mumbled. Upon hearing her comment, Alex snapped his head toward her. "She was the one who stole the scroll from Dr. Kelley. Of course it was her. She would have the knowledge of how to pull off a heist like that. But she needed Milner."

"Needed him?" Emily asked. "For what? And what heist? Tara, are you okay? I'm not following you."

"Milner is nothing but a pawn. She needed someone who could

pull Sean's and Tommy's strings, all of our strings, to get what she wanted. What was Kimberly's major in college?"

"Um, one moment," Emily said. A full minute passed before she spoke again.

During the interlude, Alex mouthed, "What is going on?"

Before Tara could answer, Emily spoke again. "Political science with a minor in... that's odd, psychology. Don't see those two together that often."

"Nothing about history? Archaeology or anthropology?"

"No. I'm sure she took a few history courses as part of the load, but nothing unusual."

"That's my point. She doesn't know much about archaeology, history, ancient cultures, or theology. She needed Sean and Tommy to figure out the clues. She had all the ingredients, but without a cook who knows what they're doing, she couldn't bake the cake."

"Okay, now you're just all over the place with metaphors. What's going on, Tara?"

Tara looked over at Alex, who was wondering the same thing. She decided to answer both simultaneously. "Milner was Kimberly's errand boy. She needed someone who could get Sean's and Tommy's attention in a grandiose way."

"I'd say that worked," Alex offered.

"Not only that, but she needed them to collect all the pieces. She's not a poker player, not a master thief, and definitely not a theologian. Only someone with expertise in all three of those could have found the answers to the riddles from the scroll."

"Scroll? Riddles? I'm sorry, you lost me."

"Don't be sorry, Emily," Tara said. "I think you just helped us figure out this whole thing. The only question I have is, why? What was Kimberly's motivation behind all of this?"

"I have no idea."

"Well, that's what I intend to find out. Thank you for your help. I really appreciate it."

Emily didn't respond.

"Hello?"

Again, silence.

"Emily? You there?"

"Sorry. Yes, I'm here. I just found something else about Kimberly. Your questions made me wonder, so I looked up what I could find about her background. Her mother *and* father were murdered when she was ten years old. All of her psych evaluations checked out, though. Just scanning some of them quickly from the FBI database, I don't see any red flags that would normally catch my eye."

"Murdered? By who?"

"Case unsolved."

"I wonder if she thinks—"

"Milner." Emily said the word without reservation.

"Do you think Kimberly believes Milner was their killer?"

"Maybe, but they were killed in Maryland. Two years before the Milner killings."

The theories flooded Tara's mind, coming too quickly for her to sort. She rubbed her right leg nervously. "Did Milner ever live in Maryland?" She waited on rusty nails to hear the answer.

"No," Emily said.

Tara slumped slightly.

"He lived in nearby Virginia. Worked there in a church. Tara, I think you may have just solved a twenty-plus-year-old cold case."

"And no one will know about it."

"I knew I liked you."

"So, Milner killed Kimberly's parents, and now she wants revenge. Sounds like she's wanted it for a long time."

"That would be my guess. The psychology degree she earned probably helped with some of it, especially when it came to studying abnormal psych—the kind that revolves around guys like Milner. Most people I've known who studied that particular topic are adept at manipulating standardized tests. New ones come out every so often, but if a person who understands their construction is able to dissect it, they can rig it to give whatever results they desire. We typically don't share that with the public."

"I can see why." Tara wanted to mention how cool it was that

Emily had access to the FBI database, but she also didn't want to sound like a fangirl, so she kept it to herself.

"That's all I have right now, but I'll keep an eye out for anything should it come my way."

"Thanks again, Emily."

"Don't mention it."

"Because it's classified?"

"Something like that." Emily left the comment dangling by a tearing thread.

"Okay, then. Like I said before, I'll keep it quiet."

"I appreciate your discretion. Call me again if you need to. We should have dinner sometime. I'm sure John would love to see you both. Maybe even Sean and Tommy, too."

Tara chuckled. "Will do."

She ended the call and set the phone in her lap.

"What did she say?" Alex asked, desperate to know the details of the conversation.

"It's not every day you get an invitation to dinner with a former president."

"What?"

"Nothing. Sorry. Emily said that Kimberly isn't Milner's daughter."

"I thought I heard something about that but wasn't sure."

"Milner doesn't have a daughter. Kimberly used him, just like she used all of us. We thought it was Milner who wanted the prophet's cloak, but it's Kimberly. This entire odyssey has been one long revenge tale for her, and now she's finally at the finish line."

Two deep lines formed on Alex's forehead, carving a V shape into his skin.

"Wait. If she wants the cloak, what's she going to use it for?"

"I don't know," she said. "That's the one answer I can't conjure yet."

"And why? Why not just go after it herself? Why go to all the trouble, the planning, all the setup? She must have connections all over the world in various agencies, not to mention underground ops dens where you find mercenaries."

"Emily and I both wondered that," Tara admitted. "It could be some kind of long-game vengeance plan like in *The Count of Monte Cristo*." With no more answers, she pressed her lips together and went back to thinking as she observed her surroundings.

She glanced past Alex at the old man in the seat across the aisle. His black button-up shirt was undone at the top, the collar hanging limp to either side. He held a paperback book in his hands, an adventure story from the looks of it. Something about an undersea treasure, though the title on the spine was difficult to make out.

"What did you and your new friend talk about?" Tara asked, giving her brain a break from the mental grind of detective work.

"Travel. He has a boat off one of the Indian islands. Said it's there for maintenance."

Tara retreated a few inches, her chin sinking into her neck. "And he just left it there to fly to the States?"

"That's what he said. Told me he had some business or something to attend to back in the US." Alex rolled his shoulders. "I didn't want to pry."

She couldn't take her eyes off the man. Something about him felt so familiar, though she was certain she'd never met him before.

"He must have quite the adventurous life," she whispered.

"Indeed. I bet he's been everywhere. Kind of like Sean and Tommy."

She shook off the mesmerized glaze in her eyes and looked down at her phone again. One detail was still glaringly absent from this entire case, and she would have given a fortune to know what it was.

"Kind of like us, now, I suppose."

"Starting to look that way. It's not so bad, getting out of the lab now and then."

"No, it's not," she said with a disarming smile. "I do miss it a little when we're not there. That lab is like our fortress. Our happy place."

"It does feel safe there. Like a child in the warm embrace of a mom or dad."

Her eyebrows lowered, and she looked at him quizzically. "Wow, look at you waxing poetic. Like, cheesy poetic, but poetic nonetheless."

He snorted. "Cheesy, huh?"

She nodded and then froze in place. "Mom and dad."

Alex didn't tear his eyes away from the computer screen. "What about them? They're fine."

"No. No. No. No." The words spewed out of her mouth. "Not my mom and dad. Kimberly's."

Alex closed his laptop and looked into her eyes. "Okay. You lost me."

She picked up her phone and shook it. "Emily said that Kimberly's parents were murdered. The killer was never caught."

"Oh," he said, elongating the word. "So, you guys think Milner was the one who killed the parents. That's why you were saying something about revenge to Emily."

"Now you're all caught up. If Sean and Tommy can locate the cloak, Kimberly is going to take it. And I don't know if I like what she has in mind as far as how to use it."

She read the question in his eyes and answered. "The power of God was attached to that mantle," Tara explained. "At least it seems to be when you look at the story of Elisha, both before and after he died. His bones resurrected a man. Think about that. A dead man raised another to life. If there was still power in those bones, maybe Kimberly isn't crazy to think the cloak would bestow the same kind of power."

"And if she gets her hands on it, you're right, there will be big trouble."

"We know where she's going. The problem is... she has our friends."

42

LADAKH, INDIA

Sean woke to a wretched, pounding headache, made worse by the back of his skull thumping against a window. His head rolled to the other side and came to rest on the top of a vinyl bus seat.

His breathing came heavily, with air pushing hard out of his nostrils. His entire body felt heavy, as though tied to a hundred tiny weights that made it almost impossible to move. Even his head seemed to be full of lead.

He blinked slowly, trying to bring his surroundings into focus. He was on a bus, he thought. Several more blinks cleared his vision, and he realized his assertion was correct.

He was sitting on a seat near the back of a bus with his hands bound with plastic cuffs. *Why are my hands tied?*

Tommy's head bobbing against the window in front of him caused memories to flood to the front of Sean's mind. To Tommy's left, Adriana sat upright, head turned to the window as she watched the terrain pass by.

That's right. Milner drugged us and brought us to—

Sean's thought cut off as he followed his wife's gaze out the window. Terror shot through him as he realized where they were.

The high mountain peaks of the Indian Himalayas spiked into the sky all around. To the left of the bus, the mountain dropped off down a steep, rocky slope.

Sean's lifelong fear of heights instantly locked up his muscles. The only ones that seemed to work were the ones in his neck as he turned away from the nightmarish visage to the other side of the bus.

"Good morning, Sean," Milner said from across the aisle and slightly behind Sean in the last row.

He must have been in Sean's blind spot.

"Forgive me," Sean groused, "if I don't look that direction."

"Oh?" Milner asked, looking out the window then back to Sean. "I didn't realize you had a fear of heights."

"Yeah, something like that."

Kimberly was in the seat nearest the driver. She looked back for a moment at the occupants, then swiveled her head around to continue looking out the windshield.

"I trust you slept well," Milner said. "That was a long flight. I must admit, I don't think I'll be doing that one again. Of course, once I have the mantle, my means of travel will certainly change. Perhaps I shall be able to ride upon the very clouds we see in the sky."

"Perhaps you'll fall and splatter on the ground, too," Sean muttered.

"What was that?"

"I said, maybe."

"Ah. Lying lips are an abomination, Sean."

"So is murder, but I guess you don't see it that way."

Adriana heard the discussion and looked back over her shoulder. She offered Sean a warm, quick smile before forcing the scowl back onto her face for their captor's benefit.

"Murder?" Milner pondered as he scooted to the edge of the seat. He rested one arm on the headrest in front of him. "You're talking about the men I killed in Atlanta?"

"Bingo."

"Well, those were hardly murders, Sean. Those men deserved to die. They were stealing from their flock, betraying their family and friends and followers, and had molested the youngest of those who trusted them most. Tell me. If you surveyed a hundred Americans, a thousand, what would they say should happen to those men? Should they be given mercy? Allowed to continue on in their sinful, disgusting ways? Or should they be given justice?"

"Justice? I'm sorry." Sean rubbed his forehead with the back of his thumb. The effects of the drugs wore off quickly after he woke, but the headache seemed to get worse. "I didn't realize someone died and made you the judge of who lives and who dies."

"That is the yoke a true prophet must bear, Sean."

"I don't recall any prophets executing people like that."

Milner's head rolled dramatically to the side, along with his eyes. "Oh, Sean. I suppose you don't recall Elijah slaughtering prophets of Baal. That was only one account. There were several in the Old Testament where the men of God, men of the cloth, were called to wield the sword of righteousness."

"Yeah, well, I didn't realize it was still 600 BC."

Milner shook his head in disappointment. "I suppose there will always be those who do not understand. But soon you will. Soon you will see the power of the Almighty in full view, manifested by me through the mantle of Elijah. I will be anointed as the next in line."

"Okay," Sean said. He turned away and looked out the window next to him, staring at the slopes that passed by only a few feet from the van's tires. He was much more comfortable with that view than the one on the other side that provided a panoramic vista of imminent death.

"Your eyes will be opened, Sean. I promise."

Sean didn't respond. He was done talking to the man. Milner was off his rocker in a bad way.

Fortunately, the older man stopped talking and looked straight ahead. The weapon on his lap kept Sean from trying anything as foolhardy as an escape, not that he was a threat. Sean would have glued himself to the seat before trying to jump from the moving vehicle rumbling along a deadly precipice.

Instead, Sean kept his gaze on the window and the alien landscape outside.

They were high up the mountain when the bus rolled around a curve and left the terrifying mountain slopes behind. The stretch of road flattened out slightly, and through the windshield, the occupants beheld their first sighting of Hemis Monastery.

The white walls of the compound on the left reflected the unimpeded rays of the sun. Orange shutters hung from most of the windows with a red gable that ran across the entire edge of the roof. Balconies dotted the façade, highlighted by yellow and red paint on the recessed walls and the railings.

A market along the street ahead and on the right housed stalls and kiosks where people sold trinkets, prayer scarves, and snacks. Some sold yak-butter candles to visitors, either to take home or to leave in the temple.

Kimberly stopped the bus away from the scant collection of vehicles parked nearest the entrance to the monastic village. The abrupt halt shook Tommy from his drowsy state. His head rolled from one side to the other, and then he finally held it up straight—sort of.

"Where are we?" he asked, the effects of the drug still playing havoc with his senses.

"Hemis," Adriana said. "The monastery Sean talked about before."

"Sean's here?" Tommy turned around and smiled drunkenly at his friend. "Hey, buddy. Glad you could make it."

"Wouldn't miss it," Sean said, feigning a jovial attitude.

Kimberly swiveled out of her seat and reached into a rucksack near her feet. She pulled out a small black box about the size of her fist. The object had a red-and-blue wire looping out of one side and into the other. Two prongs jutted from the bottom like a pair of open tweezers.

Then she removed a pair of handcuffs from the bag and stood. With both items in hand, she walked toward the back.

Sean watched her closely, wondering what she was planning with the two objects. He had a feeling he already knew.

Taking three hostages into the monastery would be difficult. He hadn't been to this particular place, but he knew others like it, and they were a maze of narrow corridors, hidden passages, alcoves, chapels, prayer rooms, and dormitories. A monastery this size would be a child's dream spot for a game of hide 'n' seek. For Sean and his friends, endless opportunities for escape lurked around every corner.

Then there was the matter of the monks.

Kimberly and Milner couldn't just walk in with guns in full view. They would have to be subtle. Such discretion could be mitigated with the cold-weather jacket Kimberly wore. The Glock she'd brandished before would fit easily into the deep pockets and out of sight of the monks.

Milner would have his own method of concealment, probably a similar coat.

That still didn't solve all their problems.

At any second, Sean and Tommy could alert the monks to what was going on. Even at the risk of being shot, it would foil the villains' plans and cause chaos in the monastery, if that were possible.

For a brief second, Sean's imagination played out the scenario like a movie. Monks running for the exits, knocking over yak-butter candles in their mad rush to leave what had moments before been a place of utter serenity. Candles would touch loose fabric, sparking instant fires that would rage through the ancient wooden frames.

Sean snapped back to reality.

He knew Kimberly wouldn't let that happen. She had a plan to keep him and Tommy on their best behavior.

She stopped at Adriana, then looked at Sean. "Boys, time for you to get out."

"Where are we going?" Tommy said, his voice steadier but still a touch off kilter.

"Come on, lads," Milner said, standing. He waved the pistol toward Sean. "Get a move on. Destiny awaits."

Sean rolled his eyes. He said nothing, though, knowing any further conversation with this madman would bear nothing fruitful. Sean eased by Adriana, who simply sat in her seat and watched him

go by. There were no words, no goodbyes, no lamenting. She sat resolute, unwilling to break for their two captors.

"Let's go, Tommy," Sean said, dragging his friend up by the armpit.
"Time to get off the bus."

Tommy stood, albeit gingerly, and followed Sean to the front.

Milner stayed right behind them with his weapon still in hand.
"That's far enough," Milner said when Sean reached the door. "Wait
there."

In the back, Kimberly ordered Adriana to get down on the floor.

"I suppose you're going to cuff me to the legs of the seat now?"
Adriana asked.

"Very good," Kimberly praised. "On your knees."

Adriana did as told and slid off the seat and onto the floor in the
aisle. Her wrists were still bound. They were barely loose enough to
allow circulation into her hands.

"Now, sit." Kimberly motioned with a twirl of the Glock's barrel.

Adriana again did as instructed and shifted onto her backside.

Kimberly bent down with the handcuffs and slapped one end
onto Adriana's left ankle. She roughly shoved the foot to the side and
looped the cuffs' chain around a seat leg, then clasped the other end
to the right ankle.

"Now, if you would be so kind as to hold this." Kimberly extended
the hand holding the black box.

Adriana took it with a breath of hesitation. "An explosive device?"

"Two for two. You *are* a smart one. I'm not shocked. Although I am
surprised a woman like you lets a couple of bumbling grunts like
those two lead you around like a dog on a leash."

"Is that what you think?"

"Just an observation."

Sean's eyes burned, but he didn't say anything to correct the
woman's insinuation. He knew Adriana wasn't buying it. She was her
own person, a strong woman with an even stronger resolve. She
didn't *need* anyone. But she chose Sean.

"I don't care about your observations," Adriana hissed.

Kimberly's lips pouted, feigning being wounded by the barb.

"Well, that's fine. But you're going to need to observe those two prongs on that detonator there."

Adriana followed the woman's gaze to the two metal pieces sticking out of the box.

"Press those together. And do not let them separate. If you do, it's bye-bye."

Adriana hesitated, fingers resting on one of the smooth contact points.

"Do it," Kimberly insisted, pointing her gun straight at Sean's head.

The woman from Madrid raised her eyes and met Sean's tired gaze. She wanted to tell him it would be fine, that she'd be okay, but the look said it all.

She pinched the metal flanges together and held them. It didn't take a tremendous amount of strength to maintain the contact between the two, but over time, it would become more difficult as the muscles and tendons in her fingers grew weaker. Adriana knew she'd have to switch hands every so often to make sure she didn't accidentally let go.

"See you soon," Kimberly said sardonically. Then she spun around and stalked toward the front of the bus. "Let's move, Father."

"Yes, ma'am, dear."

They concealed their weapons as they ushered the two hostages off the bus and onto the loose-gravel parking area next to the rocky slopes surrounding the village.

Cold air doused Sean and Tommy, sending a shiver though their skin from their toes up to their ears.

"Guess it would be too much to ask for one of those coats," Sean said.

"It won't be cold once we're in the monastery," Kimberly noted. "So, suck it up."

The chilly air shook Tommy from his drug-induced fog and he looked around with new eyes.

"You do realize that women aren't permitted in certain areas of some monasteries, right?" His question came with dose of snark.

"I'm aware," she said. "I also don't think that is going to be an issue."

She turned to Milner and nodded. "You have all three pieces attached?"

He pulled back the sleeve of his gray coat to reveal the shining wrist guard. A flap extended up over the back of his hand. The three rods were folded back against the main body of the gauntlet. The armor nearly reached up to the man's elbow.

"Wearing and ready," he said.

"Good."

He snaked the sleeve back over his wrist and strapped it down with the Velcro patch dangling from one end.

"Over there," Kimberly said, indicating the front entrance to the monastery. "Move."

Tommy and Sean shared a reluctant glance, then started across the parking area and into the village. The dry, thin air brought strange new smells to their senses. Curry, onions, and perhaps cauliflower, steamed in one of the stalls, then a whiff of grilled chicken seasoned with perhaps paprika or chili powder reached them. More steam poured out of another of the stalls, wafting up from a giant steel wok with burnished sides that indicated the cookware had been around a while.

"Any chance we can get a bite to eat?" Sean asked cheerfully as they ambled up the sloped path toward the monastery.

"Maybe after we're finished," Kimberly offered, the promise as hollow as her soul.

"You sure?" Tommy added to the antagonizing. "I'm really hungry, and these muscles don't feed themselves." He showed off his biceps with a quick flex.

Sean chuckled. Even at gunpoint, in the highest mountain range in the world, his wife in a bus holding a bomb, he could find a way to laugh.

That's why Sean wasn't friends with anyone who would say "There's nothing funny about" a situation. For Sean, finding humor in the most dangerous situations—even when facing imminent death—had helped him overcome countless perilous threats.

The group stepped onto a stone walkway cobbled with flat shale pieces sourced from the mountains. The path looked like a monochromatic mosaic that stretched from one wall to the other.

Continuing on, the four passed between three tall poles decorated with colorful sashes. Most prayer scarves—or *kataks*, as they were known—were smaller and were draped from wires in sacred places or along paths leading to a pilgrimage site. Dozens, hundreds of them, hung from over the stalls and kiosks in the village.

Sean recalled seeing even more at the Tiger Monastery in Bhutan. Those had been strung up over a vast ravine, and the memory of it shook Sean to his core. He remembered essentially hugging the steps cut into a sheer cliff as he scooted his way down the precipitous staircase. Then he'd had to repeat the same ridiculous feat going up the other side to reach the monastery.

Here, there was no such terror—not that he could see, anyway—and the road leading up to this place had been challenging enough, thank you very much.

They climbed the wide steps leading to two dark, heavy wooden doors. The scent of incense and burning yak-butter candles drifted through the open doorway. Somewhere inside, the faint sounds of chanting touched the visitors' ears.

A few tourists stood in the main courtyard off to the right, taking pictures to post on their social media feeds, showing their friends and followers how adventurous they could be. Pilgrims spun prayer wheels —metal bells engraved with various prayers of peace, health, abundance, and gratitude. It was believed by many Buddhists that the prayers carved into the metal cylinders made a very real imprint on the fabric of our reality, and thus could alter the state of fate's path in the world.

Sean wondered at the sight with new eyes. Tommy, too.

"Can you imagine Jesus coming to this place?" Tommy whispered. "Seeing their traditions, their beliefs? It had to be a shock compared to Nazareth and Jerusalem."

Sean sucked in some of the cool, fresh mountain air. "I was just thinking that, although I have a feeling Christ was open-minded. He may have come here to minister, but also to study with these people, to learn their ways and their customs from a standpoint of respect. As we all should. I believe it strengthened his own faith, his beliefs, and helped hone his spiritual journey into what it became."

"Wow. Did you write that down on the way here?"

Sean chuckled. "No. Just been thinking about it."

"You two, shut up," Milner spat. "We're going in."

Sean rolled his eyes at the cliché but didn't say what he wanted to. He'd provoked Milner enough, and right now wasn't the time. They were about to enter a place considered sacred to many, and he didn't want to set a bad tone, even though he was being held at gunpoint.

As they stepped into the building, they were greeted by a monk in red robes who was standing to the side. His hands were folded in front of him, his head shaved, and his sleeves cut off at the shoulders. The garments were folded over and tied with a belt at the waist.

"Welcome," the man said in English.

Sean tilted his head, surprised. "You know we speak English?"

The monk offered a humble smile and bowed his head. "We have visitors from around the world here. I find it helpful to be able to identify them to make them feel more at peace."

"Thank you," Sean said with a nod. He'd inadvertently taken the lead in this fiasco. Now, if he could take the guns from the bad guys, things would start looking up.

His thoughts wandered to Adriana, as she sat in the bus pinching the nodes of the bomb together. He needed to move things along for her sake.

"My friend here," Sean motioned to Milner even as he choked on the bitter words, "has something to show the abbot, if it's possible."

"Ah," the monk said. He looked fairly young, perhaps in his early to mid-thirties, but with his shaved head it was difficult to tell. His thin arms showed signs of some musculature, probably from the many chores the monks were required to complete each day. "What is this thing you wish to show him?"

Sean motioned to Milner. "Might as well show him," he said. "Would be a shame to come all this way and not cross the finish line because you were shy about showing off your prize."

"Prize?" The monk looked confused but turned to face Milner.

The serial killer shifted uncomfortably. He had to let go of the pistol concealed in his coat pocket in order to roll up the jacket sleeve.

The weight barely moved in the coat. Sean knew he was the only one who had noticed, maybe Tommy, but his friend gave no indication.

Milner unclasped the Velcro strap that kept the sleeve tight against his wrist, then pulled back the jacket to reveal the golden wrist guard beneath.

The monk's eyes widened in both awe and fear. For a man who seemed to be laden with zen, his reaction came as a surprise to Sean and Tommy.

"Yes," the monk said. "I will get the abbot right away."

He disappeared in an instant, rushing down a dimly lit corridor. A moment later, he disappeared around a corner. His feet made almost no sound as they padded against the smooth worn planks.

"So... I guess we just wait here, then?" Tommy suggested.

"Patience," Milner cautioned. "You are standing on the threshold of a new age. You will stand as witness to the salvation of the world."

Sean heard the words, but he cast a glance at Kimberly. Something was off about her, and he still couldn't place exactly what it was. He analyzed her reaction to Milner's comment. It was nonchalant, almost disregarding in nature. Most wouldn't have noticed, but Sean did. Forever the poker player and psychologist, his eye captured all body language. Hers didn't tell the story of a doting daughter who deeply believed her father to be some kind of messiah. It was of a woman biding her time.

But for what?

43
___

LADAKH

The abbot moved more slowly than the young monk who went to retrieve him. Still, there was a sense of urgency to the older man's motions as he followed his subordinate through the darkened corridor and back into the light of the monastery's atrium.

His round, pudgy face revealed a life of physical inactivity—at least for the last several years. The matching body sported thick, chubby arms and fingers and a belly that protruded slightly, though not dramatically so. Still, the man was hardly the living embodiment of the obese Buddha statue that sat off to the left of the doorway, surrounded by incense.

The younger monk stepped to the side and allowed the abbot to draw close to Milner.

"You are the one?" the abbot asked. His English wasn't as clear as the younger monk's, and it came in staccato syllables.

Milner nodded and pulled back the sleeve once more, revealing the golden brace.

The monk breathed heavily, and not just from the exertion of walking through the maze-like halls. His wide eyes told the same story the young monk's had when Milner showed him the gauntlet.

The abbot bowed his head low, with hands pressed together, and then met Milner's eyes.

"We have been waiting for you for two thousand years." His voice, full of reverence, trembled noticeably. "All these centuries, the abbots of our order kept the secret safe. A decade ago, it was truly put to the test when people came here searching for answers about Yeshua studying here."

The use of Jesus' Jewish title didn't escape Sean or Tommy.

"Yes," Milner said. "You and your brethren have done well. And now, I am here to reclaim the robe of the anointed." It pained the man to acknowledge the Buddhists' diligence and steadfastness. He believed they were heathens worshipping false gods and idols, but insane or not, Sean noted the man's self-control, the cool demeanor, and how he calculated every word, every step, to get what he wanted. He may have been crazy, but his understanding of how to navigate a delicate situation was in perfect working order.

"Of course," the abbot said. "And thank you. Please," the man motioned to another hall on the opposite side of the foyer. "It is this way."

Milner nodded and rolled the sleeve down again to cover the wrist guard.

The abbot padded across the floor and into the dim hallway with his apprentice at his heels.

"Right this way," Kimberly said, motioning with her left hand. "And keep your hands where I can see them."

She didn't have to warn Sean and Tommy about the gun in her pocket. They'd never forgotten it.

"Fine," Sean said. "Take it easy."

He and Tommy hurried to keep up with the monks and followed them into the hall. Kimberly and Milner trailed behind, watching constantly for any sign that they might do something out of the ordinary. Sean had a reputation for daring escapes.

Sean smiled at that. But his grin slowly flattened as he reflected on his own reputation for secrecy, too.

A man with a secret past, his years of work at Axis forever hidden behind the impenetrable veil of national security, Sean had won praise from his bosses and world renown from far beyond just the intelligence and archaeology communities. As his success increased, rumors about him floated around more than ever.

And in quiet moments of self-reflection, he'd often feel guilt for those times he had to walk up to the line of what was good versus what was evil. At those times, he often felt the call to withdraw again, as he'd tried to do several years before when he opened a kayak and paddle board shop in Destin.

He tried running from who he was, what he was, but a place on earth didn't exist for him to hide. Or maybe he just hadn't tried hard enough.

A guarded look over his shoulder reminded him of how closely he was being watched. How many guns had been pointed at him over the years? Heck, over the last twelve months?

Too many.

The abbot led the way through a wooden archway. Candles burned along the walls, some in sconces, others merely sitting atop running boards that ran parallel to the floor. The scent of the candles overpowered the senses with their pleasant, buttery aroma.

Sean pondered the long wait the abbot and his predecessors had endured in anticipation of this moment. For thousands of years, these men had kept the secret of the mantle's location, taking it to their graves save for passing it along to one apprentice. That same process must have happened hundreds of times through the years. He wondered if each abbot was disappointed on his deathbed, not having seen the sacred mystery come to fruition.

The monks veered right down another hall and continued straight ahead. Sean noticed a cool draft coming though one of the shuttered windows, nothing more than a sliver, but the chill poked him like a needle. He looked through it and noticed a mountain peak high above, still capped with snow in what must have been a perpetual winter at that elevation.

Halfway down the corridor, the abbot stopped at a wooden door. It looked like most of the others they'd passed, probably dorm cells or little prayer rooms. None of them featured any special markings.

This one, however, had a keyhole that the others did not.

The abbot produced a key out of the folds of his robes. It dangling from a necklace that the visitors hadn't noticed before. It was an ancient scrap of metal, a skeleton key of ancient design. The cuts and grooves appeared simple enough, but at the base, the metal opened into a loop. Inside the circle was an iron flame.

He inserted the key into the lock and twisted it. The old mechanism clicked and the door swung free. The well-oiled hinges didn't make a sound as the door opened. The abbot stepped into a humble dorm cell with a simple bed with white sheets to the left, a writing desk to the right, and a mat on the floor for praying.

The monk asked the others to wait there and stepped over to the desk. He nudged the furniture to the right and bent down. The room was dark, only lit by the candlelight radiating from the corridor, but he somehow saw what it was he needed. His forefinger and thumb disappeared into a hole, and when he retrieved the digits, they held another key similar to the one he'd used to open the cell door.

"You sure seem to have a lot of keys for a humble abbot," Sean noted. "I wouldn't think security would be paramount in a place like this."

The monk shifted his desk back to its normal place and returned to the door with the same deadpan look on his face. "Security, even among the most trusted allies, is nothing to be taken lightly." He looked into Sean's face. "Especially with something so powerful."

The response caught Sean off guard.

So it is here, he thought.

Milner grinned devilishly, like a lion eyeing a fresh, bloody steak.

"So, you've seen its power?" Milner asked. His voice trembled with excitement.

The abbot thought for a moment then shook his head. "No. None have. Only the one who brought it here has seen what it can do. And I'm not sure even he witnessed its power. I'm simply telling you what I've been told, and all those before me, for centuries. When the one bearing that bracelet arrived, we were to show the way to the garment."

"Show the way?" Kimberly asked, suddenly confused. "What's that supposed to mean?"

An eerie gaze filled the abbot's eyes. His apprentice lowered his head and said nothing.

"I cannot give you the mantle," the abbot said. "I can only show you the way to it. The one who bears the armor must go to it."

She didn't like the sound of that, but Milner didn't appear concerned. "Fine," he blurted. "Let's get to it."

"Very well," the abbot said. "Follow me."

He left the cell, this time allowing the door to stay wide open, and continued down the hall.

The corridor ran the length of the monastery. Sean and Tommy both silently took in every nook and cranny, every alcove, and each of the halls that branched off the main one.

Sean wondered if Thomas had walked this very passage nearly two thousand years ago, and if so, how this place had stayed relatively untouched by time.

The abbot and his apprentice made a sharp right at the end of the hall. Then, midway down the next corridor, they stopped at a sculpture of Buddha. It was different than the one in the front of the building. That one featured an obese man with a jovial, almost drunken look on his face. This one was slimmer, more solemn.

"What are we doing here?" Milner asked, incredulous.

The abbot said nothing, instead slipping around behind the statue into the alcove.

"Here," he said and motioned to the floor.

Milner and Kimberly both inched closer so they could get a view of what the man was trying to show them at his feet. He peeled back an old rug to reveal the outline of a trapdoor. Then he bent down and inserted his key into a tiny keyhole near the edge of the wood. He turned it, the mechanism protested with a creak, and then relented with a click.

"This is the way," the abbot said. "I can go no farther with you."

"Why not?" Milner asked, seeming to forget what the man had told him just moments before.

"It is not my place. I am but a messenger, a guide. Once you go through this door, you are on your own. I bid you a safe journey and good fortune."

Sean wasn't sure, but he felt the abbot was talking to him when he added that last part. Maybe it was the slight twitch of the man's eyes as they landed on him for a split second. *Does he know we're being held hostage? And if so, why isn't he doing anything about it?*

The abbot bent down and pried open the lid. A burst of musty air erupted out of the hole. An ancient wooden ladder was fastened to the wall leading down into the underground passage.

"You will need a light," the abbot cautioned.

"We have that covered, thanks," Milner said and produced a phone from his pocket.

He turned on the device's light and shined it down into the cavity. The ladder descended twenty feet into the mountain. The roughly hewn passage had been carved by human hands and tools.

"I'll go first," Milner stated. He motioned to Sean and Tommy. "Then you two. Then my daughter."

Kimberly nodded her agreement to the plan.

Milner shuffled sideways into the alcove, and the abbot moved aside to allow him to gain access to the ladder. Then the killer grabbed on to the first rung and started to descend.

"Careful," Tommy warned. "Wouldn't want that first rung to snap. You could fall and break your neck. That would be awful."

Kimberly flashed him a scathing glare. "You're next," she said and motioned with a tilt of her head toward the opening.

"Yeah, yeah," he complained.

Tommy moved into the alcove and hovered over it until Milner reached the bottom. From the upper vantage point, it was hard to see anything beyond the sphere of light the killer commanded, but he assumed there was another passage.

Tommy bent down and grabbed on to the top rung, then began his climb into the bowels of the temple.

"You going to be okay with this, Sean?" Tommy asked as his head disappeared from view into the cavity.

"He does have a point," Sean said. "I'm terrified of heights."

"That's too bad. You should hold on tight, then," Kimberly replied.

Sean shuffled over to the hole and looked down. It wasn't high enough to cause him to panic, but he still didn't like it.

"What? No witty comeback?" she groused.

"I'm saving it for the opportune moment," Sean quipped, then stepped onto the ladder without showing any signs of trepidation and descended into the darkness below.

The abbot stared blankly at Kimberly as she moved into the alcove and prepared to lower herself into the subterranean passage.

"Be careful," the older monk said, his voice monotone, almost insincere.

Her eyes met his. "I'm fine, thanks."

She put a foot on the top rung.

"I wasn't talking about the ladder," the abbot clarified. "There are more dangerous things down there than this simple contraption."

She searched him for an answer, but none came. "Thanks for the warning," she said snidely, then climbed down into the hole.

Above, the monk lowered the lid to the secret door and covered it once more with the old rug.

44

LADAKH

Down in the underground passage, Milner stood at the lead, shining the light from his phone toward the extending darkness. No markings adorned the walls. No lamps lit the way.

"This place hasn't been touched or seen in a very long time," Tommy said, noting the layer of dust at his feet. A collection of cobwebs dangled from the upper corners, their builders long since vanished.

"Which way do you think we should go?" Sean asked.

"There's only one way," Milner answered, not sensing Sean's sarcasm.

"Thank you for that."

Milner caught up and fired a searing glare at Sean. "Come on," he said. "Destiny calls."

"Right behind you, Captain Cliché. Is that your alter ego? What superpowers do you have? Boring me to death?"

Tommy chuckled. "I'm guessing he has the ability to stop creative thoughts in a single bound."

"Well played."

"Shut it," Kimberly ordered. She shoved the pistol into Sean's back. "Get moving."

"Relax," Sean said. "We've been in tunnels like this at least fourteen or fifteen times."

"Feels like a hundred," Tommy countered.

"I said, shut up." Her voice echoed though the passage. "Move."

Milner waited to let the two hostages pass and then fell in line behind them, letting Kimberly take the rear.

They ambled down the straight path until it ended at a right turn. Sean peeked around the corner and then turned to Milner. "Shine a light that way," he said.

Milner leaned around the stone edge, pointing the bright beam of his light into the next section of the passage.

"Quite the maze they have down here," Sean noted.

The tunnel shot away from their position and went on for another two hundred feet before the phone light surrendered to the overpowering darkness.

"Keep going," Kimberly ordered. "Why are you stopping?"

Milner glanced back at her and shrugged. "There could be some kind of trap down here or something?"

"In a Buddhist monastery?"

"You never know," Sean said, adding to the killer's trepidation.

She shoved her pistol into Sean's lower back and he grimaced at the sharp pain. "Ah. Sorry, but I think Tommy's the guy you want if you're looking to damage some kidneys. He's the one who usually takes that kind of punishment."

"Hey!" Tommy protested.

Sean stepped out into the lead and continued ahead. He inched his way forward, not entirely convinced he and Kimberly were wrong about the Buddhists and their penchant for using traps to keep treasure hunters out.

They pressed on until the corridor turned left, continued on for fifty yards, and then made another left, sending them back into the heart of the mountain.

"This thing seems to go on for a while. Maybe we should turn back," Tommy suggested.

"No one is turning back," Kimberly countered.

Their voices danced off the stone walls.

Halfway down that part of the tunnel, Sean noticed a marking over his right shoulder. The emblem painted in white resembled one he'd seen before—now being worn on Milner's wrist. He stopped and ran his finger along the outline. The paint had barely faded; a sign that either time and weather had been kept at bay, or that someone had come down here now and then to refresh it. He doubted the latter. There were many cases where archaeologists discovered ancient paintings that still looked as they might have thousands of years ago. Several such well-preserved artistic works were discovered in the famed Valley of the Kings in Egypt.

"What is it?" Kimberly asked.

"It looks like an arrow with a flame over the tip," Milner said.

"Very astute," Tommy replied.

"What does it mean?"

"I'm not sure," Sean lied, "but it must mean we're going the right way." He looked down the tunnel and motioned with a flick of his head. "Come on. Let's get this over with."

"That's the spirit," Tommy joked.

They hadn't gone thirty feet when another emblem appeared on the wall to their left. This one featured the head of an ax. Farther down, they passed more symbols, all painted white: a bear, a strange-looking fish, a fire on a pile of stones, and the last, a chariot being drawn upward with tongues of fire lapping at its wheels.

"A chariot of fire," Milner gasped as he stared at the image. "The prophet Elijah's translation into heaven."

Sean nodded, momentarily forgetting he was a hostage.

"We are here," Milner said. "In the resting place of the mantle. The place we've been searching for. The—"

"Thanks. We get it," Sean halted him. "Let's keep moving. If I'm gonna die, I'd prefer it not be from boredom."

He pushed ahead into the bleak corridor without so much as a look back.

When Sean seemed to disappear, a perturbed and confused Milner ushered Tommy to hurry and follow.

The passage went on another hundred yards before coming to an end. The walls expanded out and opened up into a thirty-foot-high chamber.

Every set of eyes stared in wonder at the incredible sight. Carved into the rock in front of them appeared to be the entrance to a temple.

Three enormous statues stood guard, each wearing different kinds of robes. Each of the stone men, however, wore the same cloak over their shoulders. The garment, chiseled from the mountain's core, was hewn to show a striped pattern with wide bars stretching from end to end. The stone figures wore sandals, designed as they would have been two to three thousand years before.

Two of the statues stood to the left of what looked to be a doorway. The other figure loomed to the right. The door was a gigantic stone slab adorned with a golden knob in its center. Circles filled with images similar to those the group had passed on the way in, surrounded the dial. The arrow of fire, the chariot, the fish, and several others were painted on stone wheels that covered a majority of the door's middle.

"What is this?" Milner asked.

"The temple of the prophets," Tommy answered.

All eyes shot toward him, waiting for a deeper explanation.

"It's pretty obscure as far as history goes," Tommy admitted. "But I've heard of this place once or twice in passing. I have to say, though, I never thought I would actually see it. I thought it was just a fairy tale. And I certainly would never have guessed it would be here."

Kimberly stepped closer to the door and reached out a hand to touch the golden knob.

The second she made contact, Tommy stopped her with a sharp, "Wait."

She frowned and glared at him. "What?"

"You don't know what that thing does or how it works. Do you?"

"It's a doorknob," she said and twisted the dial to the right.

Suddenly, several clicks echoed from inside the slab. Two of the outer rings of the door's wheel twisted and then stopped in a new position, lining up the symbols in a different order.

A loud thud nearly deafened the group as they were showered with dust and debris from overhead. The room, the very mountain, shook as the ceiling overhead dropped several feet toward them and then stopped abruptly.

Kimberly's hand still rested on the dial as she looked around, terrified.

Sean reached out and risked pulling her fingers from the device. "Why don't you let the professionals handle this one?" he said. "I'd rather not end up a pancake."

She didn't say anything, but took back her hand and shifted away from him, still brandishing the gun in case he tried to snatch it from her.

"What is this?" she asked.

Tommy took a step forward and peered at the wheel. The setup wasn't unlike the fabled Mayan calendar in some ways, though with different symbols.

"What do you know about this thing?" Sean asked his friend.

Tommy continued his study of the device. He traced his finger along the three outer rings and the painted carvings within them. "Like I said, I only heard, or maybe read, about it in passing. But I believe we have to line up the symbols correctly, or that slab over our heads will crush us."

"Elaborate," Sean quipped.

"And deadly. Not only that; if we fail, no one else will ever be able to access this again. Not without some heavy equipment."

"Or explosives. And that would be risky in here. Would probably bring down the entire passage."

"Yes, well, we're not planning on doing it that way," Milner cut in. He raised his pistol at Tommy. "So, please, try not to screw it up again."

"Uh, first of all, that was your little girl's doing."

When he didn't say anything else, Sean asked, "Was there a second? Is that it?"

Tommy shook his head. "No, that was it."

"Would you two idiots shut up and open the door?" Kimberly swore at them as she gave the order.

Milner turned to look at her with a disapproving glare. "Dear, we don't use that kind of language. Please. We are in a sacred place. I taught you better than that, didn't I?"

She feigned regret. "Sorry, Father. I'm just eager to get the mantle for you so you can begin your mission."

He accepted the apology with a nod and returned his gaze to the other two. "Please, if you will."

Tommy blinked rapidly and then turned to face the bizarre wheel. He looked over the symbols and then up at the statues. He silently counted the number of symbols he recognized from the passage leading to this place. "Nine," he breathed. There were nine that went along with stories from the prophets. *That's it. Three each.*

Tommy raised his hand, but instead of turning the knob, he twisted the outer ring until the chariot of fire pointed toward the giant stone figure of Elijah. He moved the ring inside that one until the symbol of the flaming altar lined up with the chariot. Then he moved the inner ring, twisting it so that the last image, the one of a cloud with rain and lightning, aligned with the other two.

When he was done, Tommy stepped back and looked at the wheel. The symbols for the other prophets weren't lined up properly, but he risked the deadly assumption that this was an ancient combination lock, a device that required three attempts to unhinge whatever mechanism remained hidden within.

He stepped back to the knob and reached out his hand.

"Are you sure that's it?" Milner asked, desperation cracking his voice.

Tommy spun on his heels. "Do you want to do this, or do you want me to do it?"

Milner held his tongue and swallowed. "Do it."

"Thank you. Now, please, don't interrupt me again."

Sean looked over at Milner. The man's face blushed so red it virtually glowed in the dim tunnel. "You really shouldn't bother him."

Milner only responded with a sideways glance before returning his gaze to the door.

Tommy touched the knob and twisted it clockwise until he felt resistance. He took a deep breath and exhaled to calm his nerves, then twisted again.

The knob caught for a second and then forced through whatever held it back. A heavy clack echoed from beyond the door.

Four pairs of eyes immediately looked up to the slab overhead, partially expecting it to drop farther. To their relief, the giant stone didn't budge.

"There you go, buddy," Sean encouraged. "Whatever you just did, do more of it." He pointed at the door as he spoke.

Tommy briefly considered explaining the mechanism's workings, but decided against it and went back to the next pairings. He moved the outer ring again, this time aligning a burning arrow, ax head, and bear from top to bottom. Again, Tommy twisted the dial and met similar resistance to the first, but upon exerting a tad more effort, he pushed through and heard the familiar clack from within the walls.

Sean pumped his fist, though his excitement tempered when he cast a look to his side and remembered they were being held at gunpoint. He pouted his lips and bobbed his head. "Sorry," he offered, pointing at his friend. "This is just really cool, isn't it?"

Milner frowned at him. "What is wrong with you?"

"Me? I don't know. Maybe it's the elevation. I don't usually go to high places like this. Or maybe I just really like archaeology."

"That's not what this is," Tommy corrected.

"My mistake," Sean said.

Even Tommy had to admit Sean sounded a touch funny, but he played along despite not knowing what his friend was up to.

He returned his focus to the wheel, ignoring Sean's antics for the moment, and began spinning the third combination for the figure of Jonah on the right side of the entrance. The strange fish was the first symbol on the outer ring. He fixed it into place and then twisted the second ring until the next symbol—a tree with a squiggly worm dangling from a branch—lined up with the largest ring.

Tommy paused, staring at the inner ring. He knew which two of the remaining symbols didn't fit with Jonah. That still left three possibilities. The emblems consisted of a ship, something that looked like a fireball or perhaps a comet, and a disc with lines radiating away from it.

He assumed the third to be the sun, indicating the sweltering heat Jonah endured at the end of his tale. The problem was that both of the other's were just as applicable. The fireball could indicate the prophecy of destruction Jonah gave to the city of Nineveh were they to remain steadfast in their wicked ways. But the ship also presented a viable possibility since Jonah attempted to flee the mission he was given by boarding a boat in Joppa to sail to Tarshish.

"What's the delay?" Kimberly asked after waiting for nearly two minutes as Tommy pined over the problem.

"We have an issue," he answered plainly, never taking his eyes off the wheel.

"What do you mean, an issue? I thought you knew what you were doing."

"Well, I did," Tommy began. "It looks like we have to match symbols from important events that occurred during the prophets' lives. It worked for the first two. With the third, though, all three are possibly correct."

Sean sobered momentarily. "So, eliminate one that's least likely to be correct," he offered. "Just like teachers used to tell us when we were preparing for a multiple-choice test."

"Yeah, fine. If I had to choose one that doesn't belong, it would be that symbol." He pointed at the fireball. "While Jonah's mission to Nineveh was to predict their fiery destruction, that never happened. Not in the prophet's lifetime."

"So, that leaves the other two," Sean noted.

"Correct. And both are possible. One looks like a ship, which could indicate the vessel Jonah boarded to escape the mission given to him by God. The other is the sun, which may be symbolic of the heat that plagued the prophet toward the end of the story."

Sean considered the quandary, biting his thumbnail as he ran through the story of the man who ran from God.

"Which one of those is more pertinent?" Sean asked.

Milner and Kimberly watched the exchange like a tennis match, their heads going back and forth on a swivel.

"The ship, I suppose," Tommy answered.

"You're over thinking it. The ship is the right call."

Tommy faced his friend with questioning eyes. "I don't know if we get three strikes on this one, Sean. The next wrong combination could bring that thing down on us."

In the dim passage, Sean's gray eyes shone brightly, like a wolf staring out from between dark tree trunks on a cold winter's night.

"The good news is, you only die once, Tommy."

"What?"

Sean clarified. "Whenever I'm in a tight spot, where it doesn't look like I'm going to make it out alive—"

"That's way more than we could both count on our fingers," Tommy added.

"True. But you know how I get through those moments? I tell myself that the worst possible scenario can only happen one time. We only die once, brother."

Tommy searched his friend's face for a crack, some kind of signal that he was joking, but there was no humor written there.

"Is that supposed to make me feel better? Seriously, that's probably the worst pep talk I've ever heard in my entire life."

"Yeah, well, I guess maybe that way of thinking isn't for everyone." He shrugged. "I still think it's the boat, though."

Tommy's look of disgust never left as he shook his head and turned back to the door. "Okay, the ship it is."

He twisted the innermost ring until the vessel lined up with the other two symbols. "You realize we're putting all of our lives on a coin flip, right?" Tommy glanced over his shoulder at his friend.

Milner's eyelids were nearly closed shut they were so tight. "We are doing the work of the Lord," he said. "I am his messenger, and so we will be protected."

"Okay then," Tommy said disparagingly. He put his hand on the knob and turned it. When he felt the expected resistance, he paused, second-guessing himself again. He closed his eyes and exhaled, pushing away the doubt, and then turned the dial harder.

45

LADAKH

Adriana's grip on the nodes weakened and she switched hands for the umpteenth time since being left in the bus.

She squeezed the metal prongs harder as she transferred the device from one hand to the other, careful to make sure the rested fingers had a good grip before letting go with the tired ones.

There is a way out of this, she thought. *I just have to find it.*

She'd been racking her brain for the path to escape, but nothing popped up as a viable option.

No one could see her through the windows since she was on the floor, and it was doubtful anyone would hear her scream for help. Kimberly had parked the bus far away from the rest of the vehicles, probably with that very consideration in mind.

She kept a set of lock picks in her boot, hidden under a fold just behind the zipper, but she couldn't access it without risking dropping the bomb. Adriana grunted in frustration and kicked her feet out, thinking maybe the chains could dislodge the leg holding up the seat.

That hypothesis came to a painful and sudden halt. The chain caught on the seat leg and stopped abruptly, causing the cuffs on her ankles to dig into her skin nearly to the bone. She grimaced, but didn't let out a sound save for a low grumble in Spanish, something she probably wouldn't have said in front of her father.

"That was stupid," she scolded. "You've been in worse spots than this, Adriana. Think."

Throughout her adventures, there had been many times where the odds were stacked against her. This, however, was the first she could recall holding an active detonator.

If only she had something to bind the nodes together, she could lay down the bomb, access her lock picks, and get out of this mess— maybe with enough time left over to help Sean and Tommy, assuming they needed it. The duo were good, but even the best needed help now and then.

Adriana lay down on her side and let her head come to rest on the floor. She didn't care how dirty it was at that point. Being clean didn't matter if she was dead. If the bomb went off, it would be anything but a clean murder scene.

The disturbing thought nearly made her laugh, but she kept the dark humor at bay and closed her eyes to focus. She felt the cold steel against the skin on her wrists, and the pressure of the same style of cuffs on her ankles, digging into her flesh.

It was almost meditative. Her mind focused on the moment, letting every sensation, every thought come and go, acknowledging each with a casual deference.

Whenever she meditated, she started with her toes, relaxing those extremities before working her body scan up through her legs, torso, and the top of her head. When she reached the latter, her eyes popped open.

An awkward source of pressure pushed against her skull. It was from her ponytail. When she put her head down, it came to rest against the base of the hairdo and bunched it into a small area.

"My hair tie," she realized.

Adriana continued to squeeze the nodes together as she sat up again. She used her free hand to work the hair tie out of her ponytail and pulled it loose. Her brown hair dangled freely over her neck and shoulders, loosed from its bonds. The move was tricky to pull off with her wrists bound together. Her fingers held the nodes together harder to make sure the metal didn't separate. Once she had the hair tie between the fingers of the other hand, she brought the device back down to her lap and carefully wrapped the stretchy band around the prongs, making sure it was tightly bound, pulling on the material until it was taut before wrapping it again. Doing so would prevent the hair tie from stretching and allowing a gap to open between the rods. She hoped.

Satisfied the band was as tight as she could get it, Adriana took a deep breath and exhaled, saying a silent prayer. "Here goes," she whispered.

She twisted her torso to the right and delicately placed the device on the floor. For a second, Adriana hesitated, uncertain if her plan would work. There was no other way, though. If she merely sat there and waited for Kimberly and her father to return, they would execute her anyway. This was her only chance.

Resolved there was no other way to get out alive, she let go of the nodes.

She winced for a breath, then two, and when nothing happened, she opened her eyes and looked down at the detonator. The hair tie remained in place, keeping the rods connected.

Uncertain how long it would hold, she shifted away and reached forward to her boot, unzipped the side zipper, and retrieved her lock picks.

Adriana had picked cuffs like these before, and it took her less than twenty seconds to work the pin to the right position before the cuffs on her legs loosened. She breathed a sigh of relief and stood up, careful not to kick the explosive device on the floor. She hurried toward the front of the bus, pried open the door, and jumped out.

She sprinted away from the vehicle and skidded to a stop near the top of the parking area. Adriana took in huge gulps of air, both relieved and slightly out of breath, before sticking her lock pick into the handcuffs and releasing them. The shackles dropped to the ground with a clank, and she twisted her wrists back and forth to resume normal blood flow.

A car approached, coming up the road toward the monastery. She lowered her head, perhaps a touch paranoid, and walked quickly over to a van parked near the slope heading down the mountain. The red Hyundai compact's engine rattled as it neared, and the driver pulled into an empty parking spot twenty feet away.

Adriana kept her head low and started to walk toward the monastery. It was unlikely Milner or his daughter had left anyone there to watch, but it was difficult to know. They supposedly had connections all over the world, so where were the henchmen, the guards to help make certain their mission went according to plan? Something didn't add up, and Adriana wanted to know why.

She neared the entrance to the village when a voice stopped her in her tracks.

"Adriana?" the familiar voice called.

With a befuddled frown, she turned slowly toward the voice. Standing next to the red compact car was Alex and Tara.

Her heart skipped a beat as she stepped toward them, walking at first, then at a trot.

"What are you two doing here?" she asked, reaching Tara first. Adriana almost wrapped her arms around her and squeezed her tight, but she resisted the urge. There wasn't time for that.

"We found out about Kimberly. She's not who she says she is," Tara said.

Alex rushed around the back of the car and joined the two women.

"I know, she's Milner's daughter," Adriana said.

"No," Alex jumped in. "Milner never had a daughter. Kimberly isn't related to him at all. She convinced him that she's his daughter to use him for this whole thing."

Adriana's bewilderment poured out of her eyes as she shook her head. "But why? Why would she use a crazy murderer to do all this? She could have just done it herself."

"Milner killed Kimberly's parents. He didn't realize that she was *their* daughter. Still doesn't, by all accounts."

The epiphany dropped onto Adriana's shoulders. She turned

toward the monastery for a moment, then back to the kids. "Kimberly wants revenge for what Milner did to her parents. And she used all of us to get it."

"Sean and Tommy," Alex realized. "Where are they?"

"They went into the monastery with Milner and Kimberly. They left me here in the bus, but I got out just before you arrived. We need to get in there and find them before it's too late."

"That's not all," Alex added. "We think Kimberly wants the prophet's cloak."

"For what?"

"We're not sure, but she may believe that it can bring her parents back to life. Beyond that, if the cloak is real and she finds it, she could wield unimaginable power. There's no end to the damage she could do."

"Then we have to stop her before that happens," Adriana said. "Come on. Follow me."

Car doors unexpectedly slammed shut all around the parking lot, some together, some staggered like falling dominoes.

Adriana panned the area and immediately realized her previous question was about to be answered.

Men from a mixed bag of ethnicities, wearing a variety of clothing, stepped from seven cars scattered around the lot. Each of the seven men stared menacingly at the group. Scarves covered the lower halves of their faces from the nose down to the nape of the neck.

Alex and Tara also noted the trouble, and the three naturally withdrew into a tight circle with their backs to each other.

Two more men approached, cutting off the way into the village.

"I don't suppose you two brought guns with you? Did you?" Adriana ventured.

"We had to fly commercial," Tara answered. "Didn't have time to go through the process of checking our weapons. We barely made the flight."

Adriana nodded. "Perfect." She turned her attention to the nearest of the approaching henchman. She couldn't see his lips or jawline, but there was no mistaking the eyes. Sean had told her about the man from Macau named Ling. Now, all the pieces started connecting.

"Hello, Ling," she said with an insincere cordiality. "What brings you here from Macau?"

The man inclined his head and then stopped short of the cornered threesome.

"Kimberly was afraid you might escape or that someone could come to help you. It was a long shot, but she is wise and doesn't let assumptions get in the way of preparation."

"I was wondering where Kimberly's crew was hiding." Adriana sized up Ling and the man next to him. His partner was shorter, with wider shoulders and strong legs. He was also Asian, though she couldn't place the exact country. If she had to guess, she'd have said China. His head was shaved in a way that could have passed him off as one of the monks in the monastery.

"You should have stayed in the bus," Ling said coldly.

Adriana cocked her head to the right. "You should have stayed in Macau."

Alex and Tara kept their hands up in a defensive position in front of them.

Adriana, however, looked like she was taunting the men into making a move. Her arms hung limp at her sides with one hip sticking out slightly.

Ling cracked a devilish smile. "Take them to the bus," he ordered. "Tie them all to the seats."

The rest of the men moved in, all stalking toward the tight triangle. Alex and Tara said nothing. They didn't have to ask what the plan was. They already knew.

"I have to admit," Adriana said over the howling wind cascading down the slopes, "I'm impressed you're not using your guns."

Ling shook his head. "It just so happens we don't have them with us. Difficult to get into and around this country with firearms. Not to worry," he said. "If you cause any trouble, we'll kill you with our bare hands and drop you off a cliff." He motioned with a flick of a finger toward one of the rocky hillsides.

Adriana merely acknowledged the threat with a shrug. "Oh, I always intend to cause trouble for people like you."

"How do you say in America? It's your funeral?" Ling groused.

"Let's play, then," she said.

Adriana didn't wait for him to take the initiative. She surged forward like a cat, breaking the triangle to lash out with her right foot. Ling stepped to the side, easily dodging the wild attack. He laughed at her as she withdrew.

"That's your plan?" He tilted his head back. "You're not very smart, are you?" He looked at his men. "Kill them all. Throw them down the slopes when you're done."

Adriana withdrew back to the group and waited as the rest of Ling's men closed in. She gave no indication of fear. Neither did she display the sense of excitement, the adrenaline, that came with a fight. She'd been fighting her entire life. Moments like this were what her father had prepared her for, and it was the same for Tara and Alex following their time with Sean.

These thugs may have them outnumbered, but they had no idea what they'd just bargained for.

46

LADAKH

The ancient mechanism inside the stone door let out a grinding sound that reverberated throughout the walls of the temple's entrance. The four explorers immediately looked up at the massive slab overhead, expecting it to drop and make them a permanent part of the mountain.

Instead, a heavy panel to the left of the key wheel abruptly broke free and fell into the threshold, the top stopping flush with the floor. Sean and Tommy looked at each other with both excitement and trepidation.

Tommy's breath came quickly, but now with a feeling of utter relief.

"Go," Milner urged, eager to get out from under the hanging slab that loomed over them.

Tommy didn't have to be told twice. He stepped through the doorway into the temple. Sean followed behind with their two captors hurrying after.

The vast temple atrium stretched eighty feet across. Even in the dim glow from the killers' lights, the detail of the ancient chamber appeared absolutely breathtaking.

Sean smelled something pungent nearby. His nose twitched, and following the scent, he turned and took a step toward a dark pedestal.

"Shine some light over here," he said to Milner.

The murderer could have argued not to boss him around, but he sensed something about Sean's curious request and sidled over to where Sean inspected the plinth.

Under the light, the group could see more detail, and they realized the column was made of pure gold.

It was wider at the bottom, narrowing gradually toward the flat top like a kind of pyramid. Resting at its center was a golden bowl with a narrow duct running to the wall. The golden conduit looked as though it wrapped around the entire room, though their lights were less effective on the far walls.

Sean looked into the bowl and found the source of the smell. "It's some kind of ancient fuel," he said. "Either of you have a lighter?"

Kimberly produced a small cigar torch from her pocket and handed it to him. "That better not be explosive," she said as she took a wary step back.

"I should be so lucky," he chirped.

Sean extended his hand and pressed down on the lighter's silver button. The blue flame ejected out of the hole in the top and he lowered it to the substance in the bowl. The second the flame touched it, the fuel ignited into a bright fire with yellow and orange tongues lapping toward the ceiling. The flames darted along the duct and reached the wall, spreading rapidly and lighting the room with every inch it progressed.

The line of fire reached a sconce that held a smaller golden bowl. The trail paused for a second, then fuel inside the bowl flamed up, casting a brighter glow on that portion of the chamber. The fire continued, wrapping around the room, lighting twelve oil lamps in total before it finished its journey near the entrance.

The atrium glowed in the firelight, and the full detail of the room emerged from the darkness. Two giant stone pillars, carved directly from the mountain, towered from the floor in the center of the room, stretching all the way to the ceiling as if they were the only thing holding up the mountain above.

"This is amazing," Sean whispered reverently.

"Yeah," Tommy agreed.

The smooth walls displayed no flaws or cracks. They were perfectly square, chiseled by ancient hands, though the quality appeared machine-like. To the left of the enormous columns, two more squared pillars stood, set into the wall—two on either side of two more cylindrical supports. In the center, an open doorway beckoned with a roofed section hanging out over it. On the top of the roof, dozens of stone triangles pointed to the sky.

"This looks familiar," Sean noticed, his voice still somber.

"That's because this"—Tommy pointed at the wall and doorway —"is a replica of the entrance into the temple of Jerusalem as it may have looked more than two thousand years ago."

"It's a miracle," Milner said. "An absolute miracle."

"Yes, Father," Kimberly said. "It certainly is."

Sean caught something in her voice, a strange hint at malevolence. His suspicions had already reached boiling point, but he got the distinct impression Kimberly and Milner weren't on the same side. And Milner had no idea.

For the moment, he kept the conspiracy to himself.

"Don't just stand there," Kimberly snapped. "Let's keep moving."

"Would it kill you to say please?" Sean retorted.

The comment got him a boot to the tailbone and he staggered forward toward the entrance.

Light poured out of the doorway, glowing brightly from beyond. Through the portal, the group could see that the flames had carried to the inner chamber and lit more lamps within.

Tommy stepped through first, watching the floor and walls to make sure there were no other millennia-old death traps. Nothing happened.

Sean followed, walking over the threshold and down two steps into a smaller chamber.

Three reliefs of the prophets were carved into the far wall. Each of the men stood with stoic looks on their faces, hands in various positions of prayer or offering blessings. The floor, laid with stone tiles, measured sixteen square feet.

Beneath the images of the prophets, a twelve-foot-long stone table held three identical golden boxes on its surface.

"I can't believe it," Milner said. "We found it. We found the secret chamber containing the mantle of the great prophet Elijah."

He pushed between Tommy and Sean and scurried across the floor to the table.

Sean and Tommy watched him curiously.

"Stop," Kimberly ordered.

Milner stood over the box in the center, his hands ready to pry it open. He spun around, a *how dare you* look on his face. "What? We are here. Our goal has been realized. Now we can begin our true mission."

"Why are there three?" Kimberly asked.

Milner struggled to answer the question. His head snapped back around, and he looked at each box carefully. "I... I don't know," he confessed and faced her again. "Why?"

"I think it best our friends give us that answer." She waved her pistol at Sean and Tommy. "But if I had to guess, it has something to do with the writing on the wall beneath the three prophets."

Milner followed her gaze and discovered what she was talking about. Beneath the feet of the prophets, a line of Aramaic gave warning to those who dared touch the boxes.

Likewise, each container displayed a word, also written in the same ancient language.

Milner pored over the text, as if staring at it long enough would unlock the mystery.

He spun and glowered at the two prisoners. "What does it say?" He pointed his gun at Sean.

"Sorry, pal," Sean said. "I don't speak Aramaic."

"Then I have no use for you," Milner said. His finger tensed on the trigger.

"I do," Tommy interrupted. "I know what it says."

"You do?" Sean asked.

"I run an archaeological agency."

"Yeah, but I didn't realize you knew that particular dead language."

"I picked it up," he said. "With so much travel, you gotta have hobbies on those long flights."

"Wow. You picked up a two-thousand-year-old dead language?"

"Would you two shut up?" Kimberly roared from behind them. "What does it say?"

"Speak the name that must not be spoken, and the blessings of heaven will be given to you," Tommy said, translating the text out loud. "It's a reference to the name of God."

Sean leaned close. "Seriously?"

Tommy merely nodded subtly with lips pressed together.

Sean was feeling better, the effects of the altitude sickness having worn off. He'd never really experienced that before, and he wondered why it was happening now. That was a concern for later. As long as he could fight, he had a chance to turn the tables.

Milner looked down at the boxes again, still unable to read the ancient text.

"What does that mean?" he urged desperately.

Tommy took a careful step forward and stopped behind the killer.

Milner moved to the side, keeping his gun pointed at Tommy.

With a deep breath, Tommy looked over the titles carved into the tops of the golden boxes.

"That one," he said, pointing to the container on the left, "says Adonai. The one in the middle says Elohim. And the one on the far right says Yahweh."

Milner's face scrunched in confusion. Then the light went on in his eyes. "Yahweh. The name of God is Yahweh." He rushed over to the box on the far right and unhinged the clasp from its loop. His eyes alight, joy radiating over his face, he set down the gun on the table and set his fingers under the lid. He tilted his head to the heavens and said, "I accept your blessing, Yahweh."

He placed his phone on the end of the table and held out his hands, pausing for a breath as he anticipated the glory that waited within the gilded object. With a satisfied sigh, Milner lifted the lid.

The contents of the box weren't what he expected. Instead of a glorious cloak, all he found was a small pile of sand. Then something clicked from within the stone, and the floor dropped out from under him.

Milner screamed. Grasping for the edge of the table, he managed to catch it with his fingers while his feet dangled over a black pit. The tile hung on hinges behind him, another trap placed long ago by the architects of the chamber.

"Help me! Kimberly! My daughter! Help me! Please!"

She rushed to the edge of the pit on the right-hand side and looked into the abyss. Keeping an eye on Sean and Tommy, she spoke to Milner.

"I would help you, Theodore. But here's the thing. You're not my father. You don't have a daughter. You killed my parents when I was just a child. I used you. I used you to get what I want."

"What?" Milner shouted. "Please, you have to help me!"

"You murdered my parents, Teddy," she said. "And now, it's your turn to die."

She raised the weapon and fired. The loud pop echoed through the room, sending instant ringing pain through every ear.

A bullet hole appeared in the middle of Milner's back. His fingers trembled. His legs stopped kicking, and his grip slipped from the stone slab.

Milner's body gave way to gravity, tumbling limply through the dark cavity in the floor.

Kimberly turned the weapon toward Sean and Tommy, the barrel still trickling bitter smoke into the air.

Sean nodded. "I have to admit, I did not see that coming. I mean, I knew there was something up with you, but I didn't think it was that."

"I'm glad you enjoyed the charade," she said. "Because you're going to open the next box."

47

LADAKH

When the circle of nine men approached within eight feet of the triad, Adriana knew they would make their move. Any closer, and they'd be vulnerable, if only temporarily, to a unified attack from her and her two friends.

She watched all of them, giving Ling the most attention, but as the circle tightened, he withdrew slightly behind them. He did not intend to get his hands dirty unless it was absolutely necessary.

Goading him wouldn't change that. Adriana knew as much.

What he didn't consider was that he'd just tipped the odds slightly in her favor.

At eight feet, the first two men made their move. The two who were with Ling lunged forward, but what none of them anticipated was that moving in all at once would cause a moment of chaos.

As the eight henchmen surged forward, they ran out of space and barged into each other. The clumsy attack resulted in immediate punishment.

Tara was the first to strike. Nimble and fast, she jabbed at a man who had lost his balance and stumbled toward her. His nose rammed her fist with his full momentum behind it. The crumpling sound radiated through his face a second before the blinding pain seared into his brain.

His hands shot to his face to stem the immediate bleeding. The cracks between his fingers couldn't dam the liquid that oozed through, and he dropped to his knees in front of her. The man who had bumped into him righted his balance and stopped five feet away, then twisted his body into a fighting stance, ready for another attack.

Tara remembered what Sean had taught them. *If ever in a fight where the numbers are against you, take out their wounded first. Never give a fallen enemy the chance to recover.*

She took a step forward, bending her knee while twisting her torso slightly. Then she snapped around in a whirl, her leg whipping in a deadly circle. Her foot connected with the target, plowing into the thug's left temple. He fell onto his side, unconscious or dead, but out of the fight either way.

Tara didn't let her gaze linger long on the motionless attacker. Her eyes were already on her next victim.

WHILE HIS WIFE was taking out her share, Alex faced three of his own. The men momentarily got in each other's way but corrected by narrowing their breadth to two, with one in the rear.

He knew from his time with Sean that if faced with multiple attackers, the one advantage he could truly use was confusion. The old adage of two heads are better than one wasn't true in a fight. People had different fighting styles, different ideas of how to attack, how to defend. Communication was almost never there, and if it was, it was nonverbal and vulnerable to misinterpretation.

Alex knew this as the men charged at him with fists raised. He focused his attention forward and between them so that each detail of their intent came into his periphery. Within half a second, he knew the man on the left would try to use his feet, while the one on the right planned on some kind of punch or chop.

The man to the left attacked first, sweeping his right leg as he slid forward on the gravel. Alex jumped over the leg and chopped down with his right arm just as the second attacker attempted to strike him in the chest with a devastating blow. Bone sank through forearm tissue.

The man yelped but landed on his feet in time to recover and avoid a second blow from Alex. The guy who had tried the foot sweep leaped off the ground with incredible power and extended his leg at Alex's face.

Off balance from his missed punch, Alex was vulnerable for only the slightest of moments. He deflected the kick and threw an uppercut into the attacker's groin as the man flew by and crashed onto his shoulder, injuring himself badly enough to require at least a minute to recover. He rolled to a stop at Adriana's feet just a half yard away.

Alex would have finished him if the other two weren't so quick to resume the onslaught.

The third man who had waited in reserve now joined the other, each facing Alex from opposite sides.

ADRIANA'S ASSAILANTS coordinated their efforts better than the others. They were the least eager to get into the fray, or perhaps they were simply smart enough not to rush headlong into a triangle of death.

One of the killers fell at her feet, grasping at his groin. Adriana raised her leg and shoved down her heel. The hard edge of the boot hit the man's exposed temple and dug in deep. His eyes rolled back into his head, and he stopped moving.

The three who surrounded her paused at the gruesome way she'd just killed one of their own so casually. They also allowed the mistake of emotion to come into play.

Their eyes blazed with fury as they rushed at her from three sides. Adriana moved in a blur, her hands and feet deftly twisting in a fluid ballet of lethality.

The man in the middle attacked first.

She met his reckless charge, blocking a jab to the side. She stepped forward and smashed her elbow into his mouth, knocking two teeth into the back of his throat.

His head snapped back from the blow, his lips and gums screaming in pain. To his credit, the attacker didn't fall, though it may have been better if he had.

Adriana twisted and drove her right foot down into his left knee.

His foot was planted firmly on the ground, and the knee gave an audible pop as the ligaments ripped under the devastating force. He clutched at the injury and fell onto his side, groaning.

The next two attackers weren't so foolhardy. The men split up and attacked from two sides, and with greater skill. They both attacked high at first, and Adriana had no choice but to dive-roll forward over the injured man and regroup. When the two resumed their attack, she knew it would come in tandem as before. She also knew how to deal with that scenario.

Adriana picked out the man to her left and rushed at him. She deflected a punch, then another, a chop at her throat, and then countered with a blow to his ribcage. She drove the base of her hand through tissue and snapped it hard when it struck bone.

The man staggered back, reeling for a moment, while the other immediately jumped back into the fray.

His foot snapped out and hit her in the side, sending a surge of pain up through her armpit and into her neck. She grimaced but twisted in time to catch the next kick and throw the foot aside. The attacker launched another assault, using a combination of stabbing hand movements and low kicks—the latter intended as more of a distraction, though if one landed, the consequences could have been a broken bone or, at best, a sprain.

Adriana blocked most of the efforts, though two landed—one on her right cheek and the other in her ribs. She countered with every strike, finding the attackers to be just as equal to the task.

Slowing and frustrated, one overcommitted with a lunging roundhouse punch. Adriana stepped forward to deliver a sidearm chop across his jaw. The blow might well have dazed the well-trained fighter, but the moment before she made contact, a hand wrapped around her throat and pulled her back, squeezing hard against her neck.

BEHIND ADRIANA, Tara continued the fight against another brawler. She'd taken out one, but the other opponent was much larger. She'd already struck him three times without effect, and if she'd delivered any damage, the guy didn't show it. She felt like a fly buzzing around a bull.

He bore a long scar down the right side of his face, from the corner of his eye to his jawline. It was clear he'd been in fights before, though it appeared he hadn't emerged from them due to technique. He was a brute, and his strategy was clear: overwhelm his enemy with sheer strength.

Towering over Tara at six feet three inches, he was also easily twice her weight. The man's mistake, however, was thinking he had an insurmountable advantage over her.

Tara used her size and quickness to duck under a heavy cross-punch, then another. She drilled him in the gut and ribs both times as a counter, then dove out of the way as the irritated man kicked a massive boot up at her face.

She hit the ground and rolled to her feet, already in a fighting stance by the time her spine stiffened. The giant turned toward her and smirked, then lumbered at her again. She switched fighting styles to a hybrid of Brazilian jujitsu and kickboxing, merging the flow of one with the attacks of the other. Tara knew that keeping the beastly man moving was the only way to beat him—to wear him down. He reached out for her and she swatted away the meaty fist, ducking to the side, then deflecting another jab. For a guy his size, her opponent was much more nimble than he looked, and she realized simply dancing around wasn't going to exhaust him as much as she'd hoped.

Tara kept moving, though, keeping her movements rhythmic but altering them every few steps to keep the enemy from guessing her next move.

He stabbed out with his left hand again, and she saw her opening. Tara leaped at him, aiming for the base of his neck with her right foot. She realized too late that he'd duped her into the attack. The big man twisted deftly to the right and caught her foot under his armpit, then immediately squeezed, clamping down hard on her ankle.

Tara tightened her abdominal muscles to try to whip herself free, but instead he grabbed her by the back of the neck and did the work for her, jerking her up to meet a heavy fist. She barely turned her head to avoid a direct blow to the nose, and the strike hit her on the jaw.

The world spun. She felt her limbs go weak as he raised his arm again to deliver another blow. Instinctively, she put up her hands to block, but only managed to deflect the hammer fist. Her wrists met his, though hers took the brunt of the force. Pain instantly radiated from the bones in her forearms as he raised the hand again to pummel her. Tara's eyelids blinked slowly, staring up into the attacker's dark eyes. She swallowed hard, mustered all the control she could find in her gut, and swung her right leg forward.

Her shoe made solid contact deep in his groin. The man's grip loosened, and she fell to the gravel.

He doubled over, grimacing but not felled. He let out a groan as Tara scrambled backward, retreating from the henchman.

The triangle was broken.

TWENTY FEET AWAY, Alex took on two opponents. He punched one in the face, but the other grabbed him from behind and wrapped his arm around the American's chest, squeezing hard and lifting Alex's feet off the ground. Alex felt his lungs tighten. He was an easy target now, and if he didn't get free, he'd be pummeled to death.

The man he'd punched in the face attacked again, though with a careless arrogance. He stepped up, a cocky look in his eyes, and reared back to deliver a blow to Alex's midsection. The strike would knock the wind out of Alex's lungs, and then he wouldn't be able to defend himself.

The second enemy was too close, though, and Alex kicked up his feet. He used the thug as a human wall, running up the guy's chest. Alex drove his heel hard into the man's teeth as he used every ounce of leverage he could muster to throw his weight over the top of the man strangling him.

He flipped over the killer's head and landed on his feet behind him, now with his arms in a chokehold around the henchman's neck. Alex squeezed hard and wouldn't have let go, but he saw his wife twenty feet away, on the ground, dragging herself away from a man twice her size. Fury coursed through his veins.

"No choking for you," Alex said. Then he gripped the man's head and snapped it to one side.

The body became heavy and collapsed to the ground, a knot protruding from the neck.

The other man recovered and stepped up to attack again. He stabbed with his fists, but Alex blocked and swiped them aside. The fighting intensified, both men moving their arms and feet in a blur. Alex didn't have time for this. Tara was in trouble. He caught the man's next punch by the wrist and jerked the arm down while bringing his leg up and swiveling on his opposite heel. Alex smashed the back of the elbow across his thigh to the sound of a loud crack, followed by an agonized howl.

The man dropped to his knees. Alex whipped his foot around and smashed his laces into the man's temple. The guy fell like a tree onto his side. Alex didn't check to see if he was unconscious. Instead, he turned and started toward Tara, who clawed her way backward, away from her giant assailant. Out of the corner of his eye, Alex saw Adriana in her own struggle.

TARA WAS IN HER VISION, and she caught a glimpse of Alex in the midst of a perplexing decision: Help his wife or help Adriana?

"Go," Adriana mouthed, pushing as hard as she could against her captor's arms. Her right leg flew up and struck the second attacker in the jaw as he approached to help finish the job. Teeth spat out of his mouth as he stumbled several feet backward and then fell to the ground unconscious.

Alex didn't have to be told twice. His mind made up, he darted toward Tara's attacker.

A blade flashed in the corner of Adriana's eye. She knew she had less than a second to free herself before the sharp edge dragged across her throat and spilled her lifeblood on the dusty gravel below.

48

LADAKH

"**W**hy don't you open it?" Tommy asked.

Kimberly sighed, lowered the pistol, and fired.

The bullet tore through flesh as the cacophony of the awful pop rang throughout the room, amplified by the mountain's rock. Sparks flashed twice off two walls.

Tommy yelped, then grabbed at his leg as he dropped down to one knee.

"Are you crazy?" Sean shouted, risking a step toward her.

She pointed the gun at his head. "Not another step, Sean."

"Not smart, lady. If you miss, that bullet could ricochet around the room and kill any of us, including you. We're lucky it only deflected twice."

Tommy reached down and touched the side of his leg. It felt like five wasps had stung him all in the same place. As he inspected the wound, though, he realized it was only a gash on the outer edge of the leg.

"I guess I trust my aim more than you do. Now"—she motioned with the pistol at the two remaining golden boxes—"choose."

Tommy grimaced as he stood. He looked down at his leg again and pressed his pants down so they covered the wound. It would stem the bleeding for now. He limped to the center of the stone table and stared hard at the two boxes.

Sean stayed where he was, a couple of yards away. He risked twisting his head to both sides, examining the entire chamber in hopes of finding an additional clue that would make certain his friend didn't choose the wrong box.

If he did, Tommy would die. Kimberly would open the remaining container and take the mantle. Then there would be no stopping her unless Sean could think of something. Time for that was running thin.

"Make your decision," Kimberly ordered.

She kept her pistol pointed at Sean's head and tensed her finger on the trigger as if he needed additional motivation.

Tommy sighed hard as he stared at the two boxes, each bearing a different name. Elohim had been used in Genesis; of that, he was certain. He'd engaged in discussions about the title with several historians and biblical scholars over the years. Some argued that since the word was plural, the text was referring to multiple gods, perhaps part of a unique pantheon never before regaled in myth or lore. A few considered this to be the case and spent countless hours searching for evidence of other gods buried deep within ancient Judaic legends.

On the other side of the debate, scholars argued that Elohim was only plural in certain forms and that the term had only been applied later in history by those doing their best to interpret the original texts.

In the end, the discussion yielded no real solutions, as conversations of that nature rarely did without solid proof. Tommy had his own thoughts on the matter, but he'd voiced relatively little while the others insisted on their own designs.

Now, those conceptions surfaced in a moment when the wrong decision would result in his death.

He let his eyes drift to the golden box on the left. The word *Adonai* barely left a smear in his memory. He only knew of the term from skimming through some information about ancient texts. If he'd seen it more than once, he didn't recall it, but Tommy knew how to read it and understood its meaning.

His biggest issue with the box on the left was that Adonai didn't appear in any form or translation of the Bible he'd ever seen. He'd heard of people who read the book from front to back, but Tommy had never invested that amount of time for such an endeavor. Still, he believed that if he'd laid eyes on that word, he would remember it.

What was it the writer had said about the word Adonai? He cursed himself for not recalling.

His eyes wandered back to the box in the middle. The Elohim box seemed to call to him, the name engraved on it bolder and clearer than the one on the Adonai box. He knew for sure Elohim was one of the names given to God in the Old Testament. There was no doubting that.

It had to be the one.

He shifted his feet to the center box as Sean and Kimberly looked on, one in rapt horror and the other with abject curiosity.

Tommy reached out his right hand, steadying himself with the left planted on the table. The seemingly bottomless pit, scant inches away from his right foot, gaped menacingly.

Tommy's eyelids narrowed as he gazed into the black abyss. He looked back at the Elohim box, then into the pit once more. His gaze fell on the empty container with the word *Yahweh* on it.

He'd believed that box to be the correct one, and Yahweh was certainly one of the terms given to God in the Old Testament, as far as he and many other scholars knew. If Yahweh was indeed one of the names used in the Bible, did that mean Elohim was the wrong choice, as well?

Tommy twisted to the left and stared at the Adonai box.

"You have three seconds to decide," Kimberly threatened. "Stop stalling."

Sean watched his friend divert away from the box in the middle and stop in front of the one on the left. He said a silent prayer that his friend was making the right choice.

"One," Kimberly said.

Tommy felt his heart racing. If he opened the box and it was wrong, the next thing he would feel would be air under his feet as he tumbled into the darkness.

"Two."

The name of God was to be unspoken, he thought. *To say it was a holy privilege. Adonai wasn't used. Which made sense if this was the name not to be spoken.* He hoped he was right and steeled himself against his fears. With a clenched jaw, Tommy reached out his right hand and flipped open the lid.

He winced, the muscles of his face tightening as he braced for the fall. For a second, he didn't know what happened. He dared to open his eyes to slits, still unsure if there was just a delay on the trap.

When he opened his eyes fully, Tommy gazed upon the contents of the Adonai box.

Inside the open, gilded container sat a folded brown garment.

"Step back," Kimberly commanded.

She spun toward Tommy, pointing the gun at the center of his spine. She pivoted back to Sean. "You, too, Sean. Against the wall. Both of you."

Sean remained still and watched the woman closely. Then he shuffled backward.

Tommy didn't turn around. A wild idea blinked in his mind: *Could this truly be the cloak of the prophet Elijah?* Was it possible that the fabric still contained within its fibers some of the power the great men of God wielded to produce miracles?

I could snatch it up, he thought. *Then what would happen?*

If the power still lingered, it might make him vanish as it did Elijah when the prophet finished rebuking King Ahab. If the power was gone, though... He shuddered at the thought. Kimberly would be angrier than Jezebel.

"I said, move," she demanded, right on cue.

Tommy's moment to try the fantastic had passed, and he shifted his feet, moving around to the end of the table. When he was against the wall adjacent to Sean, he pressed his back to the stone and waited for her to fire the final bullets.

Kimberly hurried forward when the two men were out of striking distance. She stopped at the box and stared down at the underwhelming sight. The rugged brown fabric looked worn and rough, but had been surprisingly well preserved over the millennia—too well preserved to have happened naturally.

Her breath caught for several seconds. When she started breathing again, she snapped her head to the side, taking a look in Sean's direction to make sure he wasn't thinking of making a move.

"Can you believe it?" she asked. "The cloak of Elijah." Her voice filled with wonder. She reached in, daring to touch the ancient fabric. The second her finger brushed against the mantle, a surge of power zapped through her body. The jolt was so powerful, it shook the pistol from her hand and sent it tumbling down into the chasm.

Sean and Tommy watched as her body shuddered. The gyrations lasted nearly ten seconds. Then, as abruptly as it began, the shaking stopped. Kimberly looked down at her hands, then at the mantle.

She grasped the coarse fabric in her hand and looked over at the two men.

Sean's eyes blazed with intent. The weapon gone, he had one thing in mind: shove her into the hole with Milner.

When Sean took a step forward, though, she flipped the cloak over her shoulder—and with a wicked smirk, vanished into thin air.

Sean caught himself charging recklessly forward and he tripped on one of the stone tiles. Tommy's reflexes were fast, though, and he leaped forward and collided with his friend, knocking both of them to the hard floor in a tangled pile.

"Where did she go?" Tommy asked, desperation seething in his voice.

Sean stood up and spun around. In the light from Milner's phone still resting atop the table, Sean saw a faint puff of dust kick up from near the chamber's exit.

"The door," he said.

They rushed toward the opening. A grinding sound echoed from the other side of the short corridor and sent a terrifying chill through the two friends.

Within seconds, a heavy thud resonated through the mountain. The two knew what would come next, and they could do nothing to stop it.

Tommy and Sean skidded to a stop just before reaching the doorway into the atrium, and a split second before the giant stone slab crashed to the floor in front of them.

Dust and debris erupted and spilled rolling gray clouds into the tunnel, forcing the two friends to retreat backward into the room where the golden boxes still sat on the table.

Sean looked over at Tommy. The light from Milner's phone cast an eerie, sterile glow onto the ceiling and throughout the room.

"She just trapped us in here," Tommy said. His cheeks drawn, jaw slack, he turned despondently toward the table with the three gilded chests.

Without saying a word, Sean followed his friend's gaze to the table. He strode over and picked up Milner's phone, careful not to slip into the hole in the floor.

"Maybe," Sean said. "Maybe not."

"What?"

"Come on." Sean started back toward the exit.

"Buddy, she triggered the trap. That way is blocked."

Sean ignored him and pushed through, waving his hand around to clear the dust. He raised the collar of his shirt over his nose to keep from breathing much of it in. When he reached the threshold, he stopped and pointed the light onto the three-foot-thick slab. The thing must have weighed a couple of tons at minimum. Sean raised the light. Through the settling motes of dust, he could see through the doorway above the giant stone.

Tommy joined his friend and looked into the opening.

"Looks like it didn't completely block the way," Sean said. "I guess it was only meant to crush anyone who screwed up the puzzle."

He handed the light to Tommy and climbed up through the narrow gap and onto the top of the stone. Then he reached down and retrieved the phone so Tommy could join him. He shined the light on the top edge for his friend, and within seconds, the two were atop the massive booby trap. Sean focused the light on the other side of the atrium. The doorway on the other side was still there, open and inviting.

The two exchanged an understanding glance and sprinted to the opening, slid over the edge of the giant stone, and plunged into the corridor with one constant thought:

Stop Kimberly Henderson.

49

LADAKH

Adriana struggled to free herself as the man grasping her pulled the knife's edge closer to her neck. Only inches away from death, she did the only thing she could think of. She snapped her head backward and crushed the man's nose with the back of her skull. The move didn't end his attack, but it weakened his grip enough that she found room to wriggle free and drop to the ground.

She rolled away to a safe distance and readied herself to fight again. Catching her breath, Adriana stood from her crouch and waited for the man with the blade to come at her again.

He blinked away the pain and wiped his bleeding nose with his forearm. He turned his body and prepared to attack, holding the knife out in front as both deterrent and threat.

Adriana twisted sideways and waited for him to make the first move. Then she saw something behind her opponent, a blur of movement near the entrance to the village. It was as if the air shimmered like a mirage from a heatwave. Then, from nowhere, Kimberly appeared draped with a dark brown cloak and running at full speed toward the bus.

Adriana nearly gasped in disbelief. A single thought took over her mind: *Where are Sean and Tommy?*

She received her answer immediately when the two men emerged from around a rocky crag, sprinting after the fleeing woman.

Adriana's attacker lunged forward, stabbing deftly with the knife in an attempt to slash her on the left side. Her temporary relief at seeing Sean and Tommy evaporated with the man's lunge. She spun on her left heel, tucked her right leg, and slung it around into the man's chest.

The hard impact drove him back, nearly jarring the weapon from his fist. He managed to hang on, though, and steadied himself for another try. The blow's dull pain radiated through his torso, adding fuel to the raging fire of an already broken nose.

ACROSS THE LOT, Alex rushed at the lumbering man with the scar on his face. He was almost on top of Tara, who scrambled backward, unable to gain enough purchase to stand.

Alex reached the assailant and leaped through the air, driving his foot into the small of his back a second before the big man was able to grab her.

The blow sent the man stumbling forward, but he managed to dive-roll over Tara and crouch to his feet just behind her. He reached out a meaty hand and grabbed her by the hair, dragging her to her feet as she struggled, kicking her feet and swatting with her hands.

Within seconds, the man had his thick arms wrapped around her throat, and one hand on her head ready to twist it and snap her neck.

Alex froze, uncertainty strangling him into indecision.

SEAN AND TOMMY pumped their legs hard as they chased after Kimberly. She called to Ling, who stood in the middle of the mayhem, observing but not taking part in the fight.

When he heard her call, Ling immediately retreated from the fray and cut across the lot in front of her to the bus.

Tommy looked to his right, briefly taking his eyes off their quarry.

He saw Tara in the grip of a massive man. While shorter by several inches, Tommy was at least as strong as the henchman.

"Catch her!" Tommy shouted at Sean, indicating Kimberly with a finger. "I'm going to help the kids!"

He didn't bother to wonder why they were here or, more surprisingly, how. He veered off to the right while Sean hurried after the woman with the cloak.

THE SCARRED MAN squeezed Tara's neck. Her face reddened, and her limbs weakened.

"Let her go!" Alex yelled. "Fight me!"

The man's head twisted forebodingly in both directions as if to tell Alex no, that they were both going to die, and she was first.

Then, seemingly out of nowhere, Tommy barreled into the man, driving his shoulder into the target's ribs like a professional linebacker.

The jarring blow shook the massive brute, causing his grip on Tara to weaken. She slipped from his arms and fell to the ground as Tommy continued driving forward until the man in his grasp toppled over.

The two men hit the earth with a grinding thud. Gravel bit into Tommy's forearms and elbows. The man he hit took the brunt of the damage, though, with hard-packed road and jagged stones digging into his flesh and scraping away the top layer of skin.

Fury erupted in the killer's eyes as he reached his right arm around Tommy's neck to attempt a chokehold.

Tommy was too fast, though, and slithered free.

The giant assailant clambered to his feet to the sound of a nearby bus engine roaring to life.

Tommy saw Kimberly jump into the open side door of the parked bus. Then the driver shifted into reverse and gunned the accelerator. The bus lurched backward with tires spinning on gravel. Tommy saw it coming and dove clear of the shuttle as the big man spun around in time to be struck by the vehicle with a sickening thump. He fell under the chassis with a yelp, which the heavy tires quickly extinguished as they rolled over him, crushing the man underneath.

Tommy tumbled onto the ground and flopped over onto his side in time to witness the grisly death. On the other side of the bus, Alex held Tara tight in his arms.

Beyond them, Adriana stood face to face with the last villain.

But where is Sean? Tommy wondered.

Tommy got his answer when Ling stepped on the gas and sped away. There, on the side of the bus, Sean clung to the side mirror with feet dragging and flopping under him.

ON THE OTHER side of the parking lot, Adriana waited for the knife wielder to make another move. Fatigue racked her body and mind, but she knew he was feeling the same effects. She would be stronger. *Always be stronger,* her father had told her long ago. *Never lose a fight because you were unwilling to leave everything on the field of combat.*

The opponent stabbed at her again. She ducked to the side.

He slashed across his body, then countered with a backhanded jab, bringing the knife tip dangerously close to her chest.

Adriana spun clear, countered with a kick to the man's shin, and dropped back once more. The kick hurt, but she'd endured far worse. He, however, limped visibly now. The blow hadn't broken a bone, but it certainly caused the nerves in his leg to scream in pain. Her pain matched his, but she controlled it, cutting off the signals to her brain until after she'd finished the fight.

He attempted another strike, coming at her with less balance than before.

Adriana waited until the last second. The blade flashed with the rays of the sun, swinging at the base of her neck. She dropped one foot back, twisted her body, and caught the man's wrist as it passed, missing his target by an inch. The momentum of the slashing movement brought his arm back toward him, and she used it, forcing the man's fist back toward his own head.

She felt a second of resistance, but it was too late. Adriana used all her remaining strength to drive the blade's tip through the man's neck just below his jaw. The knife sank deep into his head, moving upward until it lodged into his sinuses.

Shock blinked in his eyes.

Adriana shoved him away and watched as the man's body trembled, eyes staring blankly at the mountain beyond. The drama heightened as he clutched the weapon with bloody fingers, then collapsed to his knees before falling prostrate onto the gravel.

Adriana gasped for air, realizing once more that the elevation made any exertion doubly difficult.

When she gathered her wits, she remembered seeing Sean and Tommy running after Kimberly. Adriana whirled on her heels and looked across the lot at Tommy. He stood near Tara and Alex, but there was no sign of Sean. Adriana's brow tightened as she followed Tommy's gaze toward the bus as it rumbled down the road. Then she saw Sean, dangling from the side mirror.

The bus disappeared around the bend a second later.

SEAN HELD on to the metal frame of the mirror with all his might. The muscles and tendons in his forearms burned, but he wasn't about to let go. Just behind him, the slopes of the mountain dropped off, and if he lost his grip, he would tumble thousands of feet to a certain death.

Inside the bus, Ling sat behind the wheel, while Kimberly urged him on, tucking the mantle under her armpit.

The shuttle rumbled down the road and hit a switchback turn, slowing for a moment as Ling spun the steering wheel to compensate for their speed and angle of approach.

Sean kicked his legs out, trying to get some momentum to swing in through the door. Inside, Kimberly pointed at the jagged slopes now outside the bus. Sean knew what she intended.

Ling turned the wheel slightly, pushing the bus toward the wall of rock to their right. The outside of the mirror ground against the stone, sending sparks flying and glass shattering. The metal rod he held on to groaned against the pressure, but it held true.

The bus hit a bump, and for a brief second, Sean gained respite as Ling was forced to merge left. Sean wouldn't be that lucky again. He had to get onto the bus.

He knew he couldn't kick the side door open, which meant his only choices were through one of the windows or the back door.

The road ahead cleared, and Ling guided the shuttle back against the rock. This time, Sean pulled himself up onto the protruding mirror brace and at the last moment pushed his feet off the rod as Ling forced the frame into the rock yet again, obliterating it into twisted, mangled metal.

He hit the hood of the bus and rolled off the other side, nearly falling to the road. The only thing that saved him was his left hand snatching hold of the edge between the windshield and the hood. He gripped it hard and then reached out with his right hand to assist. When both sets of fingers had a firm grip, he pulled himself toward the windshield and face to face with the enemies inside.

Ling stepped on the brakes and Sean felt the momentum push him toward the front of the bus, but he didn't let go despite the strain burning in his forearms. Ling accelerated again, this time swerving left and right in an attempt to throw Sean off the hood.

Sean's legs flopped back and forth and he felt his grip begin to give way, but he managed to hold on and right himself as Ling was forced to slow down at the next switchback.

Sean didn't dare look out over the terrifying sight of the mountain vista. It was nearly impossible to avoid, but right now, his fear of being thrown from the bus was greater than his fear of heights.

He pulled his legs up beneath him and jumped toward the top of the bus. He immediately regretted the decision. The roof only offered a flat surface with three undulating ridges on its top. There was no way he could swing into a window from there.

Then he had another crazy idea.

He spread his arms and legs out wide to keep as stable as possible while Ling slowly steered the bus around the long curve.

Sean had less than ten seconds to execute the move. And even if he did it perfectly, there was no guarantee it would work.

He let go as the bus accelerated through the apex. His body slid backward toward the rear of the bus where a slight lip afforded his feet minimum stability. The soles of his shoes caught on the lip, and he bent his knees, slithering back until they dangled over the side. Sean grabbed the metal edge with his fingers and used every ounce of strength he had left.

He looked down at the latch to the back door, doing his best to ignore the road as it raced beneath his hanging feet.

Ling swerved again, jerking the steering wheel right and left, pushing the remnants of Sean's arm strength to their limits.

His grip nearly gone, Sean gave one last stab at the door handle with his left foot as he swung to the right. His foot caught on the latch, and he pushed down hard. The door came loose and swung open, bouncing back and forth with every little bump and pothole in the road. When it was fully open, Sean kicked his legs forward and let go of the narrow edge on the roof. His momentum carried him into the back of the bus and he hit the floor with a thud.

He could barely move his fingers as he tried to scramble to his feet to rush to the front, but that plan was cut short by a woman holding a brown cloak standing over him.

She kicked him in the face, his vision spiraling into a spin.

"Why. Can't. You. Just. Die?" she shouted.

Sean's legs buckled and he slumped onto his side.

She kicked again, this time landing the tip of her boot in his ribs. He grimaced from the sharp pain. Another kick landed in his abdomen, and he felt the air sucked out of his lungs for a moment. She swung her foot again, and he barely managed to block it with his forearms, but the blow still rang hard against the bones in his wrists.

Sean saw something on the floor near him, bumping up and down as the bus rumbled along the rough road. His vision spinning, he strained to focus. It was the bomb Kimberly had given Adriana. *Was that a hair tie strapped around the nodes?* Too exhausted and dizzy to wonder for long, Sean reached out and grabbed the device as Kimberly kicked him again. This time, her foot lodged in his armpit and he squeezed as hard as he could.

She shoved him backward with her boot. The cool mountain air washed over him, rushing in from the open back door. His head hung out over the edge, Sean couldn't fight anymore. His energy sapped, he only had enough left for one last play.

Kimberly swung her foot at his head, intent on ending things then and there. Sean whipped his left hand around and caught her foot. The boot hovered over him menacingly, and he struggled against her attempt to push it down against his face. He took the device in his right hand and shoved it into the folds of her boot, just behind the zipper, and looked up at her.

"You first," Sean said.

He kicked up with his feet, sending his weight tumbling out the back door while pinching the hair tie tight with finger and thumb. He balled up as much as possible as he hovered in the air for a moment, then hit the road hard and rolled.

Kimberly stumbled backward into the middle of the bus, grasping desperately at the explosive in her boot. In her panic, the mantle fell to the floor.

The device beeped three times, then a searing white light exploded into an orange ball of fire, consuming the bus and its occupants.

Sean winced as he rolled to a stop, his body scratched and cut in a dozen places from the fall. The explosion sent a concussive blast over him and he reeled a few more feet before coming to a stop near the edge of the road.

He shielded his eyes to protect against shrapnel and debris, then watched the rolling inferno careen to the right and tumble like a fireball down the mountain.

He inhaled and exhaled rapidly. He felt his heart pounding. Everything hurt.

Sean's thoughts immediately went to his friends and wife back at the top of the mountain. They might still need his help.

It was then he noticed something dark against the white-blue sky. He frowned at first, wondering what the anomaly could be.

"It can't be," he breathed.

In the air, fluttering toward the road, the prophet's mantle drifted in the air currents, sailing straight toward him.

Sean momentarily forgot everything: the fight, the multiple near-death encounters, even his wife and friends above. The cloak floated down to him, carried on the wings of invisible angels until it landed at his feet.

He blinked rapidly in disbelief. The garment appeared unharmed by the fire, as if it had never happened.

With a swallow, he reached out and touched it. A surge of energy shot through him and he felt instantly renewed. He sighed as the power died off. The sound of a whining car engine interrupted the moment, and he stood, turning to face the new threat.

Instead, he saw Alex behind the wheel of a rental car with Tara and Tommy in the back and Adriana in the passenger seat.

The car ground to a stop, crunching in the gravel.

Sean stood there staring at them for several seconds, and then held up the cloak he clutched in his fingers.

He could no longer feel the cuts and bruises, or the exhaustion from the fight. He offered a meager smile at the occupants in the car and nodded.

"What took you guys so long?" he asked as all four doors opened simultaneously.

The friends poured out of the car and rushed to him, unsure if they should hug him or keep their distance.

"Are you okay?" Adriana asked first, risking a hug with the man she loved.

Sean nodded. "Yeah. Actually, I feel like I could run a marathon right now."

She stepped back and looked at the cloak. Her eyes softened with reverence. "So, the power is still there," she said.

"Yes." Sean turned and looked down the mountain at the trail of smoke that followed the burning bus—all that remained of the lumbering vehicle that had lurched over a cliff. "And it's probably best that this particular artifact be kept in a very safe place."

50

ATLANTA, ONE MONTH LATER

Tommy stood behind the podium with a broad grin on his face. A projection screen behind him displayed several artifacts, including a copper scroll with ancient text beaten into it.

"Archaeology is the study of history," he said, letting his hands fall to his sides with palms up. He stepped away from the podium. "The excitement of it comes from discovery, not hair-raising adventures or the monetary value of what might be found."

The screen changed to scenes of workers at dig sites as they brushed away millimeters of dirt with each careful stroke. The image split into two, then again, revealing different videos of workers going about their uninspiring tasks of searching for evidence of ancient people and cultures.

"Through archaeology and anthropology," Tommy went on, "we learn about how people lived, what they did for fun, how they ate, who they worshipped. Behind every shard of clay, every motif, every building block of ancient ruins, there was a person who made it, used it, or appreciated it. That's really what we do. We study people, attempting to walk in their footsteps to gain insight into their lives."

The audience sat in rapt attention. Most of them were from local or regional universities. A smattering hailed from various newspapers and historical websites.

Sean stood off to the side of the stage. Adriana hovered close to him. Tara and Alex were seated in the front row, smiling proudly at their boss, partially because they were truly proud of him and the work the IAA did, and partly to make Tommy feel more confident.

Dr. Kelley sat on the stage behind him, nervously waiting for her turn to speak.

"In our line of work," Tommy said, looking out over the grand lobby of IAA headquarters, "the people who are most patient, most deliberate, most careful, are the ones who are rewarded with the greatest discoveries." He turned dramatically and let his gaze fall on Dr. Kelley. He returned his focus to the audience and clapped his hands together. "We in the historical community have long waited to find more pieces to the Dead Sea Scroll puzzle. There were many gaps, many holes in the story. I believe now, thanks to the work of Dr. Kerry Kelley, those holes have largely been filled. So, without further bluster," he paused and allowed the crowd to laugh, "I present to you a true hero of the historical community, Dr. Kerry Kelley."

The audience erupted in applause as Tommy turned and motioned for her to take the podium. He smiled and winked, then walked to the side of the stage and descended the steps to join his friends.

Dr. Kelley thanked Tommy for his grandiose introduction, then began her talk about the discovery she and her team had made off the coast of Gibraltar.

"I think you're starting to enjoy public speaking," Sean quipped as his friend took a place near him.

Tommy shrugged. "Meh, it's not so bad," he whispered.

"I remember when it terrified you. Wasn't that long ago."

"Yeah, well, I guess you get used to it, huh?"

"I suppose so," Sean conceded.

The two fell silent for a moment, allowing Dr. Kelley's voice to overwhelm the lobby.

"Oh," Tommy whispered, "I just got a text from Zaid before I went on stage. Said he's doing fine and just wanted to wish me good luck with the speech."

Sean nodded absently. "That guy is tougher than granite. I feel horrible we put him in that situation. But I'm glad he's going to be okay."

Tommy nodded, then changed the subject, "Something has been bothering me about all this."

"Only one thing?"

Tommy ignored him. "How did Kimberly convince Milner she was his daughter? He wasn't married."

Sean acknowledged the comment with a nod. "I was curious about the same. Turns out, he wasn't so sinless himself."

"You mean aside from the slaying of innocent people?"

"Yes. He also had an issue with lust, particularly of other men's wives. I suspect Kimberly probably used one of their names as the potential mother. After so many years, it's easy to forget certain things or confuse names."

"Especially when you're insane."

"Indeed," Sean agreed.

"It's a shame we couldn't have the mantle here," Tommy breathed, leaning close so only Sean could hear him. "Would be incredible to show that to the world. And it would solve so many questions."

"The cloak is where it's meant to be," Sean said. "And besides, we don't know what kind of power that thing has. It could be incredibly destructive."

"I know. I know. Still—"

"The prophet's cloak was meant for the one who would bring the promise of hope to the world, for a new messenger of peace." Sean shook his head. "I don't think we fit that bill."

Tommy chuckled. "I suppose not. I wonder, though. I would have at least liked to analyze it, run some tests on it."

Sean tilted his head slightly to face his friend with the left half of his face. "I don't think that power is something you want to test, buddy."

"Maybe not," Tommy surrendered and stood up on his tiptoes then lowered back down.

Sean grinned and returned his eyes to the podium where Dr. Kelley was talking about the process they used to recover the copper scroll from the shipwreck in the Mediterranean.

"I suppose some things are best left to faith and mystery," Tommy offered after a moment of contemplation.

Sean agreed with a nod. "Exactly." He inhaled deeply. "Don't worry, Schultzie. When the time comes, the right person will discover the mantle. And I don't think they'll need us to help them."

As Sean watched and listened to Dr. Kelley, his mind wandered to a monastery in Egypt, where the cloak of the prophets lay hidden in a reliquary, awaiting a new master.

THANK YOU

Thank you for taking the time to read this story. We can always make more money, but time is a finite resource for all of us, so the fact you took the time to read my work means the world to me and I truly appreciate it. I hope you enjoyed it as much as I enjoyed sharing it, and I look forward to bringing you more fun adventures in the future.

If you'd like to know about upcoming projects and special discounts on my books as well as other authors like me, join my email list at https://www.ernestdempsey.net

To keep even better tabs on all upcoming stories, follow me on my Amazon page here: https://www.amazon.com/Ernest-Dempsey/e/B00AM8UHO4/

Join me for even more great content, both from history and from fiction on my YouTube Channel: https://www.youtube.com/channel/UCIxybcjpYK7opVwlvl12a2Q

And if you want to engage with me and millions of fans around the world, hop on my facebook page for more fun: https://facebook.com/ErnestDempsey

See you soon,
Ernest

FACT VS. FICTION

Hello again, sports fans! It's that part of the story where we delve into some of the truth and some of the gray area I mixed in.

Most of the locations in this story are real. One fictional place is the town of Watasco, Wyoming and the Morrowfield Asylum. I based those on real locations, but changed the names and added a few details to enhance the story.

Wadi El Natrun is a fascinating place in Egypt, only a short drive from Cairo. It holds so much important history, but dwells perpetually in the shadows of the great pyramids and temples along the Nile. I did my best to describe this incredible location in great detail, but without boring you to death. The layout of the town-commune was as accurate as I could make it, right down to the tower where monks would hide in ancient days when under attack. The reliquary inside the monastery, as well as the corridors to reach it are real, as are the relics within. As to their authenticity, validating that is not up to me. I choose to believe, however, in the probable—not the doubtful.

I included Macau and the casino scene because I'm a big James Bond fan and I loved the scene that took place in Macao in one of those films. While the casino and games were different, I felt it only right to pay homage to what I thought was a terrific movie by including it in this story. I did my best to describe the city in accurate detail, including the incredible drop-off between the rich and poor classes of the city.

One of the sadder truths about this story is the destruction of the Tomb of Jonah in Mosul, Iraq. While this location has been traditionally accepted as the burial place of the great prophet, it isn't the only one.

Another tomb, in northern Israel, also claims to be the final resting place of Jonah: in the predominantly Muslim town of Mashhad.

Located only a few miles from Nazareth, it is very near to Jonah's birthplace of Gath-Hefer. The shrine there is still intact, along with the burial chamber and sarcophagus. Is this the true burial place of Jonah the prophet? Was it in Mosul? Or is it somewhere else entirely?

For now, at the time of writing this story, all we can do is wonder. Still, that doesn't change the fact that the loss of the tomb in Mosul is a tragedy to the historical world.

The location of the baptism site in Jordan is well-known and visited by people of multiple faiths. As described in the story, there have been places of worship constructed nearby—some old, and some built fairly recently.

It is my opinion that this place, this holy location, serves as a center point to what I believe was Yeshua's (Jesus') underlying mission: to unite all faiths under one message of love, peace, and hope. We can see it clearly at this site, a place where all may come and bend a knee under one sky that covers all, by one river that flows into all.

Lastly, the monastery at Hemis is real and can be visited—though be aware it's at a pretty high elevation. I detailed this location as accurately as I could, though the interior design and layout took a bit of creative invention on my part. I took descriptions from other writers who've been there and mixed them for what I thought would be both plausible, and technically satisfying fo the story's flow.

And of course, I had to add an underground tunnel. Because that's where treasures hide.

As to the possibility of Jesus visiting this place during his formative years, I leave that to your thoughts.

But, here are some interesting bits of information to add to the intrigue.

Back in 2009, a movie was released that documented the research into the theory that Jesus came to Ladakh and the Hemis Monastery. There have been several books, some historical, some anecdotal, that attempt to either support or debunk the notion that young Jesus may have visited this place.

Did Jesus visit India? We may never know. But there are certainly some points of evidence to observe. How did Thomas know about India where he went to minister after Jesus left? There are stories about a scroll indicating a man from the Middle East came searching for knowledge about 2000 years ago (at the time of writing this story).

Where there's smoke, there's usually something at least smoldering.

That's the best part about writing these kinds of stories. We follow the smoke and see where it leads. Sometimes, we don't get definitive answers, but as long as we continue to ask the questions, our path to a deeper understanding of the past will grow.

OTHER BOOKS BY ERNEST DEMPSEY

Sean Wyatt Adventures:

The Secret of the Stones

The Cleric's Vault

The Last Chamber

The Grecian Manifesto

The Norse Directive

Game of Shadows

The Jerusalem Creed

The Samurai Cipher

The Cairo Vendetta

The Uluru Code

The Excalibur Key

The Denali Deception

The Sahara Legacy

The Fourth Prophecy

The Templar Curse

The Forbidden Temple

The Omega Project

The Napoleon Affair

The Second Sign

Adriana Villa Adventures:

War of Thieves Box Set

When Shadows Call

Shadows Rising

ACKNOWLEDGMENTS

As always, I would like to thank my terrific editors for their hard work. What they do makes my stories so much better for readers all over the world. Anne Storer and Jason Whited are the best editorial team a writer could hope for and I appreciate everything they do.

I also want to thank Elena at Li Graphics for her tremendous work on my book covers and for always overdelivering. Elena is amazing.

Last but not least, I need to thank all my wonderful fans and especially the advance reader team. Their feedback and reviews are always so helpful and I can't say enough good things about all of them.

One such fan is Richard Elliot, who offered his expertise as an electrician for this project. I appreciate your help, Richard!

See you next time,

Ernest